The fiery brilliance of the Zebra Hologram Heart which you see on the cover is created by "laser holography." This is the revolutionary process in which a powerful laser beam records light waves in diamond-like facets so tiny that 9,000,000 fit in a square inch. No print or photograph can match the vibrant colors and radiant glow of a hologram.

So look for the Zebra Hologram Heart whenever you buy a historical romance. It is a shimmering reflection of our guarantee that you'll find consistent quality between the covers!

MOONLIGHT CARESS

With a startled squeak of surprise, Starr whirled around to face the man who stood on the bank staring down at her. Time seemed to stand still.

Even as she crossed her arms protectively over her naked flesh, she felt an unbearable compulsion to hold her hands out to Daniel Blue Eagle and bid him join her in the water.

As if her silent invitation had been uttered aloud, the silent Indian stepped into the stream and came toward her.

She knew she should stop him. But she was mesmerized by the way the moonlight played over his muscular shoulders and by the fiery glint of desire in his eyes.

He slipped his hands, hot against her water-cooled flesh, around her waist, sending electricity through her.

"I have d‑‑‑‑‑‑‑‑‑‑‑‑‑‑‑‑‑‑‑d, drawing her soft, ‑‑‑‑‑‑‑‑‑‑‑‑‑‑‑‑ngth with scorching ‑‑‑‑‑‑‑‑‑

His mou‑‑‑‑‑‑‑‑‑‑‑‑‑‑‑‑‑‑‑‑ kiss that was both f‑‑‑‑‑‑‑‑‑‑‑‑‑‑‑‑

Never ha‑‑‑‑‑‑‑‑‑‑‑‑‑‑‑ enced anything like Daniel Blue Eagle's kiss. Her head reeled. To keep from falling, she clung desperately to him, responding to every touch, every kiss, instinctively wanting more . . . .

UNTAMED SURRENDER

MICHALANN PERRY

ZEBRA BOOKS
KENSINGTON PUBLISHING CORP.

ZEBRA BOOKS

are published by

Kensington Publishing Corp.
475 Park Avenue South
New York, NY 10016

First printing: January 1986

Printed in the United States of America

DEDICATION

All my love and gratitude to

My hero, Dick, and the beautiful evidence of our love, Stacy and Lesley, who generously gave me the time;

Donna, Sherry and Mary Ben, who gave me the benefit of their expertise;

My dad, Pat, who gave me the confidence;

And to Carin, who gave me the opportunity.

Always,
Micki

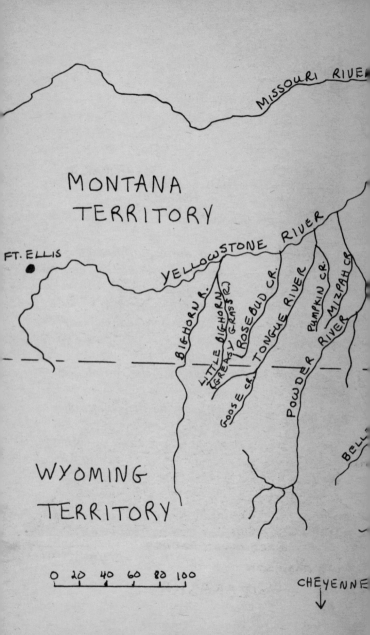

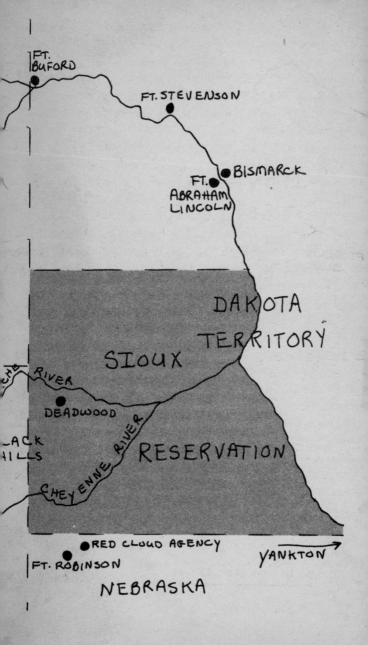

FT.
BUFORD

FT. STEVENSON

● BISMARCK

FT.
ABRAHAM
LINCOLN

DAKOTA
TERRITORY

SIOUX

RIVER

DEADWOOD

CHEYENNE RIVER

RESERVATION

LACK
HILLS

CHEYENNE RIVER

● RED CLOUD AGENCY

FT. ROBINSON

YANKTON

NEBRASKA

Chapter One

Dakota Territory—1875

"Do you, Starr Winfield, take this man, William Howard, to be your lawful wedded husband?"

The silk-clad twenty-year-old bride concentrated on the white-haired minister's thin lips, forcing herself to listen to the emotionless drone of his voice and to push aside the strange apprehension that gripped her.

"To have and to hold from this day forward . . ."

She raised her veiled face to smile at her tall blond bridegroom, elegant and breathtakingly handsome in his blue fulldress soldier's uniform. The words of the marriage ceremony repeated themselves in her mind. *From this day forward.* From this day forward William would belong only to her and she to him. But for some unexplained reason, instead of feeling elated at the thought, Starr was aware of a dull ache in the pit of her stomach when she heard the preacher say the words aloud.

"to love . . ."

Of course, to love. Hadn't she loved William from the very first time she'd seen him? What girl wouldn't love him? Not only was he handsome and extremely intelligent, he was kind and thoughtful as well. She knew she was the envy of every girl in the Territory, and had been since the Reception Ball for the officers of Colonel Custer's 7th Cavalry two years before. Since the night they had met in Stone's Hall, Lieutenant William Howard had had eyes for only one girl in Yankton. And Starr Winfield had been that lucky girl. So what was this feeling of trepidation that was making her palms perspire, her knees weak?

"honor . . ."

Oh, yes. William was above all else an honorable man, she thought, remembering the chaste kisses and embraces they had shared over the past two years. Her twenty-five-year-old bridegroom had never attempted to take any liberties with her, though as an engaged man he might have demanded more than the polite close-mouthed kisses she gave him at the end of each meeting. But he'd been adamant about waiting until their wedding night.

Wedding night! Tonight she would be truly a woman. She would learn the answers to the mysteries she'd only been able to wonder about until now. Oh, her mother had tried to tell her what to expect but had been too embarrassed to finish the personal conversation, finally leaving the room with a reassuring, "If you can manage to relax, and if he's considerate and gentle, it won't be too terrible." Relax? How was she supposed to do that!?

"and obey . . ."

Well, that was one thing she wouldn't have to worry

about. William would never order her to *obey* him. They had discussed this more than once, and they had both agreed that their marriage would be a partnership, not a master-and-servant relationship like many marriages they had both seen. That was very important to Starr since she had vowed long ago never to marry a man who would treat her as anything other than an equal. It would be especially valuable in a military family since there would be many times when William would be gone, leaving her to run their home alone.

Alone! The word triggered more anxious thoughts. How she hated to leave Yankton and her family and friends. But now there was no choice. After a brief honeymoon in St. Louis, she and William would be living at Fort Abraham Lincoln at Bismark, over three hundred miles up the Missouri River.

Starr glanced over her shoulder for one last glimpse of her parents before she became a married woman. Watching them through the gossamer bridal veil, she concentrated on memorizing their features. Her own gray eyes suddenly filled with tears when she saw that her father, Robert, a gentle giant of a man with bushy blond hair and a mustache, was taking a self-conscious swipe at his watery blue eyes, while her tiny dark-haired mother, Mary, wept openly, wiping her nose with a delicate handkerchief, trying half-heartedly to control her tears.

"Starr," the preacher whispered, drawing the bride's attention back to her groom and the importance of the ceremony. "Answer the question, Starr. Do you take Lieutenant Howard to be your lawful wedded husband?" he reminded her quietly.

Starr's mouth felt dry. Perspiration trickled down the hollow between her breasts. The high lace collar on her white silk wedding gown felt as if it were choking the life from her. And the metal stays in her corset cut into her flesh, reminding her of the freedom she would relinquish once she uttered those two words everyone in the small church was waiting to hear her say. Beads of sweat broke out on her pale forehead. She was not sure she could go through with it.

What if she refused to say the words that would make her William's wife forever? What if she simply said *no*? What if she said, *I'm sorry, William. I do love you, but I'm not ready to marry yet. I don't want to leave my mother and father. I don't want to hurt you, but I'm not prepared to be a wife and mother. Not yet. Maybe never.*

Not trusting herself to speak for fear that her mouth would give the reply her entire body was crying out to give, Starr nodded her strawberry-blonde head weakly.

"Answer, 'I do,' Starr," William whispered, his understanding smile meant to reassure his frightened bride.

"I—" she rasped uncertainly. She looked for and found gentle support in William's patient eyes. She licked her lips and tried again. "I do," she finally managed to say, her voice audible only to the people at the front of the church.

The preacher gave a satisfied nod of his head and said, "Then by the powers vested in me, I pronounce you . . ."

But before Reverend Martin could finish the ceremony, an arrow streaked through the air to enter his

12

back with a vicious zipping sound, its point immediately exiting his chest before Starr's horrified stare.

For the briefest instant, no one in the church moved. Everyone remained frozen in a bizarre portrait of horror and surprise.

Starr and William stared in shock at the bloody arrowhead protruding grotesquely from the growing red stain on the minister's shirtfront.

The wounded man looked helplessly at the wedding couple. He toppled forward into the arms of the shocked groom, just as a bullet whizzed past Starr's head and struck William in the chest.

William and the preacher fell as one at Starr's feet, leaving her standing stunned and defenseless at the altar.

To the sound of wild war whoops, the church was suddenly filled with dark-skinned men, their bodies decorated with bright war paint, their hard-muscled arms whirling rifles and murderous war clubs over their heads. As if a switch had been pulled to set things in motion, pandemonium broke out, and the congregation scattered in all directions. Women and children screamed in helpless terror; men cursed as they attempted to defend themselves and their families. But there was nowhere to go, nowhere that was safe. All the windows and exits were blocked by the savage attackers.

People were falling all around her, but still the bride could not move or understand what was happening. As she turned to take in the horror unfolding in the small church, she saw her mother struck in the head by a deadly war club, and she instantly recovered from her trance.

Seeing Mary Winfield fall, Starr sprang into instinctive action and tried to run to her mother's side, unmindful of her own safety. All thought of the wedding ceremony was erased from her mind.

But the bride was unable to reach the wounded woman before being lifted off her feet and thrown over the broad painted shoulder of one of the Indians as he fought his way through the door of the tiny church.

With the exit of the brave who carried Starr, kicking and screaming, the other warriors immediately followed, some of them with frantic women slung roughly over their shoulders. The last thing Starr saw was one of the attackers hurling a flaming torch into the midst of the dead and wounded bodies in the church.

Starr's red-gold hair whipped against her windburned cheeks, yet she was unaware of the lashes on her tender flesh. She had long since ceased to feel pain, and abandoned her futile screams for help as well as the useless struggles against the strong bare arms that held her captive. She had no idea how long it had been since she had been taken from the church, how long she had ridden across the plains in front of the half-naked brown-skinned man, or how far she was from her home.

Had it been only a few hours since she had hesitated to marry William because she had been afraid of leaving her parents to go live at Fort Abraham Lincoln? How foolish she'd been. What she wouldn't give to be there now, warm and secure in William's

14

arms. But that would never happen now, for William was dead.

They were all dead. Her parents, William, everyone. No one in the church could have escaped the brutal melee. Her heart felt as if it had been ripped from her chest, leaving her a hollow, unfeeling shell.

Starr blinked her stinging eyes. They were so tired, so dry from the continuous wind in her face. She fought the desire to close them and lean back against the painted shoulder of the Indian who had her imprisoned in the circle of his hard arms as his spotted pony sped west.

"Where are you taking us?" she asked her Indian captor, knowing it was unlikely that he spoke English, but hopeful that the sound of her own voice would keep her awake. She wanted to remember every detail of the journey. Should the occasion to escape arise, she planned to be able to lead the others back to Yankton. If she could do something for the other captives, perhaps she would rid herself of the dreadful black emptiness that held her in its grasp. Yes, that's what she would do. She would ignore her own pain and concentrate on saving the others.

They had crossed the Missouri River, but that had been hours ago. Hours of watching the tall grasses of the flat prairie swaying hypnotically in the wind, hours of looking for a marker on the endless sea of grass. But everything was the same. No trees, no houses, no towns, no other riders. Just a rippling ocean of green.

"I know we're heading west because the sun is beginning to set," she yawned, observing the huge ball of fire in the western sky, trying not to think of

15

her dead parents and William. "What are you going to do with us? You know the soldiers will come after you. They won't stand still for this. You've broken the treaty," she mumbled, no longer able to keep her head from dropping forward on her chest. Her red-rimmed eyes finally conceded defeat, and she slept.

"Treaty!" the Indian blurted out in disgust. Starr awoke with a start. "You speak of treaties? You, who try to steal our *wakan paha*, our sacred hills, for the gold they hold? Bah!" he spat.

Starr swung her head to look at the stern-faced man who held her in front of him. "English! You speak English!" she choked. "How? Where did you learn to speak our language?"

"You are surprised that a *savage* can speak more than one tongue? And how many languages do you speak, *winyan ska*?" he asked, licking his lips hungrily as his black eyes raked over her perfectly-formed features for the first time.

Never had he seen such a beautiful woman. The fact that she was white made her a valuable commodity in itself, but with her burnished red-gold hair and large gray eyes, she would be worth a great deal more in trade than the other women they'd taken from the wedding ceremony. He realized she was a rare and beautiful treasure.

"I only speak English," Starr admitted, recognizing the expression in the Indian's hard black eyes as it changed from loathing to lust. Unable to avoid an inward cringing, she hurriedly turned her burning face away from his in a weak attempt to avoid the glistening ebony glare that seemed to cut into her soul and strip her naked.

16

"Then there is something the *ikce wicasa* can teach the *wasicun* after all," he growled, taking the reins in one hand and using the other to slide up the length of her body, boldly lingering a moment on her full breasts, before gripping her chin in a painful squeezing hold. He forced her head around to face him again. "Do you agree?"

"Yes," Starr whispered, her silvery eyes wide with terror.

"You are right to be afraid of me, *winyan ska*." His laugh was vicious and knowing. He released his grasp on her jaw to slide his hand downward, encircling her slender throat with long brown fingers pressed into her delicate flesh. "I might decide to keep you for myself instead of using you to bargain with the soldiers for their word that they will keep the whites from our sacred hills."

Starr knew the hills the Indian referred to were the Black Hills in the southwestern corner of the Dakota Territory. She also knew that last year General George Armstrong Custer had announced the discovery of gold in those same hills, causing a rush of whites to swarm onto the Sioux reservation in search of the precious ore. The greedy miners were determined to ignore the treaty the government had signed at Fort Laramie in 1868, the treaty which had supposedly guaranteed all the Dakota Territory west of the Missouri River to the Sioux Indians.

"The soldiers make every effort to turn them back."

"But still the *wasicun* comes. Like a great swarm of locusts. Destroying the grazing lands, butchering the buffalo, littering our hunting grounds, trying to

17

pen the People up like animals."

Starr heard the hate in the man's tone, but she heard something else. She heard pain. Deep pain and sadness. A pain so cruel that for a moment she forgot her own anguish.

"Do you really believe this is the way to stop them?" she asked softly, never doubting that he knew she was referring to the attack on the church and the kidnapping. "Every time your people commit a hostile act, it gives the government reason to send more soldiers." Starr felt the tensing of the muscular arms which surrounded her. But she went on, praying she would be able to convince the obviously intelligent Indian of the wrong he was doing. "The soldiers will come for us and more innocent people will be killed."

"No more talk," he grunted suddenly, kicking his horse to a full gallop as he tightened his grip on Starr's slim corseted figure, making it clear that he was through with their conversation.

Starr didn't attempt to initiate further talk with the Indian, but instead tried to formulate a plan of escape. It was impossible for her to give up hope, no matter how desperate the situation.

She didn't know when she had fallen asleep, but when she awoke it was dark, the full moon high in the sky. The Indian was lifting her from the horse's back, and she was so relieved to be off the horse that she didn't have the strength to resist him.

Starr heard the sobs and pleas of the other women prisoners as they were taken from the horses they'd been astride since that morning. Trying desperately to see what was happening, she found her view blocked by horses and her captor.

"Where are we? What's happening?" she asked. She couldn't see the others, but she could certainly hear them. And she could hear their pitiful whimpers that sounded like the cries of wounded wild creatures. "What are they doing to them?" she shrieked, starting to run in the direction of the wretched wailing to help. But she was immediately stopped by the Indian.

He grabbed Starr's long hair and pulled her back against his hard length. "They are claiming the rewards they deserve after our successful raid," he said, reaching around from behind and ripping Starr's blood-spattered white silk from the high collar to her waist. "White women wear too much clothing," he growled.

"Please don't do this!" Starr pleaded. "The soldiers won't negotiate with you for our release if we're used this way!" she shrieked, trying to make the leader of the raiding party understand. "They won't want us back. Your plan will fail."

"Then we will kill you one by one until the *wasicun* leaves our lands." With deadly accuracy he slid a long knife into the hollow between her breasts and cut her corset open with one swift motion. The restricting garment fell to the ground with her dress, leaving her clad in nothing but a thin chemise and drawers.

Starr's hands flew upward to cover herself. "Please," she whimpered in a small, weak voice, realizing for the first time that her situation was hopeless. Although the Indian's speech seemed civilized, she remembered he was still a savage and would not be stopped with reason.

Strong fingers closed over her hands and pulled

19

them around to grasp them between her body and that of the Indian who stood behind her.

The vicelike grip on the girl's frail wrists cut off the circulation to her limp hands almost immediately, but not soon enough to prevent Starr from feeling the pressure of the brave's manhood, hard and thrusting against the palms of her numbing hands. Realizing what she was touching, she balled her hands into fists and tried to scream, but the only sound she could make was a sharp intake of breath.

For some reason, her mother's words came back to her. *If you relax, it might not be too terrible.* Starr laughed silently. At the time, the words which had been meant to comfort had seemed so ridiculous. But now they were all Starr had to rely on. *Relax and it might not be too terrible.* Those ridiculous words were all she had now.

Relax . . . relax . . . relax . . . she thought over and over, forcing herself to go limp, to ignore the feel of the dark hand as it fumbled over her body. But she couldn't relax. Couldn't stand still and allow this savage to touch her this way. What could she do? She couldn't escape. His hold on her was too strong. If she struggled, he would only make what was happening more painful than it already was. She'd heard too many stories about what savages did to women captives who made them angry.

Think of something else. Don't think about what he's doing to you.

What about the other captives? Did they all survive? She realized the screams had died down to pathetic moans and whimpers. She could still hear them, but only an occasional shrill cry pierced the air now. Which women had the Indians taken from the church? How many were there? Starr tried to count the captives. She was certain she'd seen a flash of familiar pink flowered calico draped over one of the brave's shoulders when they'd left the church. That would be sixteen-year-old Melanie Walters. And she had gotten a glimpse of fourteen-year-old Katie Hodges and her mother, Agatha, but were there others?

With a grunt of disgust, the Indian shoved Starr to the ground and fell on her, making it impossible for her to think of anything but his presence. All worry about the other captives was erased with the loud ripping sound of her own flimsy drawers. All concern with the past and future was obliterated, leaving her with but one thought, one basic instinctive thought. She could not give up without a fight.

Starr let an earsplitting scream as, with an unexpected surge of strength, she managed to twist her hips to the side, miraculously evading the determined brave's attack.

"There is nowhere to go. You are my woman now," he laughed, his words a chilling threat.

He lunged again.

And again, screaming with renewed vigor, she was able to move successfully and avoid his assault.

The Indian slapped the resisting girl across the face with a stinging blow meant to control her. But before he could take advantage of her temporary stillness, a series of rifle shots suddenly rang out, filling the air with smoke and flashes of light.

Starr's captor sprang to his feet, pulling her with him. She was too dazed and stunned from the blow to

21

her head even to attempt to cover herself. All she knew was that he was no longer on top of her. She didn't even realize what the shots she had heard could mean. Not until she heard a deep male voice calling out in English, "Let us have your prisoners, Gray Wolf, and I may be able to convince the soldiers not to retaliate."

"Bah," the Indian holding Starr spat onto the ground. "If it is not Daniel Blue Eagle. Or should I call you *Man of Two Faces*?"

"We are all around you, Gray Wolf. Release the women. I will return them to their families," the deep voice said calmly. To confirm his position of strength, a bullet came out of the darkness to whiz past Starr's face and embed itself in the ground beyond her.

Now speaking in his native tongue, Gray Wolf shouted to his followers, who were waiting for orders from their leader. When he finished speaking, a cheer from the renegade braves rose and he spoke in English again.

"If you wish to take our prize from us, *Man of Two Faces*," he called out, his mouth curling in disgust as if the name left a bad taste in his mouth, "you will have to fight for them." The challenge in Gray Wolf's voice carried an obvious tone of excitement.

"We outnumber you, Gray Wolf. You will lose."

"But your hands are tied. Are they not? You won't attack us since you know the *winyan* will be the first to die. No, this will not be a battle between our braves. It will be between the two of us only. A battle to the death."

"I do not wish to fight you, Gray Wolf," the voice said from the darkness. "But it will be as you wish."

22

As if reacting to some silent signal, Gray Wolf's warriors, several dragging limp captives with them, spread out to form a large circle around their leader and Starr. They were quickly joined by an equal number of solemn-faced, buckskin-clad Indians who were armed but wearing no war paint like the braves who had taken the women from the church.

A hush fell over the gathering as a tall man stepped out of the shadows and into the ring of braves.

An Indian! The man who had come to save them was not a white man but another Indian. Starr's breath caught in her throat. From his mellow, unaccented voice, she had expected to see a white man come forward to fight with Gray Wolf, not an Indian.

Moving with the grace of a dancer, the challenging Indian approached the man and woman standing at the center of the circle.

Daniel Blue Eagle stopped before Gray Wolf and his captive and ran his eyes fleetingly over Starr's frightened face, his gaze catching and holding hers for the briefest instant. But that instant was enough for the girl to realize that the Indian's eyes were not black. They were light like a white man's. Possibly blue or gray, she couldn't determine which in the bright moonlight. But they were not black like the eyes of other Indians she had seen. She was certain of that.

Instinctively, Starr looked at Gray Wolf's angry features to confirm her strange discovery. Then she looked back at the man Gray Wolf had called Daniel Blue Eagle. Both were tall, taller than the other braves, though Daniel Blue Eagle was the taller of the two, and both wore their glistening black hair parted in the center and braided in the style she had come to expect Indians to wear.

They look alike! Starr suddenly realized. *They have the same broad forehead, the same prominent cheekbones and square jaw.* Even their straight noses seemed to have been sculpted by the same artist. *Only the eyes are different.* She wondered if her imagination could be playing tricks on her.

"It has been a long time, Gray Wolf," Daniel Blue Eagle said. "You look well."

"And you," Gray Wolf responded vengefully. "It is obvious that you have fared well at the side of Man of the People. The place you stole from me with your twisting words."

"He asks about you daily, Gray Wolf. He would like to see you."

"And he will when he sees that you have sold him to the *wasicun* for a few pitiful bolts of cloth and sacks of flour. Or perhaps after I kill you this night, I will take him your scalp and assume my rightful place at his side, as future chief of our band."

With those words, Gray Wolf cast Starr into the arms of another brave and took out a long knife, which he firmly clamped between his teeth.

"I don't want to fight with you, Gray Wolf," Daniel Blue Eagle said, sadly aware that this battle had been inevitable for years.

Gray Wolf grunted in reply and took a battle stance.

Unhappily aware that he had no choice but to fight, Daniel Blue Eagle quickly stripped off his buckskin shirt and leggings, leaving himself dressed only in his breechcloth, his muscular torso glistening

24

gold in the pale moonlight. Taking a long knife and placing it between his teeth as Gray Wolf had, he accepted his war club from one of his braves.

The two circled slowly at first, both crouched low with arms outstretched. Gray Wolf made several springing false starts toward Daniel Blue Eagle who reacted each time with carefully measured sidesteps, never allowing his concentration to waver from the other man's face.

For what seemed an eternity the two stalked each other, each wanting the other to make the first move. Finally, with a wild yell that sounded as if it had come from hell, Gray Wolf flew across the space that separated the two fighters.

Swinging his war club viciously, its movement through the air making an eerie swishing sound, he barely missed Daniel Blue Eagle's shoulder. But Daniel Blue Eagle was able to avoid the deadly, rawhide-covered stone head of the war club just in time. But his balance was thrown off and he tripped, falling helplessly on his back.

Gray Wolf immediately took advantage of the other man's vulnerability and whirled around, swinging his war club as he lunged for the downed warrior.

Starr screamed, but neither of the men in the ring heard her involuntary cry. Nor did they hear the encouraging shouts of the other spectators. Each man was aware only of his own heavy breathing and the actions of his opponent.

Daniel Blue Eagle rolled to one side and to his feet, regaining his equilibrium just in time to avoid Gray Wolf's deadly lurch. But he had moved at the last instant, too late for Gray Wolf to stop his own forward drive. The attacker flew to the earth to land face down in the spot where Daniel Blue Eagle had been only the moment before.

Before Gray Wolf could rise up, Daniel Blue Eagle was on top of him, his hard knee boring into the center of Gray Wolf's back as he pulled his head up and held his knife at the base of his scalp.

The knowledge of what was about to happen cut into Starr's heart. She stuck her fist into her mouth to muffle the scream she felt rising in her throat.

The moment was rife with tension as the stunned captives and Indians waited for Daniel Blue Eagle to finish off the downed brave. No one moved.

"I will not kill my brother," the victor finally announced to the dumbfounded witnesses, knowing that by sparing Gray Wolf's life he was disgracing him before his men and that this would not be the end of their fight.

Daniel Blue Eagle dropped Gray Wolf's paint-smeared face in the dirt and rose to walk away. He nodded his head to his men who took the women captives from Gray Wolf's braves, then backed slowly from the circle, covering their leader's departure with their alert vigil until the last of the hostile braves had ridden away.

Chapter Two

"Please wait!" Starr cried out. Shrugging off the hand of the Indian who was guiding her to the horses, she ran toward the retreating back of Daniel Blue Eagle.

Totally unmindful of her own near-naked state, she was only aware that they had been saved by the strange Indian who had blue eyes and spoke English with the accent of a cultured white man. She had to thank him, had to know why.

"How can we ever thank you?" she asked, afraid to believe that these braves did not have the same vicious intentions as Gray Wolf's warriors.

There was no answer.

When she reached the tall man who stood silently gazing into the surrounding darkness, his muscles glistening in the moonlight, she stopped. She was strangely touched by something heartbreaking in his stance. "Who are you? Why did you come for us?" she whispered at last.

Daniel Blue Eagle tilted his proud head back and

looked heavenward, seeming not to notice the low groan of sorrow he let out.

The lonely, tortured sound cut into Starr's heart. Daniel Blue Eagle's strong limbs hung at his sides, anguished clenching and unclenching of his fists his only reaction to her presence.

Starr reached out to touch the golden brown flesh of one massive arm, instinctively moved by some inexplicable compassion for his mysterious suffering. But a sense of survival told her she couldn't touch the bare flesh that beckoned to her. It told her that if she succumbed to the desire that screamed from within her heart, she would be lost.

With the need to feel the hard glimmering flesh so great that her fingers burned, she willed herself to draw her hand away, flexing her fingers over and over as if trying to regain control of their actions.

But it was no use. His suffering was too real, her need too great. She couldn't stop herself or deny the need to soothe him.

Hot and dangerous, his power drew her to him as it burned its way into her soul. With her shaking arm outstretched, her trembling fingers only inches from contact now, she stood as if hypnotized by the narrow space that separated their skin.

"We'll take you to our village tonight and let you rest. Then we'll return you to your homes tomorrow," the man called Daniel Blue Eagle said suddenly, his deep voice breaking the silence and releasing Starr from his magnetic hold.

Her hand dropped to her side and she sighed in relief.

In reaction to the whisper of her breath on his

damp flesh, Daniel Blue Eagle whirled around angrily to be caught by the startled gaze of Starr's silvery eyes.

"Why aren't you with the others?" he growled, accepting the return of his buckskin shirt and leggings from one of the other braves who were nearby.

"I wanted to know what you're going to do with us," Starr mumbled breathlessly, not certain she could keep from swooning under the intense heat of his formidable glare, but knowing she must not—for the sake of the others, if not for herself.

Daniel Blue Eagle drew a deep, impatient breath, expanding his broad muscled chest to its full breadth. He expelled it slowly, as though he needed time to find the words and patience to explain the most basic matter to a simple-minded child.

Starr bristled indignantly under his disdainful expression, but as his warm breath sighed over her face and neck, she couldn't control the sudden shiver that shook her to her very core. She told herself there was a chill in the night air, nothing more.

She grew uncomfortably warm under his indifferent scrutiny as his scorching blue eyes traveled down the graceful column of her throat, along the gentle slope of her shoulders, over her full breasts down to where her slim waist curved into her well-rounded hips.

Suddenly, Daniel Blue Eagle's gaze shot upward again to the full, lush mounds thrusting against the gossamer material of a torn chemise that barely covered their fullness, as if he had to confirm what he had seen. His mouth agape, his blue eyes grew wide and then shifted nervously to the ground. Beads of perspiration broke out on his upper lip.

"You'd better wear this," he muttered, shoving his buckskin shirt toward Starr.

Wondering what it was that had caused him to act so strangely, her eyes fell to the spot that had captured the man's startled gaze. She gasped aloud. The color of her pale skin, already pink with embarrassment, deepened. One hand flew upward in an overdue attempt to hide the dark shadowy circles that showed through the flimsy white material.

She seized the offered shirt, turned her back modestly and hurriedly drew it over her head, determined to regain her composure. After all, he had said he was going to take them back to Yankton. That was all that mattered. That was all she would think about.

Blushing and looking down at the buckskin shirt to be certain that her modesty was once more intact, Starr was overwhelmed by its softness and pleasant odor. It was a heady mixture of leather, smoke, and the masculine scent of the man who had worn the shirt. It took every bit of her determination not to sigh at the wonderful sensations the intoxicating smell evoked.

Hanging well past her knees, the fringed garment had been painstakingly beaded across the shoulders and front. "It's lovely," she murmured without thinking as she ran her hands over the velvety garment. "So soft."

"Yes, it is," Daniel Blue Eagle said, finding it difficult to take his eyes away from the enticing picture the small girl with hair the color of the evening sun made in his shirt.

Daniel Blue Eagle shook his head, as if to clear his mind of unwanted thoughts. "See that you do it no

30

harm. It is very special."

His hoarse voice cracked as he spoke, but Starr did not notice. "No, I won't harm it," she promised absently as she fingered the colored beads on the shirt.

"You'd better check on the other women, since you seem to be in the best condition. Then we will go."

His words brought Starr back to the present with a crushing jolt of guilt. The others! She had actually forgotten the others for a moment. Had forgotten her plan to take care of them. Had forgotten the injury they had all suffered. She'd been too concerned with saving herself from Gray Wolf and then with Daniel Blue Eagle's intentions. She should have gone to them the moment she was able.

Silently condemning her own selfishness, Starr ran to where the other women were huddled together, each lost in her own misery. There were five of them, and their condition was much worse than Starr had ever imagined it would be. All were wearing only remnants of the clothing they had worn at the wedding; hair that had been painstakingly arranged that morning hung in damp tangled masses about stooped, defeated shoulders; and all five women wore the same dazed, pitiful expressions on their dirty, beaten faces.

None of them spoke when she approached. In fact, none of them seemed to be aware of anything that was going on. They all looked as though they had crossed into a mystical fog and were no longer the human beings they resembled.

The pink calico Melanie Walters had been wearing was hardly recognizable. Bloody and shredded by the knife of one of Gray Wolf's warriors, it covered little of the girl's battered and bruised skin, but she didn't seem to notice. Nor was she aware that there was a steady stream of blood coming from her nose, for she made no effort to wipe it away. Instead, she continued to hug her arms around her waist and rock back and forth, the blank stare on her once lovely face even more grievous than her physical wounds, for it told of injuries to her soul that would probably never heal.

"May we have some blankets?" Starr called out, choking back her own tears as she tried to clean Melanie's face with the hem of the flowered calico.

When she had done all she could for Melanie, she turned to put her arm around another of the captives. Though she and Dorcas Wimberley had never been good friends, it distressed Starr to see the proud girl so beaten and defeated. "There, there, dear, it will be all right," she promised as she smoothed the dark hair off her anguished face.

However, seeing that Dorcas was not going to respond to her presence, she turned anxiously to Agatha Hodges, thinking the older woman might be some help. But the thought had to be discarded immediately. Agatha wouldn't be able to help. Holding her daughter to her breast and humming a tuneless lullaby, she was completely oblivious to her surroundings.

Something about the way Katie looked worried Starr, and she rushed to her side to press her fingers against the point on her neck where she should have been able to feel a pulse. There was none.

Starr looked up into Agatha's blank eyes, not knowing what to do. How could she tell this mother that her daughter was dead?

"Here, let me hold Katie, Mrs. Hodges. You see to Mercy, won't you?"

But Agatha didn't answer. She just continued to rock her dead daughter and hum her eerie lullaby.

"Please, can't they have something to cover themselves?" Starr called to the Indians as she squatted down to check on twelve-year-old Mercy Green.

But seeing the child's lifeless, mutilated body lying on the ground, Starr could no longer suppress her anger. "Look what those savages did to her! She's just a baby and look what they did."

She stood and ran wildly at Daniel Blue Eagle and beat helplessly against his hard chest. "How did you let this happen? Why did you let those animals live?"

The tall Indian, his own heart aching at the sight of the two dead girls, welcomed Starr's angry blows, as though they might actually be able to make his own pain disappear.

When he had received word that Gray Wolf had taken the women from the church, he and his followers had ridden as fast as their horses could carry them, hoping to retrieve the captives before it was too late. But they had been too late, and now all he could do was take care of the remaining four and pray the consequences were not as catastrophic as he sensed they would be.

Aware that the girl's pounding was growing weaker, the feeble blows spaced further apart, Daniel Blue Eagle drew her into his strong embrace. Without thinking it odd that he felt compelled to console her, he placed her tearstained cheek against his hard chest and let her sob as his big hand soothed over her silky,

33

sweet-smelling hair.

Though she did not know what she was doing, he was very aware of it when her arms slipped around his waist to cling desperately to his strength. It was then that he realized what was happening to him. He gripped her upper arms and jerked her away roughly.

"We must be leaving," he growled, his deep voice unusually hoarse. "It is several hours to our village."

"Yes, we must leave," Starr repeated woodenly, Daniel Blue Eagle's harsh tone having shaken her back to reality. "But how will they travel? I don't think any of them can sit a horse after what's happened to them."

"They will have to ride. There is no other way. There was no time to bring travois poles," he said sternly, the coldness in his expression causing Starr to wonder if he could possibly be the same man who moments before had comforted her so gently.

He seems angry. As if he blames us for all that has happened.

"Can't you make some?" she insisted, now determined to protect the women at all costs, even if it meant facing the Indian leader's wrath.

"The poles require timber, which is not abundant on the prairie. Now, do you want to help the others to understand the importance of mounting the horses? Or shall I have my braves do it?" His voice, low and even, carried an obvious threat—a threat Starr thought better about challenging.

"I'll do it," she conceded, walking away from him to the other women.

"These Indians are going to take us home. They aren't going to hurt us. But we must ride the horses to

34

their village. Can you ride?" she asked, pulling Melanie to her feet. "Melanie! We're going home! Can you ride?" The other girl nodded numbly and allowed an Indian brave to lift her to the back of his pony before leaping on behind her.

"Come on, Dorcas. You can do it. I know you can," Starr went on urgently, drawing the lethargic girl to her feet. "Don't you want to go back to Yankton?" Dorcas still did not respond to Starr's anxious pleadings, but she didn't fight when another brave put her on his horse.

Starr took a deep breath and turned to Agatha Hodges who continued to rock her dead daughter in her arms as she hummed her lamenting lullaby.

"Mrs. Hodges," Starr whispered softly as she stooped to lay her hand on the woman's arm.

"Why, Starr Winfield! What are you doing dressed in that heathen garment?" Agatha said suddenly, her look a combination of shock and chiding. "What would your mother say if she saw you wearing that scandalous thing?"

She doesn't even realize where we are! She thinks we're in Yankton! What am I going to do?

"You'd never see my Katie in something like that! Goodness me, no! She's too much of a lady," Agatha went on, her tone rife with pompous pride. "But you never did much care what people thought about you, did you? Runing all over the countryside like a boy when you were a little girl. Then coming back from that college in St. Charles spouting off all sorts of crazy ideas about women being every bit as smart as men. I always say the family foolish enough to give a girl an education deserves what they get."

35

"Please, Mrs. Hodges. We've got to leave."

"And look at your hair. Goodness, child! When was the last time you took a brush to it? Your mama ought to be whipped for letting you run around like that."

"Will you help me fix it?" Starr asked softly, prying Agatha's hands off the dead girl's arms. "You always fix Katie's so nicely. Please come show me how you do it."

Obviously flattered by Starr's words, Agatha smiled and let Katie be taken from her arms. She took a tangled strand of Starr's hair and examined it closely. "Of course, only a devil's child would have hair this color. I always asked myself what sweet Mary did to deserve such a curse. Don't know what she expected though. Marrying that scoundrel Robert Winfield!"

Starr was too worried about the woman to be hurt or angered by her words. "Come with me, Mrs. Hodges, and as soon as we get home you can fix my hair."

"What about Katie?" Agatha said. "I can't leave Katie here alone."

"Oh, no, Mrs. Hodges. We won't leave Katie. We'll take her with us. She'll ride another horse."

"Katie can't ride a horse."

"Of course she can."

"But Katie's dead. How can she ride a horse?"

The breath caught in Starr's throat. "What did you say?"

"Katie's dead," the woman repeated matter-of-factly. Then as if the truth of her own words had slapped her conscious mind in the face, she said them again. Only this time they were a pathetic, hysterical shriek. "Katie's dead! My baby is dead! They killed her! Those savages killed my little girl!'"

With inhuman strength, Agatha jerked herself free of the Indian who had come forward to help Starr get her on the horse. "Get away from me, you filthy savage," she screamed, suddenly waving a long knife in the air and holding it as if she would attack.

The Indian beside Starr automatically lowered his guilty look to the empty sheath on his side, then looked up helplessly into the angry glare of Daniel Blue Eagle.

"Don't be afraid, Mrs. Hodges. These men have come to help us. They mean us no harm. They're taking us back to Yankton! Please put the knife down and come home with us."

"I won't go with you. I'm going to stay here with my baby!" She was now kneeling beside her daughter and smoothing the mussed hair from the pale, dead face. "I always said that Starr Winfield was a daughter of Satan, didn't I, sweetie?" she said to Katie. "Now you see what she's done? She's gone and gotten us killed. But we won't have to see her again, because she'll be burning in Hell for what she's done. And we'll be together in Heaven with the glorious Savior!" she said, the smile on her face spiteful as she glanced at Starr before lifting the knife upward to plunge it deep into her own chest. And before anyone could react, Agatha pulled the weapon out and stabbed it into her heart again. Then she slumped forward dead, her life's blood spilling over the ground and her beloved daughter.

"No!" Starr screamed, starting to lunge for the woman, but she was stopped by the strong grip of

Daniel Blue Eagle.

The already familiar feel and scent of him wrapped around her and seeped into Starr's soul like a magical life-renewing panacea, and she slipped blissfully into unconsciousness.

When she came to she was riding eastward, nestled securely between golden brown arms and against the firm wall of a heavily muscled chest. She didn't wonder who it was that held her on the horse's back. There was no doubt in her mind that she was in the arms of Daniel Blue Eagle, a place that in only a few short hours had already come to mean safety and shelter to her.

In her drowsiness she sighed and stretched like a cat before resettling herself in the rugged embrace. But in the next instant she was brought abruptly out of her pleasant state.

"Did you sleep well?" a voice asked in her ear, sending a ripple of goose flesh over her skin and reminding her that she would not be safe until they were back in Yankton, if then. Hadn't she been in Yankton when Gray Wolf's warriors had taken them? How could she be certain these Indians were any different than the others?

She ignored Daniel Blue Eagle's question and sat up straight in the soft Indian saddle. "How much further is it to your village? The others must be exhausted."

"It's not far now," he assured, unable to disguise a laugh deep in his throat. "Are you uncomfortable?"

"Of course I'm uncomfortable. What's in this saddle, anyway?"

"Buffalo hair and dried grass. I'm sorry you don't

find it to your liking. The next time I save you, I will ride bareback."

"Who are you? You look like an Indian, but you certainly don't speak like one."

"That's because I spent a good deal of my youth in a white home and was educated in the East. I have a college degree from your Harvard University."

Starr twisted around to study the Indian's face, certain he must by lying. "You don't!" she gasped.

"I do," he said, raising his black eyebrows in mock surprise at her reaction. "Don't you believe me?"

"But how?" she stuttered. She'd heard of a few Indians going to college. But to Harvard?

"My maternal grandfather was a man of great wealth and influence, and himself a graduate of Harvard. So there you have it." He chuckled and shrugged his shoulders.

"Was he an Indian too?" Her curiosity about the enigmatic Indian's background seemed to have renewed her strength and she was hardly aware of the soreness in her legs and hips anymore.

"No, he was white, as was my *ina*, my mother." Daniel Blue Eagle's voice contained a moving tone of sadness at the mention of his mother, but Starr barely noticed it. She was too excited about her discovery.

"I knew it! I knew you weren't an Indian! But why do you live with them? Wear your hair long and dress like them?"

She felt Daniel Blue Eagle's posture stiffen. "Oh, but I am an Indian," he said coldly, as if she had insulted him by suggesting otherwise. "In every way that counts, I am of the *ikce wicasa*—the People. As far as I'm concerned, there is no other blood flowing

39

through my veins than *Lakota* blood—Sioux in the words of the white man."

"But your eyes are blue," she insisted. How could he deny that he was white? Besides, she couldn't have such a conversation with a savage Indian. There had to be some reason he claimed to be an Indian.

"As were my mother's and my grandfather's. But I'm an Indian nonetheless. My father is Man of the People, a full blooded *Lakota* chief. Though, in the words of the whites, I am a *half-breed*, in my soul— my *nagi*—I am only Lakota."

"Then why do you use the white name Daniel?"

"Because it is the name my *ina* gave me. I do it out of respect and love for her."

Anxious to ask more questions, but realizing by his tone that she had dredged up unpleasant thoughts, Starr decided to change the subject. "How long will we stay in your village?"

"Only long enough to see to the others' injuries and rest a short while," he answered distantly, his mind still in the world to which her curiosity had taken him.

"Will it be dangerous for you to take us back?" Starr asked, suddenly realizing that the soldiers would have no way of knowing that Daniel Blue Eagle and his braves were not the Indians who had attacked the church.

"Yes," he answered, but offered no further information.

She felt his body tense as he suddenly straightened and leaned forward.

"What is it?" she asked, turning to see his eyes squinted in concentration, his face hard and troubled.

40

She looked to see if she could determine what it was that held his attention so completely.

In the distance, she saw what she thought might be the outlines of Indian tepees against the gray predawn horizon. But why would that upset him?

Daniel Blue Eagle held his hand up to silently signal his followers to stop. He turned to them and spoke in their language, a language Starr could not understand. But she could read the concern in his tone and the anxiousness in the eyes of the other braves as they listened to his words. And she was afraid, almost as afraid as she'd been when Gray Wolf had taken her from the church.

Worried, the group started forward. Only now, they spread out to form a line that would eventually encircle the small village.

"What's happening?" Starr whispered at last. But instead of answering her question, Daniel Blue Eagle clamped a hand over her mouth so tightly that she thought she would pass out.

When he felt her relax, he released the hold just enough to make it possible for her to breathe more easily, but he kept her mouth covered with his hand.

They rode the rest of the way into the village like that, his hand on her mouth, her eyes wide with fright and apprehension about what the change in Daniel Blue Eagle's manner might mean.

She kept her eyes on the still village, but before long she realized there was furtive movement in the area. At first she thought it was just the breeze moving the tall prairie grasses. Then it looked like round gray boulders rising up out of the grass. Finally, she realized the moving figures she was seeing

41

were human beings. There were people coming from the village toward the mounted Indians.

Daniel Blue Eagle dropped his hand from her mouth, but still his posture remained tense as the line of braves approached the greeting party coming from the village.

Slowly, Starr became aware of a mournful wailing in the distance. It seemed to be coming from the village. A woman crying? No, it wasn't a woman. It was many women. Crying!

Starr turned to look at Daniel Blue Eagle, her expression questioning, worried. But he seemed to have forgotten her presence, so great was his anxiety.

When they finally reached the cluster of moaning women, one older woman came forward to meet the men. She babbled excitedly, pointing repeatedly to the village and using her hands to tell her story.

The braves listened in stone-faced silence to what the woman said, but Starr could tell by their expressions that their anger would be hard to suppress, no matter what had caused it.

The fear that had plagued her from the moment Daniel Blue Eagle's demeanor had changed so suddenly grew to unfathomable proportions. She sensed that something so terrible had happened that her own life would forever be altered by it. Yet she did not know what it was. She could not imagine what could have happened in this little Indian village that would affect her in such a way.

Chapter Three

"There must be some mistake!" Starr insisted when Daniel Blue Eagle finally told her what the woman was saying. But his angry blue eyes burned into hers, telling her that there was no mistake, a new hate in his expression. She grew weak with the knowledge that he blamed her people for what had happened. More afraid than she'd ever been in her life, she knew she still had to defend her countrymen, had to make him believe that no decent, law-abiding white could have committed such atrocities.

"It must've been someone else! United States soldiers are in the Dakota Territory to protect people. They don't ride into defenseless villages and slaughter them. They wouldn't kill helpless women and old people! And the children! Only monsters would do something like that to little children! Don't you see? It had to be someone else! Someone completely evil! Perhaps desperate prospectors who think starting trouble will gain them access to the Black Hills! Or even another tribe of Indians who want you angry

43

with the soldiers so you'll go to war!''

Daniel Blue Eagle kept his stony silence as he leapt from the horse and roughly pulled Starr to the ground. With a deliberate lack of concern for the pain his hold on her was causing, his strong fingers dug harder into the tender flesh of her upper arm as he shoved her forward, forcing her closer to the horrible sight that had greeted them.

"No! I can't look!" she cried, squeezing her burning eyes shut and turning her head away from the ghastly vision that in only a few seconds had managed to scar itself into her memory.

Starr's head was violently jerked around with such fury that a paralyzing pain shot through her neck. The grip on her hair was so tight that she was certain the tangled masses would be yanked from her scalp. Still she refused to open her eyes.

"You will look!" Daniel Blue Eagle growled, giving her head a hard shake until she opened her eyes. "You will look and remember! See what your brave soldiers have done to these defenseless people!"

"I know soldiers didn't do this," Starr whimpered, no longer aware of the pain his hold was causing. All she could feel was the ache in her heart, the violent urge to double over and vomit. "They didn't," she repeated, her eyes wide with horror at the gory sight.

The murderers had laid out the scalped and mutilated bodies in the center of the village, and Starr knew that as long as she lived she would never see another sight so vile or so cruel.

"Do you honestly think this is the first time this has happened?" Daniel Blue Eagle asked, his words more accusation than question.

44

He twisted her head toward a dead man who still held a red, white and blue American flag in one hand, a white flag of peace in the other. Both flags were filthy, tattered, and covered with blood and bootprints. "Believe me, it is not!"

Next he forced her to focus on a young mother, not much more than a child herself. The cradle board containing her tiny dead baby was still strapped to her maimed body, and Starr clutched at her own heaving belly as she struggled to turn away from the horror. But still he forced her to look.

"More than once your soldiers have attacked and murdered peaceful bands. At Ash Hollow they killed a hundred Lakota who were trying to parlay, and at Sand Creek, Colorado, one of your great soldier heroes, Colonel Chivington, led a thousand troops against Black Kettle's band of six hundred Cheyenne, mostly women and children, while they were innocently waiting to conclude a peace treaty. The longknives left one hundred seventy-five of the *ikce wicasa* dead and mutilated that time!"

"Please," Starr finally begged, clamping her mouth shut tight in a last ditch effort to keep down the contents of her stomach; but he didn't seem to hear her.

"It is only fortunate that most of the women and young people were out digging wild onions and were able to hide until they saw us returning," he said coldly, forcing Starr to take a last look at a dead five- or six-year-old boy who lay nearby. With that, Starr could no longer control her body's revulsion to the horror before her. She vomited violently, as if in so doing she could purge herself of the poisonous mem-

45

ory the appalling bloodshed had left on her soul.

Daniel Blue Eagle watched her coldly and was silent for several minutes before Starr realized that his grip on her hair and arm had relaxed.

Her own heart aching with sorrow and the need to make amends for the senseless cruelty, she turned to face him. But she was unprepared for what she saw in his expression.

The civilized man who had fought so bravely to save them from Gray Wolf's warriors the night before had disappeared. She was now facing a man filled with so much anger and pain that the sight of his contorted features filled her with new fear and she gasped aloud. If there had been any doubt about Daniel Blue Eagle's Indian heritage before, there was none now; and viewing his tortured features, she was afraid that any love he had ever held for his white ancestry had been destroyed by the irrational brutality.

"I would give anything for this not to have happened," Starr whispered, choking back her tears as she laid a consoling hand gently on his bronzed arm. "If only I could do something to help."

Daniel Blue Eagle studied Starr's slender fingers, pale and soft against his hard brown flesh, before looking up in startled surprise. He was stunned to realize that he had a painful and unexpected urge to accept her gently offered comfort.

Suddenly, as if burned by hot coals, he gave his arm a hard shake to remove the touch that was burning its way over his skin and throughout his body, directly to the heart of his manhood.

Though the shock of his reaction to the light pressure on his arm threw him for a moment, he was able to recover quickly. With years of the strictest training behind him, he was an expert at disguising his feelings, so when he spoke again, though his voice was hoarse and low, the gleam in his blue eyes remained cold and ominous.

"Oh, you will help," he said. "You will see to it that the men responsible for this are punished."

"Yes!" Starr agreed urgently. "When we get to Yankton, I'll testify that these people were killed in cold blood."

She didn't see the humorless laugh in his icy stare. "They will know of this ruthless massacre in Yankton, but it will not be you who tells them," Daniel Blue Eagle said softly, the gentle even tone of his voice seeming even more dangerous than if he had shouted.

"I don't understand," Starr gulped, the germ of a new fear beginning to dawn in her mind. "Of course, I'll tell them. Do you think I would let this terrible thing go unreported? Just as soon as I get back to Yankton I'll—"

"You're not going back to Yankton."

"Of course, I am. You said you were taking us home."

"That was before your soldiers came into my village and killed my people. Now you will stay with us until the guilty troopers are located and hung."

"But we can't stay here. I must go home and find out about my family. They will be worried about me," she lied, knowing her words were untrue since everyone in the church was dead. "And my husband!" she added urgently. "I have to go to my husband."

Starr noticed a taut muscle in Daniel Blue Eagle's jaw tighten when she mentioned William, but she

47

thought nothing of it and went on urgently.

"Please take us home as you promised. I give you my word that I'll dedicate myself to seeing that the guilty persons are brought to justice!"

Daniel Blue Eagle studied her long and hard. Then without further words, he turned and walked away, leaving her standing in the midst of mourning women who had already begun to prepare the dead by wrapping their bodies in buffalo robes.

Starr looked around helplessly for a moment and then ran after Daniel Blue Eagle. "Don't you walk away from me like that. We aren't through talking!" she demanded, the pressure of all that had happened in the past twenty-four hours finally breaking through her numbed sense of disbelief. Until that instant it had all seemed unreal, as if she would wake up any minute from the bad dream. But now she knew there would be no merciful awakening. It was all true! And she was in a fight for her life. He had to understand.

Daniel Blue Eagle stopped in mid-stride and turned slowly to face the enraged woman. "Understand this!" he said evenly. "You are in a Lakota camp now. And in a Lakota camp the man determines when the conversation is ended. I will choose to ignore your foolish outburst this time, but should you repeat it, I will have you tied up for the remainder of the day. Do I make myself clear?"

"You make yourself perfectly clear, Mr. Blue Eagle! It is clear that you are no less a savage than that beast, Gray Wolf! If you keep us here against our will, you are as guilty as he is!" she goaded foolishly, her feet set squarely apart, her clenched fists on her hips. "So, for all your education and feigned talk of

48

peace, you are still nothing more than a hostile savage, are you?"

The muscle along Daniel Blue Eagle's square jaw twitched perceptibly now, but Starr continued heedlessly.

"What makes you think you're the only one who has been injured? Yesterday was my wedding day! It should have been the happiest of my life. Instead, I saw my parents and bridegroom cut down by ruthless savages, my friends and neighbors butchered and burned by those same fiends. Now you have the gall to insinuate that I'm to be punished for this." One hand made an ineffectual sweep toward the carnage at the center of the village.

Angry tears streamed down her wrathful, sunburned face but she could not back down. Not now. Not when she'd finally found the courage to unleash all the anger she felt.

And Daniel Blue Eagle experienced yet another surprising stab of feeling.

Damn fool, he cursed himself silently, growing more and more angry at his ridiculous weakness by the instant. How dare she speak to him in such a manner? *Only a white woman could be this stupid.* He was certain no Lakota woman would ever behave so unwisely.

He became increasingly aware that the busy funeral preparations surrounding them had stilled. Everyone in the village was waiting to see what he would do. None of them had ever seen such lunacy—or bravery—in any female, especially a white female.

Then, too, there was a certain faction who watched eagerly to see how the half-white son of their chief,

Man of the People, would handle this situation. They were the ones who were already making plans to join Gray Wolf's band of hostiles to seek their revenge for the brutal massacre should Daniel Blue Eagle let his white blood affect his decision to pursue a course of retribution.

With eyes narrowed furiously, he examined Starr's upturned face, hoping for a sign of remorse in her expression. There was none. He had known there would not be.

Daniel Blue Eagle had no choice. The woman with hair the color of autumn leaves and the temper of a rabid she-wolf had challenged him before the others, and he could not turn away from that challenge—not if it would lose him the respect of the other men of the tribe, not when he had to keep them from the warpath that could only lead to their total destruction. Now was no time to be soft.

Without further words, Daniel Blue Eagle allowed himself one exasperated shrug, slung Starr over his shoulder and carried her, kicking and screaming, into a nearby tepee and threw her to the ground.

"Let me go!" she screamed. "You can't do this to me, Daniel Blue Eagle!" she cried out, twisting and bucking as he held her pinned to the ground with a knee in her back while he deftly wrapped narrow strips of rawhide around her wrists and ankles.

Grabbing a fistful of matted red hair in his hand, his hard knee still pressing into the small of her back, Daniel Blue Eagle lifted Starr's upper torso, arching her back painfully. "The next time you forget to show me the proper respect, you will be tied to a post and whipped," he growled viciously and dropped her face in the dirt.

"They'll hang you for this," she threatened weakly, but no one heard her. Daniel Blue Eagle was gone, and she was alone. Totally alone. "You can't do this to me," she protested pitifully. But not only could he do it, he had, and she knew she would never see her home again.

Drawing her weary, battered body into a tight ball on the ground where she lay in the dark tent, she finally gave herself over to the despair that had been building since the moment the Indians had burst into the church the day before. No longer did she feel the need to pretend a courage she didn't have, and at last she cried.

She cried for herself, for her sweet parents, for her dead husband, for Agatha and Katie Hodges, for Mercy Green, for Melanie and Dorcas, for the little Sioux Indian boy who would never grow to adulthood, for the old man with his useless flags, and for the dead Indian girl and her tiny baby. She cried for all mankind, both Indian and white, and when at last her tears were spent, she slept.

Hours later, when she awoke, Starr was aware of the overwhelming silence that surrounded her. She strained her ears for sounds of life, but there was nothing but silence, deafening silence. Even the ever-present sound of the wind rustling across the prairie and the hum of the insects seemed to have ceased. Where were the barking dogs she had heard earlier? Where were the wailing women?

Struggling to a sitting position, she was only vaguely aware of the numbness in her hands and feet. She cocked her head to listen again. Surely they wouldn't have left her. He had said she would be kept as a hostage until the murderers were punished. They wouldn't leave her behind to die of starvation or in the jaws of some wild animal. They wouldn't. There would be no purpose.

"Is anybody there?" she called out, the panic in her voice impossible to disguise. "Where is everyone? Can anyone hear me?"

The inside of the tepee had become a sweltering oven. The limited supply of air within felt smaller with each breath she took. Her breathing became increasingly more rapid. The walls of buffalo hide seemed to be closing in on her. She had to get out. She had to have air. Starr managed to force herself not to think about the burning in her throat and lungs.

With great effort, because her hands were completely useless, she crawled across the flattened grass that made up the floor of the large Indian lodge. She was determined not to stop until she reached the flap entrance of the tepee, the tempting lure of fresh air pulling her forward until she was finally within inches of the doorway.

All she had to do now was open the flap and she would be able to breathe again!

Suddenly, a frightening thought occurred to her. What if he was waiting outside for her to do just that? What if he was playing some diabolical cat and mouse game with her? Well, she could be as devious as any savage.

Her hands still tied behind her back, Starr toppled over on her side again and squirmed her way around so that her face was directed toward the flap, her nose a scant inch from its bottom edge. Slowly, ever so slowly, she moved her face toward the curtain that covered the doorway. Gingerly, she touched her nose to the smoke-scented hide with the intention of pressing it open along the ground so that she could get her mouth into a position to suck in glorious, hard-won air. No one would ever notice.

"At last," she gasped, giving the flap a final nudge with her nose and chin. But the opening was blocked!

"Are you going somewhere?" the familiar voice of Daniel Blue Eagle cooed softly. Starr felt the flap over the doorway snatched away from her face and found herself nose to toe with an Indian moccasin.

Despite her panic at being discovered, she greedily sucked in huge gulps of air as she rolled helplessly over onto her back and looked up the buckskin-clad length of Daniel Blue Eagle. "I thought you had left me," she finally gasped, unable to control the rapid rise and fall of her heaving chest.

"I told you I was keeping you," he rasped irritably, raking his hungry gaze over her perfectly-proportioned and defenselesss body. Though she was dirty and disheveled, she caused an ache in his loins that was becoming increasingly difficult to deny.

"It was so quiet," she whispered, her eyes closed lethargically.

"We were attending our dead."

Suddenly, he hunkered down on his heels, grasped her by the upper arms and jerked her to a sitting position, causing her head to snap back painfully. Her head reeled and her vision blurred.

"Do you understand your position now?" he

ground out, holding her limp form so that she had to look at him, willing her not to fight him and make it necessary for him to punish her further.

Starr searched his intent azure eyes quizzically, and for an instant she thought she saw a glimmer of sorrow and regret in their frosty depths. Then it was gone, and all she saw was the stony mask. Of course, it had been her imagination. This man felt no regret. He was a brutal and vicious animal. He had no feelings. He held no remorse for what had happened to her and the others. He had no intention of ever taking them back to Yankton.

"Yes, I understand!" she hissed, wishing with every fiber that she had the courage to spit in his face. But even if she were that daring, her mouth was too dry. She would have to wait for her revenge on Daniel Blue Eagle. And it would be much more subtle and permanent than the mere insult spitting in his face would be, but she would have it. She would have her revenge if it were the last thing she ever did.

"Good," Daniel Blue Eagle said, not missing the glint of rebellion that refused to be extinguished from her tone. "We'll be breaking camp shortly. You'll find those more comfortable for traveling," he mumbled, indicating a bundle of tanned skins with a tilt of his dark head as his brown fingers nimbly loosened the rawhide bindings on her ankles and wrists.

Starr ached to rub the red marks the leather thongs had left on her pale skin, but she refused to give Daniel Blue Eagle the satisfaction of knowing how miserable she was. Even if she couldn't fight him physically, she swore she would find other ways to make him regret the day he had gone back on his promise to take her and the others to Yankton.

So instead of massaging the circulation back into her tingling extremities as she longed to do, she reached for the bundle of clothing on the ground. "I'm sorry that I got your special shirt dirty," she said caustically, not bothering to hide the fact that not only was she not sorry in the least but that it gave her great pleasure to see the grass and dirt stains scattered over the garment. "I'll wash it," she added sweetly, her tone dripping with saccharine sincerity.

Yes, she would be the docile, well-behaved captive he expected her to be, and then when her chance came, when he least expected it, she would have her retribution. And that sweet, sweet moment of final revenge would be worth any amount of humiliating groveling she had to suffer to reach that goal. She inadvertently licked her lips in anticipation.

Daniel Blue Eagle studied the girl, finding her change of tactics from shrieking rebel to subdued prisoner interesting, if not amusing. Of course, she didn't fool him, not a bit. He knew she was a long way from giving up, and he couldn't help but admire her spirit. But at least this way she would behave in front of the others and he wouldn't be forced to punish her repeatedly. Still, he made a mental reminder not to turn his back on her.

"Am I to be allowed any privacy?" she asked humbly, almost able to hide the last bit of defiance in her voice.

His black brows raised suspiciously, but Daniel Blue Eagle only smiled in agreement as he bowed out of the tepee, letting the flap fall back over the doorway.

Not only music soothes the savage beast, Starr thought with satisfaction as her lips turned up in a sardonic smile and the revengeful plan for destroying her enemy continued to grow in her mind.

Moments later, clad in soft moccasins and a deer-skin dress that reached almost to her ankles, Starr took a deep, steadying breath and drew back the tent flap. She had been able to fingercomb some of the tangles from her hair and had used one of the rawhide strips that had bound her hands to tie her hair into one thick braid down her back. Reluctantly admitting to herself that the unfamiliar clothes and makeshift hairstyle were more comfortable than anything she had ever worn, she stepped into the sunshine and fresh air.

It took her pupils a moment to adjust to the glaring noonday sun after the long hours inside the dark lodge. However, as if there were an invisible line forcing her to seek him out, the moment she regained her vision her eyes homed in directly on Daniel Blue Eagle where he stood on the other side of the camp with his back to her.

Sensing her presence, Daniel Blue Eagle looked up from what he was doing and turned toward her, only to be assaulted anew by her rare loveliness. Her bright hair shimmered like gold in the rays of the warm sun, and standing against the backdrop of the dun-colored tepee, she presented a sensuous portrait of fire and determination. God, how he wanted her.

Across the camp, Daniel Blue Eagle's piercing blue eyes locked with and challenged her smoky gray ones, and before Starr could stop herself she lifted her chin a fraction, jutting it in silent defiance, just as he had known she would do.

Then she realized how close she was to revealing her hostility. It was too soon after she'd been granted this cherished reprieve, and it never occurred to her that he would not do as he had threatened at the slightest infraction. No, now was not the time to rebel. She was not ready to give up her precious freedom of movement again.

She dropped her gaze to the ground and waited subserviently in the tepee entrance.

Daniel Blue Eagle smiled inwardly at the play of emotions that had crossed her face in that instant. He walked toward her, unaware that he was not the only brave in camp who was enthralled by the young captive's pale beauty, not the only warrior who had visions of having the girl lying naked and moaning with passion beneath him.

Watching through a thick curtain of wispy lashes, Starr waited as Daniel Blue Eagle crossed the space that separated them in a few easy strides. Her breath caught in her chest. He really was magnificent. A magnificent male animal, lithe and dangerous. A wild bronzed animal whose fine nostrils were flared as if he had picked up the scent of his mate and would destroy any who challenged his possession of her. What would it be like to be the mate of that primitive animal who approached her? To lie with him? To feel his strength against her?

Starr shuddered with embarrassment at her wanton thoughts and she blushed.

"Are you more comfortable now?" he asked as he approached her.

"Yes, thank you," she whispered, her voice a weak

tremble. He was so close she could feel the heat of his body and smell his familiar scent of leather and smoke. What was happening to her? She was certain she would faint if he didn't step back from her, if the new sensations she was feeling didn't ease.

Daniel Blue Eagle looked down at the bent head and fought the desire to take her back into the tepee and make her his. But something told him that once would not be enough, that once he had her he would never be able to let her go. He knew that if he ever gave in to the temptation, he would no longer be the captor, but the slave.

"You will help my father's sister, Prairie Moon, take down our lodge," he said matter-of-factly and strode away before he could give away his painful desire.

Starr's head shot up to ask about Melanie and Dorcas, but he was already out of sight and had been quietly replaced by the short dark Indian woman who had greeted the rescue party that morning.

Then the most amazing thing happened. The leathery-faced woman smiled. The woman had actually smiled—a crooked, gentle smile that displayed a mouthful of stained and broken teeth. But it was the most beautiful smile Starr had ever seen, and she felt its warmth surround and hold her, giving her hope for the first time since they had ridden into the camp that morning.

Chapter Four

Starr heaved a sigh of relief as she carefully secured the last smoke-flap pole in a hollowed out spot. Wiping her work-roughened hands on her buckskin dress, she stepped back to survey the result of her efforts.

The tepee she and Prairie Moon had erected and taken down every day during the week stood at least fifteen feet high; she noted with pride that it was tilted at exactly the proper angle to allow the most standing room at the back. With the door flap correctly positioned to face the east and the tepee's bottom edge pegged securely to the ground, the sinew-stitched buffalo hide lodge looked as good as any of the many that were rapidly going up around her.

A fleeting thought of what Daniel Blue Eagle would think of her accomplishment leapt unbidden into her mind. She shook her head in an attempt to erase the unwanted memory of the blue eyes that seemed to haunt her. *I don't care what he thinks, just as long as he leaves me alone!* Determined not to think about Daniel Blue Eagle, she turned her attention to Prairie Moon, who had already begun the supper fire.

"Here, let me do that," Starr insisted, putting her arm around the older woman and leading her toward the tepee. "You've been too sick to be up and about," she said, using her hands to talk to the woman, who had suffered all day with stomach pains and coughing spasms.

Prairie Moon smiled the snaggle-toothed grin Starr had already come to love and tried to go back to the fire, insisting in her own language that she was feeling better now; but the younger woman would have none of that.

"Look!" she exclaimed, sweeping her hand toward the lodge and patting her own chest. "I did the tepee alone. You've taught me well, Prairie Moon. I will fix our supper. You rest," she pleaded, kneeling down and patting the ground for Prairie Moon to sit. "I'll have a tasty stew ready in no time!" she promised.

Starr returned to the fire Prairie Moon had already laid and had it going almost immediately. She smiled to herself as she put water into the cooking pouch attached to four poles she had erected over the fire. If anyone had told her a week ago that she could ever live like this, she would have laughed at them. Yet, here she was, boiling the water for supper by using a forked stick to drop hot, fist-sized stones into a pot made from the lining of a buffalo's stomach.

Once the water began to boil, Starr added strips of dried buffalo meat, pieces of the prickly-pear cactus they had been lucky to find that day, wild onions and peas from one of the beaded food bags Prairie Moon had called a *parfleche*, and a root vegetable that looked like a turnip. Again thoughts of Daniel Blue

Eagle filled her mind. Where was he?

The last time Starr had seen the blue-eyed Indian was when he had turned her over to his aunt, ordered her to help take down the lodge, and ridden out of camp without looking back. That had been a week ago. A week of moving west, of cooking with primitive utensils, of no proper bath. A week of worrying that she would never see civilization again, and of wondering what would become of her and the other captives.

She had seen Melanie and Dorcas a few times, but neither of them would talk to her. They seemed to blame her for their plight. Both young women had been taken in by braves who had lost wives in the horrible massacre that first day, and neither of them had shown any signs of adjusting to the Indian way of life. In fact, each day, they seemed to be more wasted than the last.

It tore at Starr's heart to see Dorcas and Melanie, even from a distance. She knew she had to do something for them, but what? What could she do for the two? They not only refused her assistance but were not even willing to help themselves. What could she do to make them understand that by giving up they were killing themselves? What could she do to make them even want to live?

It's obvious they don't care if they live or not, she observed silently as she walked toward Prairie Moon, who sat in the shade of the tepee, her head nodding.

Starr smiled at the dozing woman, thinking, *How can she have come to mean so much to me in such a short time? We don't even speak the same language.*

Squatting down beside Prairie Moon, Starr placed

a cool hand on the woman's feverish forehead, unintentionally rousing her from her light sleep. "Let me take you inside to lie down, Aunt. Then I will bring you a dipper of cool water before you sleep. I will tend to everything else while our supper cooks." Prairie Moon offered only token resistance as Starr led her inside, where the girl quickly rolled out a sleeping mat for the sick woman.

When Starr stepped out of the lodge into the light, a strange feeling of apprehension swept over her. Though the summer day was sweltering, odd prickles of goose flesh broke out on her arms. She sensed she was being watched and swung her head around.

Daniel Blue Eagle! she realized, unable to disguise the excitement that colored her features when she recognized the man coming toward her. She had forgotten how tall he was, and how strikingly handsome.

Unconsciously, she wiped her hands off on her dress and reached up to try to straighten her mussed hair, which for convenience she now wore in two braids. She wished more than ever that she'd had a place to bathe during the week on the move. Knowing she smelled as terrible as she looked, she wanted to run and hide. She didn't want him to see her like this, but she couldn't pull her gaze away from the approaching figure.

Starr closed her eyes and opened them again, but he was still there, looking neither left nor right as he ambled toward her with long, easy strides.

"I have returned, Firebird," he said softly, standing so close in front of her that she had to tilt her head back to see his face.

If he just didn't smell so good, Starr groaned inwardly, unable to stop herself from inhaling his familiar scent.

Trying to ignore the pounding in her chest, the tingling in her limbs, the tightening in the pit of her stomach, she looked down at his moccasins rather than chance being trapped by the dangerous gaze which boldly burned its way over her. She had to remind herself that he was her enemy.

"I can see that," she said, her voice low, her words carefully controlled, lest they give away her fluttering heartbeat.

"Are you well?" he asked politely, drinking her in with his eyes, wondering how she could still make his blood boil when she was so dirty and disheveled. Cleanliness was one of the few white man's habits that he adhered to. But then, dirty or clean, this woman was different than any he had ever known. Although she was a beauty, it was not her physical appearance that made him ache with need for her, but something else. Something almost tangible. *She's a fighter, a survivor! The kind of woman a man could rely on to stand beside him at all costs.*

Starr threw her head back suddenly to look at Daniel Blue Eagle with surprise. She couldn't believe that he had really asked her if she was well. As if they were old friends meeting in her mother's parlor!

"Oh, I'm fine," she answered, the smile on her face chilling. "I'm just fine and dandy. I've had a wonderful time on this little trek across the Territory! I don't know how to thank you for making it possible for me to be here!" she said through her frozen grin, keeping her teeth clamped tight in an effort to keep the lid on her temper. She knew that once she unleashed it on

63

this man she would not be able to stop, and that would mean her own destruction. "I've particularly loved not bathing for days at a time! The crust of dirt on my skin makes the mosquitoes go elsewhere for their meals!"

Secretly pleased to find that her spirit had not been affected by the hardships she had endured since he had seen her the week before, Daniel Blue Eagle pretended not to notice the display of anger. "And Prairie Moon? How is she?"

The mention of Prairie Moon brought Starr's boiling temper down to a slow simmer, and as she spoke of his aunt's health, her concern for the older woman replaced her anger. "She's been ill today. She has terrible stomach pains and has coughed a great deal. I was finally able to force her to rest while I put up the tepee and started our supper, but I don't know how long I can keep her down."

"I will look in on her," he said, surveying the hide structure she had worked so hard to erect. "You put the lodge up alone?" he asked.

"Yes," she said, her back straightening proudly, expecting him to compliment her efforts, despite the vow she had made that what he thought made no difference to her.

"Hmp," he grunted, lifting the door flap and disappearing into the tepee.

Starr wheeled around and stomped over to her cooking fire. "He could've at least said it looked good. Or 'Thank you for taking care of my aunt,' " she grumbled furiously as she attacked the bubbling liquid in the pouch with a long buffalo-horn spoon. "Hmp," she grunted, mimicking Daniel Blue Eagle. *I'll give him 'hmp'*, she thought to herself.

"I think she'll be all right after a few days of rest," Daniel Blue Eagle said as he reappeared in the doorway. "I'm hungry. What have you fixed for me to eat?"

Starr swung around so fast that a long braid whipped over her face, leaving in its wake a stinging track across her cheek and nose, but she ignored its sting. Instead, she glared at Daniel Blue Eagle, her blistering retort only held in check by the hair-trigger control on her temper.

Biting her tongue to keep from speaking, she returned her concentration to the buffalo stew that she had been so proud of only a few minutes before. *What does he think there is to eat? Steak and mashed potatoes?* She asked herself silently, unaware of the tear that trickled down her face. *Or maybe he thinks I stewed a chicken! And perhaps for dessert, he'd like a slice of the fresh peach pie I baked this morning!*

"I asked you a question, Firebird," Daniel Blue Eagle said from directly behind her, startling Starr and causing her to jerk forward and bump the cooking pouch.

She was trapped between the boiling stew and his body—his body seeming the more dangerous of the two. Still she managed to keep her control. "Hmp," she said, refusing to admit how hot she was so close to the fire—both of them!

"You will answer me," he ordered, wondering even as he spoke why he was insisting on making her feel degraded. Wasn't it her spirit that he admired? Would he feel the same way about her if that spirit were broken? Maybe that was it! If he could break her spirit, he would be able to free himself of her.

However, Daniel Blue Eagle knew that even if he managed to force her to bow to his will, no man would ever break the spirit of this woman. Like a bed of hot coals hidden beneath a pile of gray ashes, her spirit might seem to be extinguished; but like the coals, it would remain alive and burning under her calm exterior, ready to burst into flame at the first opportunity.

Hadn't she survived the past week with more spunk than he'd ever imagined a woman could possess? She had actually put the tepee up alone! Ordinarily, it took two experienced women an hour to put up one, and she'd done it alone! But he wouldn't let her know how impressed he was with her achievement. She would see his respect for her as a sign of weakness, a weakness she would not hesitate to use against him. He knew from experience that white women were manipulative and could never be allowed to gain the upper hand. No, he would keep his thoughts of admiration to himself.

"I asked you what you have prepared to me to eat, Firebird," he said gruffly as he yanked her head back by the braids.

"Stew," she answered, refusing to fight his hold on her.

"Good," he said, releasing his grip on her hair. "You may serve Prairie Moon first. Then you will serve me." He turned and walked away to see to his horse.

Oh, I'll serve you all right, she grumbled inwardly as she ladled the hot stew into a bowl for Prairie Moon, taking care that the woman got plenty of the nourishing meat and vegetables. *If his is too watery, it won't be my fault! How were we to know he would be here to eat?*

When Starr had finished gently spoon feeding Prairie Moon, she was surprised to see that Daniel Blue Eagle had not returned to the lodge. Giving the stew one more quick stir, she bent to pick up a wooden bowl. Her eye caught on the salt pouch in the side of a beaded *parfleche*.

Slowly putting the bowl down, she looked around to be certain she was alone and reached toward the food bag. *It would serve him right if I did*, she told herself, idly fingering the beaded pocket. *He couldn't prove it was intentional*, she thought, lifting the flap of the salt pocket. *It would just mean I'm not a good cook*, she convinced herself, dipping her fingers into the salt to remove a generous amount of the seasoning.

The last thoughts of adverse consequences banished from her mind, she made her decision and quickly tossed a fistful of salt into the cooking pouch and vigorously stirred the bubbly contents. *It'll be worth going without supper to see the look on his face.*

"I will eat now," Daniel Blue Eagle announced as he approached the lodge to sit on the ground near the doorway. It was too hot to go inside. Besides, he didn't want to disturb his aunt's rest.

"Yes, Daniel Blue Eagle," Starr said humbly, fighting the vengeful grin that threatened to give away her intentions. "I hope my humble efforts meet with your approval. This is the first time I've cooked without Prairie Moon to show me what to do. I only hope I remembered all she taught me."

Daniel Blue Eagle eyed the girl suspiciously, but said nothing when he accepted the offered bowl of piping hot stew. He held it up to his nose and gave a discerning sniff as he peered into the bowl. He raised his eyebrows in conditional approval. Though the stew was a little thin, its aroma was very appealing and he was quite hungry.

He glanced sideways at Starr, who stood with her head bowed, anxiously waiting for him to take the first bite with his buffalo-horn spoon. The flushed look of anticipation on her dirt-smudged face touched something inside him. She really was trying to please him. Perhaps he would tell her how pleased he was with the way she'd cared for his aunt and what a good job she had done erecting the lodge.

Daniel Blue Eagle gave Starr a reassuring smile, held the bowl to his lips, and without further hesitation drank the hot liquid in one long gulp.

With the attack on his taste buds so sudden, so unexpected, it was all he could do not to gag. As it was, with his eyes watering profusely and his throat burning unbearably, he reached anxiously for a cup of water. The cup was empty. He opened his mouth and released a tortured gasp.

"I would have water," he wheezed, trying to make his voice sound as normal as possible.

"Oh, yes, water," Starr answered eagerly, grabbing his horn cup and dashing to the buffalo pouch water container. It was all she could do to keep from laughing aloud, but she managed to stifle her pleasure as she turned back to the Indian who was now eying her knowingly. A chill of apprehension shud-

68

dered through her body.

He has no way of knowing it was intentional, she assured herself for the hundredth time as she handed him the cup.

Starr watched while Daniel Blue Eagle drank the whole cup of water without stopping. He held it out to her, indicating that he wanted more. "Bring your bowl and come eat with me," he said, studying her carefully as she reached for his cup.

The girl's gray eyes opened wide in horror, telling Daniel Blue Eagle the answer to his question. "I have already eaten," Starr hurriedly lied, the panic in her voice impossible to disguise.

"Then you will eat again. Surely, my aunt has taught you that it is improper for a Lakota woman to eat before the men have had their fill."

"I—I didn't know you would be here to eat," she protested, growing weak under his knowing gaze.

"Nevertheless, you will eat with me now," he said, his smile cold as he nodded his head in the direction of the fire and the ghastly stew.

Realizing she had no choice but to eat the salty fare, Starr turned away and walked slowly to the cooking pouch. If she refused to eat, he would know for certain that her seasoning error had been deliberate, and her punishment would no doubt be severe. She had to make him believe it was an accident. She dipped a scant ladle of stew into her bowl.

"Be sure and have plenty," Daniel Blue Eagle called out cheerfully. "We must keep your strength up! I don't want you getting sick too!"

Starr glared angrily over her shoulder at the smirking Indian before turning back to the pot to dip a

69

second helping into her bowl. *You may have won this battle, Daniel Blue Eagle, but mark my words, you won't win the next one so easily!*

"Go on and eat," Daniel Blue Eagle urged as she sat down.

Starr picked up her spoon and dipped out a small piece of meat. She held it to her lips for a moment, finally managing to plop it into her mouth. It wasn't too unbearable, she decided as she chewed it thoughtfully.

"No, not that way," Daniel Blue Eagle laughed heartily. "Drink the liquid down first, like I did. Then you go back and eat the meat and vegetables.

"But I—"

"I said drink," Daniel Blue Eagle growled, his voice now cold and hard, no longer pretending politeness.

"I—I don't think I can," Starr stammered weakly as she lifted the bowl up to her lips.

"I think you can," Daniel Blue Eagle returned, grabbing a fistful of her hair to tilt her head back as he forced her lips apart with the edge of the wooden bowl and poured the bitter stuff down her throat.

She tried to turn her head away, tried to remove the bowl with her hands, but still he forced the vile liquid into her mouth. "Drink it, Firebird," he ordered. "Drink it and remember this moment the next time you consider wasting precious salt and food on one of your childish pranks." With that he released his hold on her, threw her bowl to the ground and stalked angrily away.

Her eyes watered blindingly; a fire raged in her throat; and her stomach churned angrily. But she

70

forced herself to wait until the arrogant man was out of sight before she ran to the water pouch and frantically used her cupped hands to scoop enormous gulps of the soothing liquid into her mouth.

Finally, when she had quenched her unbearable thirst and had cleaned up the remains of the disastrous supper, Starr straightened up and looked around helplessly, not certain what she should do now. Had she let her unreasonable temper get the best of her one time too many? What would Daniel Blue Eagle do to her? If she were fortunate, forcing her to drink the salty stew would be all the punishment he planned for her. But somehow, she suspected the stew would only be a taste of what he had in mind. Dejectedly, she went into the tepee, checked on Prairie Moon who was sleeping peacefully, and lay down on her own mat to stare at the bit of starry sky she could see through the smoke hole.

In the middle of the night, Starr awoke with a start. She had heard something. Blinking to accustom her eyes to the darkness, she sat up and glanced around the moonlit tepee. Everything seemed normal. There were no strange noises now, only the familiar sound of Prairie Moon's gentle snoring. What had it been?

Suddenly, her eyes lit on an unfamiliar shape, and her hand flew to her mouth to squelch the scream that rose in her throat. She and Prairie Moon were not alone in the lodge. Sometime during the night a third mat had been spread on the ground, and Starr immediately knew who the broad-shouldered form lying on his side and facing away from her was. Daniel Blue Eagle was sleeping in their lodge!

Knowing she would never be able to go back to sleep with the sound of his breathing so close, Starr rose and silently crept outside.

The shimmering sliver of moon that hung suspended in the dark velvet sky amid the sparkling jewel stars of the summer night was the most beautiful and the saddest thing she had ever seen. She couldn't help but remember the night walks she and her parents had taken, the three of them racing to be the first to spot familiar constellations.

There's the Big Dipper, she remembered her mother's voice saying excitedly. *There's the North Star!* a little girl's voice joined her mother's in her memory. *And Hercules! Daddy, I found Hercules! So you did,* a deep voice praised. *What about Cygnus? I'll give a shiny penny to the first one who spots the Swan, Cygnus! I see it!* the little girl from the past squealed. *Give me my penny, Daddy! I saw it first! Can you see it, Mama? Yes, my love. Mama sees it!*

Holding her hands over her ears in a futile effort to block out the painful memories, Starr ran away from the camp. She didn't know or care where she was going. It didn't matter. She knew only that she had to run, had to make herself so tired she wouldn't be able to think about the past, wouldn't be able to hear those voices, and wouldn't long for a life and people she might never know again.

Coming to the narrow stream where she had drawn water when they had first set up the camp, Starr threw herself down on the ground and wept. But not until her tears finally subsided did she slowly become aware of the sounds around her, the crickets, the occasional bark of a dog in the distance, the gurgling

72

of the brook, the rustle of the breeze in the grass.

Looking around curiously, it suddenly occurred to Starr that as she lay on the ground feeling sorry for herself, she was missing a perfect opportunity. What was it she'd been thinking about Melanie and Dorcas not helping themselves? Why was she lying there sobbing like a child when the clear clean water was calling out to her, when there was nothing stopping her from having the bath she had been longing for?

Taking a hasty glance around to assure herself one last time that she was alone, Starr stepped out of her dress and moccasins and ran into the thigh-deep water. It was colder than she had anticipated, but the chill that rippled through her body invigorated her, brought her to life, gave her hope as the water swirled around her legs. Quickly unbraiding her hair, she sat in the water and lay her head back to allow the luxurious current to wash the dirt and smell from her naked skin and hair.

Daniel Blue Eagle had not been able to sleep, having tossed and turned restlessly for what had seemed like hours. When the girl left the tepee, he assumed it was to relieve herself and that she would be right back. However, when she didn't return, he began to worry. Was she stubborn and foolish enough to try to run away? Surely not! Didn't she know what Indians do to runaway captives? A wry grin crossed Daniel Blue Eagle's face. Somehow, remembering the salty stew with a twinge of remaining indignation, he didn't think that bit of knowledge would stop his fearless prisoner if she wanted to leave.

Quietly rising, taking care not to wake Prairie Moon, Daniel Blue Eagle left the tepee and walked toward the stream. If she did run away, she would probably head east—if she knew which way east was! More than likely, she would have no idea and would head in the wrong direction, west into the mountains or south toward the Badlands; but on the chance she did know which way to go, he decided to walk east first to see if he could pick up her trail.

Daniel Blue Eagle was so intent on searching the ground for clues that he was nearly to the stream before he heard the gentle splashing in the water. Instinctively dropping to a crouch, his eyes narrowed alertly as he scanned the area, bringing them to rest on the recumbent form shimmering just beneath the surface of the moonlit stream.

As if hypnotized by the beautiful vision before him, he stood and slowly walked toward the water, unable to shift his entranced gaze away. "Hello, Firebird."

With a startled squeak of surprise, Starr whirled around to face the man staring down at her from the bank. Time seemed to stand still.

Even as she crossed her arms protectively over her naked breasts, she felt the unbearable compulsion to hold her hands out to Daniel Blue Eagle and bid him to join her in the water.

As if her silent invitation had been uttered aloud, Daniel Blue Eagle stepped into the stream and came toward her.

She knew she had to say something, anything, to stop him; but she was so entranced by the magnificent man approaching her that when she opened her mouth to speak it was too late. She was too mesmerized by the intensity of his beautiful face, by the moonlight and shadows on the hills and valleys of his

74

muscular shoulders and chest, and by the fiery glint of desire in his eyes.

He slipped his large hands, hot against her water-cooled flesh, under her arms along the sides of her breasts, sending electricity racing wildly to her brain and limbs. And though her arms still protectively covered her breasts, she had no desire to fight him as he lifted her out of the water to stand before him.

"I have dreamed of this," Daniel Blue Eagle murmured softly. As he spoke, he slid his hands up the length of her arms to clasp them behind his neck before he drew her soft pliable body against his hard length.

"You have?" Starr whispered, her voice catching in her throat. Her heart pounded against her ribs so hard that she thought it would burst, but still she did nothing to free herself.

"When I was nineteen I danced the sun dance, and my dream vision showed me a great eagle with blue feathers who carried on his back a pale goddess with hair the color of the evening sun. I never knew what the vision was telling me, not until this very moment," he confessed as his mouth descended to capture hers in a kiss that was both worshipful and tender.

Starr's lips parted of their own volition to welcome his tongue into the warm interior of her mouth. Never had she experienced anything like Daniel Blue Eagle's kiss, and her head reeled under its drugging influence. To keep from falling, she clung desperately to him.

Her fingers dug into the corded muscles of his neck and burrowed hungrily into his thick black hair as she instinctively pushed herself against him to join her tongue with his.

Kissing was a white custom that Daniel Blue Eagle had never fully appreciated, but now he found he could not kiss her hard or long enough. His mouth devoured hers, his tongue seeking and tasting every hidden crevice there, as Daniel Blue Eagle lifted Starr into his arms and carried her to the bank where he lowered her to a bed of moist grass. Only then did he find the strength to break the magnetic seal of their lips.

Kneeling beside her, Daniel Blue Eagle locked gazes with Starr as he quickly removed his breech-cloth, freeing his swollen desire.

Starr's eyes opened wide, her look an odd combination of fear and passion. What was she doing here? How had she let this happen? Had the moonlight cast a spell over her? She had to get away from him.

Turning her head to the side so she wouldn't have to see the look on his face or the startling evidence of his masculinity standing proud and erect, she moaned, "Please don't—I can't—I mean, I've never—" she stammered almost incoherently.

"Don't be afraid, Firebird. This moment was meant to be. Everything we have experienced in the past has been directing our lives to this," he said, caressing her shoulders and neck to catch her chin and turn her head back to him. "You are mine. You are my *winyan*, my woman, given to me in my dream vision by the Great Spirit, *Wakan Tanka*. From that day forward, you have belonged to me," he said, his voice hypnotic as he searched her frightened eyes. "Only me."

"No!" Starr cried, jerking her head away in a final

attempt to free herself from the moonlight trance that held her in its grasp. She had to escape from his gentle hold, his compelling eyes. "I'm not yours! I'll not be the possession of any man!" she hissed as she rolled away from him and into a sitting position. She reached shakily for her buckskin dress. "I'm nothing to you but a captive, a slave. You don't even know my name!" she muttered, more angry with herself than with Daniel Blue Eagle. "How do you have the nerve to say that I'm your woman?" she scolded irritably, unable to look at the astonished man.

"I'm going to forget that tonight ever happened," she announced with resolve. "And I would hope that Harvard was able to civilize you enough that you will do likewise," she added and stomped back to the camp, leaving Daniel Blue Eagle staring after her.

"No, Firebird," he said softly. "I'm not that civilized. Nor are you. Neither of us will forget tonight, for this is our destiny." But Starr had already disappeared into the cluster of tepees and did not hear his proclamation. "You will belong to no other. You are mine."

Daniel Blue Eagle lay back and stared at the dark sky, unaware of the narrowed black eyes that watched him angrily from a cluster of shrubs only a short distance upstream. "You will not have her, Daniel Blue Eagle. She will not be your woman!" the mysterious intruder vowed menacingly before disappearing into the night.

Chapter Five

"What did you say?" Starr gasped at the lovely Indian girl who stood in front of her. "Who told you this?"

"Daniel Blue Eagle sent me," the girl said in halting English. "Are you not pleased to be given this honor?"

Starr studied the dark-skinned, black-eyed girl in flabbergasted silence for a moment before she was able to speak. "Pleased? Honored?" she finally said in disgust, her face so flushed that the Indian girl thought surely it would burst into flame. "No, Gentle Fawn, I am not pleased. Not one bit. Where is Daniel Blue Eagle? I must talk to him immediately!"

"He is praying and purifying himself in the *oinikaga tipi*, the sweat lodge," the girl answered meekly. "You cannot see him now."

"We'll see about that!" Starr fumed, stalking out of her tepee. "Where is this sweat lodge?"

"But you can't see Daniel Blue Eagle before your

wedding ceremony. It could anger *Wakan Tanka*, the Great Spirit, and bring unhappiness to your marriage," Gentle Fawn protested weakly.

"Where is the lodge, Gentle Fawn?" Starr repeatedly evenly, deliberately saving the full force of her fury for the man in the purification lodge.

"Daniel Blue Eagle will be angry with me," the girl wailed.

"I'll take full responsibility. Now tell me where it is!"

With her head bowed, Gentle Fawn hesitantly pointed toward a small beehive-shaped structure made of bent willow trees and covered with buffalo robes. It sat apart from the rest of the camp. "It is bad luck to see him on your wedding day," the girl warned one last time.

"Don't you concern yourself with that. This is not going to be my wedding day, so there is nothing to worry about!" Starr assured with more conviction than she felt as she headed toward the designated lodge.

"Daniel Blue Eagle," she said through gritted teeth as she stood at the entrance to the lodge. "May I speak with you?" she asked humbly. The chanting from within stopped suddenly.

The walk to the sweat lodge had given Starr a chance to gain control over her actions and to remind herself that Daniel Blue Eagle was not a man who had any patience with hysterics. Surely she could reason with him if she kept her volcanic temper under wraps. After all, it wasn't as if he were totally uncivilized.

"We will talk after the ceremony, Firebird," the

79

familiar voice called from inside the closed round structure.

"We must talk now," she insisted, clenching her fists at her sides until her knuckles turned white as she concentrated on keeping her voice calm and even.

"Not now, Firebird. I have spoken. Go back to the tepee and prepare for our wedding," he ordered softly, his voice low and trancelike.

"But we can't be married. I already have a husband!" she said in a rush of words, knowing that poor dead William would forgive her for the lie. "Don't you remember that?" She noticed that her voice had risen slightly, now sounding shrill and, desperate. She took a deep breath, determined more than ever to keep her self-control.

"The marriage was never consummated, Firebird. Even if the man you refer to were alive, by the law of the white man or the law of the Lakota, he would still not be your husband. *Wakan Tanka* has saved you for me. He wishes no man but Daniel Blue Eagle to call you 'wife'. Now go and prepare for our wedding ceremony. I will come to you soon." She heard the hissing sound of water being poured over hot stones, and the chanting inside the sweat lodge resumed as if she had never spoken. She had been dismissed!

Surely an educated man couldn't hold with such preposterous superstitions. He couldn't possibly believe that the 'Great Spirit' had destined them for each other in a young boy's dream.

"This is ridiculous. You simply can't do this! You can't force me to marry you. I'd rather die!" she shouted, no longer caring who heard her.

Unable to contain her fury any longer, she took an

80

irate step forward and reached for the door flap, determined to meet Daniel Blue Eagle head on. Abruptly brought up short by strong hands on either arm, Starr looked from left to right and found herself staring into the flat black eyes of two stone-faced braves who were not much taller than she was.

"Put me down!" she ordered the brawny men indignantly as they lifted her into the air and carried her kicking and protesting toward Prairie Moon's lodge, her feet dangling uselessly inches above the ground.

Moments later, Starr found herself back in the tepee and surrounded by several old women she didn't know. Prairie Moon and Gentle Fawn were there as well. They all chatted amiably in their strange tongue as they stripped off her deerskin dress, giggling and pointing at the strange thatch of golden-red hair at the juncture of Starr's legs.

Shocked beyond belief, Starr backed away from the giggling women, instinctively trying to cover herself as she did. But the women continued to chat happily as they easily removed her hands and held her still for a better look. One woman reached out to curiously touch the triangle of bright-colored hair, then jerked her hand back, twittering excitedly.

Throughout the remainder of the preparations, the 'bride' fought her 'handmaidens' at every step, though they seemed to be oblivious to her struggles. There was going to be a wedding, a celebration, a feast, and preparing the bride was an honor, a happy part of the festivities they had no intention of being denied.

Giving Starr's feeble protests little heed, the women

wrapped her in a buffalo robe and walked her to the stream where they made a privacy circle around her in the water and bathed her.

"Please don't do this," she pleaded with Prairie Moon when they were back in the tepee. Prairie Moon only smiled her warm grin and continued to comb through Starr's golden-red hair with her gnarled fingers and a hairbrush made from the rough side of a buffalo tongue.

"Gentle Fawn," Starr started, "please make them understand that I can't marry Daniel Blue Eagle! I don't belong here. I'll be leaving as soon as the men who attacked your village are caught!"

"I do not know why you are so sad, Firebird," Gentle Fawn smiled apologetically. "But there is nothing you can do. If Daniel Blue Eagle wishes to have you as his first wife, he will have you. It is a great honor to be chosen as the first wife of the first son of Man of the People. Many maidens had hoped to have that honor. But he has chosen you." Starr didn't notice the curl of Gentle Fawn's lip as she said the word 'you'.

"First wife?!?" Starr shrilled. "What do you mean 'first wife'?"

"It is the custom for a wealthy brave to have more than one wife. Did you not know this?" The girl's eyes opened wide in disbelief. "Is this not the way with the *wasicun* also?"

"No, of course it isn't! And I have no intention of being part of some savage's—some savage's—some savage's harem! I've got to get out of here!" Starr proclaimed, catching the women who brushed her hair off guard and jerking away from them.

"But you have on no clothing," Gentle Fawn reasoned, fighting the desire to laugh at the thought of the naked woman with the sickly pale skin running from the tepee and trying to escape. "And where would you go?"

"You've got to help me, Gentle Fawn!" Starr cried breathlessly as she tugged on the Indian girl's arm. "You are the only one who can understand me. You're the only one who knows how much I don't want this wedding to take place."

"I will try to help you escape, Firebird, if that is what you want. But I cannot promise that it will be today," Gentle Fawn whispered softly, knowing that the other women did not understand her words but that there might be someone outside the tepee who could. "Now, eat this and it will give you the strength to face what is to come," she reassured as she slipped Starr a button-shaped bit of food and guided her back to her sleeping mat where the women waited to finish grooming her. "Do not let the others see you eat, since you are supposed to be fasting," she warned, wheeled around and left the lodge.

Secretly consuming the acrid tasting bite of what she thought was nourishment, Starr allowed herself to be lowered back down to the mat. In only a few minutes she found herself relaxing, confident that Gentle Fawn would find a way to help her.

Closing her eyes as the women rubbed oils made of sweet scented wildflowers on her body, over her breasts, under her arms, in her navel, between her toes, within the folds of her body, she wondered at her sudden immodesty as the women's hands touched her so intimately.

But there was no time to ponder her feelings for soon she was floating out of the tepee through the smoke hole, like a curling thread of smoke. Over the camp she soared, high into the sky where she could see into eternity from the back of a giant eagle with feathers of blue.

Is is possible? she wondered in her dream state. *Am I destined to be Daniel Blue Eagle's wife? Of course not!* she argued with herself. *I could never live like this. And I couldn't bear the thought of Daniel Blue Eagle—I mean my husband—with other wives. I don't belong here.*

Starr opened her eyes drowsily at the prodding of Prairie Moon. "Prairie Moon," she sighed, giving the older woman a drunken smile before her head fell back on the mat again.

"You must awaken, Firebird. It is time," Gentle Fawn said, her voice sounding cold and angry.

Not at all like a gentle fawn, Starr thought, giggling idiotically as she tried to sit up.

"You will have to go through with the ceremony, but it will not be long before I will find a way to send you back where you belong," the Indian girl whispered into Starr's ear as she helped the drugged bride to stand.

"Thank you, Gentle Fawn," Starr said, giving the girl's arm an affectionate pat as she mumbled her slurred words. "You're a good friend."

"Yes," Gentle Fawn answered.

Prairie Moon came forward and brushed through Starr's long gold-red tresses which had been left unbound, jabbering enthusiastically as she did.

"She wants you to know that you are wearing the

dress she wore when she was a bride fifty years ago," Gentle Fawn told Starr, the look in her black eyes impossible to read.

Looking down, Starr found herself dressed in the softest, most beautiful dress and moccasins she'd ever seen in her life. The white deerskin wedding clothes had been carefully beaded with suns, moons, stars, and other symbols of good fortune. When she looked into Prairie Moon's beaming face and smiled her teary appreciation, the older woman grabbed the girl's hand and held it to her own wrinkled cheek.

"Thank you, Prairie Moon," Starr murmured, laying a cool palm on Prairie Moon's shoulder. She wondered what the sweet, gentle woman she had come to love so much would think when she left. "I'm very honored," she said humbly.

"By giving you her marriage dress, she is saying she thinks of you as her daughter," Gentle Fawn explained matter-of-factly.

"Thank you, *Ina*," Starr said to Daniel Blue Eagle's aunt, using the Lakota word she knew to mean mother.

The effects of the drug Starr had been given were beginning to wear off, but she still retained a strange feeling of detachment. And she couldn't shake the sensation that she was floating through the heavens, looking down on the Indian camp, watching this all happen to someone else.

The women who had bathed and dressed Starr enclosed her within a human circle and escorted her across the village to a large red tepee that stood in the center of the camp. Starting to chant, the women slowly backed away from Starr, leaving her standing alone and unsteady before the tepee door.

She looked over her shoulder, to find that the chanting women had been joined by many others, all crowding forward to get a glimpse of the bride. Before her sluggish brain could question what was happening, the flap on the red lodge lifted up and a tall Indian wearing decorated buckskins and an elaborate eagle-feather war bonnet stepped outside. He spoke to her in the Lakota language, and she glanced helplessly at Gentle Fawn who stood to one side.

"He asks if you are the one who would be his new daughter, the one who his son, Daniel Blue Eagle, wants to marry," Gentle Fawn translated softly.

"What do I do?" Starr asked, her drug-induced calm completely obliterating her fear and anger.

"Nod your head and say, *ohan, Ate*."

"*Ohan, Ate*," Starr obeyed, not knowing the words meant *yes, father*.

The drums began to beat, and chanting voices rose to a deafening hum as a very old man stepped out of the red lodge. "It is Red Sky, our *wicasa wakan*, our holy man," Gentle Fawn whispered as the wrinkled old man wrapped in a star-covered blanket began to sing and shake a gourd rattle over Starr and the crowd.

Then everything grew quiet. Not a baby cried. No one coughed. Even the camp dogs were silent.

Before Starr could wonder what would happen next, two young children came forward to lift the flap of the red tepee and Daniel Blue Eagle stepped through the door opening.

Dressed in white deerskin leggings and shirt, he wore a war bonnet like his father's, and Starr could

86

not suppress a gasp of surprise as the magnificent warrior moved toward her, his long steps quickly covering the space that separated them, his blue eyes never leaving her flushed face.

Continuing to chant his singsong words, the medicine man stepped forward and positioned Daniel Blue Eagle beside Starr, entwining their arms and clasping their hands together over the long stem of a peace pipe. He looked from one to the other as he sang the words to the marriage ceremony. Then continuing his chant, he turned away from the bridal couple and shook his rattle over a knife that a young boy held out to him. Holding the knife aloft, he again faced Starr and Daniel Blue Eagle and quickly made cuts on the inside of each of their forearms.

Starr looked at the rush of red that flowed from the two wounds and wondered dazedly why she was bleeding, why she felt no pain, but she did and said nothing.

The holy man lifted their entwined arms up for all to view before placing the two bleeding cuts together and winding a rawhide strap tightly around the two arms, binding Daniel Blue Eagle and Starr to one another. When he had tied a knot in the rawhide, a cheer rose from the crowd, and though Starr felt nothing, she imagined Daniel Blue Eagle gave her hand a reassuring squeeze when the medicine man lowered their arms.

She looked up at him, her expression quizzical, but she could read nothing in his piercing blue eyes, and she looked back to Red Sky who was unfurling a red blanket which he quickly draped over the bridal couple's shoulders.

Continuing to sing, he danced around them one more time and shook his rattle over the blanket. Then it was all over. The red blanket was removed, the rawhide strap was untied, and happy people hurried forward to congratulate them and lay gifts at their feet.

"Come, Firebird, and we will complete the remainder of the ceremony in private," Daniel Blue Eagle whispered into Starr's ear when the last of the congratulations were received and the wedding guests were all happily eating the feast the women had prepared.

Her head was almost clear of the drug, and suddenly the seriousness of what had happened hit Starr full force. She had actually married Daniel Blue Eagle! Married a virtual stranger, an Indian, a savage, a man who didn't even know her name!

Starr's eyes opened wide and she stared at Daniel Blue Eagle, as if seeing him for the first time. Was he really her husband? Why hadn't she fought him?

In the moment of desperation, a saving thought occurred to Starr. He had said the marriage was not a marriage until it was consummated. That was it. She could not allow it to be consummated before she escaped!

"I'm hungry," she said, taking a determined step toward the food spread for the guests.

"We will eat later," Daniel Blue Eagle said as he pulled her back against his hard body, finding it necessary to stoop to speak into the shell of her ear.

Chills radiated from her ear over her neck and breasts to the heart of her womanhood, and Starr had to fight the desire to succumb to his plan. "I want to eat now," she insisted breathlessly.

"Our fast will be ended after our marriage is consummated," Daniel Blue Eagle said, knowing what she was doing and having no part of her diversionary tactics. He was hungry too, but his was a hunger of a different nature.

"You know the whites don't recognize Indian marriages as legal," she tried weakly.

"I know," Daniel Blue Eagle said, growing tired of her feeble attempts to stop him. Without further ado, he swooped her into his arms and carried her toward their lodge. "But the *ikce wicasa*, the People, do. And that is what I am, one of the *ikce wicasa*."

A cheer rose from the wedding guests as the bride and groom disappeared into the tepee. The drums and singing grew faster and more frenzied, and women beat on pieces of wood with bones.

No sooner had they entered the darkened tepee than Daniel Blue Eagle set Starr on her feet and drew her to him to kiss her.

"Please, unhand me!" she gasped, turning her head away from him so that his kiss missed its target and landed on her cheek, but she was unable to slip out of his embrace. "I don't care what mumbo jumbo that medicine man jabbered, we're not married!"

"I've been more than patient with you, Firebird, but my patience is growing thin," Daniel Blue Eagle smiled. "We are married in my eyes, in the eyes of my father, and in the eyes of the People, and this marriage will be consummated, here and now."

He took her jaw in his hand and made her face him. The look in his blue eyes was hard and cold but Starr countered with her own icy glare. She told

89

herself she would never back down, would never stop fighting this unreasonable savage and his outlandish marriage.

"I can take you by force or you can give yourself to me willingly, but you will not leave this lodge until we are truly man and wife!"

"Then you will take me by force, Daniel Blue Eagle, for I will never submit willingly to the likes of you!"

Daniel Blue Eagle studied Starr for a long moment, his expression contemptuous and disbelieving, hers determined and unrelenting, and he couldn't help but admire the girl's courage. But by God, she was his wife and he would have her. He could have raped her and used her as a slave, but he hadn't. Instead, he had given her the respect and honor of marriage, and he was not going to be denied his rights.

Continuing to hold her face clamped in his strong hand, he squeezed her jaw painfully and lowered his head to bring his mouth within a fraction of an inch of hers. "Never?" he asked, brushing his lips over Starr's tightly clamped mouth, sending an unwanted flutter of excitement through her body. "Never is a very long time, Firebird," he laughed.

Starr's anger and fear grew by leaps and bounds, and it took all her control to keep from screaming, crying, begging; but she wouldn't give him the satisfaction of knowing how afraid she was. She vowed she would not show her fear. So with superhuman resolve, she tightened her lips and forced herself not to look away from the man whose face was so close to hers that she could smell his clean, sweet breath, and feel its warmth moving the fine hairs on her skin.

She quaked with fear, but he would never know how frightened she was. She knew that if he wanted to take her there was nothing she could do; the difference in their sizes told her that; but if he did insist on consummating this illegal marriage, it would be an unfeeling piece of wood that he took, not a responding woman.

"Never," she reiterated through clenched teeth.

"I enjoy a challenge," Daniel Blue Eagle said, his lips still not quite touching hers as his tongue slid along the outline of her mouth. His free hand pulled her hard against his length and caressed her back and buttocks, sending painful tremors of excitement coursing through her blood.

Starr's eyes fluttered closed, but she managed to force them open with a start. She couldn't let herself fall under the spell of his touch, or cling to his muscled back to keep from falling. She mustn't respond to the way the soft contours of her body seemed to fit so naturally against his firmer shape.

"Stop it!" she ordered. "Since this will be an animal coupling, I see no need to suffer your crude kisses and fondling."

"Very well," Daniel Blue Eagle said, putting her from him, fighting the need to wince when he saw the dark red marks on her face that his fingers had made. "Take off your dress."

"What?"

"I said take off that dress."

"I will not!" Starr gasped, backing away from him, all thought of pretending not to fear him gone from her mind. Suddenly, the tepee that had seemed so large when she had put it up was very small. There was nowhere to go to get away from him.

Daniel Blue Eagle took off his own white shirt and tossed it to the side. "I said off," he growled, stepping out of his leggings and taking a menacing step toward her.

"No!"

"A Lakota bride does not tell her husband 'no'." With one determined motion, Daniel Blue Eagle snatched the beautiful white deerskin marriage dress over Starr's head and threw it aside, leaving her standing naked in front of him.

Starr gasped in surprise and tried to cover herself.

Daniel Blue Eagle froze, his admiration for her pale nakedness impossible to disguise. "How can any woman so beautifully made be such a shrew?" he asked, more to himself than to Starr.

"A shrew?!?" Starr shrieked, raising her hand to slap the insulting look from his face, but he saw it coming and caught her wrist in his strong hand.

"Don't ever strike me, Firebird," he said, the warning in his voice not penetrating her scalding anger. She raised her other hand and struck him on the cheek, leaving a stinging handprint on his chiseled flesh.

In an instant, he clamped her wrists together and wound a length of rawhide around them before throwing her to the sleeping mat. "What are you going to do?" she whimpered, knowing she had pushed Daniel Blue Eagle too far this time. If only she had been able to hold her temper!

"What I came in here to do," he snarled.

Without taking his eyes from Starr, he stood and

found a stake which he hammered into the ground above her head. Then he secured her bound hands to the stake, leaving his bride stretched out like a fine feast, a feast he had no intention of leaving until he had had his fill.

"Is this the only way savages can get a woman to lie beneath them?" she asked, wondering even as she spoke why she couldn't hold her tongue.

"God, woman," he growled. "Your mouth will be the death of you!" *Or me*, he groaned inwardly. "You wanted an animal coupling, you will have it!" he threatened, stripping his breechcloth from around his slender hips and freeing his shaft, long and erect, for her frightened gaze before falling on top of her.

Raising up to look into Starr's terrified face, he laughed and grabbed a plump breast in each hand to roll and pinch her nipples until they were hard as he ground his hips against her lower body. "Say something, Firebird. Tell me what a savage I am!" he ordered angrily.

But Starr could not speak. She could only stare into the blue eyes of the man above her. Then his mouth fell on hers, roughly forcing her lips and teeth apart with his tongue as it filled her mouth, plundering and ravaging its tender interior with all the anger and frustration she brought out in him.

Starr was not certain when her own mouth began to soften and respond to Daniel Blue Eagle's kiss. She couldn't be sure when his cruel taunting hold on her breasts became gentle adoring caresses, but she did feel the hotness between her legs, warm and wet as it made her quiver for relief, and she was appalled.

"Firebird," Daniel Blue Eagle moaned. "Don't

fight me. Be my wife today, forever," he groaned, not even aware that he had spoken.

Sliding downward, his mouth burned a blazing trail over Starr's arched neck to her underarm, exposed and defenseless with her hands tied above her head. Nipping and biting the sensitive flesh, he moved to straddle Starr's hips. With his tongue burning wet spirals over the hollow of her arm, his hands on her breasts imitated the circling motion of his tongue under her arm, quickly bringing her nipples to hard points of desire; and he was not surprised to feel the gentle thrusting of her hips under his buttocks.

Daniel Blue Eagle gave a satisfied smile as he felt the instinctive rising of her female mound beneath him, pushing, begging, offering, and he rotated his own hips on her, causing Starr to writhe beneath him, arching her aching breasts toward him as she did.

Cupping the undersides of her full breasts in his large hands, Daniel Blue Eagle pushed them together, creating a deep shadowy cleft in which he dipped his tongue to taste her sweetness. Licking his way over her pale flesh he hesitated only a moment before sucking an erect nipple into the warmth of his mouth to tongue the sensitive nub to pebble hardness.

Starr could no longer fight the delicious languor enveloping her, and though she tried to chide herself for enjoying her wanton feelings, she was unable to suppress the moan that escaped from deep in her throat.

Daniel Blue Eagle sucked harder on her nipple and then trailed his wet kisses over to her other breast. "You like that, don't you?" he chuckled with satisfaction.

His words of victory brought Starr to her senses like a blast of winter air in her face, and she squirmed beneath him, renewing her futile efforts to escape his mouth with fresh energy. "I hate it. And I hate you," she spat angrily.

"Then, I'll have to see what I can do to change your mind," he threatened, giving both her nipples a painful pinch as he slid down her body to lick and nibble his way across her belly.

Starr wiggled and twisted to escape his mouth and hands. But they were everywhere, tasting her tingling skin, sending a tidal wave of desire flooding through her. She was horrified by what he was doing, and even more horrified that she was fast losing the will to fight him. How could this be happening?

While he continued to nip and bite the tender flesh of her stomach he slid his hand between her legs to open her thighs. Starr's eyes opened wide. Until today, no one had ever looked at that part of her, much less touched her there. Even she had never touched that most private part of her body except while carrying out the most necessary matters of hygiene. Yet, this man, this stranger, this savage who insisted he was her husband, was stroking and probing her there as if it were the most natural thing in the world.

"Please, don't do that," she whimpered, trying to twist away from his disturbing touch.

Without answering her, Daniel Blue Eagle slid his hands around her hips to lift her upward and slide a folded buffalo robe beneath her.

"You're very beautiful here, Firebird," he said, his voice husky as he ran his fingertips over her displayed femininity. "I like the way you feel, all warm and moist. You must never be ashamed to have me see you, touch you, taste you," he groaned, dipping his head to kiss the object of his admiration.

"No, don't," Starr gasped as the tip of his tongue touched the satin of her womanhood and burned its way along the quivering length of her. Her heart beat violently and her panic rose to the point that she was certain she could bear no more of the delicious agony he was perpetrating on her, but still he did not cease. He pleasured her until she thought she would die. If only she could. If only she could die then and there— if not from the humiliation she felt, then certainly from shame for the immoral way her own wanton body reacted to his licentious lovemaking.

Then suddenly, without warning, it was happening. Her entire body felt as if it were going to explode into a million tiny pieces, her every sense concentrating on one purpose—the volcanic tension building within her core. She knew without a doubt that she was dying, and in that last moment before she was hurled into the beyond, she prayed she would be forgiven for this, her weakest hour.

Her body jerked spasmodically against Daniel Blue Eagle's mouth as he squeezed her round bottom and lifted her upward to savor every sip of the sweetness of her sex before he slid back up her limp, perspiration-misted body to kiss her mouth once more.

But she wasn't dead! She was alive and had senselessly responded to Daniel Blue Eagle's unnatural lovemaking, like the savage he was. The disgrace of her actions was too much for her, and with a wild scream she struggled to escape further contact with his mouth, desperately turning her head from side to side. But she could not free herself. Her hands were still tied, and his weight over her was too great to fight.

With his muscled chest crushing her breasts, he captured her mouth again, this time with such burning force that Starr felt her last modicum of strength leave her, and she went limp, helplessly succumbing to the weakness and immoral desire that swept over her again.

Her mouth opened of its own volition and Daniel Blue Eagle did not hesitate to enter its warmth to suck the velvet of her tongue back into his own mouth. Delicious desire undulated through Starr's weakened body, and she was jolted with the shameful awareness that she actually liked, wanted, craved the feel of his mouth and hands on her, that she no longer wanted to stop what was happening.

Was this love? Was that why she no longer wanted to fight him? Was that the cause of the ache that was building in her loins again? No, of course not. It was lust. Disgusting, vile lust! How could he make her feel like this? She hated him for what he was doing, for what he was making her feel.

Daniel Blue Eagle raised up to look into Starr's confused eyes and said, "It may hurt this first time."

With that, he separated her legs and took the plunge into her body, unable to keep from wincing when he saw the shock and pain that contorted her beautiful features.

Starr felt as if she were being torn apart. Daniel Blue Eagle's largeness filled her sheath to capacity, and she squeezed her eyes tight to fight the tears.

Daniel Blue Eagle's movements stilled to give Starr time to adjust to his size as he gathered his trembling, frightened bride into his arms. "I'm sorry, Firebird," he whispered, fighting to control his throbbing manhood within her warm body. "I didn't want to hurt you," he swore, kissing her face and damp eyelids.

Then slowly, with his gentle murmurs in her ear, his slight motion inside her, she began to feel a new kind of pain, a marvelous, sweet pain that made her own body want to match its movements to his, and she was no longer afraid or ashamed. Only the moment mattered.

As their rhythm increased, Starr became distantly aware that her wrists were no longer bound; but she didn't use her freed hands to fight her captor as she would have only moments before. Instead, she wound her arms around Daniel Blue Eagle's broad back to pull him into her, harder, deeper, as they moved together, their pleasure building to the grandest heights imaginable until their passions finally burst, hurling them both to the heavens.

"My name is Starr," she murmured as she floated weightlessly from the pinnacle to which he had taken her.

"I know, but to me you will always be Firebird. My woman, my wife, my Firebird," he whispered as they both drifted into an exhausted sleep, their limbs and bodies still united in passionate embrace.

Chapter Six

"We'd never make it. We'd all be dead before the day was over," Melanie Walters said woodenly the day after Starr had unwillingly married Daniel Blue Eagle. The girl was on all fours half-heartedly razing the remaining meat and fat from a fresh buffalo skin pegged to the ground in front of her. "We may be slaves, but at least we're alive," she sighed, taking a final swipe at the hide with her flesher before sitting back on her heels to observe her work. "And we're not hungry or thirsty," she added, looking to her master's first wife, Bead Woman, for approval. "Sooner or later someone will come for us and I have every intention of being here, still alive, when they do! We just have to be patient."

"No one is going to come. It's up to us to save ourselves," Starr insisted, her voice a whisper although she knew Bead Woman understood no English. "Daniel Blue Eagle told me that the Army has no intention of seeking out and punishing the soldiers who attacked the village, so he's not going to take us back. Our only chance is to leave when the men are out of the camp and find our own way home."

"Home?" Melanie laughed bitterly, running the back of her hand over her forehead to wipe the sweat from her eyes. "Home to what? To our dead families? Home to all the handsome young men who won't want us for wives because we've been whores to the Indians? Besides, Spotted Shoulder doesn't treat me that badly. He doesn't beat me like Yellow Whip does Dorcas. At least he hasn't so far. But he told me that if I ever try to leave him, even once, not only will he take the whip to me but he'll cut off my nose!"

"Yellow Whip beats Dorcas?" Starr choked in alarm.

"He beats all of his wives when they displease him. But Dorcas has learned how to keep Yellow Whip happy so he doesn't beat her as often as he did at first. Of course, his other wives detest her. Not only does she not do her share of the work, but their husband makes no secret of the fact that he prefers a slave's bed to theirs!"

"I can't believe what you're telling me," Starr gasped.

Eyes which had been dull and lifeless since the young women had been taken from the church suddenly lit with malice as Melanie continued to relay her shocking gossip. "I understand he takes her every night—sometimes several times a night!" she told Starr confidentially, shuddering involuntarily at the thought. "How horrible that would be to have a filthy Indian grunting and rutting on you constantly. But she says she prefers that to curing buffalo hides and cooking. I'd rather do my share of the work! At least Spotted Shoulder treats us all equally and I only have to put up with his animal lust every three or four days."

"How many wives does Spotted Shoulder have?" Starr asked, unable to understand how Melanie could bear the thought of sharing a man with other women.

"There are five of us," Melanie answered matter-of-factly. "But usually one or two are spending time in the women's lodge during their monthly flow, if they are fortunate enough not to be with child."

Melanie's words brought Starr a new fear. What if she had conceived a child during her wedding night? If she was pregnant with Daniel Blue Eagle's child, she would never be able to get away from him. The Sioux loved their children above almost everything else. "Don't you see, Melanie? We've got to leave before one of us becomes pregnant," she pressed urgently.

"Believe me, I'd like to get out of this village, but not enough to try to cross the plains by myself. Besides, how do you know every one of us isn't already expecting? Don't tell me Daniel Blue Eagle hasn't already spilled his seed in you!" Her lip curled with contempt when she thought of how fortunate Starr had always been. The handsomest boys had always liked her the best; she'd always had the prettiest clothes, the most flawless skin, the most doting parents; and now here they were captives and Starr had been chosen by the chief's good-looking young son, while she and Dorcas had been given to short squatty warriors in their forties.

"You're probably already carrying his brown-skinned brat in your belly, Starr," Melanie threw spitefully over her shoulder as she followed Bead Woman to check on the hides being cleaned by

Spotted Shoulder's other wives.

Was it possible? Could she already be pregnant with Daniel Blue Eagle's child? Surely not, but the possibility made her all the more determined to escape before the possibility could become a fact.

But I can't leave Melanie and Dorcas here. I have to convince them that we'll spend the rest of our lives as prisoners in this Indian camp if we don't take the chance and try to escape soon, Starr told herself as she walked toward Yellow Whip's tepee where it was said Dorcas slept all day while the other women worked. She didn't hold out much hope that she would be able to persuade the lazy girl to attempt the dangerous escape across the plains, but if there was any chance at all, she knew she had to try. If she could convince Dorcas, perhaps together they would be able to change Melanie's mind.

Standing before the entrance to the tepee, Starr took a deep prayerful breath and started to announce herself. "Dorc—" But before she could complete her call, she heard a familiar voice. Her heart leapt into her throat.

She whirled around to see Gray Wolf approaching her, his stride long and confident, his black eyes darting appreciatively over her. "What are you doing here?" Her angry voice covered the fear she felt at the sight of the warrior.

"I've come to congratulate you on your wedding, my sister," the tall brave smiled, not bothering to disguise his desire as his gaze swept over her.

"I'm not your sister, and when Daniel Blue Eagle sees you, he will kill you for daring to approach me or this village again," she threatened boldly, realizing that now was not the time to protest the legality of her marriage to Daniel Blue Eagle.

Gray Wolf laughed hard. "Hasn't Daniel Blue Eagle told you that we are brothers?"

"I don't believe it," Starr choked, searching her mind for anything that might have told her the two were related. Of course they looked alike except for their eyes, but all Indians seemed to have those similar features. "When he called you his brother, I thought he meant that you were both Sioux."

"Only one of us is truly Lakota," Gray Wolf said, the bitterness in his voice undisguised by the smile that remained on his face. "However, despite the fact that his mother was white and mine Indian, we are brothers. Both of us are sons of Man of the People. So that makes you my sister, my brother's wife," he added with a look that said he saw her as anything but a sister.

"It can't be!" Starr gasped, cringing as she took a step backwards in an effort to escape Gray Wolf's insulting examination.

"But it is," Gray Wolf assured her and took a step toward her. "And you may be interested to know that I've decided to return to my father's band for a while. Should my sister need me, I will be nearby," he said, his promise sounding like a threat to Starr.

"I won't need you and don't want you to be anywhere near me," Starr rasped, using every effort to control the quiver in her voice.

"You never can tell. My older brother might be killed and leave you with no one to protect you. It would be my duty to take you into my tepee as one of my wives—a duty I would not hesitate to fulfill. Or he

103

might decide to divorce you! Then where would you go? To me, of course!"

"Divorce?" Starr gulped. How could someone she wasn't legally married to divorce her?

As if answering her unspoken question, Gray Wolf said, "If you displease him and he puts you out of his tepee, we consider the marriage ended, and another brave can claim you. You are fortunate that you are so pleasing to the eye. You won't be without offers, but it will be my tepee you will come to live in."

"That will never happen. Never!" Starr screamed, turning blindly to run away from the arrogant Indian who talked so calculatingly of having his brother's wife for his own.

Starr didn't pay any attention to where she was heading. She only knew she had to get away from Gray Wolf, away from the smell of buffalo hides, away from the sounds of playing children and barking camp dogs, away from the memories of the night before.

Running heedlessly away from the camp, Starr glanced back over her shoulder frequently, hardly aware that her feet were taking her up one hill, and then another, until she could no longer see the Indian village. All she knew was that Gray Wolf was still behind her, his hard face laughing at her attempt to escape. He seemed to be walking at a leisurely pace, yet no matter how fast she ran, he was always right behind her, one of his long strides easily equaling two or three of her shorter steps.

Starr looked frantically for a place to hide, but though there was timber in the area, it was still sparse and there was no place that was safe. Willing herself to ignore the cramping pain in her side, the inability to draw enough oxygen into her lungs to support her expended energy, she concentrated on moving her feet even faster.

More concerned with the distance between herself and Gray Wolf than with where her flight was taking her, Starr looked over her shoulder again, not even letting up slightly on her desperate pace as she did. But he was still there, and despite her increased speed, he was ever closer.

Her pursuer was rapidly gaining on her, but the expression on his face was no longer amused. Now it was alarmed, angry, concerned.

"Stop!" he bellowed, suddenly breaking into a fast run. No longer playing a game, Gray Wolf quickly overtook the terrified girl. He took a running dive, seeming to fly through the air to grab Starr around the waist and pull her to the ground. Together they rolled back down the incline, the girl screaming her protests loudly as they tumbled in a tangle of brown and white limbs.

"Let me go," she screamed when they finally rolled to a stop at the bottom of the hill, but before Gray Wolf could answer, they were joined by a third person.

"Get away from her, Gray Wolf," Daniel Blue Eagle ordered.

Both Gray Wolf and Starr looked up in surprise to see her husband bounding down the hill toward them, his knife drawn.

"When we fight this time, the fact that you are my brother will not save your life," he yelled, his teeth bared in an animal snarl as he took the last few steps that would bring him to the two who lay on the ground in a compromising position.

"I'm sure you won't believe this, but I just saved your wife from killing herself," Gray Wolf sighed as he rolled off Starr's prone body and stood up. Though he didn't draw his own knife, his hand was poised at his side, ready to defend himself should it be necessary. "I stopped her from falling into the ravine the only way I could," he said, motioning toward the top of the hill with his head, never losing eye contact with his brother or letting down his guard.

Daniel Blue Eagle glanced in the direction Gray Wolf had indicated, wanting to believe the younger man, but hesitant to do so. The hill they had rolled from did drop off suddenly at its peak. Daniel Blue Eagle knew that for a fact. But still what were they doing together? "Is this true?"

"You forget that I am Lakota too, my brother. I would not break our taboo against incest and touch my sister any more than I would refuse your challenge if that is what you want. But if we fight, I want it to be for our conflicting beliefs, not for a crime I did not commit."

"I would like to believe what you say, Gray Wolf, but I find it difficult. How do you come to be this far from the village with your sister, my wife?" Daniel Blue Eagle asked suspiciously.

"I spoke to her in the camp, offering my congratulations on your marriage. She was frightened of me and ran away. I followed her to reason with her, to assure her that she had nothing to fear from me. Then when I saw the direction she was heading, I managed to catch up with her before it was too late. You should be grateful to me. I saved your foolish wife's life."

"Are you all right?" Daniel Blue Eagle said, speaking to Starr for the first time. "Did he hurt you?"

"No, it was as Gray Wolf said." She couldn't tell him all that Gray Wolf had implied with his suggestion that she would end up with him. Seeing the angry fire burning so brightly in Daniel Blue Eagle's eyes, she knew that if she did, he would attack his brother without further hesitation. And this time the battle would be to the death. There would be no holding back and Daniel Blue Eagle might not be the victor! She couldn't chance it, couldn't risk losing him. "Seeing him brought back painful memories and I foolishly ran."

A smile of satisfaction slid over Gray Wolf's stern countenance before he spoke again. "Well, do we fight or not?"

Daniel Blue Eagle looked long and hard at his younger brother, then shook his head as he replaced his knife in its sheath at his side. "I still have no wish to fight with you, Gray Wolf," he said, bending down to lift his bride into his arms.

"Perhaps another time," Gray Wolf laughed and turned to go. "You ought to show your wife the ravine she nearly went into. The next time she gets an urge to run away, she might think twice about it," he called over his shoulder and started back toward the camp, leaving Daniel Blue Eagle and Starr alone.

"Are you sure you're all right?" Daniel Blue Eagle asked, searching her eyes for the answer.

"Really, I'm fine," she insisted, her voice trembling, though she made great effort to control its tremor. Using every bit of self-control she could muster to resist the overwhelming desire to relax her head against his strong chest, she told him, "You can put me down now. I can walk."

"We'll go look at that ravine first," Daniel Blue Eagle said, ignoring her protests as he started up the hill with his wife held protectively in his arms. "I want you to know how much danger you were in. You could have been killed. Do you understand?"

Starr nodded her head numbly as she looked into the deep gorge at the top of the hill. Though it was not more than six feet across, the frightening split was very deep, its sides steep and raw. It was as though giant hands had tried to tear the earth open to reach the stream that flowed at the base of the cruel cleft, appearing at the one end of the divide and disappearing back into its underground world three hundred feet downstream.

Realizing the fall she had barely escaped, Starr's head began to whirl and her vision blurred, but she was unable to tear her eyes away from the horror before her. Then her stunned gaze was drawn to the carcass of a buffalo that had obviously met with the fate meant for her, and she couldn't stop the scream that escaped her throat before she buried her face against Daniel Blue Eagle's shoulder.

Starr inhaled deeply, determined to blot out the horrible sight as she breathed in the wonderful smoke and leather smells that were as much a part of Daniel Blue Eagle as his black braids and azure eyes. Unconsciously, she tightened her arms around his neck, totally unaware of the shudder of relief that rippled through her body as she relaxed in the security of the

108

man's embrace. A strange feeling of well-being crept over her. Nothing could hurt her as long as this man held her. Nothing and no one.

They stayed that way on the edge of the ravine for a long time, her arms wound tightly around his shoulders, his own muscled arms clutching her fiercely against his chest, as if to let go would be to lose her.

"That could have been you, Firebird," Daniel Blue Eagle groaned at last, his words catching in his throat. "You might have been killed. I could have lost you."

Starr lifted her head and looked into Daniel Blue Eagle's anguished face, her own tearful expression puzzled. What she saw in his eyes stunned her even more than the dangerous gorge. At that moment, Daniel Blue Eagle's pain was so visible that she could almost believe he really cared what happened to her. She could almost convince herself that the wetness she saw glistening in his eyes was caused by something other than the bright autumn sun.

Starr's hands rose to cup Daniel Blue Eagle's tortured face. Her thumbs circled idly over the prominent cheekbones as she searched his sculpted features, still afraid to believe what she saw.

The anguish displayed so openly in his expression tugged at Starr's heart, filling her with the need to nurture and console, making her forget that she was this man's prisoner.

With his face trapped between her palms, she hesitated only slightly before she raised her lips to brush each of his blue eyes shut with feather-light kisses on his lids. She gathered courage with each kiss as her mouth ghosted over his tanned cheeks, along his jaw line, to his strong chin and full lower lip, where she lingered only a moment, before continuing her loving exploration.

Starr drew back slightly and examined Daniel Blue Eagle's features again, her eyes focusing helplessly on his well-shaped mouth. Her comforting kisses had eased his torture but she was surprised to find that they had inadvertently replaced it with an anguish of another nature.

His mouth was slightly open and his breathing was becoming ragged, causing his chest to rise and fall rapidly against her body. Or maybe it was her own irregular breathing she heard. But that was impossible, because she had stopped breathing.

Realizing that she was holding her breath as she watched him, she let it out in a sigh that whispered over him just as he breathed in, taking the very air she had breathed into his own lungs, taking her spirit into his body and making it one with his before returning it to her to inhale. Just as their blood had been blended in the marriage ceremony, just as their bodies had been united on their wedding night, their souls now became one.

Gently, giving Starr the sense of floating, Daniel Blue Eagle lowered her to the ground, and she had no desire to stop him, no desire to stop what she knew would happen—what she with all her heart wanted to happen.

With his upper body over hers, he raised up, resting on his elbows so that his hands were free to unbraid her hair. Sighing as he loosed the plaits, he combed his fingers through the silky, sweet-smelling tresses, finally fanning the thick strands out into a glorious golden-red crown on the flattened brown buffalo grass beneath her.

Warmed beyond reason by the rapture on Daniel Blue Eagle's face as he arranged her hair around her, Starr licked her lips and reached for the fastener on one of his braids that hung between them. She untied first one, then the other, combing her fingers through the plaited hair until its shiny, raven-colored strands were loose and free.

Unable to wait any longer for the feel of his mouth on hers, Starr threaded her fingers into the hair at Daniel Blue Eagle's temples and clutched handfuls of the straight coarse hair, using her grip to pull his face down to hers.

Finally the waiting was at an end. At last his mouth was on hers, crushing her lips against her teeth as his tongue filled the inviting sweetness with its passionate hint of what was to come. Starr sucked gently on his tongue, her own meeting his eagerly, sparring with it, teasing it, luring it further into the warm cave of her mouth.

Starr's hips began to move suggestively, almost as if she danced to a melody only she could hear, and when Daniel Blue Eagle put his hand on her stomach, she arched her hips, rising up to meet his touch, begging him to fill her emptiness. Already the ache in the pit of her belly was becoming unbearable. Her only thought was to relieve the pressure that was consuming her.

Daniel Blue Eagle's callused hand slid up under the deerskin dress, and his hard warm flesh glided over her skin.

Lifting her upward, he raised her dress, exposing

first her long slender legs. Her gently-rounded hips, the flat white belly that prickled with goose flesh under his intense examination were next to be divulged to his greedy eyes, and finally her lush breasts were warmed by the sun and his radiant gaze.

Molding and shaping a plump breast in his rough hand, Daniel Blue Eagle bent his head to draw one of the distended peaks into his mouth, spiraling its tip with his tongue until he had worked it into a tiny button. Then his mouth worked its magic on her other breast as his hand slid between Starr's thighs to take the bud of her desire between his fingers to pinch and tug and twist until she was writhing helplessly against his hand.

Starr felt as if she had been hurled into the air. She was one with the clouds she could see floating above her, and she wanted that feeling to last forever. But all too soon, she was tumbling over the edge of the earth in quivers and contractions.

She cried out as she clutched Daniel Blue Eagle's head to her breast and held him hard against her, never wanting to let go.

When the explosive tremors had nearly faded away, Daniel Blue Eagle kissed his way up to Starr's mouth as he moved his buckskins aside and rolled over onto her waiting body, to fill it with his strength as his tongue filled her mouth.

She experienced no pain with their coupling as she had the night before. Instead, there was only pleasure. Instinctively she bent her knees, leaving her feet flat on the ground so that she could lift her hips to meet each of Daniel Blue Eagle's masculine thrusts, each one taking his organ deeper into the warm folds of her body.

Still he had not given her all of himself. He was afraid he would hurt her. But as he drew closer and closer to his own climax, he could no longer hold back. He had to feel the moist warmth of her femininity around all of him.

Daniel Blue Eagle rained kisses over Starr's face and neck as he caressed her legs. Placing the heels of his hands on her knees, he bent her legs up so that her thighs lay against her breasts, her knees at her shoulders.

No longer able to hold anything back, he pressed into her, filling the tight hollow of her womanhood to capacity.

Over and over he drove into her body, kissing her face as he did, murmuring Indian words of love into her ear. Again the tension of her desire began to grow, and she tried to hold on to these moments spent in heaven. But there was nothing she could do to stop it, and when the final explosion came, it shook Starr beyond understanding, splintering her emotions into a million stars to be scattered throughout the heavens.

She cried out her passion aloud, but Daniel Blue Eagle didn't hear her, for he too had reached the convulsive pinnacle of ecstasy and was calling out his own release.

Neither Starr nor Daniel Blue Eagle spoke, as together they drifted down from the exquisite zenith of their lovemaking.

With a final shudder that shook him from head to toe, he rolled over onto his back to lie beside Starr, the length of his body pressing hot against hers from shoulder to foot. Resting one forearm across his forehead, he closed his eyes, seeming to sleep. But Daniel Blue Eagle was not asleep, and his other hand drew idle circles over Starr's belly and legs, each caress spiraling closer to the center of her desire.

Sickened and embarrassed by the fire she felt rebuilding within her body, Starr rolled over onto her side, curling herself into a ball as she turned away from Daniel Blue Eagle. She had behaved like a harlot, like one of the whores Melanie said they were. How would she be able to face him again? She was glad she had no mirror because she was certain that she would never be able to look at her own reflection again without hating herself. Letting him take her in broad daylight in plain view of anyone who came along was bad enough, but she had actually responded and enjoyed it. She hadn't wanted it to end. She had wished it could go on forever!

Daniel Blue Eagle turned on his side, shaping his body to hers as he draped a brown arm and leg over her.

"Now we are truly man and wife, Firebird," he whispered in her ear, unmindful of the chills that shook Starr's body. "You gave yourself to me willingly. Now no one can take you from me. You are mine for all eternity."

Starr turned in his embrace to look into his blue eyes. "But I'm still your prisoner," she said, her voice surprisingly even.

"You are my wife, not my prisoner," he protested, propping himself up on his elbow and resting his head on the fist of his dark-skinned hand.

"Then if that is true, you will let me go. You will take me home," she said softly, holding her breath as

114

she awaited his reaction to her words.

Coldness glazed his eyes. Her request had hurt him more than he could have believed possible. "That I cannot do, Firebird," he growled.

"Take us back to Yankton. I give you my word that once Dorcas and Melanie are safe and we've talked to the authorities about the massacre, I will do whatever you say. I will come back to your village and be your wife for as long as you want me. I'll never ask another thing of you, Daniel. I'll work hard and will never refuse you anything. I swear that if you grant me this one thing, I will be a good wife to you. Please," she begged, sitting up to face him, her imploring expression almost more than Daniel Blue Eagle could bear.

"I will not bargain with my wife for her obedience, Firebird," he said sternly. "It will be as I have said. The others will be returned to their people when the murderers who killed our people have been punished. As for you, my wife, your place will be with me," he said as his mouth came down hard on hers in an urgent kiss, as if he could force her to care for him with sheer strength.

He pushed her over on her back, his kiss bruising and fierce, and at first Starr struggled against him. But as his hands roved over her body, she felt herself weaken, returning his kiss and caresses in kind. Even as she wrapped her arms around him, she vowed that the next time he came to her she would resist him.

But right then the urgent ache deep in her womb was the only thing that mattered. She knew that only Daniel Blue Eagle could fill her need.

Chapter Seven

In the weeks that followed, the tribe moved every three or four days to provide fresh grazing for the horses. Each move took them further west and further from home, but Starr never forgot her vow to find a way to help Melanie and Dorcas, even if it meant forfeiting her own life and freedom.

And though they did not speak of her suggested bargain again, Daniel Blue Eagle knew that his wife still had not resigned herself to the fact of their marriage, nor given up the hope of gaining her freedom.

The women of the village were busy preparing for the winter days that would soon descend on them. Already the nights were uncomfortably cold, making extra blankets necessary. Everywhere Starr looked, there was industrious activity going on. Strips of buffalo meat were hung out to dry into jerky; women prepared and sewed animal hides the men brought back from each hunt; drafty tepees were patched to protect the inhabitants within from the winter winds;

and warm clothing was made. Buffalo hides with the fur left on them were sewed into blankets and robes; and the women of every lodge took pride in the number of *parfleches* they were able to fill with the dried meat and vegetables their families would need to survive the winter. And Starr was no exception, though she continued to seek a way to escape with Melanie and Dorcas.

During the month and a half she had been in the Indian camp, she had managed to collect and dry more than a dozen kinds of wild fruits and vegetables, and an even larger variety of stalks and roots. She had filled her *parfleches* to bursting with wild rose hips, milkweed buds, wild onions, peas, chokecherries, persimmons, fruit of the prickly-pear cactus, as well as the root vegetable Daniel Blue Eagle told her the *wasicun*, the white man, called 'prairie turnips.' She had even discovered that fresh sweet thistle stalks tasted like bananas when they were peeled and when dried would add wonderful flavor to winter soups and stews.

Using a stone maul to pulverize strips of jerky into a powder, Starr sat on her knees in front of her lodge with Prairie Moon. Though the older woman had learned only a few words of English, and Starr was just beginning to understand the language of the Lakota Indians, the two had developed their own means of communication, and neither had any trouble understanding the other.

"I think this is fine enough," Starr said, using the edges of her hands to gather the powdered meat into a pile in the center of the flat pounding stone before picking some of it up for Prairie Moon to see. She absently let it sift through her fingers onto the stone, studying it for overlooked lumps.

"*Washtay*," Prairie Moon agreed, nodding her head up and down as she ground and pounded dried wild cherries, pits and all, into a mush that would be combined with fat and the buffalo jerky Starr was beating to make *pemmican*, a nutritious food that would be stored in the rawhide *parfleches* she and Starr had made for the winter food supplies.

"*Washtay*," Starr said, pointing to the crushed cherries. "*Washtay*—good," she translated for her own benefit as well as for the older woman.

"Good. *Washtay*—good," Daniel Blue Eagle's aunt repeated proudly, emptying the ground fruit into a wooden bowl with other fruit and powdered meat, before tossing another batch of cherries into her mortar and attacking them energetically with the stone pestle.

Starr couldn't control the sigh that escaped as she put more strips of meat on the stone in front of her and began to beat it with her maul.

She knew she had to find a way to get Dorcas and Melanie out of the camp, and soon. Every day she spent in the company of Prairie Moon, every night with Daniel Blue Eagle, she was risking liking the free nomadic life of a Lakota Indian too much to be able to give it up when the time came. Already she found herself treasuring each new discovery she made, taking special pride in each new skill she mastered. If she waited much longer, she wouldn't be able to give it up.

Starr assaulted the dried meat with new vigor. If it were just herself that she was responsible for, she could stay or go. The choice would be simple. There would be no reason to go back to Yankton. Her family was gone, and she knew what kind of reception she could expect from the upright citizens of the town. Starr shuddered involuntarily, remembering a scene from her childhood.

The soldiers had found a woman who had been a prisoner of the Indians and had brought her to Yankton, together with her two half-Indian children, one just a baby. Though the townspeople had not really shunned her when she came into town—their Christian consciences forced them to make a show of welcoming her home—they had never accepted her back into their midst. Many made it a point to move to the other side of the street rather than meet her on the boardwalk and have to speak, and her visits into town always brought stares and whispers, the gossips' faces hiding none of their contempt. Starr could still remember the tragic woman, caught between two worlds, belonging in neither. Her sad eyes had haunted Starr a long time, even after the woman had finally given up trying to live with her people again and had disappeared, presumably having returned to the Indians.

But no matter how cold a reception she could expect, she still felt obligated to help Dorcas and Melanie however she could. They both continued to find life in the Indian camp a torturous existence, although they knew what awaited them in Yankton if they returned there. What would become of them when the winter snow and ice covered the ground if she didn't get them out of here?

Yet what about Prairie Moon? She had a responsibility to her also. Who would take care of her when her arthritic hands were too inflexible to do her share of the work? Already the woman's swollen joints were stiffening with the cooler weather, and though she never complained, Starr knew she was in pain a great deal of the time, especially in the morning before the sun had had the chance to warm the air. In another month she would not be able to put up her tepee alone. If Starr left, the independent woman would eventually have to trust herself to the charity of the other tribeswomen.

If only Daniel Blue Eagle had other wives, she mused, then shook her head vigorously at the thought. She didn't even want to think about that. As long as she was the only woman he called wife, she could almost believe that their marriage was real, and could almost convince herself that she wasn't doing anything wrong when she lay in his arms at night and responded to his every caress.

There has to be another way! she told herself with determination. *If only he would accept my bargain, I could stay and take care of Prairie Moon, and Melanie and Dorcas could go home.*

Suddenly, Starr felt as if she was being watched, and the familiar tingle that ran through her told her that Daniel Blue Eagle was near. She looked up from her work, her anxious gaze drawn to the other side of the camp, fully expecting to see the man who called himself her husband, though he had been out hunting wild game with the other braves from the village for two days and wasn't expected to return before the next evening.

He was there, just as she had known he would be,

120

watching her from afar as he often did, the pleasure in his blue eyes hidden from none. It was always that way. She never failed to sense his presence moments before he came into view.

The village had burst into an explosion of activity with the return of the hunters. No longer questioning the power that drew her to him, Starr put down her maul and rose to meet Daniel Blue Eagle. They walked toward each other, oblivious to the people milling all around them.

"We did not expect you until tomorrow," she said when she reached him, her polite tone not quite disguising the pleasure she felt. Fighting the urge to embrace him, she blushed and looked at the toes of his moccasins. Of course, it was a foolish impulse. She couldn't throw her arms around him. Instead, she took the reins of his horse out of his hand and turned back toward their lodge.

"We killed much game," he answered matter-of-factly. "We will celebrate tonight. There will be much for you and my aunt to do while I am gone."

"Gone? You are leaving again?" Starr's tone remained conversational, not showing the disappointment she felt at his announcement.

"My father and many chiefs from other bands are going to the Red Cloud Agency for talks. We must leave tomorrow."

"Will you reconsider taking Dorcas and Melanie with you?" Her tone was low and even, though she could feel her heart pounding her excitement loudly in her ears. It would solve everything if he could be convinced to do it. The two young women would be taken care of by the soldiers, and she, herself, could stay behind and care for Prairie Moon. She ignored the fleeting thought that the older woman was not the only reason she wanted to stay. "Please," she added urgently, coming to a halt beside the man and stopping him in the path with her hand on his arm, the intense look in her eyes imploring him to do as she asked.

Daniel Blue Eagle's eyes ran over the small red-haired girl. The beseeching expression on her face was almost more than he could bear, and he wanted to pull her into his arms right then, no matter who would see.

"You know that is impossible, Firebird," he said, his voice sad and tired. "I've made a vow and must stand by it. Spotted Shoulder and Yellow Whip would be very displeased if I took their women away. They would say I'm using my position as the son of Man of the People to keep you while I ask them to give up their captives."

"Then I could go with you too. You could take us all to show the soldiers your good faith. But when Dorcas and Melanie are safe at the Red Cloud Agency, I could come back with you, not as your captive, but by choice. If you do this for me, Daniel Blue Eagle, I will never ask another thing of you."

"I can't, Firebird." Unable to bear the sight of the disappointment in her face, Daniel Blue Eagle resumed walking toward their tepee, leaving Starr standing alone behind him. If there were any way he could free the two women, any way at all, he would— if for no other reason than to guarantee that his wife would stay with him willingly. He longed for a time when he could leave the village and not be cursed with wondering if she would still be there when he returned.

Starr had to quicken her step to catch up with Daniel Blue Eagle. He was giving her no choice. Didn't he know that she would have to make every effort to escape now? No matter how much she wanted to stay, she had to leave him.

She approached the tepee as Prairie Moon was greeting her nephew. She watched the reunion sadly, knowing now what she had to do. Maybe Prairie Moon would be all right. Perhaps Man of the People's wives would take care of her. From what she had seen of the two women, however, it would be simply out of duty, not as an act of love. Starr wiped her eyes and nose with the back of a slender wrist and set to work unsaddling Daniel Blue Eagle's horse. She wouldn't cry. She wouldn't!

That night with Prairie Moon soundly asleep in her own smaller tepee, Daniel Blue Eagle made love with his wife more tenderly than ever before. And Starr responded with more passion than she had ever imagined herself possessing. Knowing it would be their last time together, that she would be gone when he returned, she held back nothing. She felt as though she needed to inscribe every precious moment indelibly in her heart, as if the memories they created that night would have to last her a lifetime.

"How long will you be there?" Starr asked when their appetites had been temporarily appeased. She snuggled closer against Daniel Blue Eagle's side as she spoke, her head resting on his shoulder, his arm wrapped around her and caressing her upper arm. She traced her fingers over the muscles of his chest and flat stomach, teasing his flat brown nipples, dipping into his deep navel, examining the raised scars on his chest. She kissed the nearest reminder of the sun dance from seven years before, feeling the pain in her own heart that he must have suffered when he'd been lifted off the ground by rawhide ropes attached to pegs inserted into his flesh.

"I don't know how long we will be away, Firebird. Will you miss me?" he asked softly, wondering why he had asked, knowing he was leaving himself vulnerable to her rejection. He had never caught her in a lie and knew she would tell the truth now, even at the risk of his anger.

"I will miss you, Daniel Blue Eagle," Starr admitted for the first time, either to him or to herself. She was certain that leaving him would be the hardest thing she had ever done. She tried to tell herself she didn't want to go back home because she wouldn't be accepted by the people there after she had lived with the Indians. She wouldn't allow herself to consider the real reason she had put off an attempt to escape for so long. But Daniel Blue Eagle had made the decision for her when he refused to release the others. She had to go, for Melanie and Dorcas. She had already waited too long. She had to get them to safety before winter. "But you won't be gone for long, will you?"

Studying the top of Starr's bent head out of the corner of his eye, Daniel Blue Eagle slid his hand up and tangled his fingers in her hair. He couldn't believe what he was hearing. Was she actually beginning to care for him? True, she had been a good wife, always treating him with respect, never failing to see to his every need, but that could be because she feared punishment. A wave of shame rocked over Daniel Blue Eagle as he remembered the way he had treated her that first day in the camp.

"It may be as much as a month. Maybe more, maybe less. The whites want the Indians to stay on the reservations. They want our roving bands to give up the hunting grounds in the Montana Territory to starve to death on the reservations where the buffalo no longer roam. The government says we don't need the buffalo because they will feed the People and teach them to farm. But the tribes who have tried to live on the reservation are half-starved and constantly cheated out of food and clothing by the agents. The meat they give them is usually rotten by the time they get it and the flour and grain are not fit to eat. And it is rumored that if we refuse to give them our Black Hills they will take them from us, killing peaceful and hostile bands alike if we are caught off the reservation."

"Are we in the Black Hills now?"

"No, they are south of here. They are sacred to the Indian, a place to commune with the gods. Yet, the whites want to destroy them in their search for gold. Already there are over ten thousand prospectors in the area. The hostile bands harass and kill them when they come across them, but for every white man that is shot, three more come to replace him. President Grant has ordered the Army to arrest them when they come onto our lands, but the civil courts release them as fast as they can be taken in. It's only a matter of time until they don't bother to apprehend them at all."

"What will that mean to the Lakota?" Starr asked, looking into Daniel Blue Eagle's sad eyes. She didn't know what answer she expected, but she was unprepared for the one he gave.

"It will mean war," he said in a voice that cracked as he spoke. "There will be nothing we can do to stop it. I believe it will mean the end of the People as we know them now. There are too many whites, and too few of us."

"It can't be that bad. Surely, you can talk to the People and tell them what will happen if they resist!"

"I've tried, Firebird. My ideas have caused a split in my own band."

"If you are ordered to the reservation, will your father's people go or will they resist?"

"I don't know. Some will, some won't. Already many have left our band to join Sitting Bull, the Hunkpapa medicine man. As the injustices against the People accumulate, all the bands of the Lakota lose young braves every day. Hunkpapa, Minneconjou, Brule, Yankton, Santee, Two Kettle, Sans Arc, Blackfoot, and of course ours, the Oglala, gather together to resist. Maybe the commission they are sending to talk to us will be wiser than we are and will be able to help solve our problems. But I don't have much hope. I doubt Sitting Bull will even come," he said with resignation.

Starr leaned over and kissed Daniel Blue Eagle's lips lightly, wanting desperately to ease some of his sorrow, some of her own, knowing there was only one way they could both forget, even for a few minutes, what the future had in store.

Again they made love, this time with a frightening

126

frenzy. Finally, they both collapsed, falling into a restless slumber, his body still joined with hers.

Starr stood beside Prairie Moon as together they watched Daniel Blue Eagle ride out of the camp with Man of the People and his brother, Gray Wolf. She swallowed her tears as she strained to watch the three until they had completely disappeared. Even after that, she concentrated on the spot she'd last been able to see them, as if he might come back for her. But of course he didn't. He was gone, and she would not see him again.

If anything good could be said about what was happening, it was that Man of the People and his two sons were a united front again. They still didn't agree on the outcome, but Gray Wolf, still a staunch supporter of killing any whites who came onto their lands uninvited, had developed a wait-and-see attitude about the latest commission the president was sending to deal with them. And Daniel Blue Eagle had come to realize that if the whites continued to encroach on their lands, they would be forced to defend themselves, or live the lives of political prisoners on the reservation. Either way would mean death and the end of the Lakota way of life.

Finally forcing herself to concentrate on what she had to do, Starr bent and spontaneously kissed Prairie Moon on the cheek, telling her, "I will be back. I have to visit with Gentle Fawn and my friends, Melanie and Dorcas."

The older woman nodded her head and patted the girl's arm.

Starr didn't know if she understood or not, but she had to assume she did. It was time to move on. There was no time left to teach Prairie Moon to speak English.

Rushing across the camp to Gentle Fawn's family's tepee, Starr planned what she would say. The Indian girl had promised to help her escape. She hoped that she hadn't changed her mind. Without Gentle Fawn, she didn't have a chance of getting away.

The lovely Indian girl looked up from the hide she was softening by pulling it through a hole in a bone to make it more malleable. She could tell by the look on Firebird's face that this was not a social call. Could it be the time had come? The time when she would no longer have to see her with Daniel Blue Eagle in the place she should have occupied? She smiled with satisfaction, the beautiful smile not quite reaching her obsidian eyes. She had nearly given up hope that the pale woman would seek her out again. She had begun to consider other, more violent, ways of destroying Firebird.

"Good morning, Firebird," she said sweetly, taking care to show none of the resentment she felt for the woman Daniel Blue Eagle had chosen before her. Because of the pale-skinned female, the best Gentle Fawn could hope for now was to become the first wife of a lesser warrior, or to be chosen as Daniel Blue Eagle's second wife—a position she would never settle for. She was the daughter of a chief's first wife. She would be no man's second wife. She would be his first wife, or nothing. And she had no intention of settling for nothing.

"Can we talk?" Starr asked the girl she thought

was her friend. They both glanced from side to side at the other women nearby.

Gentle Fawn put down her work and told her mother and sisters that she would be back. Together she and Starr walked away from the camp toward a copse of trees, already losing their red and gold leaves in preparation for their winter sleep.

Starr glanced around cautiously before she spoke. They were alone. "You said on the day I married Daniel Blue Eagle that you would help me escape. I need directions to find the nearest settlement of whites that have come onto your lands. My friends and I will go there and ask them to take us back to Yankton."

"You have chosen your time to leave wisely, Firebird. I thought perhaps you had changed your mind about going."

"I wanted to be certain Prairie Moon had enough supplies put up for the winter. And too, I only found out last night that there are whites all over the area. I wasn't certain we could make the journey all the way across the Territory, but I'm sure we can manage to ride two or three days to safety. Will you help me? Where is the closest gold camp?"

"That would be a place they call Deadwood. It's to the south. When will you leave?" she asked eagerly, finding it difficult to hide her happiness. If the stupid white girl didn't get lost and die in the hills before she reached the wild camp, the loathsome prospectors would make her into one of their whores. Either way, that would be the end of her marriage to Daniel Blue Eagle.

"I'd like to leave in the morning, just as quickly as

129

I can prepare Melanie and Dorcas for the trip," Starr answered, looking to the south and wondering how far Deadwood was.

"Are you certain you want to take the others with you?" Gentle Fawn asked, her eyes shifting nervously. She couldn't let that happen. The other two would slow Firebird down so much that Daniel Blue Eagle might be able to find them before they could get away. Or worse still, they might get only a few miles from the Lakota village and give up. They'd be back in the camp before anyone knew they were gone.

"Of course I'm taking them. I can't leave them behind."

"I understand, Firebird, but do you think it is wise? You will be able to travel faster alone and could get to Deadwood in one day at the most if you aren't slowed down by those two." She lied adeptly about the length of the four-day drip. "If you take them, you will spend all of your time pampering them and listening to them complain. Also three horses would leave a trail that would be easier to follow. I think you should go alone. You could find someone to help you, and I could bring the women to meet you, say in three days."

"I really could travel faster alone. I don't think they even ride. You say this Deadwood is not more than a day from here?"

"At the most," Gentle Fawn continued. "Traveling alone, you might be able to make it in even less time."

"I could get an early start tomorrow morning and be back here by evening on the next day."

"Only you will not have to come all the way back. I will meet you two hours south of here. With so many of the men out of the camp, we do not want the soldiers to know where we are."

"No, we don't want that," Starr said, shaking her head as she remembered the massacred Indians she had seen on her first day in the camp. "But how will you know where to meet me?"

"I'll ride part way with you tomorrow to be certain you are headed in the right direction, and we will decide on a meeting place then."

"Thank you, Gentle Fawn. It is a good plan. I am in your debt."

"You owe me no thanks, Firebird. I am only doing what I think is right," she said truthfully. *In fact, I owe you my thanks for your cooperation in making your disappearance so easy for me!*

Before the two young women returned to the village, it was arranged that they would ride out of the village four hours before sunup, in order to give Gentle Fawn time to get back into the camp before her absence was noticed.

During the hours that followed, Starr spoke to both Melanie and Dorcas, finally convincing them that this would be their last chance to escape before winter, and the least dangerous way to carry it out. Relieved that they would soon be free, they both agreed to ride out of the camp with Gentle Fawn when the time came to meet Starr and their rescuers.

The rest of the day was spent stashing a two-day supply of food in saddlebags and scraping the meat and fat off the hides Daniel Blue Eagle had brought back. She was relieved that Deadwood was only a day away, because it meant she wouldn't need to take a buffalo robe for sleeping on the ground. The added weight would only slow her down, and she needed every bit of speed she could muster. She didn't want to be alone in the hills one moment longer than absolutely necessary.

Though she was not able to sleep that night, when the time for her departure came, it was a wide-awake Starr who stole out of the camp. Carefully secreting her supplies under a blanket wrapped tightly around her shoulders, she eyed the buffalo robe on her sleeping mat and reconsidered taking it with her. Already the temperatures at night were dropping to within a few degrees of freezing, and until the sun came up to warm the earth, it was going to be cold. As if to reenforce her thought, she let out a sigh, aware that her warm breath formed a cloud of mist when it hit the cold night air. Still, she'd better leave the robe behind to give Prairie Moon additional warmth this winter, since Starr wouldn't be here to help her make another.

Taking a final glance around the tepee that had been her home for a month and a half, Starr wished with all her heart that it could have been hers forever.

"But it just wasn't meant to be," she mumbled to herself and crawled out of the tepee. She didn't look back as she scurried to the place where the tribe's horses grazed.

Picking out one of Daniel Blue Eagle's horses that looked a little bigger and better fed than the others, she quickly saddled him. She tied a lark's-head knot in the middle of a rope, the way she had done hundreds of times since she'd been with the Lakota, and slipped it around the horse's lower jaw to make his bit. Just as she draped the rope ends along either side of the horse's neck to be used as reins, her accomplice, Gentle Fawn, joined her.

Starr hurriedly slung her beaded saddlebags over the horse's back and mounted. "I'm ready," she said with resolve, nudging the horse forward with the heels of her moccasin-covered feet. She didn't look back at the camp, knowing that if she did, she might lose her courage and return to the safety of Daniel Blue Eagle's tepee, letting Melanie and Dorcas worry about saving themselves.

Chapter Eight

Riding at a steady pace, Starr turned her face toward the rising sun, hoping desperately to absorb some of its warmth into her chilled core. She was glad she had thought to slip a pair of Daniel Blue Eagle's buckskin trousers on under her dress. *At least I'm not as cold as I could have been*, she told herself as she pulled her woven blanket closer around her, refusing to think about the buffalo robe she had left behind.

The hours since she had left the Oglala Sioux village had been miserably cold, especially the last two after she and Gentle Fawn had parted by the stream where they were to meet the next afternoon when she returned with help.

They had traveled east only a short distance before turning south to follow the base of a line of pine-capped buttes that stretched along the miles toward the Black Hills. The tall chalk-colored limestone and clay spires looked less frightening in the morning light but were still intimidating, jutting so sharply from either side of the deep coulee in which she traveled.

Carefully concentrating on the trail before her, she couldn't fight off the frightening premonition that suddenly quaked through her chilled body. What if she took a wrong turn? It would be so easy to do. Between each of the buttes that lined her trail, there were other trails, some narrow, others as wide as the one she was on. She had already more than once reached forks where she had to guess which trail was the way to Deadwood. Once she had chosen the wrong turn and found herself trapped in a dead end, making it necessary for her to retrace her path to the main trail.

Starr made certain that the sun remained on her left shoulder, hopeful that she wouldn't get turned around in the maze if she always kept the sun's position in mind. Still, she should have come to the butte that Gentle Fawn had told her to watch for a little after sunrise, the one with the deep vee-shaped groove cut in the top of it.

The sun had been up for an hour now but she had seen nothing that resembled the butte Gentle Fawn had described. Could she have reached it sooner than the Indian girl had anticipated and missed it in the dark? Or what if she had gotten on the wrong trail and not realized it? Should she go back and see if she had made a mistake?

Starr stopped her horse and looked back over her shoulder to consider her choices. She wouldn't panic. It was probably just ahead. After all, she had lost all that time when she had taken the wrong trail in the pre-dawn darkness. She was just overly anxious. She would continue south. She had come too far to go back and try to determine where she'd gone wrong, if she had.

Throughout the morning, Starr watched for it, studying every flat-topped hill from every angle as she passed it, but she never found the odd-shaped butte she was looking for, and by the time the noonday sun was at its highest in the sky, she realized she wasn't going to find it.

Spotting a patch of grass in an adjacent coulee, Starr led her horse to it and staked him out so that he could graze—and she could eat her lunch while she decided what to do. She knew she couldn't turn around and go back because there was a strong chance she would get more lost than ever if she did. That meant she would just have to forge ahead, keeping herself alive by the skills and instincts she had developed while living with the Indians. She wished she had insisted on bringing Melanie and Dorcas with her so a trip back to the village wouldn't be necessary. But it was too late to think about that now. Thoughts about how she would find her way back to retrieve the other two would have to come later. Not now. There would be time to think about that after she reached Deadwood. Right now she had to concentrate on just one thing: staying alive. Nothing else mattered.

All through the rest of the day, Starr kept her horse headed south, her confidence growing when she noticed that the concentration of tall buttes on either side of her was thinning out. At least she had managed to keep to her course and had worked her way a little closer to the Black Hills and Deadwood.

However, just after sunset, a new worry seized her. Searching for a place to spend the night before darkness completely surrounded her, she came to an intersection of trails. She sat up straight in her saddle and looked around, immediately alert to every sound, every smell, everything in her line of vision.

Starr realized she was not alone in the area. A large number of people and horses had recently crossed over the trail that met hers. And it hadn't been very long ago.

Sweat broke out on her brow as she studied her surroundings nervously, as though she expected to see other human beings on the trail with her, but she was alone—or so it seemed.

By the looks of the shoeless horse tracks and moccasin footprints, Starr realized that there was a large party of Indians moving west, probably agency Indians leaving the reservation to join Sitting Bull and the wild Sioux in the Yellowstone country. And not much time had elapsed since they'd been here. The horse manure on the ground was fresh, some of it still steaming in the cool evening air. If she had been here an hour earlier, she would probably have ridden into the main concentration of their band!

Leaping from her pony, Starr led him into a crevice between the sheer wall of a butte and a tall boulder that must have once been part of the larger hill before melting snow and rain had cut a path between them. There was barely enough room for the horse and young woman in the narrow space, and when the gray horse whinnied his complaint, she had to pinch his nostrils shut to silence him, shushing him as she patted his neck to calm him.

"We'll wait until dark, and then we'll cross to the other side. They must be camped near here, so you'll have to be very quiet. If their horses hear us or pick up our scent, they will alert the whole tribe, and we won't have a chance," she whispered to the horse who was slowly settling down under her soothing caresses.

She listened carefully for the sounds she knew would mean the Indians were still nearby. She heard nothing. Perhaps they had not stopped for the night after all, making their getaway under cover of darkness. Besides, they would want to get out of the coulee before morning. Not only were the high bluffs perfect for ambushing people on the lower ground, but if a rainstorm came up suddenly, the trail could quickly become a deadly torrent washing over and destroying everything in its path.

Starr instinctively looked at the clouds floating across the sky and tried to determine if it was going to rain.

In spite of the fact that she was eager to put the Indian crossing behind her, Starr patiently waited until the last of the twilight was gone and the surrounding darkness was almost total.

She stepped cautiously out of her hiding place, taking one careful step at a time, uncomfortably aware of every sound she and the horse made, certain they were loud enough to call attention to her presence. Step. Stop to listen for signs of detection. Step. Stop. Step.

When she finally reached the intersection, she stopped again to look in both directions, ready to scurry to the other side if it was safe.

Then she heard it, a soft rumble at first, like distant thunder. She looked to her left, aware that the rumble was growing louder. It was coming down the cross trail directly toward her. Ever louder and closer, until its roar filled the entire canyon.

Tugging desperately on the reins of her reluctant horse, she managed to get back to her hiding place and conceal herself only an instant before the riders sped past her, heading down the same trail the tribe of Indians had taken earlier. Evidently the fast-riding warriors were the rear guard and probably the last of the traveling band. Still, she would take no chances and waited another hour before she crept into the open again.

This time there were no mounted latecomers, and she made her crossing safely. She knew now that she would have to travel through the night to put as much distance as possible between herself and the Indians before daylight, so she shared the remainder of her dried fruit and vegetables with her horse, thinking he needed it more than she did, and mounted again.

Keeping to the shadows created by the giant buttes along the edges of the trail, she felt as though she made pretty good time. But by the time the moon had risen, reached its apex and had started its decline again, the hard day of riding, on top of two sleepless nights, began to wear on her. She could hardly hold her head up, and the way her horse kept stumbling on rocks in the trail, she could tell he was tired, too. Even though she hated to risk stopping, she decided she would have to find shelter in a small niche in a hill where she could rest for a while. She rode another half an hour before she found a place that seemed safe.

Starr staked out her horse in a patch of dry grass near the tiny cave she had found. Wrapping her blanket more securely around her slender body, she crawled into the hole in the side of the hill and curled herself into a tight ball. She didn't even notice the cold dampness of the cave floor or the growling noises her stomach was beginning to make. She would eat tomorrow in Deadwood. Surely, it couldn't be much farther. *It's probably just over the next ridge*, she assured herself. *Just over the next ridge*.

"Well, whatta we got here?" a man's loud voice boomed, bringing Starr awake with a jolt.

Sitting up suddenly, she needed no time to adjust to

where she was. Instantly alerted to danger, she drew her knife as she peeked out of her hiding place in the direction from which the voice had come. She was shocked to realize that it was daylight—she felt as though she had just closed her eyes. But it was definitely no longer night and the sun was shining brightly on a group of men gathered around her tethered pony.

"This sure ain't no white man's pony," another man said, examining the saddle and saddle bags on the horse's back. "Wonder where the varmint is hidin'," he said, looking around suspiciously, his revolver already drawn for action.

The first man who had spoken tilted his head wisely in Starr's direction and drew his gun too, aiming it at the cave where she hid. Starr's heart leapt into her throat. She tried to back deeper into the cave, knowing even as she did that she was trapped. There was nowhere to go.

"Awright, Injun. Git on out here with yer hands up!" a third man hollered, his gravelly voice coming from directly outside the entrance to Starr's cave. "I'll give ya three ta git yer ass out here, an' then I start shootin'."

"You'd git five, but ol' Calam can't count no higher'n three," the second man laughed, joining his comrade outside the cave, certain now that they had nothing to fear from an Indian who was alone and hiding in a hole in the side of a hill. It was probably some old chief who had crawled away to die. He had heard they did crazy things like that. "Come on out with your hands up, Injun. Start countin', Calam."

"One," she heard the raucous voice of the one called Calam shout out.

Starr took a deep breath and hid her knife in her sleeve.

"Two."

"Don't shoot. I'm coming out," she called, crawling on all fours toward the entrance.

"What the hell?" the first man cursed, realizing the voice of the 'Indian' they had cornered belonged to a woman. "It's a squaw. We've captured us a squaw! Look at us! Guns all drawn like we was gonna take on the whole Sioux nation, and we got us a helpless squaw." He shoved his gun into his holster and walked away from the cave's entrance, too soon to see Starr's head appear in the opening.

"I'll be gawdamned," the man with a luxurious mane of blond ringlets cursed. "You gotta see this, Bill," he said, returning his own revolver to its holster.

"You ain't no Injun," the man who'd been counting accused, spitting the juice of his tobacco on the ground beside his boot. "What the hell're you doin' here, gal?"

His curiosity roused by his friend's comments, the man called Bill walked over to see what all the fuss was about, his mouth dropped open when he viewed the frightened face of the strawberry-blonde white girl on her hands and knees before him. "Where'd you come from, little lady?" he asked gently, stooping his large frame to the ground to get a better look at her, his eyesight not what it used to be, though he would admit that to no one.

"My name's Starr Winfield," she started breathlessly as she accepted the tall man's assistance to stand on her shaky legs.

"Well, Miss Starr Winfield, it's nice to meet you. Do you mind tellin' me and my friends what you're doin' out here alone and dressed in them clothes?" The man's smile was warm under a long droopy mustache that curled inches past his jaw. Actually, he was quite good-looking, with his thick shoulder-length chestnut hair and dark brown eyes that seemed to dance with amusement when he spoke, as if he didn't take too much, himself especially, seriously.

"My friends and I were prisoners of a tribe of Sioux. I heard there were whites in a place called Deadwood, so I escaped to go for help. My friends are still there. I promised I'd come back for them. You aren't going north by any chance, are you?"

"No, but we'll be glad to accompany you to Deadwood," the man with the long blond ringlets said, bowing to her as he took her hand and kissed it. "Colorado Charlie Utter at your service."

Starr couldn't help giggling. This whole situation was preposterous. She was filthy, smelling worse than her horse, and this charming dandy in his brocaded vest and neat black suit was treating her as if she were wearing a beautiful gown. "I'm charmed to meet you, Mr. Utter," she managed to say, thinking she wished she smelled as good as he did, and that her fingernails were as clean!

"Allow me to introduce you to Wild Bill Hickok," he offered grandly, indicating the brown-haired man with the fabulous mustache.

"Mr. Hickok," Starr said, taking his offered hand and firmly shaking it.

Hickok continued to hold her hand in his as he introduced the other man who stood watching the three as if he was not certain how to take this unexpected turn of events.

"And this here's our good friend and drinkin' buddy, Calamity Jane," Hickok said, bestowing another of his infectious grins on both women.

"Calamity—*Jane*!?!" Starr gasped, studying the woman's homely features, her thick figure, realizing suddenly that there were curves under the ugly brown coat that would not be on any man. "I—I thought—" she stammered awkwardly, embarrassed by the fact that she was staring but unable to stop.

"Well, you thought wrong," Calamity Jane growled, deciding she didn't like the skinny girl at all. She especially didn't like the way Wild Bill and Colorado Charlie were making so much fuss over her. And she didn't like it one bit that Wild Bill Hickok couldn't seem to take his eyes off the scrawny thing. "I may be a female," she said, taking off her hat and freeing a curly mass of dirty copper-colored hair that she kept tucked under her man's hat, "but I kin outfight, outshoot, outride, outdrink an' outchew the best o' men," she bragged, laughing raucously as she slapped Wild Bill on the back and spit another stream of tobacco juice on the ground. "Cain't I, Wild Bill?"

"You sure can, Calam," he agreed. "Can't think of anyone I'd rather have on my side in a fight."

Calamity, who stood much taller than Starr, looked down her squashed nose at the stunned girl, the expression on her face saying, *Now you know how it is between me and Wild Bill, and if you get in my way you'll be sorry.* Then she turned her adoring tobacco-stained toothy smile toward Wild Bill Hickok and practically blushed with girlish pleasure.

Starr not only got the masculine woman's message, but she agreed with Wild Bill. She wouldn't mind having Calamity Jane on her side in a fight either!

"Well, little lady, you want to join up with us and head into Deadwood?" Wild Bill asked.

Before she could answer, Colorado Charlie offered her his arm and led her to her horse.

Realizing the second meeting with the commissioners from Washington was about to begin, Daniel Blue Eagle rubbed his eyes and shook his head sadly. He could see that no agreement would be reached at these meetings and that they had been a waste of time. He was very disappointed. He had hoped that by not breaking the Fort Laramie Treaty of 1868 they would be able to keep their hunting lands and still avoid a war. But he could see now that his thinking had been idealistic and foolish.

The whites would make a pretense of paying for what they took, whether the Indians wanted to sell or not. But in the end, they would get what they wanted. A wave of sadness engulfed him, for he knew that many, both Indian and white, would die in the process, and there was nothing he could do to stop it. War was inevitable.

Daniel Blue Eagle looked around from where he sat on the ground beside Man of the People and the other chiefs who faced the commission. He felt vulnerable without his arms or horse, but he had wanted to be beside his father at these talks, so he had put down his gun.

The council was surrounded by thousands of Indians who had gathered for the conference, having worked themselves into a frenzy over the government's offer to buy the Black Hills. Daniel Blue Eagle felt as if he were sitting on a barrel of explosives.

There were many chiefs who would agree to sell, but they were fighting among themselves over an asking price, unable to reach an understanding. And while they were haggling over how much the Black Hills were worth, the wild Indians from the unceded territory around the Powder and Yellowstone Rivers were threatening to kill any chief who signed the paper to sell.

Daniel Blue Eagle was suddenly brought to attention by the sound of gunfire. He swung around in time to see groups of riders from the wild bands rushing headlong toward the commissioners and chiefs gathered for the council.

Brandishing repeating Winchester rifles, shooting haphazardly into the air, the shouting groups rode circles around the council tent, each time coming closer to the unarmed men in the center.

The interpreter tried to keep the unprotected council calm, telling the frightened men that it was normal behavior for such an important meeting, but the commissioners were not convinced. All the color drained from their faces, and they frantically searched for a place to hide. But there was none. They were surrounded.

Daniel Blue Eagle wasn't convinced either. He stood up and turned to face the screaming warriors, shielding his father with his own body as he did. The crazed braves were shouting threats to the chiefs and commissioners. Some were even shooting over the heads of the commissioners, and there was nothing he could do to help the frightened whites and chiefs of the council.

A warrior Daniel Blue Eagle recognized as Little Big Man from Sitting Bull's Hunkpapa band in the Yellowstone country suddenly rode in the small space between the commissioners and chiefs. With two revolvers in his belt, a rifle in one hand and cartridges in the other, he was already stripped for battle.

"I will kill the first chief who speaks of selling the Black Hills," he shouted savagely in the Indians' language.

Out of the corner of his eye, Daniel Blue Eagle saw the soldiers who were guarding the commission mount their horses and aim their guns at the renegades. They waited for the order to fire. But it didn't come, for at that same moment, Indians rode their own horses in front of the soldiers, surrounding the commissioners and shutting out the soldiers.

"All hell's breakin' loose!" one of the whites shouted, certain they were dead men.

But just then, Young-Man-Afraid-of-His-Own-Horses led his own wild Oglala into the middle of the fray, making a protective inner circle between the commissioners and the riled Hunkpapas.

Daniel Blue Eagle's mouth dropped open, for Gray Wolf was standing beside Young-Man-Afraid with the Oglalas challenging the Hunkpapas.

Bravely stepping to the center of the council, Young-Man-Afraid shouted to the angry warriors, his authoritative voice booming over the sounds of war whoops and gunfire. "Go back to your lodges until your heads are cool," he ordered. And surprisingly, the Indians began to scatter.

Though some of the hostiles followed the council members and their mounted champions back to the Red Cloud agency, still shouting and threatening to kill the commissioners, a savage battle had been averted by the Indians' bravery.

The angry hostiles soon departed for home, but the others, determined to reach some sort of agreement, met for four days until they came up with a price to ask for the Black Hills. They wanted seventy million dollars. The commissioners quickly refused.

Finally, after two more days of discussion, the commissioners came back with their counter-offer. They were authorized to offer $400,000 a year for the mining rights in the Black Hills or $6 million for an outright purchase. The Indians quickly refused, ending the talks, making the council an utter failure.

Dejected, Daniel Blue Eagle, Man of the People, and Gray Wolf started home with their braves. Though they felt that their efforts had been useless, they had not come away from the council empty-handed, for there was a new closeness between the three that had been missing for many years.

"You and Young-Man-Afraid surprised us all when you stepped in and chased Little Big Man and his followers off. I thought we were dead, standing there in that tent with no guns, no knives, and nowhere to go." Daniel Blue Eagle could laugh now.

"I was very proud of you, my son," Man of the People said, his somber expression not disguising his pride. "It was a very brave thing to do. If you had taken a *coup* stick with you, you would not have been able to keep count of all your *coup*."

"Don't misunderstand my motives, father. I still believe we will have to fight the whites, but cutting down an unarmed peace commission would prove very little. It would just bring the whole United States Army down on the People."

"What do you believe they will do now, my sons?"

"I think they'll stop making any effort at all to keep the prospectors out of the Black Hills. They tried to buy them, we refused to sell, and now they will wash their

147

hands of it, not even making a show of protecting the Indians' lands. We will have to fight them or give up the land. And if we do that, they will only find something else of ours to steal."

"And what does my older son think?"

"I agree with Gray Wolf, though it saddens me deeply that fighting is the only way. If we let the whites take our hunting grounds, leaving us with only the inedible filth the agents pawn off as food, the People will starve to death. We can't give up our hunting grounds," Daniel Blue Eagle said, the sorrow in his voice heartbreaking. He knew he had failed. Failed his father, failed the People.

He had been so certain he could find a way to prevent war.

Chapter Nine

"If'n we ain't safe from the Injuns in Deadwood, we ain't gonna be safe nowhars west o' the Missouri," Calamity Jane observed wisely as she popped a new chaw of tobacco into her mouth. "This here entrance is so tight that the only way two wagons could pass each other along here is if'n one was ta fly!" she exaggerated, as she always did.

It was true the mile-long entrance to Deadwood Gulch was the only way to get in and out of the dead-end canyon where the illegal prospecting town was located, but it wasn't quite as narrow as Calamity indicated. There was room for two teams to pass. Barely, but they could pass.

" 'Minds me o' the time I was a scoutin' fer the Army an' a hundert an' fifty redskins was breathin' down my neck," she roared, slapping her leg as she sat back in her saddle, preparing to begin one of her long tales of her adventures. Starr was beginning to suspect were not exactly true, but they still fascinated her, and they were a way to pass the time.

"There I was boxed in a canyon with a entrance even tighter than this one. It was so tight that the redskins would have to line up ta git through it. Anyways, I looks 'round me an' says, 'Calamity, ol' gal, ya done got yerself in a heap o' trouble this time.' I didn't know what ta do. There was a hundert an' fifty o' them an' only one o' me, an' all I had was a knife and my trusty six-shooter. Only thing was, there was only one bullet left in it."

"What did you do?" Starr asked, her eyes open wide with anticipation, in spite of the fact that she knew the rowdy woman probably wouldn't know the truth from a lie.

"What did I do? Well, what do ya think I done? I found me a hidin' place and crouched down real low, jest countin' the seconds til them redskins lined up an' come through that skinny entrance ta git me. I waited. I could hear'm outside makin' their Injun noises while they decided what ta do. The sweat was pourin' off my face, almost blindin' me when it dripped inta my eyes. The knife in one hand and the gun in the other, I waited for 'em ta come through that skinny entrance. My finger itched ta pull the trigger. Still I waited. I knew I couldn't hurry or give 'way my hidin' place or they'd be all over me. Know what I done?"

"What?" Starr asked, almost believing the woman's convincing performance.

"I aimed real careful at that entrance til the first Injun finally showed his painted red body in the openin'. I wiped the sweat outta my eyes, took a deep breath an' fired my only bullet." She held her hand out and demonstrated her steady aim, even blowing

150

the smoke off her imaginary gun barrel before putting it back into her imaginary holster. "An' that's how come I'm here today, cause o' that one shot!" she bragged with a big grin.

"How could killing one Indian save you?" Starr scoffed good-naturedly.

"Oh, I didn't kill *one*. Lined up like they was, an' my bullet bein' so fast and true, it passed right through the whole line of 'em, sendin' all hundert an' fifty of 'em toes up with that one bullet! That's how come I'm called the fastest female gun in the West."

Starr rolled her eyes and smiled, shaking her head in mock disgust at her own gullibility. She'd done it again. She'd let herself get caught up in one of the outlandish tales Calamity and Wild Bill liked to tell, each trying to top the other with a bigger lie.

Word had spread like wildfire that the famous lawman, gambler and gunfighter, Wild Bill Hickok, and the notorious Calamity Jane were on their way into town, and the four riders were met with wild cheers along the main, and only, street in Deadwood when they arrived. Calamity and Wild Bill gloried in the reception, waving to their fans, and Colorado Charlie eagerly joined them for his share of the adulation.

Dropping back so the three could have their time in the limelight, a wave of sorrow rocked Starr as she looked along the narrow, saloon-lined main street of Deadwood. It was filled with logs, lumber, stumps, and boulders, and hundreds of men who moved from saloon to saloon. A few buildings had been slapped together out of raw pine, but many of the business establishments were nothing more than tents.

Jammed with horses, wagons, mules, oxen, burros—in addition to the people and other litter—the town had an eye-stinging, suffocating shroud of dust and stench hanging over it.

No wonder the Indians didn't want to share their sacred hills with these carriers of filth and destruction. If these wild people were loosed in the beautiful Black Hills, it would only be a short time before they had destroyed the rest of the land the way they had Deadwood Gulch.

Well, the first thing she needed to do was find someone to go back for Melanie and Dorcas with her, and then she'd be able to leave this eyesore of a town. She wondered if Daniel Blue Eagle knew about Deadwood. What would he think if he saw what the prospectors had done to the steep wooded hills of the canyon? It made her want to cry for the Sioux, and for Daniel Blue Eagle.

It still hurt Starr to think of Daniel Blue Eagle, and she tried to drive thoughts of him from her mind. She'd been partially successful at forgetting him when it was necessary to give all of her concentration to surviving during the perilous journey into Deadwood—a journey that Gentle Fawn had told her would take one day but had in fact taken five—but now she couldn't stop wondering about him.

Where was he? Had he gotten back to the village yet? Was his conference successful? Had he found a way to save his lands? Did he know she was gone? Was he angry? Hurt? Would he even care? Would he come looking for her?

A chill of apprehension trembled through her, though the September day was warm. Even now that she was safe in the protected canyon with its high sides, she couldn't escape the fear that he would come for her.

On the other hand, she thought fatalistically, taking another critical look around the celebrating town, *just how safe am I here?*

Remembering the peaceful Indian village she had left with its hard-working women, giggling children, and brave men, she couldn't help comparing the two places. This was supposed to be civilization, and the Indians were supposed to be the savages.

Starr kept her gaze on Wild Bill's back to keep from seeing the curious and leering faces that watched her ride down the center of Main Street.

Already, her presence was drawing lewd comments from the drunken men that lined the street, and she frantically wished for a kind understanding face. She missed Prairie Moon. Why had she left her? She should have known better than to do something so daring and foolish. Why hadn't she waited for someone to come for them, instead of taking the matter into her own hands. At this point, she didn't even think she would be able to find her way back to the village alone, and she saw no one in the boisterous dirty town she could ask to help her. So what had she accomplished? Nothing! Not a single thing. Not only was she unable to help Melanie and Dorcas now, but she might not even be able to help herself!

"Mabel, this here's Starr Winfield," she heard Wild Bill say, and she hurried forward to meet one of the few women she'd seen in the town. "We found 'er along the trail. Seems she 'scaped from some Injuns north o' here. Do ya suppose ya could take 'er in for a day 'r two til she decides what she's gonna do?"

The bosomy blonde pursed her painted lips and looked Starr over from the dirty matted hair on her head to the bottom of her moccasined foot. "I ain't runnin' no charity house," she warned, shrewdly taking in the girl's fine features. *Clean 'er up a bit and git some decent clothes on 'er an' she'll be a right nice addition to the shop.*

"Oh, I'd work," Starr assured the woman, certain that there was no job she wouldn't be able to do. Cooking, cleaning, sewing. She'd so anything!

"Well, I guess we could give 'er a try. The boy git tired o' the same gals, an I ain't had no redhead 'round here since Pepper married that gambler. Men do like a fiery redhead fer a change. Wisht yer hair was redder though, not so washed out an' blonde lookin', but I guess it'll have ta do til I kin git my hands on some henna."

"Henna? Boys? Men?" Starr gasped looking helplessly from Mabel to Wild Bill. "Just what kind of work are you expecting me to do?" she accused, a horrifying realization dawning on her.

This woman expected her to work as a prostitute!

"What kind o' work do ya think yer gonna do? Ain't but one thing fer a gal ta do in a minin' camp. Ya want the job 'r not?" she said to Starr. When Starr didn't answer, the woman shrugged her shoulders and turned to enter her tent bar. "Come see me some time, Wild Bill," she called out as she left.

Starr looked helplessly at Calamity Jane.

"What're ya makin' sech a fuss 'bout?" Calamity laughed. "There's a whole lot worse ways ta make yer spendin' money."

"But I can't," Starr started, turning her distraught face toward Wild Bill and Colorado Charlie.

"There oughta be somethin' else she could do, Wild Bill," Colorado Charley protested. He wouldn't mind a go at little Starr himself, once she got cleaned up, but somehow she just didn't seem like the type.

"Wait a minute, Mabel," Wild Bill called out.

"Yeah?"

"Ain't ya got somethin' else she could do? Like cookin', 'r cleanin'. How 'bout tendin' bar? You could teach 'er ta do that, couldn't ya?" he asked, blessing Mabel with one of his charming smiles that could melt the coldest heart. "It'd be good fer your business ta have a pretty little gal out front, wouldn't it? Advertising your goods, so ta speak," he laughed. "Whatta ya say, Mabel?"

"I can cook and sew," Starr interjected optimistically.

"Well," Mabel sighed, thinking she wouldn't mind being on Wild Bill Hickok's good side. In a place like Deadwood, it couldn't hurt to have a friend who was one of the fastest guns in the West. Besides, she could always work on the girl. Sooner or later she would give in. "I s'pose I could give 'er a try. But you better 'member ya owe me one, Wild Bill," she said with a suggestive grin on her red lips as she rested her hand high on his strong thigh and gazed meaningfully into his brown eyes.

"I ain't about to fergit, Mabel. I do owe ya one, and I'll be 'round one o' these days to pay up," he promised. Nudging his horse forward, he turned in his saddle and tipped his hat at Starr and Mabel and headed down the street toward the Number Ten

155

Saloon, flanked by Calamity Jane and Colorado Charlie Utter.

"You jest do that, Wild Bill," Mabel called after him and then turned to Starr, who sat waiting for the woman to tell her what to do. "Well, don't jest sit there. Let's git you cleaned up 'fore the miners git here ta spend the gold dust they done took outta the hills today. I'll have ta teach ya how ta use the pennyweight," she added with disgust in her voice, leaving Starr to dismount and hurry after her.

Mabel's living quarters behind the bar were in one of several small tents owned by the woman, each canvas structure only big enough for a straw mattress and a nightstand. Keeping her eyes straight ahead as she followed behind Mabel, Starr tried not to think about the kind of place she was going to be working in, but her surroundings made it impossible to forget. She would have to be deaf and blind not to realize what was going on.

The tent next door to Mabel's had the flaps down, but lewd grunting noises and squeals of pleasure could be heard from within, embarrassing Starr to the point that she thought she would be sick. As repulsed as she was by what she knew must be happening within the tent, she was unable to keep from glancing in that direction. But just as she looked toward it, the flap lifted, and a short fat prospector stepped outside, adjusting his fly as he did, satisfaction obvious on his whiskered face.

Starr couldn't suppress the gasp of shock that rose in her throat and hurried turned her head away. But the view there was no more settling. The tent on the other side of Mabel's was open and had a tall brunette standing in the entrance. Dressed in a dirty pink-flowered wrapper that gapped open to the waist to display a generous portion of bosom, the woman stood with one bared fleshy leg propped on a packing crate, and was smoking a cigarette.

"Who's the new girl, Mabel?" she asked, eying Starr to determine if she would be much competition.

"I think we'll call her Heavenly Nights," Mabel laughed, the sound very crude.

"Glad to know ya, Heavenly. My name's Frenchie," the brunette offered.

"But my name's not—" Starr started, but Mabel interrupted her.

"Yer name's whatever I want it ta be, if ya wanna keep yer job. Ya understand?"

"Yes, ma'am," Starr replied, promising herself she would look for other work the first chance she got. She couldn't stay here, though she felt guilty for her lack of appreciation. Wild Bill Hickok didn't have to find her a job at all, but she couldn't help wondering how the man could leave her in a place like this.

"Here's the tub," Mabel said, pulling a wooden foot tub out from under her four-poster bed, the only real bed and the only bathtub in her operation. "You kin git water down that way," she grumbled, pointing toward the back. "I guess ya kin wear one o' my gowns til we decide what to do with ya. I'll be back fer ya in a hour. Be dressed an' ready ta work up front, or I'll send yer customers back here. An' the fellers what come back here won't be inner'sted in how good you kin pour a drink!" she threatened, her throaty chuckle sending chills down Starr's spine.

Starr stared after the laughing woman for a long

157

moment, and then sprang into action. She wasn't going to give anyone a chance to catch her alone in here. She'd be ready in forty-five minutes, to be on the safe side. Snatching a pail out of the wooden tub, Starr ran for the river to fetch her water.

Thirty minutes later, she stood toweling her hair dry with a blanket Mabel had left for her, when she heard a young voice outside the tent. "Ma sed bring ya this here dress ta put on, Miss Heavenly."

Wrapping the blanket around herself, Starr hurried to the entrance and lifted the flap to find a little tow-headed boy about six years old standing there. "Thank you," she smiled, wondering what could possibly become of a child raised in a place like this. Bending down, she cupped his thin face in her soft hand. "What's your name, little man?"

"Ain't got no name, ma'am. Folks jest calls me Boy."

"No name? Why not?"

"Ma ses this way I kin pick whatever name suits me, an' I don't have ta be stuck with no name I don't like."

Taking the shiny red dress from the child. Starr ruffled his shaggy blonde hair and smiled her gratitude. "Well, I suppose that makes sense."

"I'd best be gittin' back, Miss Heavenly. Ma told me ta tell ya ta hurry," he shouted over his shoulder as he dashed back to the large tent that served as Mabel's Deadwood Gulp Saloon. Watching after him and noticing how his little bare feet stirred up large clouds of dust, Starr couldn't help but think that the only thing worse than Deadwood after a long dry spell would be Deadwood after a heavy rain.

Removing the blanket she had wrapped around herself, she tossed it on the bed and held up the red dress Boy had brought her. She shook her head doubtfully. It looked very small and short. It was difficult to imagine Mabel's generous figure stuffed into the skimpy dress. In fact, Starr had doubts that it would even fit her own slender body.

Making an effort to ignore the torn black lace on the skirt and the stains under the arms of the red satin garment, Starr stepped into it and quickly laced it up the front. She winced as she held her breath and tried to pull the front edges of the bodice together, but she couldn't make them meet.

Stretched near the point of ripping, the dress was impossible to close up the front, leaving a long vee of pale flesh exposed from the edge of the shockingly deep decolletage to a point three inches above her waistline.

A glance down at herself brought a gasp of horror to Starr's lips. She realized that the dark shadow of her navel showed at a point where the opening of the dress was only an inch wide, but that was not the worst. At its widest point, the split in the bodice not only exposed the deep shadowy cleavage between her full breasts but barely covered her nipples. Even if she'd been able to close the bodice, the neckline would have shown too much of her bosom. Surely there was some mistake. This was a prostitute's dress, not a bartender's garment. She couldn't wear it.

Just as Starr reached up to untie the tight laces across her breasts, thinking to find her deerskin clothes and sneak out the back, Mabel lifted the tent flap and came in with a pair of black pumps in her

159

hand.

Starr turned to face her, her expression trapped and guilty.

"Well, now, that looks real nice, Heavenly," Mabel said sweetly, her pleasantness effectively disguising her surprise. The deerskins certainly hadn't done the girl justice. But now realizing how well the girl was endowed, the madam thought better about her earlier reluctance to take her in if she wasn't going to work the tents.

Mabel could easily see that Heavenly Nights could be a very profitable property. And she made herself a promise to treat that property with kid gloves until she could be broken in. *An' in the meantime, it won't do business no harm ta be givin' the boys a look an' a 'casional feel o' the merchandise. Them fools'll be swillin' the drinks like crazy jest fer a chance ta look at them young tits poppin' outta her dress. By the time she's ready ta come out, they'll be lined up at the flap o' the tent with gold dust bulgin' in their pockets. That's not all that'll be bulgin'! This little gal is gonna make ol' Mabel a bundle!* "I brung ya some shoes," she said, shoving the black slippers at Starr.

"I can't wear this dress, Miss Mabel. It doesn't fit me!" Starr protested.

"Sure it does, honey. It fits you jest fine. Why, you'll have them miners droolin'. Ya won't be able ta keep their mugs filled fast enough."

"I can't," Starr insisted, turning her back on Mabel and untying the knot at the top of her laces. "I'm leaving."

"No, ya ain't. Yer gonna stay right here an' do

160

what I say or I'm gonna put ya up fer grabs. Coupla them miners might be willin' ta pay real high ta take ya up ta their shacks on the hill and bang ya ta their hearts' content. I jest took ya in as a favor ta Wild Bill Hickok. Yer jest lucky he brought ya ta me. Anywhere else, ya woulda already been flat on yer back under some humpin' prospector. Now, let's see what we kin do with yer hair," Mabel said, the sudden change in her tone chilling Starr to the core as she sat down on the edge of the bed and let the woman arrange her hair.

The black-clad gunfighter leaned back against an abandoned wagon and crossed one ankle over the other in a seemingly casual pose, the way he'd done for two days now. He was unconcerned with the stares and questioning looks he was drawing as he put the cigarette he had just rolled into his mouth, struck a match and held it to the tip of his smoke. He inhaled deeply. With calculated indifference, he exhaled slowly as he watched the open front of the Deadwood Gulp Saloon from under the wide brim of the black Stetson hat that hid his face.

"Hey, mister, did ya hear Wild Bill Hickok's down at the Number Ten?" a friendly prospector called as he passed by.

"Thanks," the stranger grunted, never averting his gaze from his quarry in the Deadwood Gulp.

He had been told that Hickok was in town from the moment he had ridden into Deadwood. Assuming that the stranger was in town to challenge the legendary gunfighter to a showdown, the enthusiastic citizens of the wild town didn't want to miss the chance to see some blood spilled, no matter whose it was. But they were going to be disappointed, because Wild Bill wasn't the man's target.

The Deadwood Gulp was particularly busy this afternoon. Everyone said it was because of the new girl Mabel had hired. Heavenly Nights was the name she used. Prospectors were fighting to get to the bar, just for a chance to see her up close. It was said that she had the face of an angel and the body of a wanton, a body every man in Deadwood was hoping to know intimately, though so far Mabel was saying the girl wouldn't be working the tents. The word was that the smart proprietress of the Deadwood Gulp was going to charge a whole gold mine for the first to experience a *heavenly night* with Miss Heavenly Nights. The stranger leveled his cold stare on the subject of his thoughts.

At first glance from across the street, she had looked like any other whore. Painted lips, rouge, suggestive sway of her hips, gaudy display of bosom and legs. But at second glance, a man would have to be blind not to see the exceptional beauty that lurked beneath the garish makeup and clothing. It was the kind of beauty for which a man would kill to hold in his arms. And once he had possessed her, he could continue to kill to keep her.

Slipping a thumb and forefinger in the pocket of his leather vest, he pulled out the trappings for another cigarette—paper and tobacco pouch. His eyes never leaving the saloon across the street, he deftly rolled his smoke, then ran the tip of his tongue along the edge of the thin paper so it would stay closed.

162

Putting it between his lips, he reached for a sulphur match, striking it on the rusty wheel on the wagon behind him. But he didn't hold the tiny flame to his cigarette, because his attention was suddenly diverted.

Something was happening across the street. He stood up straight to be certain, unaware that the match in his hand was still burning, until it had burned down to his fingers. Brought abruptly back to his immediate surroundings as the flame touched his tanned fingers, he cursed, shaking the match out and tossing it, as well as the newly rolled cigarette, to the ground.

The time had come to move.

Concentrating on his motive, he stepped into the street and started across.

Keeping his head ducked low, he peered out from under the brim of his hat, his icy gaze following the girl in the tight red dress as she stepped out from behind the bar and left the tent that housed the Deadwood Gulp Saloon.

"Don't be gone long, sugar," a drunken miner called out.

"We're gonna be mighty thirsty by the time ya git back."

The stranger didn't hear the girl's reply as she disappeared around the corner to go back to the smaller tents behind the saloon, but it didn't interest him, anyway.

"Well, howdy, good-lookin'," Mabel cooed as she wiggled up to the gunslinger and grabbed his arm, cushioning his biceps between her mammoth breasts. She'd been watching him watch her place for two

163

days now and had almost given up on getting him to come over.

"I want a woman," he said, his voice cold and hard, sending an unexpected chill over Mabel.

She studied his features carefully. Handsome. Not pretty handsome like some dandy, but rugged and masculine. Hard. Mabel's first instinct was to service him herself. She wouldn't mind being ridden by some young stud with his looks and build, but something in his cold eyes told her this one had a mean streak in him. It could be deadly to tangle with him.

"What's yer pleasure? Blonde? Brunette?"

"Redhead. The one that works behind the bar," he said coldly, dropping five twenty-dollar gold pieces into the woman's hand, one at a time.

"I'd like ta help ya out, mister," Mabel said hesitantly, eying the gold pieces hungrily. "But she ain't a workin' gal. She's a personal friend o' Wild Bill Hickok an' he don't want 'er workin' the tents," she explained, offering his gold coins back to him, the expression of regret on her face easy to read.

The stranger clamped his fingers around the woman's flabby wrist and added five more gold coins to the first five in her sweaty palm.

"Wild Bill'd kill me, an' you too. Why don't ya let me innerduce ya ta Frenchie. She'll show ya a real good time. She's my best gal. Trained in Paris, France, she was." Mabel was finding it difficult not to close her fingers over the money in her hand and take her chances. "Why, fer this much, I could give ya Frenchie and New Orleans Lil fer the whole night. How 'bout it, mister? Frenchie and Lil fer two hundert dollars."

164

"I told you what I want," he said coldly, adding another five gold pieces to the mounting stack in her shaking hand.

"She's gonna fight ya," Mabel said, her gaze never leaving the gold.

"You let me worry about that," the man in black said, adding still another hundred dollars.

"I don't want no rough stuff in my place. I take good care o' my girls."

"Here's five hundred," he said, adding another hundred and closing her fingers over the coins. "There'll be another five hundred when I leave."

"Soon's she gits back, I'll send her back ta my tent, the one with the bed in it."

"Make it fast," the man growled, and wheeled around on his heel, leaving a confused Mabel five hundred dollars richer—make that a thousand dollars richer!

She glanced around nervously to make certain no one had noticed the transaction. Not only did she not want to risk being robbed, but if Wild Bill asked any questions, she could always claim ignorance. She'd say the girl told her she was sick and wanted to go lie down in the tent. She could pretend that she didn't know the man was going back there. She'll say she thought he was with Frenchie.

"Heavenly," Mabel called out cheerfully to the returning bartender. "Will ya go ta my tent an' git me a pair o' boots from under my bed. The ones I got on 're rubbing my bunions something fearful." She spoke to Starr where no one could hear her.

"Yes, ma'am," Starr said, eying the woman suspiciously. "I'll be right back."

"You jest take yer time, sweetheart. Ya been workin' awful hard the last couple o' days. Maybe ya should lie down an' rest for a bit b'fore ya come back ta work. I kin handle things in here."

Now Starr was suspicious. Mabel had something up her sleeve, but what? The girl studied the older woman's puffy, smiling face but couldn't read anything there. She was probably just being imaginative. Mabel wasn't all that bad. After all, she'd been true to her word and not tried to force her to work in back with the other girls. If it just weren't for the revealing dress she was forced to wear, Starr could have tolerated tending bar in the Deadwood Gulp Saloon—until she could find a way to go back for Dorcas and Melanie.

Maybe she would lie down for a minute. It would give her time to think of a way to get out of Deadwood and away from the hated red satin dress, away from the woman who had taken control of her life, the woman who told her when to eat, when to sleep, when to relieve herself! God, she had to get away. She couldn't stand much more of this. It didn't matter where she went as long as it was out of Deadwood Gulch!

Chapter Ten

Starr didn't see the man when she first lifted the flap and walked into Mabel's tent, allowing it to drop behind her. It was dark inside, and it took her eyes a moment to adjust, but she had a strange feeling something wasn't right, not right at all. Instinct told her to leave, but instead, she turned to reopen the tent flap so she could better see what was wrong.

It was then she heard a rustle in the darkest corner of the tent, and her head jerked up in startled surprise.

Starr wheeled around to see what, or who, was in the tent with her. It was then the dark figure of a man stepped out of the shadows. Shrinking back from his approach, she gasped aloud. She knew she should scream, tried to scream, but the only sound that escaped her lips was a wheezing gulp for air. And before she could recover from the shock enough to sound an alarm, the intruder spoke, his voice terrible and frightening.

"Hello, Firebird," he said softly, the controlled

anger in his tone chilling Starr's flesh.

"Daniel Blue Eagle!"

Her first instinct was to run to him and throw her arms around him. He'd come to her! He would take her away from this evil place. He would take her home with him! Home! Home to the village and everything that was good and pure. Home to their tepee.

But though she would have run to him across the space that separated them, planted a million kisses on his face, told him how glad she was to see him, Starr did none of these. True, the man in the tent was the man she had known as her husband, but it was now a stranger who walked toward her through the semi-darkness with deliberate stalking steps. A stranger with hate and disgust burning in his blue eyes. Hate and disgust for her.

"How did you find me?" she whispered, unable to stop her gaze from raking over the man she had thought never to see again, greedily taking in his hard sculptured features, his broad shoulders, his trim waist and hips. How could she ever have left him? How could she have thought anything was more important than what they shared? She had betrayed this man for two spoiled, selfish girls who refused to make any effort to help themselves, and now she could see in Daniel Blue Eagle's face that it was too late to make him believe she was sorry.

"Did you think I wouldn't?" he asked, now standing in front of her, so close she could smell the wonderful leather and smoke scent she loved. His steely blue eyes bored into hers, hypnotizing her, making it impossible for her to look away. "Do you know what our Comanche brothers do with a wife that is unfaithful, Firebird?"

"No," she gasped as he grabbed a fistful of her hair and bent her head back, arching her neck uncomfortably.

"They cut off their noses, making them undesirable to all men, marking them for life. Do you think that is what I should do with you?" he asked.

"I haven't been unfaithful to you, Daniel. I haven't," she choked. Her eyes, already filling with tears, were wide with fright. "There's been no other man."

"Don't lie to me, Firebird. Look at you! You've become a whore, and yet you have the audacity to tell me you haven't been with another man!" he spat out viciously, almost unable to control the tears he felt welling in his own eyes.

"I'm not lying, Daniel. I don't work in the tents. I only serve drinks in the front," she protested, strangely detached from the two small hands that rose to caress away the pain and anger in his face.

"Is that why you hurried back here so fast when your boss sent you? Because you don't work the tents?" he accused, slapping her hands away from his face as if her touch were vile and offensive to him. God, how he wanted to believe her, but there was too much evidence staring him in the face. "Who'd she tell you was in here? Your special friend, Wild Bill Hickok?"

"She sent me for a pair of shoes," Starr defended herself weakly, knowing even as she spoke that her answer was not plausible.

"You didn't come in here for shoes, Firebird. You

169

came in here to whore, and that's just what you're going to do," he growled, jerking her head farther back, pulling her hair so cruelly that it made her eyes sting. "I paid a high price for you and I'm going to get my money's worth."

Daniel Blue Eagle bent down and buried his face in the curve of Starr's neck and shoulder, nipping painfully at the tender flesh with his teeth. She heard a muffled laugh that sounded strangely like a sob as he ravaged her arched neck. His bites became more hurtful.

"Please, Daniel. Not like this. Not here!" she pleaded as his hands opened the laces of her dress front and bared her breasts to his pleasure.

"Why not, Firebird? Does it bother you to bed your husband in the same bed Heavenly Nights entertains her customers? Or is it just one special customer? Who is he, Firebird? It's Hickok, isn't it?"

"Wild Bill saved my life on the trail. He's only a friend. He isn't a 'customer'," she insisted, becoming aware of the distant rumble of passion that was beginning to build within her loins and hating herself all the more for her weakness.

Daniel made short work of the bodice laces and dress, tossing the offensive garment onto the ground in a soiled heap of red, leaving Starr standing before him naked and defenseless.

He viewed her critically, denying the heat he felt rising in him at the sight of her beautiful breasts and pale skin—the body he had loved so many times, the woman he had worshipped. Now they were defiled and used. She was no longer an Indian goddess, but a

170

white man's whore.

With a groan of repulsion, Daniel grabbed the spread off Mabel's bed and used the rough cloth to wipe across Starr's lips with relentless pressure. "You may be a whore, but it doesn't mean I've got to look at you with that stuff on your face." As if he could rub away the pain he had felt since he had first discovered his half-dressed wife in the Deadwood Gulp Saloon, he scoured her face hard until the last of the paint was gone, leaving Starr's fair skin chafed and stinging from the harsh cleansing.

"Come here, Firebird," he ordered, tossing his hat on the chest and flopping his powerful body down on the bed. The challenge in his blue eyes was cruel. She saw that he had cut his hair, but at that moment the fact didn't register in her thoughts. All she could think of was her need to make him believe her.

"Daniel, there's never been any man but you," she sobbed, stepping forward to look down at him, unconcerned with her own nakedness. "You must believe that!" she wept, the tears now streaming freely over her burning red face.

Damn her! I just took a whore's dress and makeup off her, and she still denies it. She's been displaying her wares to anyone who wants to look, and she expects me to believe her. He groaned inwardly and reached for her.

"I don't want to hear any more of your lies!" he growled, grabbing her wrists and pulling her down beside him. "Talk's not what I want right now!"

Starr placed a protesting hand on Daniel Blue Eagle's chest and looked into his cold face, her anguished expression beseeching, lost. "Please, Dan-

171

iel. Not like this. I was so glad to see you. Don't destroy what we had."

"You already destroyed it, Firebird. But if you're really glad to see me, why don't you show me how glad?" he laughed harshly, pushing her hand downward where she found his trousers stretched tight with his desire.

Feeling the turgid muscle grow under her touch, Starr realized that an equal need was mounting rapidly within her own body, and she was appalled by her wanton reaction.

How could she want him after the terrible things he had accused her of? But she did. God help her, she did. She wanted him even though he hated her. She wanted him even though he would take her and then leave her. She wanted him one last time. She had to be with him this one last time.

Starr hesitated only an instant, and then with sad resignation, she knelt on the bed beside Daniel Blue Eagle.

Her fingers trembling, she negotiated the opening on his black trousers, freeing his hardness at last. Her breath caught in her throat as she wrapped her hands around him.

Unable to deny her own desire, she instinctively matched the motions of her hands to the primal beat that thrummed relentlessly in her veins. And when the hunger to be filled with him reached the point of being unbearable, Starr raised up and straddled him, her womanhood hovering precariously over the hot trusting spear of his sex.

Splaying her hands on the hard muscles of his chest, Starr held herself above him. She looked into his icy blue eyes and said one last time, "I'm not a whore, Daniel. There has been no one but you." With those words, she let her hips drop onto him, sheathing him deep within the dark grotto of her femininity.

Starr rose and fell on Daniel Blue Eagle's hardness, each descent forcing him further into the moist warmth of her body, until he was moaning for release and helplessly rolling his head from side to side in exquisite agony. Still she kept up her attack, never slowing her pace as she rode him closer to the edge.

"Oh, my God," he groaned, rolling her over onto her back to drive his final thrusts into her, spilling himself in a violent, convulsive flood of ecstasy.

Daniel Blue Eagle collapsed on Starr, pressing his sweat-slicked chest to her rapidly rising breasts. He reveled in the feel of her arms wrapped around him, holding him tightly to her. He was home at last and he could forget what had brought them to this point. But she spoke, bringing it all back.

"Please believe me, Daniel. You're the only man I've ever known," she whispered softly, her words sounding like a prayer unintentionally uttered aloud.

"I wish I could," Daniel Blue Eagle said with an exasperated sigh. He rolled to a sitting position and impatiently adjusted his trousers. "Get dressed, and we'll be on our way."

"Are you taking me with you?" she asked, shocked. After the way he had treated her, the things he had said, she had expected him to leave her behind.

"You're my wife, Firebird. And I will tell you when you are not. Get dressed."

"Mabel took my clothes. That's how she got me to

173

wear that awful thing. I have nothing else to put on," she told him, stooping to pick up the hated red dress.

Daniel Blue Eagle's long arm shot out and snatched the dress out of her hands, ripping it in half before she even realized what had happened. "If I ever see you in something like that again, I'll kill you," he groaned through clenched teeth, his eyes already searching Mabel's tent for something to cover his wife's nakedness.

His gaze fell on the chest beside the bed. Throwing the ruined red dress to the floor, he crossed to the scarred piece of furniture and jerked out the top drawer. Opening the drawers one by one, he pulled out the contents angrily and tossed them onto the ground. A smart businesswoman like Mabel wouldn't come to the Dakota Territory without something beside her own body fat to keep her warm when winter came.

Finding nothing but flimsy nightgowns, underthings, and cheap gowns in the drawers of the chest, he looked around, his search zeroing in on the bed. He drew a flat trunk out from under the four poster. The fact that it was locked did nothing to deter Daniel Blue Eagle. He quickly broke the lock with the butt of his gun and rummaged through it until he found what he was looking for—a flannel shirt and a pair of jeans. Without looking up, he pitched the clothes to Starr and turned back to the trunk, digging deeper until he came up with a pair of sturdy boots and two pairs of socks. "See anything else you need?"

Starr nodded mutely and pointed shyly to a pair of drawers and a camisole that Daniel Blue Eagle had discarded as useless. She wanted them, though it occurred to her that she had been without under-things for so long that she might have to get used to them all over again.

Glancing at the lacy white things with disgust, he shrugged his shoulders and grumbled, "Take them and let's get going."

Moments later, Daniel Blue Eagle and Starr stepped out of Mabel's tent and walked past the bar to where his horse was tied. Placing his hands at her waist, he lifted her onto the horse and leapt on behind her. He kicked the horse in the sides and sped down Main Street toward the exit from Deadwood Gulch.

Though neither of them spoke, their thoughts were the same. They both prayed they would never have to see Deadwood again.

Just as they neared the passage out of the canyon, they heard a woman screeching hysterically after them. "He's got Heavenly Nights. That stranger stole one o' my girls!"

They both turned their heads to see a red-faced Mabel jumping up and down in the middle of the congested street, waving her fists angrily into the air. "Somebody git 'er back. That gunfighter took Heavenly!" she shrieked to the drunks that staggered out of her saloon to watch the retreating horse and riders. "Somebody go tell Wild Bill."

Starr felt Daniel Blue Eagle's grip on her tighten at the mention of Wild Bill Hickok's name, and she knew he still didn't believe she hadn't been with the other man. When she had said he still wanted her for his wife, that he was taking her with him, she had let herself hope that he did believe her after all. But as usual, she had only been fooling herself.

For the next few hours, the two rode in silence, not stopping to rest until long after darkness had settled over the rough terrain. Lifting Starr from the horse, Daniel Blue Eagle ground-tied the animal by dropping his reins in a grassy glade near a patch of cottonwood trees. He walked away from Starr without looking back at her.

"There's a cave near here where we'll be safe for the night," he said, bending to gather long grass for the horse to munch when they took him into the cave. Silently following his example, Starr began to pick grass too, using the front of her large shirt as a basket, the heaviness in her heart unbearable.

Later, when the man, woman and horse were safely ensconced within a two-chamber cave in the side of a hill, Daniel Blue Eagle offered Starr *pemmican* to eat and pointed toward a narrow underground stream running along one wall of the cave where she could get water to drink. Without speaking, he dropped a blanket beside her and then disappeared through the narrow entrance to the cave, leaving her alone in the darkness.

Deciding to take advantage of her momentary privacy, Starr added another stick to the tiny fire Daniel Blue Eagle had lit and went to the back chamber to relieve herself. The horse, seemingly unaffected by carrying the double weight on the hard ride from Deadwood, was lazily munching the grass they had picked, his bulging brown eye watching her curiously as she moved around the dark area.

When she spread the blanket on the ground, thinking to be asleep when Daniel Blue Eagle returned, she suddenly got a whiff of the cloying perfume

Mable had insisted she wear. Unable to bear the sickening odor a moment longer, Starr gave a quick glance toward the cave entrance, then rushed over to the underground stream.

The 'stream', she noticed with only mild regret, was hardly more than a trickle entering the cave from a waist-high hole in the wall, splashing into a pool and then disappearing back into another wall only a few feet away, but it looked wonderful to her. If only she had had a bar of soap, it would have been perfect. But as it was, the fresh running water would have to do.

Quickly divesting herself of the shirt and jeans, Starr knelt at the edge of the pool and scooped the icy cold water up into her face. A chill shook violently through her with the shock of the frigid water on her skin, but it didn't stop her. She continued to splash the clean mountain water over her face and shoulders, as if its purity could wash away the memories of her time in Deadwood and the cruel accusations Daniel Blue Eagle had made.

Just as she was drying her hair with the flannel shirt, Daniel Blue Eagle reentered the cave, stopping unnoticed at the entrance to watch the beautiful woman. At the sight of her standing beside the small fire, his heart ached.

Wearing only the newly-acquired camisole and drawers and boots, she was bent over the fire, her arms upraised. She was rubbing her hair vigorously with the shirt. The flickering flame of the fire played over her creamy skin, giving it a golden sheen, and he ached to go to her.

But the man didn't move, not even daring to

breathe lest she look up and deny him the exquisite vision.

She seemed oblivious to the way the thin camisole and drawers clung to her curves where water had splashed on the front of her, making the thin covering totally transparent in those spots. Nor was she concerned with the way her raised arms stretched the gossamer material tight over her breasts.

Daniel Blue Eagle felt hynotized.

Still unaware of his presence, Starr straightened up and turned her back to the place where he stood in the shadows. She shook out her long damp hair with a movement that used her whole body.

Daniel Blue Eagle's enraptured gaze fell helplessly to the two softly rounded mounds that gleamed through the translucent drawers. This time a grasp did escape, but Starr didn't hear him. She was too engrossed in what she was doing.

He watched with fascination as she found a forked stick and used one of her boots to pound it into the ground beside the fire, draping the flannel shirt over it to dry. Then he couldn't help being disappointed when she stood as close to the fire as she could bear and plucked at her clinging underthings, pulling them away from her skin in an attempt to dry them as quickly as possible.

"You're going to be cold if you don't get your clothing back on," he said, stepping out of the shadow as he spoke.

Starr's glanced up in surprise as he made his presence known. "How long have you been standing there?" she accused, able to tell by the look in his eyes that he hadn't just come in.

"Long enough to know you're going to be sick if you don't get your hair dry before you sleep," he returned, picking up a damp golden strand and studying it. "Don't you know any better?" he mumbled, idly wrapping the curl around his forefinger and running his thumb over its silk.

"I needed a bath. I had to get the stink of Deadwood off my skin," she defended, refusing to back away from him. She met his gaze defiantly, thinking how odd it was that the icy bath had given her back her gumption. With reminders of Deadwood clinging to her body, she had felt beaten, almost as if she had deserved his vicious treatment in Mabel's tent, almost as if where he had found her had been totally her fault. But now she knew she wasn't the only one to blame. If he had released Melanie and Dorcas as she had asked, she would never have left him. So it was his fault as much as hers that she had ended up in the Deadwood Gulp Saloon.

Starr reached up and snatched her hair off his finger, her gray eyes chilling as she kept her gaze leveled on his face. He had degraded her enough for one day. She wouldn't allow him the chance to do it again. He could believe and think what he wanted about her, but she wasn't going to be used to relieve his lust again. And she could see that was where his caress was leading. She was never be his whore again.

Turning away from him, she tested the flannel shirt for dryness before taking it off the forked stick and putting it on. She hurriedly buttoned it up the front and looked around for her jeans. They were on the ground where she had left them. Only Daniel Blue Eagle stood between her and them.

Starr looked at the jeans, then at the man, then back to the jeans again. Throwing her shoulders back, she licked her lips and took a deep breath.

"Excuse me," she apologized haughtily as, her chin held high, she breezed by him to pick up the discarded pants. She came so close to him that she could feel the warmth of his breath as he exhaled, but he didn't reach out and grab her as she passed.

Relief washed over her, only to turn to a strange unexpected disappointment. She'd been so sure he would touch her and had planned to put him in his place by denying him access to her body. But he hadn't even reached for her, had only watched her with his cold blue eyes.

Starr stepped quickly into the jeans and spread the blanket on the ground. Unable to look at the man who watched her, she lay on her side with her back to where he stood. "Good night, Daniel Blue Eagle," she said coolly and closed her eyes, feigning instant sleep.

"Good night, Firebird," he returned, lowering himself to her blanket.

Now it would come, she thought. Now he would turn to her and try to make love to her, but she would refuse him. For the first time since their wedding night. And this time she would make her refusal stick. Starr held her breath in anticipation. But though she could feel him beside her, the length of his body only inches from her back, he didn't reach out to her.

There was a rustle of clothing and the blanket, and Daniel Blue Eagle turned onto his side, his back to her.

Starr opened her eyes in surprise. She should have been relieved, but she wasn't. She stared past the fire into the darkness. What was wrong with her? She should be exhausted, yet she didn't feel like sleeping. With great effort she closed her eyes again, forcing them to remain that way, but every time she relaxed they popped open again. She rolled over onto her back and stared at the dark ceiling. Now she was cold. She'd never get to sleep.

Looking out of the corner of her eye at Daniel Blue Eagle's still form, she listened to his breathing. It was slow and even. *What can it hurt if I just move a little closer to him to get warm? He won't even know*, she rationalized as she inched first a leg, then an arm, then her hips, then her shoulders until she was almost against his strong back. Already she could feel his warmth seeping into her chilled body, but it wasn't enough.

If I roll over on my side facing him, I can pull the edge of the cover over my shoulders, she convinced herself, reaching for the blanket corner and carrying it with her as she rolled toward Daniel Blue Eagle. *Much better*, she realized contentedly as she fought the urge to wrap an arm around his waist and shape her body along the length of his. Her lids dropped closed, and she teetered precariously between sleep and wakefulness.

"Why did you go there, Firebird?"

Daniel Blue Eagle's low voice startled Starr into full consciousness. "I thought you were asleep," she gasped, rolling onto her back, embarrassed that she'd been caught snuggling up to him. He would think she was looking for something besides warmth.

181

"Why did you go?" he asked again. "Was life as my wife so terrible that you preferred a place like Deadwood?"

She could hear the hurt in his voice and she hated herself for wanting to respond to it. After all, he'd been heartlessly cruel to her. He didn't deserve her compassion. She had tried to explain, but he hadn't listened. He had just jumped to his own conclusions and thought the worst. She ought to tell him she preferred anywhere, even Deadwood, to living with him; but no matter how she had been wronged, she couldn't bring herself to lie to him deliberately, knowing they would both be hurt by her falsehoods.

"I thought Deadwood was only a day from the village and that I could find help for Melanie and Dorcas there. You wouldn't release them, so I had no choice. I was going to bring back someone to take them home."

"And you, Firebird? Were you going to go home with them?"

She couldn't give him a straight answer, couldn't say that she hadn't wanted to leave. He'd never believe her anyway. "I didn't think you'd want me after you found that I had helped them escape."

"But when you got to Deadwood you decided not to go back to the village. Why?" he asked, rolling over onto his back to stare at the black ceiling.

"It wasn't like that. I was lost, and it was so much further to Deadwood than I expected. Wild Bill Hickok, Calamity Jane, and Colorado Charlie Utter found me and brought me to Deadwood. By the time we got there, I wasn't certain how to get back to the village, and I had no way to support myself. Wild Bill got Mabel to hire me. She tried to make me into a prostitute, but when I refused, Wild Bill convinced her to use me as a bartender. He thought he was doing me a favor, and I guess he was to a certain extent, but it was horrible. I hated it, but I didn't know what else to do. I've never felt so alone or so helpless. She took my clothing and made me wear that red dress. I was only there for three days, but they were the worst three days of my life."

Daniel Blue Eagle covered his eyes and took a deep breath of frustration. He wanted to believe her. But could he? "Do you know what I felt when I rode into that hellhole of a town and saw my wife working in that saloon? Do you know what it did to me to stand across the street and hear those drunken prospectors make lewd suggestions to my wife? I wanted to kill all of them. And you. But I couldn't, because it would have meant my own exposure and I couldn't risk getting myself killed before I could report what I've seen to my father. So I just stood across the street watching you, the hate gnawing at my gut."

Yes, she did know what he felt. She knew how she had felt just thinking of sharing him with another wife, so she could easily understand the torture he'd experienced believing her to be intimate with other men. She didn't question what it meant that they both felt such possessiveness for each other. She couldn't, because to do so would mean examining her own feelings too closely. And she wasn't ready for that.

"I'm sorry I hurt you, Daniel," she whispered as her hand found his clenched fist between them. She caressed the strong fingers open until she could inter-

183

twine hers with his, not objecting to the pain when he squeezed her hand hard, as if hanging onto it like a lifeline. "I was wrong to leave. I only pray you can forgive me and believe me. There's been no one else."

Daniel Blue Eagle didn't answer her but rolled over on his side, turning her away from him and pulling her body against his. Nesting her round buttocks in the curve of his hips, bending his knees against the backs of hers, and draping his arm over her to cup a full breast in his hand, he nuzzled his face against the nape of her neck and went to sleep. And so did Starr, secure for the first time in over a week.

Chapter Eleven

When Starr opened her eyes in the morning, she saw that the fire had burned itself out, but she was still warm. She squirmed contentedly in Daniel Blue Eagle's embrace, loving the weight of his leg draped over hers, the warmth of his hand tucked under her breast. It was impossible to stay angry with the man who had held her in the warm security of his arms all night long.

She turned in his arms to face him, placing small kisses on his eyes and nose.

Daniel Blue Eagle opened his eyes lazily and smiled at his wife's playful busses before he remembered that he hadn't decided if he believed her story or not. He only knew that whether she was telling the truth or not, he wasn't ready to give her up. He hadn't had nearly enough of her. "We'd better be leaving," he groaned regretfully as Starr rolled him over onto his back with her own body and held him there with her slight weight.

She was making it very difficult for him to stay mad.

"I don't want to leave yet," she whispered, continuing her assault of butterfly kisses on his face and neck. She didn't even wonder about her unusual forwardness. She only knew that she felt free in the cave. Free to be herself, free of other people's opinions of what was right

185

and wrong.

"Don't you want to stay here a little while longer?" she teased, rubbing her lips back and forth on his partially opened mouth.

"Yes," he admitted, tangling his hands in her wild mane and holding her head still so he could catch her roving mouth with his hungry lips. He kissed her long and hard, his tongue filling the whole inside of her mouth.

"Yes," Starr agreed. "Oh, yes." Rising up, she quickly unbuttoned his shirt and displayed his broad chest to her eager gaze. She didn't know where to start. She only knew she wanted him, wanted to show him how she felt, wanted to put her mark on every inch of his flesh.

Trailing a line of hot, moist kisses down the cord of his neck, Starr showered Daniel Blue Eagle's shoulders and arms with her kisses. Her kisses burned over his chest, her tongue darting to taste and savor his muscled flesh.

She memorized him with her senses, tasting the wonderful salty flavor of his skin, becoming drugged by the uniquely male scent of him, feeling him body change and squirm under her touch, and delighting to the sound of his ragged breathing in her ears.

Circling a nipple with her tongue, she said, "Shall we leave now?"

"You witch," Daniel Blue Eagle groaned, throwing her over onto her back and hurriedly unbuttoning her shirt and slipping her arms out of it. He drew her to a sitting position and raised the camisole over her head, tossing it aside. With hungry determination he bent his head to devour her breasts, and Starr sighed her pleasure aloud as she pulled his head hard against her.

His kisses were rough, they were tender, they were heaven, they were hell, but Starr loved every one, swearing to herself that she would suffer the tortures of eternal damnation before she would ever leave Daniel Blue Eagle again.

It was at that moment, when she was holding his head to her breast, as he drew her nipple deep into his mouth, that she realized she loved this man.

She loved him! Loved him like she never thought it would be possible to love another human being. She felt his pain, gloried in his joys. She actually loved him. When had it happened? How had she come to love her captor? No, he wasn't her captor. He was her husband, the man she wanted to spend the rest of her life with. If only he could love her too. But Starr knew that he thought of her only as the fulfillment of a dream, a possession. That was the reason he'd been so angry about Deadwood—because he thought someone else had taken something that belonged to him. But it didn't matter what he thought, she had enough love for the both of them, and she would love him, work beside him to help his people, and have his children.

Giddy with the discovery, Starr placed her hands on Daniel Blue Eagle's cheeks and pulled his head up from her breast so she could see his face. She looked deep into his passion-drugged blue eyes and smiled, her gray eyes mysteriously forgiving.

A puzzled frown clouded Daniel Blue Eagle's face, but before he could examine the meaning of the strange light in her eyes, she drew him to her and kissed him, her own tongue filling his mouth, running along the tender flesh between his teeth and lips, under his tongue, in the hollows of his cheeks, until she knew every secret niche

187

and ridge like she knew her own mouth. "Take me now, Daniel," she pleaded.

Hurriedly stripping off her jeans and drawers and the remainder of his clothing, Daniel Blue Eagle rolled between her open legs and waited only an instant before sinking into her warmth. "Ahh," they groaned in unison, both knowing the feeling of being the only place in the world where they were safe from strife.

Daniel Blue Eagle rested his forearms on either side of Starr's head and tangled his fingers in the cloud of hair that framed her face. "Don't ever leave me again, Firebird," he said, his voice at once a plea, a threat, and an order.

Starr raised her hands and smoothed the lines from his handsome forehead and made her promise to him. "No, Daniel, I will never willingly leave you again. I will be your wife for as long as you want me," she vowed, wrapping her long limbs around him and hooking her ankles together behind his back, as if she could bind herself to him permanently.

"That will be forever," he growled, beginning to move on top of her, filling her with his strength until the only sounds in the dark cave were the gentle stirring of the horse in the next chamber and their united breathing.

Feeling her desire begin to churn and seek release, Starr dug her nails into Daniel Blue Eagle's back. She lifted her hips upward to greedily take all of him within her. Her whole body was on fire and still he relentlessly stoked the flames.

Certain she had died and gone to heaven, she opened her eyes lazily, fully expecting to see the angels, but the face she saw brought her more joy than any angels ever could.

Daniel Blue Eagle had stopped his motions on her and smiled down at her. Though she could feel that she was still full of him, that he had not been satisfied, he seemed happy, as though he had derived his pleasure from hers.

When he withdrew from her, she tried to stop him, but he hushed her, as one would settle a restless mare. Taking a breast in each hand he kissed first one and then the other before lavishly swabbing the sensitive flesh of her stomach with his velvet-rough tongue.

Kneeling between her legs, he used his thumbs to expose the delicate tip of her sex. He took the swollen bud in his mouth and teased it with his lips and tongue until Starr was mindlessly lifting her hips toward him, offering herself to him.

With small groans of ecstasy, she grabbed fistfuls of his thick straight hair and held him to her until she again exploded in fireworks and dropped her raised hips back to the blanket.

Again Daniel Blue Eagle entered her, and this time there was no holding back. He slammed into her time after time until they were both delirious, and at last he filled her with the fluid of his passion as the convulsing muscles of her body wrung him dry.

Drifting down from the pinnacle of ecstasy, Starr wrapped her arms and legs tighter around the man she loved, the man who was her husband.

Daniel Blue Eagle collapsed on her, his face burrowed in the curve of her neck, his nose near her ear, his hot breath sending chills over her, though they were both damp with perspiration.

"I'm so glad you came for me," she sighed, remembering how afraid she'd been in Deadwood. "Did Gentle Fawn tell you where I was?"

"Gentle Fawn," he asked, raising up on his elbows to look at her. "What's Gentle Fawn got to do with this?"

Still refusing to believe the nagging hunch that the Indian girl had deliberately misled her about the distance to Deadwood, Starr experienced an uncomfortable pang of guilt. She had unintentionally gotten the girl into trouble.

"She had mentioned a place called Deadwood to me, and I thought she might have figured out where I would try to go," Starr quickly improvised, but not quickly enough. Daniel Blue Eagle had noticed her hesitation and detected the look of panic that flickered in her eyes when she realized she'd said something she shouldn't have.

"I see," he said, the knowing gleam in his eyes telling Starr she hadn't fooled him. "No, it wasn't Gentle Fawn who told me. I haven't been back to the village. It was just by accident that I found you."

A wave of disappointment ricocheted through Starr. He hadn't come for her on purpose. "Then why were you in Deadwood?" she couldn't resist asking, mercifully managing to speak with an even voice.

"We wanted to know how many *wasicun* were there and how well protected they were. I'm the only one who can pass for white, so my father sent me."

"Oh," she sighed, unable to keep from wondering if he would have bothered to come for her if he'd gotten back to the village and found her missing. *Probably not*, she told herself as she squirmed under Daniel Blue Eagle, indicating that his weight was becoming uncomfortable on her.

He rolled to the side. "But if I'd gone to the village

first, I still would have come for you, Firebird," he said, as if he had read her thoughts.

Starr's heart soared at his words.

"We can use hostages more than ever now."

Starr's spirit plunged to the rocks of despair.

"The talks did not go well at all, and I'm afraid it's only a matter of time until the whole Sioux Nation is at war with the United States Army."

"Surely it's not that serious," she grumbled as she gathered up her clothing and began to dress herself, wondering what she had expected him to say. Had she really thought he would profess his great love for her? Starr smiled at her unrealistic wishfulness.

"It's only a matter of time until the *wasicun* overrun the Black Hills and destroy the last good hunting grounds on the reservation. The agency Indians will be forced to live on the supplies the agencies hand out and will starve to death, and the wild Sioux of the West will never give up their freedom without a fight. The Hunkpapas tried to start something at the conference. Believe me, it's going to happen. Already the People are buying up rifles at the agencies in preparation for what is to come."

"The government sells the People guns?"

"The Army has no idea what goes on at the Indian Bureau, and the hacks and swindlers who run most of the agencies have no idea what the Army is doing."

Starr looked around her sadly, already feeling a personal loss. During the few minutes they'd spent making love they had been free. Free of the problems of the world. Free to enjoy each other without worrying about the consequences. Just a man and woman loving each other. Husband and wife. Equals. Now his words had brought them back to where they were before. Separate people from different worlds—worlds that were bound to collide.

He was an Indian preserving his lands and protecting his people the only way he could, and she was his white captive again, bound to find a way back to her own people.

Neither of them spoke as they prepared to leave behind the idyllic moments they had shared. As soon as they were dressed and had made certain there were no live coals hidden in the ashes of their fire, Daniel Blue Eagle left the cave ahead of Starr, who was leading the horse.

Just as the sunlight hit Daniel Blue Eagle's face, Starr heard a heavy thud and saw him tumble forward outside the cave.

"What is it?" she shrieked, dropping the horse's reins and running to the fallen Daniel Blue Eagle, who was lying on his face rubbing the back of his neck and moaning softly.

But before she could check him for injuries, a raspy voice spoke from behind her. "Ya'll right, Miss Heavenly?"

Whirling around to meet Daniel Blue Eagle's attacker head-on, she screamed at the unshaven prospector, "Who are you? Where did you come from?" The fire in her eyes was deadly, but the man was too surprised to realize it. He had thought she'd be glad to see him.

"We come from Deadwood ta save ya from that there stranger," he defended proudly, grinning widely to expose a mouth full of broken and rotten teeth.

"Who's with you?" she asked, already trying to

decide what kind of chance she would have if she jumped at the man and tried to knock his gun out of his hand.

" 'Member me?" a man Starr recognized from the Deadwood Gulp said as he stepped out from behind a boulder. She certainly did remember him. He had given Mabel a lot of trouble when she wouldn't send Starr to the tent with him. She cringed when she remembered the vile man's threats to have her. "We thought ta be 'round when ya broke down an' shared yer favors. Didn't seem fair fer that stranger to be the only one gittin' ta ya after ya been gittin' the whole town o' Deadwood horny with them great tits ya been showin' off."

"You don't understand. He's not a stranger. He's my husband. We got separated and I was just working for Mabel as a bartender until he could come for me. She didn't hire me as one of her girls," she explained, killing time until she could think of something to do. Out of the corner of her eye, she saw that Daniel Blue Eagle was rousing slightly.

"Then why was Mabel sellin' chances on who was gonna be the first ta take ya ta the tent, fer a whole night?" the man who'd hit Daniel Blue Eagle said knowingly. "We know ya was jest workin' up front ta up the ante."

"I don't know what you're talking about," she promised, just as the semi-conscious Daniel Blue Eagle groaned and rolled over on his back.

The man with the drawn gun lifted it and aimed at Daniel Blue Eagle's head. "Say goodbye to yer ol' man, if that's what he is." He clicked the hammer back.

"No," Starr screamed, stepping in front of the drawn

193

pistol just as it fired.

Her eyes opened in shock as she looked at the man who'd shot her, and then she pitched forward, sliding down the front of him to lie in a crumpled heap at his feet.

The prospector's mouth dropped open as he saw the blood form on the ground beside Starr, and he looked helplessly at his partner and then back to Starr. "I—I didn't mean ta shoot 'er," he explained to no one in particular. "It was a accident. A accident!"

"You danged fool. What's the matter with ya? Ya done kilt Heavenly Nights. Now we ain't never gonna git ta stick 'er." He went for his partner's throat, but before he could put his hands on the man's neck, a growl that sounded like it originated in hell cut into the morning stillness.

Both prospectors looked in the direction of the ungodly yowl in time to see Daniel Blue Eagle, only partially recovered from the blow to his head, fly across the space that separated them, his knife drawn and deadly.

The shock of accidentally shooting Starr, coupled with the unexpected attack, caused the men to react slowly. The one whose shot had felled Starr was the first to feel Daniel Blue Eagle's wrath as the Indian jabbed his knife into the man's heart with deadly aim. Giving the blade a vicious twist, Daniel Blue Eagle raised a booted foot and put it in the man's groin to kick him backwards and off his knife.

Certain the first was dead, or would be very soon, Daniel Blue Eagle gave him no further thought as he turned to the stunned prospector who still lived.

"Wait a minute, mister," the dirty man protested,

backing away from his menacing attacker. "Can't we talk?"

Those were his last words. Daniel Blue Eagle hurled his weight into the man and immediately inflicted a fatal injury on the man's neck.

Watching the dead man carefully, Daniel Blue Eagle withdrew his knife and coldly wiped it on the man's filthy shirt. He gave his first victim one more quick glance and then rushed to Starr.

He turned her over and held her in his arms, clutching her to him, oblivious to the blood on his hand.

"It hurts, Daniel," she moaned weakly, sounding like a wounded child. It tore at his heart. She put her hand to her side and then brought it up to view the red on her palm. "I'm bleeding," she announced with vague curiosity in her tone.

"Why, Firebird? Why did you step in front of that gun?" he scolded, his voice a loving reprimand as he swiftly ripped open her shirt and camisole to examine her wound.

"I couldn't let them kill you," she said, the brave smile on her pale lips trembling as he touched the torn flesh left by the bullet. "You didn't tell your father about Deadwood yet." *And because I love you*, she told him silently. *Because I couldn't bear the thought of living without you. Because I'm your wife, and you're my husband.*

Probing the injury carefully, Daniel Blue Eagle quickly determined that the bullet had torn along the flesh over her ribs, miraculously exiting without contacting any vital organs. Though there was a lot of blood and she might have a nasty scar, she was not hurt seriously. If they could just keep the infection out of her

195

wound, she would probably be all right.

But infection was the big problem. That and stopping the bleeding.

Without hesitation, he tore the camisole the rest of the way off her, folded it into a thick pad and put it on the bleeding wound, placing her hand over it with instructions to keep it there. Despite her protests, he stripped off her jeans and drawers and began to rip the drawers into long bandages. Sitting her up, he wound the bandages around her ribs, holding the wadded camisole in place as he did.

"There, that ought to do until we can get to the village," he grunted, sitting back on his haunches and critically examining his handiwork.

"Except for one thing," Starr laughed, finding the pressure of the tight bandages had not only stopped the bleeding but had also eased some of her discomfort.

"What?"

"I'm cold," she confessed, looking down at her nude body and then up into the surprised blue eyes that only now noticed her exposed flesh. "Do you suppose I could have my jeans back?" she asked, drawing the edges of the shirt together over her breasts, though there were no buttons left on it.

Daniel Blue Eagle's tanned skin darkened several shades. "Sorry about your, uh, other clothes," he mumbled as he handed her the jeans. "I had to stop the bleeding," he explained sheepishly.

"That's all right," she smiled, intrigued by his sudden embarrassment. "Going without drawers under my clothing is definitely preferable to bleeding to death."

Daniel Blue Eagle, who had not fully recovered from his bump on the head, studied the smiling redhead quizzically. Why had she done it? Why hadn't she let the white prospectors kill him and take her back to Deadwood? Was it possible that she cared for him just a little bit? Was it possible that she wanted to stay with him? She had said she wouldn't leave him again, but he hadn't let himself believe her at the time. Perhaps he could now.

Somewhere in the back of his mind he heard her saying, "He's my husband." Had she really said that to the prospectors? Or had it been a dream? He rubbed the back of his head thoughtfully, wincing slightly when his fingers brushed a large bump at the base of his skull.

"Let me look at that," Starr suggested anxiously, finding that her concern for Daniel Blue Eagle had given her the strength to stand up.

"It's nothing."

"Well, let me look anyway," she coaxed as if talking to a child.

She led him away from the dead bodies and made him sit down on a nearby boulder. Gently using her fingers first, she quickly located the sticky lump on his head, then parted his curly black hair for a more careful examination. "Ooh, that looks like it hurts," she groaned, wrinkling her nose as she felt for the extent of his injuries. She sighed in relief when she finally determined the wound was not too serious. Though the knot was large, his scalp only had a small cut on it. As her father would have said, he had quite a 'goose egg.'

"You stay right there and I'll go get some water to clean the cut," she said, patting him on the shoulder and reentering the cave where they'd spent the night.

"I'm really all right," he protested when she reappeared in the entrance with the horse behind her.

197

"You're the one that was shot, not me."

"But your doctoring was so good that I feel like new," she laughed, ignoring the light-headedness she was beginning to feel. "Here, put this on the back of your head and it will help the swelling go down," she promised, placing a cold wet rag at the back of his head. She'd torn it from the tail of her shirt.

"Then I think we'd better be leaving before more of their friends come looking for us," she said, her words coming slower and slower as Daniel Blue Eagle's face blurred before her eyes, then doubled, then disappeared all together as her lids fluttered shut and her body folded to the ground.

When Starr awoke, the sun was high in the sky, and she and Daniel Blue Eagle were riding north away from the Black Hills. She looked around sleepily, thinking that the harsh terrain looked vaguely familiar. This must have been part of the trail she had traveled on her way to Deadwood.

The pain in her side was increasing with each jolting step the horse took, and she grimaced to keep from crying out. She wouldn't think about it.

"How far are we from the village?" she winced, thinking to concentrate on where they were.

"About four days," he replied, looking down at her head where it leaned back against his shoulder so trustingly. "How do you feel?"

Four days! That couldn't be. "I'm fine," she lied, more interested now in where the village was than in her own comfort. "Did they move?"

"They planned to stay in the same place until I rejoin them. The hunting is good, there are plenty of grazing areas for the horses, good clean water, and it's protected from attack from the soldiers by steep embankments."

"I thought it was only one day from Deadwood."

"What made you think that?"

"I don't know," Starr evaded his question, deciding she would talk to Gentle Fawn before she made any accusations. What reason would the girl have to lie to her? Yet it would seem that Gentle Fawn had deliberately sent her on a five-day journey into a strange, deadly terrain with only a two-day supply of food and a thin cloth blanket. Why? If Wild Bill and his friends hadn't come along, she could have died on the trail.

Was that it? Did Gentle Fawn want her dead? But why?

Turning her head around to focus her puzzled gaze on Daniel Blue Eagle's stony face, the answer to her question assaulted her in a mind-exploding awareness.

Gentle Fawn wanted her dead so she could have Daniel Blue Eagle!

She had sent Starr out alone, planning for her to die on the trail!

"Ohh," she moaned disgustedly, more from the shock of additional proof of her own stupidity than from the Indian girl's betrayal.

"What is it?" Daniel Blue Eagle asked, the concern in his voice reminding Starr what a gentle, caring man her husband was, a man with a great weight on his shoulders.

She couldn't add to his worries by telling him about Gentle Fawn. She would have to take care of the Indian girl herself.

"My side is hurting," Starr answered, not lying in the least. She could no longer ignore the burning pain that radiated through her entire left side. "Can we stop for a few minutes?" Her voice was a whisper as she tried to hide her pain from the man who supported her so tenderly in his arms.

Daniel Blue Eagle looked around quickly, spotting a grove of cottonwoods off to the side. "We'll stop there," he said as he nudged the horse off the trail. "I need to check your bandages anyway."

Starr managed a breathy laugh. "I'm so sorry to tell you this, my husband, but I have no more underthings for you to tear into bandages," she coughed, grabbing her side as she did and pressing against it in an effort to ease the pain.

The breath caught in Daniel Blue Eagle's throat. His heartbeat accelerated erratically. She had called him her husband! Had she finally acknowledged their marriage? He put his hand on her chin and turned her face to him, the expectant look on his face full of hope.

But what he saw drove away all thoughts of anything but keeping her alive. Her gray eyes were puffy and glazed, her skin paler than he'd ever seen it, her lips dry and starting to crack. He laid his palm on her forehead, his panic increasing by the instant. "Damn!" he cursed, berating himself for not realizing her condition sooner. She was burning up with fever.

Lifting her half-conscious body from the back of the horse, he carried her to a patch of grass that was cool to his touch as he lowered her to it. Hurriedly removing his own shirt, he tore the sleeves out of it, then ran to a nearby stream and dipped the sleeves into the cold water.

Daniel Blue Eagle wrung out one of the rags and wiped it over her face, squeezing drops of the cool water onto her lips and into her mouth.

"More," she mumbled, smacking her lips for more water.

"Yes, my love," he agreed anxiously, his deep voice shaking with fear and worry. Wiping the wet cloth along her lips again to dribble more water into her mouth, he kept up his gentle ministrations until the first sleeve had grown warm from the contact with her skin, switching then to the second cooler piece of his shirt.

Daniel Blue Eagle draped the cold cloth over her forehead and told her he would be right back, but she was not even aware that he left, for she had dozed off into a fitful sleep, filled with nightmares.

Chapter Twelve

"Daniel? Daniel Blue Eagle, where are you?" Starr called out in her sleep, the panic in her voice rising in hysteria. "Don't leave me here alone. I'll be a good wife, I promise. Just don't leave me here!"

Daniel Blue Eagle ran to the shelter where Starr slept, the worry on his tired face evident. "What is it, Firebird?"

"Where are you?" she cried, tossing her head from side to side as she fought to escape from her nightmare. "Please, don't leave me."

"I'm here, Firebird," he assured, gripping her hand tightly in his and kissing her fingers as he had done hundreds of times in the past two days. He smoothed her hair back from her forehead and lay down beside her to take her into his arms. "I won't leave you, Firebird."

At the sound of his voice, Starr seemed to settle down, and her whimpers finally eased when she felt his arms enclose her. She squeezed his strong fingers, as if holding onto him for her very life, and drifted back to sleep.

She'd been this way for two days now, and Daniel Blue Eagle was at his wit's end as to what to do for her. If the fever didn't break soon, she might die. From a flesh wound! His wife might die from a minor flesh wound, and nothing he'd done seemed to help her.

Daniel Blue Eagle had bathed Starr's feverish skin over and over again, fighting a losing battle against her fever. And he had changed the bandages on her wound so many times that his black *wasicun* shirt and pants, as well as the buckskin shirt he had meant to change into when he got out of Deadwood, had all been ripped into bandages, leaving him with only his leather leggings and breechcloth. Then when all the clothes they could spare had been made into bandages, he had even washed and dried the dirtied bandages and reused them until they were in threads.

He had tried everything, even packing the wound with a poultice he had concocted using wild plants he found growing nearby. He had used a metal cup he had brought her as a gift from the agency to boil part of a rabbit he had shot so he could feed her the nourishing broth. But that hadn't worked either. Nothing had. In fact, she was getting worse.

There were fewer and fewer moments of consciousness and rationality, and when they did occur, they lasted for shorter and shorter periods. He knew he needed to get her back to the village where the women could care for her properly, could perform their *washtay pejuta*, their good medicine, but he had been afraid to move her because every jar seemed to open the wounds again.

He had finally controlled the bleeding by crudely sewing the edges of her wounds closed with an awl fashioned from a rabbit bone and sinew from the same creature, so it now looked safe to move her.

They would leave in the morning. When she had called out for him he'd been building a *travois* on which to carry her. Though the ride would be rough, lying on the platform pulled by the horse would be a lot safer than sitting on the horse's back, but a lot slower, too.

Gently prying his fingers from hers so that he could return to his work, he noticed for the first time that her hand didn't feel quite so warm as it had, that her breathing seemed to be less labored. He looked at her more closely.

Beads of sweat were popping out on her forehead, which had been so hot and dry for so long.

"Firebird! Your fever's breaking!" he shouted excitedly, picking up a wet rag to mop at her brow. "It's breaking," he called out to no one in particular. To the cottonwood trees, to the hills, to the gods, to *Wakan Tanka*. His Firebird was going to be all right!

"Daniel," she croaked weakly, the ache in her parched throat making it difficult to speak. "What are you shouting about?" she smiled, her red-rimmed eyes fluttering open and shut.

"Thank God," he rasped, gathering her into his arms and clutching her to his chest. He shook his head from side to side, unable to stop the tears that formed in his eyes to blur his vision. "I thought I'd lost you," he confessed, suddenly looking away lest she see the trails of wetness on his face.

But he had turned his head too late, and Starr had

204

seen the tears. Or at least she thought she had.

She reached up and ran the back of her fingers over the tanned flesh of his cheek, then brought her hand to her mouth to rub her knuckles along her lips, flicking her tongue out to taste the salty dampness there. She didn't know what to make of it. Indians weren't supposed to cry. Men weren't supposed to cry. It was a sign of weakness, wasn't it?

Yet, Daniel Blue Eagle had cried, and she saw more strength in him in that moment than she ever believed possible.

Of course, he was embarrassed by his 'unmanly' show of emotion. She could tell by the way he kept sniffing his nose and wiping at his eyes with the heel of his hand without looking at her. He didn't want her to see. But she had. And she would never forget, though she wouldn't admit to him that she remembered.

"May I have some water?" Starr asked him, closing her eyes to give Daniel Blue Eagle a chance to regather his composure.

He was back in a minute with the shiny new metal cup brimming with cold spring water. Gingerly lifting her to a sitting position, he held the cup to her lips to allow her to drink.

"Thank you," she laughed as his overzealous care resulted in water dribbling out of the corners of her mouth and down her chin and neck.

"How do you feel?" he asked anxiously, setting the cup aside and lowering her down to the blanket again.

"I feel like a herd of buffalo trampled me—several times."

"Where do you hurt?" he asked, the worried frown on his face touching Starr's heart. He hurriedly lifted the shirt and began unwinding her bandages.

"I just feel stiff and achey all over. I think it's from lying on the ground for so long. How long have we been here, anyway?" She liked the way he bit his lip and frowned as he concentrated on her injuries.

"We've been here two days," he grunted as he pulled freshly washed bandages from a nearby saddlebag. "But now that you're better, we can leave tomorrow. Your wounds are on the mend," he commented, unable to hide the relief he felt on removing her bandages and seeing healthy new tissue beginning to close the openings in her side. At least his crude surgery hadn't caused more infection.

Once the fever broke, Starr's recovery was rapid, and by the time they arrived in Man of the People's village a few days later, she was able to walk beside Daniel Blue Eagle though he had fought her all the way, insisting that she should stay on the travois.

The word had spread rapidly that Daniel Blue Eagle and Firebird were approaching the camp; and by the time they were close enough to see the tepees clustered along the various ravines that crisscrossed the broad depression where the camp was headquartered, the men and women of the tribe had rushed out to greet them. A smiling Prairie Moon led the welcome.

"Good, good," she said over and over again as she patted Starr's hand and held it to her wrinkled cheek.

"*Ohan, Ina*, it is good to be home," Starr said, draping one arm around Prairie Moon's shoulders and wrapping the other around Daniel Blue Eagle's

206

waist for support.

As the well-wishers greeted Starr and Daniel Blue Eagle, she looked for one particular face in the crowd. But Gentle Fawn was nowhere to be seen.

Dorcas and Melanie were there, though they both looked disappointed when they saw that Starr had come back with no help. She smiled at them as they watched her from the entrances to their tepees, but neither of them acknowledged her. They both turned their backs and reentered their lodges. Well, she would worry about them later on. She had something more important to attend to.

Gentle Fawn!

As if Starr's thoughts had brought the Indian girl out of hiding, Gentle Fawn suddenly stepped into the path to greet the returning pair. Despite the fact that she spoke to Daniel Blue Eagle first, the girl's apprehensive gaze remained on Starr. How much had the woman with Daniel Blue Eagle figured out? What had she told her husband?

"Daniel Blue Eagle, it is good to have you and your wife back among us," Gentle Fawn said evenly.

"Thank you, Gentle Fawn," Starr answered for her husband, the smile on her face saccharine sweet. "It is so good to know that our friends cared enough to worry about us."

Gentle Fawn's black eyes opened wide. She was unaware that her surprise caused her to noisily gulp. She narrowed her gaze on the smiling white woman. Was it possible that Daniel Blue Eagle's stupid wife had not figured out that she'd been betrayed?

But the brief instant of relief Gentle Fawn felt was quickly dashed with Starr's next words.

"We have so much to talk about, don't we, Gentle Fawn? I had quite an adventure, but then you expected that, didn't you?" she asked pleasantly, her own gray eyes narrowing into steel spears of accusation.

"I'm very glad you are safe, Firebird," Gentle Fawn insisted, hoping that her fears were causing her to read something into Firebird's words that wasn't there.

"Are you?" Starr asked, arching her eyebrows suspiciously, just enough to leave no doubt in Gentle Fawn's mind that her deception had been discovered. "Oh, you don't have to tell me that. I can see that you are. It's so wonderful to have friends one can trust, isn't it, Daniel Blue Eagle?" she said, looking away from the astonished Indian girl and up at her tall husband.

"It's good, but we shouldn't stand here any longer. We need to get you to the tepee so that Prairie Moon can care for your wounds," he insisted, impatient to make certain that her healing had not been thwarted by their journey.

He swept her into his strong arms and she draped hers around his neck, allowing him to carry her the rest of the way to their tepee as he explained to the others in the Lakota language what had happened to Starr.

Entering the tepee with an anxious Prairie Moon on his heels, Daniel Blue Eagle could not suppress a sigh of relief as he gently lowered Starr to a sleeping mat. Unconcerend with his aunt's presence, he squatted down beside his wife where she sat on the mat and took her face between his two palms. "We're home,

Firebird." His words, low and intimate, echoed the glorious feelings that were swelling in her heart.

"Yes, Daniel, we're home," she sighed, not resisting as he helped her to lie back.

"I will now go and tell my father what I saw in Deadwood, and then I will return," he promised softly, leaving her in the capable hands of Prairie Moon.

Prairie Moon quickly opened the flannel shirt and unwrapped the bandages Daniel Blue Eagle had put on Starr that morning.

"*Washtay*—good," the old woman mumbled over and over as she poked and probed at the wound in Starr's side, nodding her head approvingly. She was obviously pleased with Daniel Blue Eagle's work.

"My husband is a good *pejuta wicasa*, isn't he?" Starr smiled, remembering the gentle hands that had nursed her since she'd been shot, and blushing at how naturally she had accepted his intimate care.

"Good medicine man, my nephew," Prairie Moon agreed, the broad grin on her face obvious evidence that she was pleased that she'd been able to surprise Starr with the new words in her vocabulary.

Of course, Starr had taught the words to her, but there had been no way until now to tell how much Prairie Moon had retained. "Oh, Prairie Moon, what a wonderful surprise! I'm so proud of you!"

Before Prairie Moon had left Starr's tepee, she had bathed the injured girl, brushed her hair, doctored her wounds with special healing powders and clean bandages, fed her and, best of all, brought her clean clothes.

When Daniel Blue Eagle returned to their lodge,

he too had bathed and changed clothing, but Starr couldn't help but notice the weariness in his posture, the dark circles under his eyes, and she ached to relieve his pain as he had hers.

She held her arms out to him from where she lay on the mat, and he went into them eagerly, laying his head at her breast and sleeping almost instantly. "There, there, my dear husband. You sleep. Let me watch over you this night, as you have watched over me in the past," she cooed softly, smoothing her hand over his hair and shoulders as she spoke.

Lovingly cradling him against her warmth throughout the night, Starr told Daniel Blue Eagle of her love over and over again, knowing that just this once it was safe to confess what she felt, for he didn't hear her.

Daniel Blue Eagle and Starr had been back in the village for a week, and Starr's condition had improved daily. She had tried more than once to get up to do her share of the work, but Daniel Blue Eagle and Prairie Moon had been adamant about making her rest.

However, after a week of doing nothing, she was more than a little bit bored.

"I don't care what you say, Daniel Blue Eagle. I'm going to cook our supper tonight. Taking care of the two of us is too much work for Prairie Moon," she told her husband as he attempted to keep her inside the tepee one more day.

"I don't want you to overdo and open your wound again," he told her, still holding onto her arm.

"There's plenty of time to work when we return from our fall buffalo hunt. Right now, I just want to be certain you're fully recovered before you do anything too strenuous."

The loving concern in his voice tugged at Starr's heart, and she was tempted to do as he said, just to make him happy. But enough was enough. She had to get out!

"I won't do anything 'too strenuous' by tossing a few vegetables and bits of meat into some boiling water," she laughed, patting his tanned fingers where they rested on her forearm.

He gave no answer, but the worry in his face made Starr's heart ache with love. She stood on her tiptoes and kissed his cheek. "I promise I won't do too much," she assured him and ducked out of the tepee before he could protest further.

She loved being pampered, but it had to stop. The other women were even beginning to talk about the way Daniel Blue Eagle coddled her. And the men would lose respect for him if he treated his wife that way much longer.

Besides, if they were going to survive during the winter, there were still many things to do. She had already lost nearly a month because of her foolish actions. There was no more time to spare. She had work to do, and that was that. Waving Prairie Moon away from the fire she was building, Starr took over the supper preparations.

When Daniel Blue Eagle joined her outside the tepee, he studied her for a long time without speaking, his arms folded across his chest, the expression on his face serious. Starr was concentrating on taking

211

a mental inventory of the winter supplies she already had in her *parfleches* and listing what she still had to do, so she wasn't bothered by his silence. In fact, when he finally spoke, his voice startled her, causing her to jump involuntarily.

"We'll be gone for five or six days on the buffalo hunt, Firebird."

Though he stopped talking, his tone caused Starr to turn and look at him expectantly, as if waiting for the *and*.

"I know that, Daniel Blue Eagle," she smiled patiently, waiting a minute for him to continue. But when he remained silent, she turned back to the stew over the fire.

"Can I trust you while I'm gone?"

Starr's head lifted, but she didn't turn to face her husband. Instead, she absently circled the ladle in the boiling liquid in the iron cooking pot Daniel Blue Eagle had gotten at the Red Cloud Agency.

"Trust me? Of course, you can. I told you I won't do too much too soon."

"That isn't what I mean, and you know it, Firebird." He crossed to the fire and turned her to face him, impaling her with his intense blue gaze.

She stared at him, stunned. She knew exactly what he was talking about. Still she opened her eyes and feigned innocence. "I don't know what you mean."

Daniel Blue Eagle gave an exasperated sigh that wafted over Starr's face, making it difficult for her to keep from embracing him. "Will you try to leave me again?"

"Don't you think I've learned my lesson, after all that's happened?"

"I hope you have, but I still want your word. Give me your word that you won't run away again." His grip on her arms tightened, and the tone in his voice was urgent.

Starr wanted to tell Daniel Blue Eagle that she would rather die than ever leave him again, but she couldn't. She just couldn't! She couldn't ignore her responsibility to Melanie and Dorcas. No matter how undeserving the two were, no matter how they had treated her, she still felt she had to help them find a way home.

"I told you I'd never willingly leave you again," she said, quickly rationalizing that if she left, it wouldn't be by choice, so she wasn't lying to him. It hadn't even been by choice the last time. It had simply been something she had to do.

"I know you did, but that was when you were so relieved to get out of Deadwood that you'd say anything to keep me from taking you back there. I want you to tell me again. Right now. Look at me and give me your word you won't try to leave while I'm gone." His strong fingers dug into her arms. He held his breath as he waited for her answer.

"Daniel, I give you my word that I won't leave while you're away," she promised, giving him a reassuring smile and doing her best to look him directly in the eyes.

His sigh of relief told her that he believed her and still trusted her. After everything that had happened, he trusted her on the basis of her word. The knowledge caused such an ache in her heart that she unconsciously put her hand on her chest to stop the painful pounding.

She tried to convince herself that she had nothing to feel guilty about. She wasn't really lying. Certainly nothing would happen during the next week that would force her to make a choice between her word to him and her responsibility to Melanie and Dorcas. But somehow, none of her rationalizations eased her mind. She still felt as if she were lying, and it hurt. It hurt very much. More than the wound in her flesh. More than thinking of never seeing her Yankton home again.

The day after Daniel Blue Eagle and most of the men from the Oglala tribe had left the village, Prairie Moon came hurrying to the tepee where Starr sat beading a new deerskin shirt she was making to surprise her husband, to replace the one he had shredded into bandages to dress her injury.

The expression on Prairie Moon's wrinkled old face was wild and distraught, her eyes so wide with fright that Starr became alarmed and put down her work to rush to meet the woman. "What is it?" she asked anxiously, but Prairie Moon was talking so fast in her own language that Starr couldn't understand what she was saying.

The agitated Indian woman moved her hands hysterically, pointing all the time toward the south. She was obviously trying to tell Starr something important, but the excited words were coming out of her mouth so quickly that Starr could only pick out a few of the words.

One word she recognized for certain was *wasicun*, the Lakota word for the white man; and another word

214

the older woman said over and over was *shica*. Starr thought that meant bad.

"*Shica wasicun*?" Starr asked nervously, gripping the woman's leathery face between her palms and forcing her to look at her. "Are you saying bad white men are coming?"

"*Ohan*—yes," Prairie Moon nodded eagerly. "Bad, bad, bad!" she repeated ominously, the fear in her eyes frightening Starr.

"Where? Show me where they are, Prairie Moon," she said, noticing that other women in the village were gathered together and looking toward the southern entrance to the camp, the sound of their excited talking happy, not afraid. Yet Prairie Moon would not be dissuaded from her purpose.

"No," she said decisively. "You, me, hide. Bad men go." She was already shoving at Starr in an attempt to get her safely into her tepee.

Starr allowed herself to be herded toward the lodge, thinking to get Prairie Moon calmed down before she looked into what it was that had upset her so dreadfully. But before they got inside, she heard the distinct sound of white men's voices.

Swinging her head around in surprise, Starr saw the women of the village eagerly surrounding two buckskin-clad white men leading a string of donkeys loaded with bundles of merchandise for trading.

"Howdy, ladies. How've ya been? Ya ready ta do some tradin' b'fore winter sets in?" she heard one gravelly voice ask pleasantly. "We got calico, real iron pots, fancy blankets, all sorts o' pretties fer ya."

"An' things fer yer men, too," the second man added. "Tobacco, colored feathers, hunting knives."

215

"They're white traders, Prairie Moon," Starr said with a great sigh of relief, now able to smile again. "You had me thinking the soldiers were coming to kill us all," she shamed her friend good-naturedly. "But it's just two harmless traders. Let's go see what they have. I certainly would like a bar of soap for myself and a few special beads for Daniel Blue Eagle's new shirt," she said, already wondering what she could trade to get the items she desired.

Starr moved away from Daniel Blue Eagle's aunt.

"No!" Prairie Moon protested vehemently, grabbing Starr's arm and tugging at it urgently. "*Wasicun shica*! Bad. Bad," she insisted, shaking her head so adamantly that her graying braids whipped out from her head.

Seeing how important it was to Prairie Moon, and afraid the old woman would suffer some sort of attack if she didn't get her way, Starr stopped where she was, reluctantly staying back with Prairie Moon to watch from a distance as the traders pulled wonderful things from their packs that caused enthusiastic *oohs* and *ahs* from their enthralled audience.

Then, suddenly it hit her. The solution to her problems. The traders could take Melanie and Dorcas back, relieving her of her responsibility to them. It was perfect.

But what if they won't go? she asked herself, a worried expression replacing the elated one of the instant before.

Then I'll assume that, like me, they prefer to stay here, she mused logically. "Either way, my duty to them will be fulfilled!" she said to no one in particular.

Just as she would have ignored Prairie Moon's determined protests and gone to talk to the traders about taking Melanie and Dorcas with them when they left, the two white women rushed forward to see the traders. By the excited expressions on their smiling faces, Starr knew they'd had the same idea she'd had.

She finally relaxed, not realizing until that moment that she'd been so tense, her shoulders drawn up so high, her knees locked so inflexibly, her fists balled with such determination. In fact, as the tightness eased from the muscles throughout her body, she had to concentrate on breathing again, on unclenching her teeth.

Starr nodded her head with satisfaction and turned away from the scene in the middle of the village to take Prairie Moon into her own tepee to rest. She would tell Melanie and Dorcas good-bye after the older woman was settled.

Stepping out of Prairie Moon's lodge a few minutes later, Starr was surprised to find Gentle Fawn waiting for her. It was the first opportunity the two had had to talk since the day she and Daniel Blue Eagle had returned from Deadwood, and she was amazed that the Indian girl had been the one to seek out the meeting. *Might as well get it over with now while Daniel Blue Eagle is gone.*

"Gentle Fawn," Starr said evenly, the smile on her lips not reaching her cool gray eyes. "What do you want?"

"I came to tell you that the traders have agreed to take you and your friends back to Fort Lincoln."

"You'd like that, wouldn't you, Gentle Fawn?"

217

"I only want for you to be back with your own people. Is that not what you asked me to help you do?"

"With such a dedicated friend as you, I don't need any enemies, do I?" Starr chuckled, the smile on her face chilling.

"I do not understand," Gentle Fawn claimed, her black eyes darting nervously from side to side. She couldn't meet the cold gray eyes that were watching her with—With what? With amusement? Pity? She wasn't sure how to combat that. If she'd seen hate or anger, she would have known what to do, but this!

"Oh, I think you understand quite well, Gentle Fawn. And so do I," Starr said knowingly as she crossed to her own tepee and sat down in front of it, picking up her sewing as she did. "Did you think I wouldn't realize how you betrayed me? Or did it make any difference what I discovered?" Starr continued to speak to the gaping girl in a pleasant conversational tone. "No, of course, it made no difference, because you didn't think I'd live long enough to get to Deadwood, did you? You planned for me to die between here and there." Starr could tell by the look on Gentle Fawn's face that her suspicions had been right.

"I didn't!" Gentle Fawn protested angrily. "Ask your friends. I took them to our meeting place the next day as you and I agreed. We waited for hours, until we could wait no more. I was very worried about you, Firebird. You can ask them!"

"I'm certain you were. You were worried that by some dumb quirk of fate I would realize what you had done soon enough to find my way back before it

218

was too late. I've no doubt in the world that you were worried. But your concern was for yourself, not for me. You were afraid I'd be able to make the five-day journey on two days' worth of food and with one thin cloth blanket. You were afraid that somehow Daniel Blue Eagle would find out how you had tricked his wife before you could step in and take my place."

"It is not true, Firebird! I hope you haven't repeated these ugly lies to Daniel Blue Eagle. He would be very angry with you for saying such terrible things about the daughter of a dear friend, the daughter of a chief," she defended angrily, certain she could take the offensive away from the pale woman who sat there smiling so smugly and sewing as she made her accusations.

Starr's smile now reached her eyes and she laughed aloud. "No, dear, I haven't mentioned this to my husband. You wouldn't be standing here talking to me if I had. In fact, you'd be lucky to be alive if he knew what you tried to do to me. My husband is very protective, and he wouldn't be happy at all if he knew."

Gentle Fawn stared aghast at the white woman. When had she become so brave?

"In the future you will stay away from me, away from my husband and away from Prairie Moon. Unless you wish for me to tell Daniel Blue Eagle."

"He won't believe you," Gentle Fawn defended weakly, knowing she was defeated for the moment.

"Oh, I think he will, Gentle Fawn. And so do you."

The two women stared at each other for several long moments, each sizing up the opposition with undisguised hatred before the Indian girl spun on her

219

heel and walked away.

"By the way," Starr called after the retreating figure. "I won't be leaving with the traders. My place is here now. Here with my husband. From now on, the People are my people."

Gentle Fawn stopped in mid-step. For a full two seconds, she stood frozen, her fists clenching and unclenching angrily, and then she hurried away without looking back at Starr. But she knew Daniel Blue Eagle's wife was still smiling. And she hated her more than ever.

"To think that I used to believe she was beautiful," Starr muttered to herself, giving a disgusted shrug of her shoulders and starting to work another beaded star onto Daniel Blue Eagle's shirt.

Chapter Thirteen

Sleep was almost impossible for Starr that night. She was too elated with the way things had worked out. The traders would take Melanie and Dorcas back to civilization, while she herself would be able to stay with the man she loved and take care of him and his aunt.

Only one tiny worry nagged at her. She knew that she had not had her last encounter with Gentle Fawn. And she was certain that the next time the girl would be more determined to destroy her than ever before. Still, as long as she knew who her enemy was, she was confident that she was strong enough to meet head on whatever evil the envious Indian girl could hurl at her.

Starr had just dozed off when she heard an unfamiliar rustling noise. It was in the lodge with her. At once alerted to danger, her eyes flew open, glancing frantically around in the darkness.

"Daniel Blue Eagle? Is that you?" she asked cautiously, pulling herself to a sitting position as she hurriedly scanned the interior of the lodge.

"No, it ain't yer Injun, sugar. My name's Walleye Jacks. I'm one o' the traders."

"What are you doing here?" she asked, making every effort to seem calm, as if it were an everyday occurrence to awaken with a stranger groping around in her tepee.

"We're fixin' ta take off b'fore the whole camp gits up. I come ta git ya."

"There must be some mistake," Starr said, her instincts warning her that the man was preparing to move toward her. "I'm not going with you. I'm staying here," she told the dark shadow that stood in the center of the lodge, on the opposite side of the dying fire.

"But she said ya'd be ready ta leave with us."

Starr, of course, knew who 'she' was. "Well, I'm sorry if you've been put to too much trouble, but Gentle Fawn lied to you. I'm not going back. I've decided to stay here."

Why didn't he leave? Why did he just stand there across the fire with the lights and shadows playing over his bug-eyed face? Starr shifted nervously to her knees, poising herself for an attack.

Finally, the man moved toward the entrance to the lodge, and a wave of relief swept over the apprehensive girl. But her reprieve was short-lived, for he didn't leave. "Zeke, she says she ain't goin' with us," he whispered to someone outside.

There was the sound of more rustling as a second man brushed aside the door flap and joined the first inside Starr's tepee. "You'll both have to leave, or I'll scream and alarm the entire camp," Starr warned.

"There, there, Miss Starr. We jest wanna help ya git away from these here savages. Yer family's worried 'bout ya," the first man coaxed, his grin ghoulish in the dim moonlight that seeped in through the smoke flap in the top of the lodge.

He took a step to the left to skirt the fire and came toward her. At the same time, the second man moved to the right.

"Stop right where you are," Starr ordered, whipping Daniel Blue Eagle's revolver from beneath her buffalo robe, "or I'll blow both your heads off."

The traders froze in their tracks. "Come on, Miss Starr, put that thing down. We don't wanna hurt ya," the man called Zeke said, his oily voice revolting Starr.

"And I don't want to hurt you, but if you take one more step in my direction, I'll kill you," she said to the man, keeping her voice even, despite inner trembling that threatened to give her away.

Never taking her eyes off the two, Starr stood up, praying that in the dark they couldn't see her hand shaking as it held the gun on first one, then the other. Separated the way they were, she could probably hit only one if they decided to jump her, but she had to hope that neither would make a move. The gamble would be too great for either man. "Now, get out of here," she growled, her courage growing at the same rate as her anger, a luxury she could afford now that she had the upper hand.

How dare they come in here and do this to her? "Go on! Out!" she shouted angrily, using the gun to indicate the way.

The two traders glanced at each other and then

223

back at Starr. They realized the girl meant business and scurried out of the lodge ahead of her. "What'll we tell yer family?" Jacks asked her when they all three got outside.

"I have no family. They were all killed, so you don't have to worry about that," she snarled, her expression growing impatient. "Now get your things and leave our village."

"Well, ya sure got somebody back there. Somebody who offered a mighty healthy reward ta git ya back," the one Walleye Jacks had called Zeke said, turning back to face Starr with an annoying smirk on his face. "An' we mean ta collect that reward, Miss Starr Winfield. Yer goin' with us whuther ya want to 'r not."

"I most certainly am not, and if you don't get going in the next thirty seconds, you're not going either!" she threatened bravely, cocking the hammer on the revolver. "I'll kill you and feed you to the buzzards, and we'll keep your packs to make our lives a little more comfortable."

"Ya ain't gonna shoot nobody, Miss Sta—." That was all Starr heard before she felt a crashing blow to the back of her head and she pitched forward, surrounded by blackness.

When Starr regained consciousness, her ankles and wrists were bound and she was slung over the back of a donkey like so much baggage. She realized she was gagged, and the taste of the foul rag inside her mouth made her want to wretch.

Trying not to think of the pain in her head, the numbness in her hands and feet, the sickening taste in her mouth, she laboriously lifted her head to look around.

It was still dark and the train of donkeys was moving slowly out of a canyon. She tried to understand what was going on. What could have happened? How long had they been gone from the village? Had anyone noticed their absence yet?

But it hurt too much to think, and she let her head drop again in limp defeat. However, hanging upside down was just as bad, maybe even worse. It hurt to move her eyes from side to side, and the blood pounded painfully in her temples as the rough gait of the donkey bounced her head against its side.

Was this where it was all to end? Was she never to have a chance to show Daniel Blue Eagle how she felt? Would he live his life always believing she had lied to him? She had no doubt that Gentle Fawn would tell him his wife had left willingly. And after the Deadwood foolishness, what else was he to believe?

Starr closed her eyes and listened to the night sounds, the crunching of the donkeys hooves on the gravelly terrain, the wind in the pine trees, the song of a mysterious night bird, the creak of the packs on the animals' backs.

I should've shot them when I had the chance, she scolded herself bitterly. But there was no more time to feel sorry for herself.

She heard something! Her head shot up alertly, her eyes straining in the darkness.

There had been a sound, different from the others, and in spite of the pain in her head, she arched her neck and continued to examine the land within her view. There *was* something out there, though she could see nothing.

The sound was subtle.

Yet it was there! She felt it. Its presence was almost tangible. They were being watched, stalked.

Starr jerked her head around to see if the others had noticed the scurrying, shuffling sound, but the two traders and the two white women seemed unconcerned.

Just the wind in the buffalo grass. I'm more aware of it because my head is closer to the ground, she told herself, unconvinced. Still, she couldn't shake the feeling that something was going to happen and continued to carefully scrutinize the dark sides of the trail.

Then she noticed that the crickets had stopped their chirping, and the night bird no longer sang. A donkey brayed nervously and balked. But still the traders ignored the signs of danger. They were only concerned with putting as much distance as they could between themselves and the Indian village before daylight.

They had done a very foolhardy thing, stealing white captives from the Indians. When they had ridden into that village and found those women, two of the six they'd seen reward posters on, they had hesitated, knowing how dangerous a venture it would be. But when they'd discovered that the captive named Starr Winfield was in the village too, they had known what they had to do. The reward for her alone was four times that for the others. The combined reward for the three women would more than equal two or three trading expeditions into the Indian villages and illegal mining camps in the Black Hills.

The strange sound had stopped, and Starr began to wonder if she had imagined it. Could it be that the pulse pounding so loudly in her head had distorted her hearing?

Just when she had almost convinced herself there was nothing out there watching, she heard the sound again! And this time there was no doubt in her mind. There was definitely something or someone skulking in the darkness.

Starr looked up quickly and squinted with intense concentration on the dark brush along the sides of the trail. This time the rustling sound had been accompanied by something else. She was certain she'd seen a furtive movement out of the corner of her eye, but when she looked, everything was still. No stealthy mountain lions or bears waiting to leap out at them.

She glanced at the traders and women again, but they behaved no differently.

Was her mind playing tricks on her? Or was it possible she had lived among the People so long that she'd actually developed a keener sense of hearing than other whites?

The night bird began to sing its eerie mournful song again, only this time the odd melody was pitched lower, a difference only the most sensitive ear could have heard. The bird quickly received an answer from another bird on the opposite side of the trail.

Trying to twist her head in the direction of the second call, Starr heard still another. This one came from in front of the moving train of pack animals. Suddenly, there were two from behind them. More from each side. One so close to her face she should have seen it. She did.

She saw it! But it wasn't a bird that came into sight. It was a human being rising up from the ground. Not one, but two. No, it wasn't two. It was several. Not several. Many! Many people coming toward the donkey train from all sides.

The traders cursed. Melanie and Dorcas gasped loudly. But all Starr could do was watch the drama that was unfolding before her eyes.

The entire train of merchandise-loaded donkeys was surrounded by stony-faced Indian women and old men, each of them armed with a rifle or a drawn bow and arrow. Every weapon was directed at the two white traders.

"Give us back what is ours," a woman's voice said in halting English. Though her words came slowly, as though she was mentally translating what she wanted to say one word at a time, there was no doubt that she meant what she said. Her tone was hard. Cold. Determined. Frightening to everyone in the traders' party, except to Starr.

Prairie Moon! My God! It's Prairie Moon and she's speaking English!

"Move aside, old woman." The trader, Zeke, gave the order with a bravado he couldn't possibly have felt with fifty arrows and rifles pointed at him, even though they were held by women and old men. Every white man feared being killed by Indians. For the Indians didn't just kill a man. They disfigured and mutilated him afterwards and hid the parts of his body, believing that a man who wasn't whole would stay that way in the afterlife.

Prairie Moon ignored the man. "Guns here," she

yelled, pointing to the ground.

The traders unwisely hesitated, and at the barest nod of an old chief's head, all the Indians' arms were raised in readiness.

Zeke and Walleye Jacks threw down their firearms without further delay.

The instant the traders were unarmed, the Oglala 'warriors' relaxed their vigil—only slightly. A few of the women lay down their weapons to rush forward and untie Starr and take her off the donkey. They helped her walk on trembling legs to where Prairie Moon stood bravely challenging the traders, her rifle steady in her hands. Her wrinkled old face beaming with pride was the most beautiful sight Starr had ever seen. She hurried forward to hug the old woman.

Other women jerked the traders and Melanie and Dorcas off their mules, then prodded them back up the trail the way they had come, beating the men with sticks as they walked them toward the village.

"Wait a minute," Starr called out, her voice cracking painfully with her first words since the gag had been removed from her mouth. "Let them go," she called out in the Lakota language. "If we kill them, the white soldiers will find a way to punish us. Let them each have a mule and enough food to last them until they reach the Missouri River. We'll keep their other supplies and donkeys as payment for their lives."

"But they should be punished," one woman shouted angrily.

"In the future, we won't be able to trust any traders," another pointed out.

"The wife of Daniel Blue Eagle speaks wisely," an

old chief called Running Fox said very quietly.

Starr and the others turned to watch as the very old man came forward. Though his posture was bent with age, his step slow, his skin so wrinkled that one could only wonder what he might have looked like in his youth, she realized the white-haired chief's eyes were clear and intelligent, and his voice was still strong and vibrant, its low resonant quality capable of commanding the respect of any who heard him speak.

"The *wasicun* will use any excuse to break our treaty. I say let these traders go, as Firebird suggests," he said, directing a brown-toothed grin of approval toward Starr.

"What about them?" one of Yellow Whip's wives asked, indicating Melanie and Dorcas with a nod of her head. "I wouldn't mind seeing the end of the lazy one," she said about Dorcas.

"Yes, what about us?" Dorcas said in English to Starr. "If we stay here, our men will kill us for trying to escape. Tell them to let us go too, Starr. Please."

"But how do we know we can trust the traders?" Melanie asked, obviously not certain that she wouldn't be better off going back to the village and taking her chances with Spotted Shoulder.

"I think you can trust them to get you home safely, Melanie," Starr nodded knowingly. "There's a reward offered for your return, so unless they want this venture to be a total loss, they'll take good care of you."

"I would like for my friends to be allowed to go with the traders," Starr said, turning back to the women and men around her. "They are not happy in the village and want to return to their own people."

"But if we let them go, my husband, Spotted Shoulder, will be very angry with his other wives for not stopping them," Bead Woman protested anxiously. "He'll give us the punishment she would have received."

"Not when he sees what a good bargain we made in trade," the old chief pointed out. "Two worthless white women for all these fine goods and donkeys. To make up for their losses, we will allow Yellow Whip and Spotted Shoulder to share half of everything, while the rest of the families in our tribe will divide the remainder among themselves."

There was some grumbling among the women, but still none of them would argue with the wise old man. After all, he had been a great chief at one time, and though he was now old, his wisdom continued to be highly respected.

So, it was agreed that they would release the traders and the women with enough food and supplies to get them to the Missouri River, where they would be able to flag a riverboat to take them to safety.

"What of you, Firebird?" Running Fox asked. "Do you wish to leave us and go back to your people also?"

"No, *Tunkashila*," Starr returned affectionately, using the word for grandfather to address him. She tenderly helped the old man to one of the donkeys for a ride back to the camp. It was obvious that to lead the daring rescue had been a great strain. "I will stay here with the Oglala. They are my people now."

The old man nodded his approval and gratefully allowed himself to be assisted to the back of the donkey that had carried Starr out of the village.

By the time the men returned from the hunt, the traders' goods had been divided to everyone's satisfaction, and though the wives of Yellow Whip and Spotted Shoulder still feared their husbands' wrath, they were very pleased with their generous shares of the new belongings, as Starr was with hers. She had chosen a donkey and a pair of eyeglasses for Prairie Moon, a bar of castile soap, a hairbrush and two pairs of drawers for herself, and beads for Daniel Blue Eagle's new shirt, as well as a cloth shirt and pants for him. She was also given flour and a bolt of green calico. And she hadn't been able to resist one final luxury that none of the other women had wanted. She was now the proud owner of a wooden tub for bathing.

Anticipating Daniel Blue Eagle's return at any moment, Starr patted her hair, securing her braids with colored ribbons at the bottoms. She tried to ignore the flutter of excitement she felt tripping through her, tried not to think about how good it would be to lie in his arms that night, tried not to admit how much she had missed him and how much she loved him. But then her happy thoughts turned to worry.

Would he be as happy to see her as she was him? Or would he be so angry at her part in the release of Melanie and Dorcas that he would punish her? He might even divorce her!

I won't think about it, she swore silently. *He may not say it, but I know he feels something for me. He wouldn't have cared for me so tenderly when I was sick and wounded if he didn't*, she assured herself, making a useless attempt to boost her sinking confidence.

But there was no more time to speculate on what would happen, for suddenly he was there, and her heart leaped into her throat. How could he do that to her? How could just the sight of him make her want him so much that her body began to react even before they had touched?

She felt his eyes on her and looked up to catch his hungry gaze meeting hers across the camp. She could tell that he was feeling the same thing as she, and her breathing grew even more rapid in anticipation. God! Would she be able to wait until dark to have him love her?

Had anyone noticed the look on her face? Surely her heart was pounding so loudly that the whole camp knew what she was thinking! Starr's tanned skin darkened with embarrassment, and she looked away in a useless attempt to think of other things.

She glanced nervously at Prairie Moon and Running Fox who were sitting on the ground rolling cigarettes with the trappings he'd acquired from the white traders' packs. Starr smiled affectionately at the old people who had seemed to discover each other for the first time on the night they'd rescued her from the traders. In fact, now that she thought about it, she realized Running Fox had had most of his meals with them since that night and had brought several small gifts to Prairie Moon—the cigarette makings and a ridiculous flowered bonnet he'd gotten from the traders. What she would do with it, Heaven only knew, but it was obvious the woman treasured it greatly and would never give it up. In fact, it was hanging in a place of honor in her tepee.

Smiling about the romance she suspected was budding, she turned her eyes back to where Daniel Blue Eagle and the other men stood surrounded by the women excitedly greeting them, and her smile broadened. She couldn't help herself. Her heart was too full of joy and happiness.

Despite the fact that he stood in the midst of a crowd, Starr's eyes could see only her husband, who stood taller than everyone else in the camp. Her heart swelled with pride and love. Pride in his handsome features, pride in his broad-shouldered physique, pride in his beliefs, pride in his tenderness, and especially pride in the fact that he was her husband.

Daniel Blue Eagle smiled back at Starr. Her wide gray eyes were sending a message that made it impossible for him to stay away from her an instant longer. He politely separated himself from the group of hunters and greeters and hurried to where his wife stood waiting before their tepee, unmindful that his long, purposeful stride was causing a number of grins and knowing snickers among the people who saw him.

But he didn't notice. Nor did Starr.

When he reached their tepee, he stood before her, so close that she had to tilt her head back to see his face. Neither of them spoke. They were too busy relearning each other's features, intent on adoring each other with their eyes.

Starr inhaled deeply, growing intoxicated on the familiar scent she'd missed so much.

Daniel Blue Eagle didn't touch Starr, yet she felt his touch as surely as if he'd put his hands on her, caressing her face, her neck, her breasts, her belly, and her legs.

Finally, when neither of them could bear the longing another second, they turned as one and walked without speaking toward the entrance to their lodge. No words were necessary. Their eyes said it all.

Once inside the tepee, Starr turned to Daniel Blue Eagle, hesitating only a moment before she stepped forward and lifted the lower edge of his shirt upward and pulled it off over his head. Taking a step back, she removed her own dress in one swift movement, her intense gray eyes losing contact with his only during the brief instant when her dress passed over her face.

Her nipples, already peaked with desire, sprung free of the deerskin garment, and Daniel Blue Eagle's breath caught in his chest at the sight of her beautiful body. He tried to speak, but his voice cracked. "Firebird, I—" he started.

However, Starr didn't want the fragile moment spoiled with words, and she lay four fingers gently against his lips and said, "Shh," as she took a strong brown hand in hers and drew it up to her mouth to place a kiss in the center of his broad palm.

Daniel Blue Eagle's tongue flicked out along a finger that rested against his lips, and a sting of passion ran along Starr's arm.

Eying him hungrily, she imitated his actions, taking a teasing taste of his hand as he had hers; and when he couldn't suppress a low moan, she was pleased to know he'd been just as affected as she.

But Daniel Blue Eagle was determined they were not going to rush this time together, no matter how desperately his body cried out for him to pull her against him. No, he had thought of nothing else for days, and he was going to savor every moment of it.

With their gazes locked in passionate challenge, Starr mirrored Daniel Blue Eagle's erotic actions. With painstaking deliberateness, they each licked lazily along the fingers pressed to their lips. Their tongues circled and traced the edges, creases and tips of each other's fingers, dipping deep between them at their base, until all the fingers of both hands had been bathed with burning wet caresses.

Starr savored the taste of Daniel Blue Eagle's hand as she released her hold on his wrist and dropped her own hand to his chest. Daniel Blue Eagle freed her other wrist and, with a groan, brought his hand down to massage her breast, now matching his actions to hers. Yet their bodies were still inches apart and their mouths had not touched.

Starr made the first move to end their self-induced torture and lowered her hands along his ribcage to his slender waist, where in a single action she peeled away his breechcloth and leggings, at last freeing his manhood from the restraint of his clothing. Now it was her turn to sigh.

Glowing a golden brown in the sunlight that filtered through the tepee's flap, Daniel Blue Eagle was magnificently beautiful. Broad shoulders narrowing to slim hips over long muscular legs, he was all Starr could ever have wanted in a man. Her husband's physique was flawless, and a shiver of breathless anticipation rippled through Starr at the thought that in moments she would be one with him again.

Unable to ignore the evidence of Daniel Blue

Eagle's desire, Starr dropped to her knees before her husband. She wanted to touch all of him, taste him, brand him hers.

Realizing what her desire was crying out for her to do, Starr was finally able to partially free herself from the hypnotic hold his body held on her. Uncertainty filled her, combating her desire.

She looked up the long length of him, to find his passion-glazed blue eyes on her, but the surprise she saw in his expression frightened her for a moment, made her wonder if she should deny her desire to know all of him.

Perhaps a wife wasn't supposed to touch her husband there. Would she repulse him if she did? Yet she hadn't been repelled when he'd touched her, kissed her so intimately. She had loved it. Wouldn't his reaction be the same? After all, they had responded the same way to other caresses. Why would this be any different? Only better.

In the end, desire won in Starr's mental battle. Easing the tormenting need to know all of Daniel Blue Eagle with her hands and mouth made taking the chance worthwhile.

Extending her hand tentatively toward his jutting manhood, Starr brought her fingers to within a fraction of an inch of his throbbing flesh, so close she could feel the heat radiating from him.

There was no sound in the tepee. Even the sound of their breathing had stopped. In fact, they both held their breath as they waited on the edge of paradise for her skin to contact his. And when it did, when her fingers brushed him with bashful feathery strokes, he cried out his joy. *"Ohan, ohan,"* he gasped, throwing his head back as his hands gripped her shoulders.

Her boldness grew with his reaction, his obvious pleasure, and she wrapped her fingers around the tightly-stretched skin and allowed herself the luxury of moving her hand gently along the satiny column.

"Ahh," he groaned, his fingers digging painfully into her shoulders.

Starr could no longer stop herself from experiencing all of him. Her remaining inhibitions were cast aside, and with a movement so quick that it might not have happened, she flicked her pink tongue out to touch the tip of his strength. Then again. And again. Until her mouth closed over him.

Daniel Blue Eagle could bear no more of her sweet torment. He scooped her off the ground to settle on his throbbing manhood.

Her long legs wrapped around his waist, her ankles locking behind his back, and together they completed their journey home to the paradise they'd both dreamed of during their separation, the place their lovemaking would take them again and again throughout the night.

Chapter Fourteen

"Tell me about your mother," Starr said as she idly circled her fingertips over Daniel Blue Eagle's flat stomach as they lay temporarily replete. Her hand glided over his chest to cup his chin and turn his face toward her. "What was she like? Was she happy with your father? What happened to her?"

Daniel Blue Eagle kissed the tip of his wife's nose and smiled. "That's a lot of questions for one time. Why the sudden curiosity?"

Starr was embarrassed. How could she explain that she loved him so much she wanted to know everything there was to know about him and his life before she came into it? "I don't know. I just wondered. Would you rather I didn't ask?"

"No," he chuckled at the contrite expression on her face. "I wouldn't rather you didn't ask. My mother was a sweet and gentle woman who loved my father very much."

"What was her name?"

"Felicity. Felicity Edwards. But my father called

her Little Dove."

"How did she meet your father?"

"She taught at a mission school, and he was one of her students. He had a great hunger to learn the white man's ways so that he could help the People find a way to live in peace with them. He studied very hard, even after school hours. And when she noticed his eagerness to learn, she began to bring books out of her own personal library for him to read. She was very fair and beautiful, and he was tall and handsome."

"I can believe that," Starr interrupted, raising up on an elbow to caress her husband's sculptured face and place a light kiss on his lips. "How else would they have made such a handsome son?"

Daniel Blue Eagle frowned with feigned annoyance and said, "Do you want to hear this or not?"

"I'm sorry," she apologized. "I'll be quiet," she promised, snuggling down into the curve of his arm with her head on his shoulder. "Please go on."

"As I was saying," he teased, "she was beautiful, he was handsome, and they were both eighteen years old. They fell in love and wanted to be married, but her father, my grandfather, refused to give them permission. They ran away together and lived in the Black Hills, where I was born."

"What about Gray Wolf's mother? Your father had more than one wife, didn't he?"

"Yes, Man of the People was married at age sixteen to another. It's not unusual for a Lakota brave to have more than one wife."

"But how did your mother feel about it? Didn't she hate it?"

Daniel Blue Eagle directed an understanding smile at the top of his wife's head. "No, she didn't hate it. My mother and Autumn Flower were like sisters, and when Autumn Flower died giving birth to Gray Wolf, my mother took him to her breast and raised him as her own."

Starr was very touched by the genuine goodness of Felicity Edwards. And she hated that part of herself that could never be that good or that understanding. She was certain that if Daniel Blue Eagle ever took another wife, she would never think of her as anything but an enemy. Certainly not a sister! Instead, she would want to scratch her eyes out at the very least.

As if he could see the doubts about their own marriage in Starr's bent head, Daniel Blue Eagle laughed and tilted her head back so he could see her worried face. "Don't worry, Firebird. I'm not my father. One wife is enough for me, especially one who welcomes me home from the hunt as you do," he grinned and kissed her mouth, running his tongue over her lips enticingly.

"Who said I was worried?" Starr denied, with no idea how evident the relief was on her face. "Now go on with your story. What happened next?"

"When Gray Wolf and I were eight, Little Dove had a baby girl. We were all very happy because she had had several babies die, and she had especially wanted a little girl. She named her Faith."

"What happened to your sister? Where is she now?"

"Little Faith is dead, Firebird. She was only four when she died."

241

"Oh, I'm so sorry, Daniel. What happened?"

"Now Daniel Blue Eagle's voice grew more emotional. "When I was twelve years old, soldiers came into our village and spotted my mother's blue eyes and realized she was white. They insisted on 'saving' her from the savages she lived with. She tried to make them understand that she was there by choice, but they wouldn't listen. They were determined to take her back to her father near Yankton. When she realized she would have to go with them to straighten things out, she packed up all three of us—Faith, Gray Wolf and me—and surrendered herself. Of course, Gray Wolf's skin and eyes were darker than Faith's and mine, and the soldiers didn't believe he was hers. They wouldn't let her take him."

"Did you say they took you to Yankton?" Starr asked incredulously, remembering the woman and the two half-Indian children from her childhood.

"Near there. We only went into the town a few times. It was too painful for my mother and too frightening for us."

"I know it was," Starr said, hugging herself to her husband, wanting in some small way to make up for the terrible experience in 'civilization'.

"Anyway, my grandfather was glad to see my mother and loved my sister and myself as he would have loved any child of his daughter's. With him, I never felt I was a half-breed, as I did everywhere else in the white world. But he never let us go back to see my father."

"But Faith. What about Faith?"

"She was taken by a fever when she was four, and my mother never smiled again," he said, the break in his voice telling Starr that he was trying hard not to cry. "Then in another two years she was dead, too. She gave up every hope when she lost Faith. She knew then that she would never see my father again and just stopped wanting to live."

"Oh, Daniel, I'm so sorry," Starr sobbed, rolling over onto her back and drawing his head down to her breast so she could cradle him in her arms. They were silent for a long time, lost in their own thoughts. Finally, Starr spoke. "Is that when you came back to your father's village?"

"Yes and no," Daniel Blue Eagle said, moving to his back again and resettling her in his arms. "My grandfather felt so guilty about what he'd done to my mother that he promised he'd let me go back to the village, but only during the summers. During the other seasons, I was to get an education so I could help the People, which had been my mother's dream for me. And that's what I did. Though I'm not certain that a half-breed, even one with a law degree from Harvard, can do much to help."

"What about your grandfather? Is he still alive?" Starr still couldn't believe that for several years she and Daniel Blue Eagle had lived near each other and that she'd actually seen him those few times on the streets when she was six or seven years old. It was as if Fate had given her a preview of her husband so that she could better understand him.

"No, he died a few years ago. He left me everything. I can use his money to help the People, but of course, I have no use for the other things." Suddenly, Daniel Blue Eagle had a thought and laughed out loud. "What do you think your neighbors would think if they realized that local property owner Daniel Edwards is a half-breed named Daniel Blue Eagle?" He smiled, though there was no happiness in his tone. "Or that his wife was none other than the proper young Miss Starr Winfield from one of the town's best families?" he added, imagining the stunned expressions on the righteous faces of the townspeople.

"That would be a sight worth seeing," he went on, unaware that Starr had stiffened in his arms. "When things with the Lakota people are on a little less shaky ground, we just might go back to Yankton and set up housekeeping for a while. What do you think about that?"

So that was why he had married her, and was so determined to keep her. Hurt and confused, Starr moved away from him and stared at the reflections of the fire flickering off the walls of the tepee, which had suddenly grown cold. She had actually let herself believe that silly story about his dream vision and convinced herself that he might even love her just a little bit. But she knew now she'd been lying to herself. There'd been no vision at all. He felt nothing for her. He had only married her to have his revenge on the people of Yankton who had hurt his mother fourteen years before.

"That's why you married me, isn't it, Daniel Blue Eagle? To get back at the people of Yankton who shunned you and your mother."

Daniel Blue Eagle saw his wife's hurt but he couldn't help the smile that came to his face. He'd hurt her without meaning to. Of course, her assumption was ridiculous; but the fact that she'd been hurt by his words told him that their marriage meant more

244

to her than she had admitted. "You don't really believe that, do you, Firebird?" he said, turning her face toward him so they could see each other's eyes. "That thought never occurred to me until this very moment."

She looked deep into his gentle blue eyes and wanted so much to believe he felt the same way about her that she did about him. But he'd never said he loved her, so what was she to think? "I don't believe you," she said, her lips trembling as she tried to keep from crying.

"Then I'll have to prove it to you," he said, his voice a teasing threat as he buried his mouth in the sweet hollow of her neck.

"Stop that," Starr ordered, pushing at his face and doing her best not to laugh.

"Stop what?" he asked. "This? He took another bite of her neck. "Or this?" He filled a hand with a plump breast and squeezed it. "Or this?" He threw off the cover and straddled her hips, wrapping his hands around her ribcage to tickle her unmercifully.

"Don't tickle me," she squealed, struggling to free herself from Daniel Blue Eagle's attack.

"Do you believe me now?" he asked sternly, his mouth open and his teeth clicking together as if planning where to bite her next.

"Yes," she giggled in defeat, forcing the unpleasant suspicion to the back of her mind.

"That's better," Daniel Blue Eagle said as his mouth came down on hers to erase any final doubts with a deep kiss before taking her once more to their own private paradise.

* * *

245

"Why would Man of the People want to speak with me?" Starr asked Daniel Blue Eagle warily. She concentrated her guilty attention on pounding a piece of buffalo meat on the stone before her. She couldn't look at her husband's stern face, because the anger she'd glimpsed on his handsome features when he returned to their tepee told her he had just found out about Melanie and Dorcas.

"I'm certain you know. Why didn't you tell me, Firebird? Is that what last night was all about? Did you think I would punish you when I found them gone? I should have known there was a reason my little wife suddenly became so insatiable."

"Insatiable?!?" she gasped, slamming down her mallet and looking up at him, anger burning in her eyes. She couldn't believe what he was saying. He actually thought she would have given herself to him so freely to avoid a punishment. Suddenly, everything they had shared during the long, wonderful night of lovemaking was made to be dirty, and she was ashamed. Ashamed and angry. Ashamed that she loved a man who could think so little of her and angry that she'd let him use her like the whore he thought she was.

"That's it, isn't it, Firebird? That's why you lured me into the tepee the minute I came back. You didn't want me to find out until you'd made me so crazy with desire that I wouldn't care!" he accused.

Starr stood up and glared into her husband's burning blue eyes, the gray fire in her own matching his, spark for spark. "Now, you look here, Daniel Blue Eagle. I didn't lure you anywhere, and you know it. You came of your own free will. As a matter of fact, you couldn't wait. You're the one who was insatiable! Not me! And as for the subject of Melanie and Dorcas, it just never came up. I didn't even think of them! If you think last night was because I was intentionally trying to keep something from you, then you're nothing but a—a—an ass!" she sputtered angrily, turning on her heel and stomping away from him with her head held high.

"An ass?" Daniel Blue Eagle growled, the realization of what she had said hitting him like a tornado. "Don't you walk away from me, Firebird," he ordered, standing his ground. "We're not through with this."

"I have an appointment with your father," she returned haughtily over her shoulder and continued to walk toward Man of the People's tepee. If she was going to be punished for the escape of Melanie and Dorcas, then she might as well make her crimes complete. "I'll talk to you later."

Remembering why he'd come for his wife, Daniel Blue Eagle hurried to catch up with her and walk beside her. He glanced down at her proud head, the determined expression on her face, and was attacked by a pang of regret.

Standing outside Man of the People's tepee, Starr waited. If the door had been open, she would have gone directly in, but since it was not, it was correct to announce herself. "It is Firebird, *Ate*," she called out, using the newly-learned Lakota language to the best of her ability.

"And Daniel Blue Eagle, Father," Starr's husband added.

"Enter, my children," Man of the People answered,

the welcome in his tone sending a strange feeling of surprise through Starr. She had expected him to sound angry.

Since it was correct for the man to enter the lodge first, Starr waited for her husband to step inside before she followed. As was the custom for guests, Daniel Blue Eagle stepped to the right of the doorway, Starr to the left, and they waited for Man of the People to ask them to sit.

She hadn't realized other people would be in the lodge with Man of the People, and was surprised to see eight. Her eyes flitted nervously over the stony faces gathered around the fire. It was obviously some sort of a council to decide her punishment, and she was stunned to see Gentle Fawn, Prairie Moon and Running Fox among them. She shot a questioning glance up to her husband, but Daniel Blue Eagle didn't seem to notice.

"Come, Firebird, you will sit beside me," Man of the People said in English, smiling as he patted a mat to his right. "You, my son, will sit here," he said in Lakota, indicating the seat to his left.

Not certain what the strange reception meant, Starr swallowed hard and moved to sit beside Man of the People at the rear of the tepee. Knowing it would be terribly rude for her to walk between the other guests and the fire, she walked behind them. They all, in turn, leaned forward to make room for her.

Confused, Starr took her seat beside her father-in-law. Since a proper Lakota woman would never sit cross-legged as her husband and the other men around the fire were doing, she sat on her heels.

Man of the People took special note of his daughter-in-law's perfect manners and smiled his pleasure to the others in the lodge, who had also noticed and were equally impressed.

"So, Firebird," Man of the People began, again speaking in English to make his daughter-in-law more at ease. "It would seem there was much excitement in our village while we were out killing the buffalo."

She looked uncertainly at her father-in-law, at Daniel Blue Eagle, then to Prairie Moon and Running Fox. But none of them gave any indication as to what she was supposed to do. She was evidently on her own. Was Man of the People's statement an invitation to speak or not?

"Yes, Father," she finally decided to say, looking down at the tightly clasped hands in her lap. At this point she had nothing to lose.

"We've already been told what happened, but we would like to hear the story in your words."

Starr raised her eyes hesitantly, and the first person she saw was Gentle Fawn. The hate in the black eyes that met hers was so obvious, so open, that it made Starr flinch involuntarily. There was no telling what the spiteful Indian girl had told them. And there was no doubt in Starr's mind who Man of the People and the other chiefs would believe.

Not trusting herself to say what she meant in Lakota, though she had developed a reasonable understanding of the language, Starr spoke in English. "When the traders came into the village, the other women rushed to meet them, but I didn't go because Prairie Moon told me they were bad. I stayed in my tepee, thinking to stay hidden until they left. But that night I was awakened by one of them in my lodge. He

249

said he had come for me. I told him I wasn't going, but his partner joined him and they insisted. I was very afraid, so I aimed my husband's revolver at them and made them leave. I followed them outside to be certain they left, and I was hit on the head and lost consciousness. The next thing I remember was awakening on the back of a donkey. I was bound and gagged. That's when the women and old men came for us."

Man of the People translated Starr's words for members of the council who did not understand, then turned back to the nervous girl. "Did you see who hit you?" he asked gently.

"No, I didn't," she answered, unable to bring herself to voice her suspicions about Gentle Fawn.

"But you think you know who it was, do you not?" he said.

Starr's head jerked up to look at him questioningly. "I think so," she finally said. "There is one in this village who resents me greatly, but I prefer not to say her name."

"That won't be necessary. We know who she is. My sister, Prairie Moon, was a witness to Gentle Fawn's part in your abduction," Man of the People assured her gently, patting her hand and turning his attention to the Indian girl whose mouth dropped open in surprise. "What do you have to say to this accusation, Gentle Fawn?" he asked in his native language.

"She lies," Gentle Fawn spat angrily at Prairie Moon. "That old woman has never liked me and would do anything to make me look bad."

Gentle Fawn's father laid his hand on his daughter's arm. "Do not make it worse for yourself, child," he warned, his voice rife with the disgrace and embarrassment caused by his youngest offspring.

"Father! You cannot believe an old woman over your own flesh and blood!"

"I have known Man of the People's sister, Prairie Moon, for many years, and have never known her to lie or to falsely accuse another of wrongdoing, Gentle Fawn. Perhaps if you confess your crimes, the chiefs will find it in their mercy to go more easily on you."

"What punishment do you think would be suitable for the woman who betrayed your wife, my son?" Man of the People asked Daniel Blue Eagle, who watched Gentle Fawn sadly. The deep hurt was very evident in his eyes.

He'd always liked the feisty young girl and had even entertained an idea that she might marry Gray Wolf one day. But now that would be impossible. Man of the People would never sanction a marriage of one of his sons to a woman who'd betrayed a member of his family. "I will defer to my wife's opinion on this," Daniel Blue Eagle said, then added lightly, "After all, she's the one who got the bump on the back of her head."

Everyone politely laughed, as all eyes turned back to Starr, who was looking at her husband with amazement. This council had been called to decide a punishment for Gentle Fawn, not for her! She couldn't believe it.

"It is very unusual, my son," Man of the People said, his stern expression not disguising the spark of understanding in his black eyes. "But it will be as you wish. Firebird, what do you believe should be done about Gentle Fawn?" he asked in English.

Starr studied the Indian girl, her angry face now that of a frightened young child, and she knew she could not live with herself if she sought vengeance against her.

"I think we should consider Gentle Fawn's age and understand that young people often do foolish things they later regret. I'm certain Gentle Fawn already regrets her actions, and I believe she should be forgiven."

Man of the People translated, and there was a collective gasp from the others around the fire.

"Perhaps if she had a husband of her own, she would have something to occupy her thoughts besides her dislike of me."

Man of the People studied his daughter-in-law's bowed head, and his respect for her grew. Not only had she stayed with them of her own free will, but now she was willing to forgive her enemy. His son had married quite a woman—not unlike another he had known so many years ago, he thought sadly. He relayed Starr's suggestion to the others and then added, "Is it agreed then? Gentle Fawn will choose a husband and marry soon."

There was a consenting murmur from those present.

"And if I fail to choose a husband?" Gentle Fawn asked tentatively, the last touch of rebellion exposing itself in her tone.

"Then your father will choose for you," Man of the People promised sternly, cleaning out his pipe to indicate that their meeting was at an end.

"Which shouldn't be too difficult," her father added as he prodded his daughter toward the tepee entrance. "With all the young men who've been coming to visit you for the last year, I'll just give you to the one who brings me the best gifts."

Starr and Daniel Blue Eagle started to rise, but Man of the People detained them. "Wait for a moment, my children."

They sat back down, both watching Man of the People curiously.

"Now, tell us, Firebird, why did you choose not to go with the white traders when they took the other two worthless ones?" Man of the People asked, already knowing the answer, but wanting the girl to tell Daniel Blue Eagle why she had stayed. He'd seen the way she looked at her husband, but he knew his son believed she had stayed behind for no other reason than fear of reprisal if she were caught.

Starr glanced at Daniel Blue Eagle who sat watching her with aloof indifference, the expression on his face impossible to read. How could she tell them the reason why she'd stayed, why she never wanted to leave? But how could she lie?

"I gave my word to Daniel Blue Eagle that I wouldn't try to leave while he was gone, my father."

"And that is the only reason?"

"What other reason could there be?"

"Perhaps the fact that you have grown to care for certain of the Oglalas more than you would admit," he suggested wisely.

"True, I wouldn't want to leave Prairie Moon without someone to take care of her, and the fact that I—I—" She looked out of the corner of her eye to see that Daniel Blue Eagle's posture had straightened and that he was watching her intently. But the look in his eyes was still disbelieving and cold.

"Yes? Go on," Man of the People encouraged. "What other reason besides Prairie Moon and your reluctance to go back on your word? The fact that you what?"

"The fact that I—I—I like it here," she confessed in a rush of words. "I've come to think of the People as my people, and of Prairie Moon and Man of the People as my family."

"And your husband? Do you not think of him as your family too?"

"Yes, Father, I do," she whispered, burning under Daniel Blue Eagle's stunned gaze. "I think of my husband as my family, though I'm certain he still thinks of me as a captive to be used for revenge on the white people."

"Is this true, my son? Is your wife nothing more to you than a hostage to be used against the whites?" Man of the People asked his son.

"No," Daniel Blue Eagle croaked, his voice barely audible.

"I'm sorry, I did not hear you," Man of the People said, the expression on his wise face innocent.

"I said no," Daniel Blue Eagle returned angrily. "I do not think of Firebird as a captive."

"Then how do you think of her? Do you think of her as part of your family as she does you?"

"Yes," Daniel Blue Eagle admitted after studying his wife's bowed head for long moments. Starr raised her gaze to meet her husband's intense blue eyes in amazement. He was no longer speaking to his father but directly to her. "I think of her as my family. She is my wife, a part of me, the fulfillment of my dream vision. She's the air I breathe. Without her I am not whole."

"On our wedding day, I too had a dream vision, my father," Starr said to Man of the People, though she continued to watch her husband. "And Daniel Blue Eagle is the embodiment of that dream," she whispered softly, admitting to herself for the first time that her wedding day dream had meant she would love Daniel Blue Eagle forever.

"Then why do you not tell each other these things, instead of telling them to an old man who has better things to do with his time?" Man of the People laughed and stood up to leave. "But be quick about it," he told the two who still gazed into each other's eyes trying to absorb the meaning of the words that had been exchanged. "If you're planning to repeat last night's disappearance, use your own lodge." With a satisfied chuckle, Man of the People left them alone.

Chapter Fifteen

The breakdown of the peace council at the Red Cloud Agency in September resulted in an end to all attempts by the Army to keep the prospectors out of the Black Hills, and by October of 1875 the gold rush was on again in full force. One newspaper reported that there were five men leaving for the Black Hills every minute.

Needing a scapegoat for the blatant robbery of the Indians' lands, the government looked for a way to break the Laramie Treaty of 1868 and blame the Sioux. They had been insulted when the Indians refused to sell to them and were determined to make them pay, one way or the other. They noted that the 1868 treaty called for the Sioux to be on the reservation and decided that the wild Indians of the unceded area around the Yellowstone and Powder Rivers were in violation—although those tribes, whose main wish was to be left alone, had not signed the Treaty and were not legally bound by it.

On December 6, 1875, the Commissioner of Indian

Affairs sent runners from all the Sioux agencies to notify the wild bands in the unceded area that they were to report to the reservation by January 31 or they would be considered hostiles and "treated accordingly by the military force."

But January 31, 1876 came and went, with no wild Sioux coming into the reservation. Chief Crazy Horse of the wild Oglala said it was too cold and the snow too deep to move his people, while Sitting Bull of the Hunkpapa told them he might come in the spring. Whether the Indians believed the government was serious or simply making another idle threat, it was obvious they had no intention of turning themselves in.

On February 7, the Secretary of the Interior brought the nontreaty Sioux to the attention of the Secretary of War and the Army.

That was all General Philip H. Sheridan needed. For years he had wanted a free hand to deal with the Sioux but had constantly been thwarted by peace movements and commissions. But this time would be different. Nothing would stop him now.

Starr was aware of the undercurrent of danger that controlled their lives, since her husband frequently told her what had occurred during his occasional trips to meet with the chiefs of other bands. Yet it all seemed so far removed from her that she couldn't really appreciate the seriousness of the situation. Not until late in March.

Starr awoke that morning with a smile on her face. She was too happy to worry about anything other than the expression on her husband's face when she gave him her wonderful news. Today was the day she would tell Daniel Blue Eagle that he was to be a father in the fall. She rolled over onto her back and absently ran her hand over her still-flat belly and pictured herself round with child, Daniel Blue Eagle's child. What would the baby be like? Boy or girl? Black hair or red? Blue eyes or gray? *Blue! Our baby must have his eyes. And strong. This baby will have to be very strong to face whatever lies ahead.* "But you don't need to worry about that, little one," she said to the babe in her womb. "Your mama and daddy are very strong, and you will be too," she promised.

Throwing back the heavy buffalo robe that had kept her warm during the night, Starr shuddered with the shock of the cold morning air as she had every morning during the cold winter. Yet, there was something different this morning. The air didn't seem so cold or so biting. Pulling a smaller robe around her shoulders, she walked over to the door flap and lifted it to peek out.

The sun was shining so brightly that she had to squint to see, but she was able to determine that the snow on the ground was melting and that it was warmer outside than it had been in months. A good sign that this would be a wonderful day.

Starr automatically glanced toward the tepee beside hers and smiled at the contented sound coming from within. As always, Prairie Moon and Running Fox, her husband of four months, snored in blissful unison. Thinking how glad she was the older couple had discovered each other the night the traders had tried to steal her from the camp, Starr's own happiness doubled. In fact, she decided, her life was perfect.

Prairie Moon and Running Fox were there, Daniel Blue Eagle was coming home today, and Starr was going to have a baby.

"It's almost too good to be true," she thought aloud, suddenly shaken by a chill of apprehension. Just then, however, a saving flash of red in the snow caught Starr's attention, and she rushed to see what it was that offered her a welcome diversion from the unexpected sense of foreboding.

"Oh, look," she said to herself "a flower! A tiny red flower," she sighed emotionally, eagerly squatting down to use her bare hands to brush away the snow that surrounded the harbinger of spring.

What a good sign for the day I'm to tell my husband of the sweet flower growing within me, she thought happily as she walked back to her tepee, glancing over her shoulder for one last, quick look at the brave flower that had fought all the odds to live in a world still cold and deadly with winter. *Just like the baby in me, that little flower survived where others less strong would have perished.*

It was colder outside than she had realized, and Starr hurried inside to add fuel to the fire in her lodge and to heat some water for a bath. Though it was still too cold to take a real bath, she was determined to cleanse herself since this would be such a special day. Daniel Blue Eagle had been gone three days, and she wanted to look and smell her very best when he returned. She would brush her hair down around her shoulders the way he liked it and would wear the new beaded dress and leggings she'd made herself for this occasion.

Uncovering and washing only a small part of her

259

body at a time, Starr managed to bathe before the water grew cold, and then slipped her new dress over her head. She smiled when she tied the leather strings at her waist, hiding the excess material in deep tucks she had included to make room for her soon-to-expand belly, making the large dress seem to fit her as any other dress did.

After carefully brushing her hair until it shone, Starr fingered the beaded design on the front of the dress, wondering if Daniel Blue Eagle would recognize its significance. She remembered how, with fingers stiff from the cold, she had painstakingly created a picture of a large blue eagle and a small white bird with a red head at the eagle's side.

Hours later, though her hands were busy stirring water into cornmeal, Starr watched the door impatiently. Why didn't he come? Why did he have to pick today to be later than expected? The apprehension that had plagued her intermittently through the day rose up to haunt her again.

Deliberately concentrating on the dough she'd kneaded too much already, she decided she would go ahead and cook the bread. Surely he would be there by the time it was done.

But long after the cornbread was cooked and cold again, hours after the liquid had boiled out of the tasty stew containing all of Daniel Blue Eagle's favorite things, and when the only light inside the lodge was the fire in the center, he still had not come.

Long after she should have given up her vigil, Starr sat watching the tepee door and waiting. She pulled the buffalo robe tighter around her, refusing to listen to her own terrible thoughts. *He's all right*, she

260

assured herself over and over again. He had to be. She was going to have his baby; she couldn't lose him now. She told herself he couldn't have been injured. Surely she would have known if he'd been hurt. She'd have felt his pain. Yes, she would have known.

It had to be something else that had kept him. Perhaps the Cheyenne village he was visiting on the Powder River was further away than he had anticipated. He might have been late getting away and decided to stay one more night. Yes, that was it. He would come the next day. Maybe in the morning. Why, he might even be there when she woke up.

Convincing herself that the time would go faster if she slept, Starr curled up in the buffalo robe and closed her eyes. But it was no use—she wasn't sleepy. Anxious, frightened, worried, yes. But not sleepy.

Think about names for the baby, she told herself sternly. But not one came to mind. *Plan what you must do to prepare for the baby*, she tried again. *I'll need a cradleboard and*—She couldn't think of anything else. It was useless. Here she was trying to plan for the future when all she could think of was that without Daniel Blue Eagle she had no future. She sat up and resumed her anxious watch, staring at the closed door flap.

Her head nodding helplessly on her chest, she finally closed her eyes just before dawn.

When Daniel Blue Eagle entered the lodge and saw his wife sleeping where she sat huddled at the rear of the tepee, a sad smile came to his weary face. Viewing the ruined dinner of the night before, he realized she must have sat up all night waiting for him, and he felt his heart contract cruelly. How would he ever tell her

261

what he had to tell her?

He stooped and gently laid Starr back on the sleeping mat, sliding down beside her and rearranging the buffalo robe over both of them, drawing her warm body against his chilled one.

"Daniel Blue Eagle," Starr mumbled groggily as she snuggled and shaped herself to her husband's contours. "I was worried about you."

"I know you were, sweet wife. I'm sorry I worried you,' but we'll talk about it later. I'm here now. Go back to sleep."

"But I have something to tell you," she insisted, now more alert.

"Not now, Firebird. I'm so tired, I just want to sleep. I know we have a great deal to talk about. But later, all right?" He pulled Starr against him and kissed the top of her head before he drifted off to sleep.

When he awoke several hours later, it was close to noon and Starr was cooking. Daniel Blue Eagle rolled over on his side and watched her, memorizing her every feature—the way she hummed a tuneless little melody when she worked, the way her hair gleamed in the sunlight when it was left unbraided as it was now. And he never tired of watching her test her recipes. She would dip a bit from the pot, blow on it three times to cool it and then sip it into her mouth. Then frowning in concentration, she would roll her eyes upward and make a funny little tasting noise with her lips as she decided what was missing. Often she would add a pinch of salt or some other herb and then repeat the whole process again, until she had the flavor just the way she wanted it.

"Firebird, come talk to me," Daniel Blue Eagle said softly, motioning to the spot beside him on the sleeping mat.

"Good morning, sleepyhead. I thought you were going to sleep all day," she answered, directing a radiant smile in his direction. "Are you hungry?"

"I will be, but first we must talk." The look in his eyes was serious. It sent a storm of fright through Starr's body.

"What could be more important than keeping your strength up?" she asked, busily stirring the stew in the iron pot before dipping some into a bowl for Daniel Blue Eagle. She stalled. Something told her she didn't want to hear what he was going to say. "We'll talk after you eat."

"Firebird, put down the bowl and come here," he ordered her softly. He knew what she was doing and wished he didn't have to tell her. "I'm afraid this can't wait."

"You sound so serious, Daniel Blue Eagle. I'm not sure I want to hear what you have to say," Starr said as she poured the stew back into the pot. She tried to keep her voice light and teasing. "Let me tell you my news first. It'll wipe that serious frown from your long face."

"We can't put it off any longer, Firebird. You have to listen to me," he said, holding his hand out to her.

She took his strong fingers in hers and allowed herself to be drawn down beside him. "But—"

"No *buts*, my talkative wife. I must speak and you must listen." He smiled but the sad grin on his face did nothing to ease Starr's misgivings.

"All right," she murmured, holding her breath for

263

whatever bad news he had brought her.

"You know I went to visit our friends the Cheyenne, who are camped along the Powder River. The day I was to leave their village, a troop of soliders attacked us."

He felt Starr stiffen in his arms at his words and patted her reassuringly before going on. "At first we saw that we had them outnumbered and fought against the first company who rode in on horseback. But after a while other companies of soldiers approached from another direction and began shooting at us. We had to abandon the village and retreat into the trees along the river and the hills."

"Oh, Daniel, are you all right? Were you hurt?" Starr asked, sitting up straight and looking anxiously for any injuries. When she was convinced he was unharmed, she asked, "Were many of your Cheyenne friends killed?"

"I'm fine," he promised, taking her hands in his and kissing them as he held her in his arms. "Not as many of the Cheyenne were killed as could have been. Since the commanding officer didn't have his men surround the village before attacking, we were able to get away. Once we had escaped, the Army looted the village, evidently planning to use all the food for their own men. But the Cheyenne weren't ready to give up yet and began to attack the looters from a high position above them. Evidently the officer realized he couldn't load up the supplies and fight at the same time, so he had his men fire the entire village. All their lodges, buffalo robes and food were destroyed, leaving the entire tribe homeless and without food to keep them alive until spring. They managed to retrieve their ponies from the Army, but they lost everything else."

"What will become of them?"

"Most of them headed toward Crazy Horse's camp, three days north of where they were. I brought some with me. The sad thing is that they were peaceful and had every right to be where they were. The Cheyenne aren't even under orders to go to the reservation. When asked why they'd been attacked, one soldier who was taken alive told them that Colonel Reynolds had thought theirs was the village of Crazy Horse. Before the Cheyenne killed him, he told them that the Army's plan is to conduct a series of surprise attacks throughout the unceded lands. They'll attack and destroy Sioux villages one at a time during the winter when we are camped in small bands and aren't expecting them. They've decided the way to destroy us is with more 'victories' like the massacres at Ash Hollow, Sand Creek, Washita, and the Tongue River, where everyone, not only warriors, was killed.

"What will happen, Daniel Blue Eagle?" Starr asked apprehensively. She could almost anticipate his next words, and as much as she didn't want to hear the answer, she had to ask.

"The People, especially the Oglala and the Hunkpapas, will be outraged. All we wanted was to be left alone to hunt and live on our lands without the whites destroying everything that was dear to us. We're caught in a vice. The miners come from the east and west and the south. Do you realize that at one time the Sioux roamed this country from the Arkansas River to Canada, and that all we've been left with is the reservation and our hunting land in the Montana Territory? Now they want to steal that from us, too. With the soldiers being sent to kill us, there is no choice but to fight back. Gray Wolf was right all along. It is war, Firebird," Daniel Blue Eagle groaned, pounding his fist angrily on the ground. "There is nothing to stop it now."

"What will we do, Daniel?" Starr asked, laying her head against his chest and wrapping her arms tightly around him. The soldiers could be out there right now, waiting to attack and plunder this very village. "Will we go back to the reservation?"

"I will take you back to your own people, Firebird, and then I will meet my father and the People at the camp of Crazy Horse near the mouth of the Powder River."

Starr sat up and looked at her husband, startled, hurt and angry. She had never considered that he wouldn't want to keep her with him. "But the Oglala are my people, Daniel. I belong here with them, with you. You can't send me back. There's nothing for me back there."

"You will be safe there, Firebird. You must go."

"What of the other women? What of Prairie Moon? Are they going back, too?"

"Firebird, don't. You're making it harder than it has to be."

"Well, that's just too damned bad. You're not going to get rid of me that easily, Daniel Blue Eagle. I don't want to go! Haven't I proven to you by now that I'm as much Oglala in my heart as you are in yours?"

"Yes, you have, Firebird, over and over again," he smiled, brushing his dark fingers over the tears trailing down her face. "But now you must go back to your own people and be one of them again."

"Don't do this to me, Daniel Blue Eagle. Don't condemn me to a life like your mother's. She didn't want to go back, and look what it did to her. It killed her. She died of a broken heart, Daniel! Please don't send me. Let me stay. I'm your wife."

"I'll release you from our marriage, Firebird. Go back to Yankton and make a different life for yourself," he said softly. "I won't have time to worry about you once the war actually starts."

Starr stared incredulously at Daniel Blue Eagle's stony face. *I'll release you from our marriage*, he'd said, just as easily as he had told her he didn't want to eat a few minutes before. Was that all she had meant to him?

That's all she'd been, someone to see to his comforts! Now she was going to be in his way, so he was prepared to throw her away. Why not? She would be easy to replace with the next willing female. Well, if he could cast her aside that easily, she wouldn't fight him.

"When do we leave?" Starr asked Daniel Blue Eagle, gathering her last bit of pride and walking over to the fire to stir her stew. She dished a portion into her bowl and sat down to spoon it methodically into her mouth.

"We leave in the morning," he answered, studying her a moment longer where she sat across the tepee from him. "Do I get something to eat?"

"Get it yourself. Since you no longer have a wife, you may as well get used to taking care of yourself. I'm not going to do it any more. I'm only going to worry about me."

Daniel Blue Eagle smiled at the angry fire in her eyes. Had there ever been another like her? How he wanted to go to her and take her in his arms to kiss away the hurt and anger. He wanted to tell her that he would come for her as soon as he could, but how could he? The chances were that he would be killed in the next few months. He couldn't leave her with any hope that they'd ever see each other again. It would only make it harder for them to part. No, it was better to make the break a clean one that would enable her to go back and marry a man of her own kind—something he knew she'd never do if she felt herself still married to him. And there was no longer any doubt in Daniel Blue Eagle's mind that she considered herself his wife.

"I suppose you're right," he said, serving himself and sitting down to eat his meal as silently as Starr was eating hers.

Long after Daniel Blue Eagle had finished eating and had left the tepee, Starr sat unmoving in the same spot, staring at nothing in particular. Where would she go? What would become of her and her baby? Could she possibly face a life without Daniel Blue Eagle in it? What had she done wrong? She'd been so sure he had loved her. But if he had, how could he send her away?

That's it! She told herself, jumping up excitedly. *He's sending me away because he loves me. He wants to protect me!*

"Then why didn't he say that instead of saying I'd just be in his way?" she asked herself aloud.

What if I'd told him about the baby? What would

268

he have done then?

"He'd have just been angry that I would try to use an innocent baby to hold him to a marriage he obviously wants out of!"

Or if he really does love me, he'd have been even more adamant about getting me to safety, she told herself hopefully.

"Don't be a fool, Starr Winfield!" she scolded herself angrily. "Face it, he's tired of you, and that's the pure and simple truth of the whole matter!"

It was hard to believe that two people who always had so much to say to one another could travel across the prairie for two days without speaking, but that was what Starr and Daniel Blue Eagle did. Mile after mile they rode in silence, lost in their own private thoughts.

At least a hundred times one or the other of them would have turned the horses around and headed back to the Indian village they had left behind. But of course neither of them could do that. Daniel Blue Eagle had to see his wife to safety, even though it meant making her hate him, and Starr had begged for the last time. She refused to do so again. So they rode on toward Fort Abraham Lincoln at Bismarck, the silence between them deafening.

Starr spent a great deal of her time planning what she and her baby would do. Of course, marrying again, as Daniel Blue Eagle had suggested, would be out of the question. No matter what he did or how he felt about her, in her mind she would always be his wife.

Though she fought it at first, she had finally decided to accept some of the money Daniel Blue Eagle had pressed on her. After all, she had more than just herself to think of now. She had a baby to care for. She would use the money to go East. New York, or maybe Boston. She might even consider Chicago, since it was only about ten days by rail from Bismarck. Anywhere would be all right, as long as it was a place where no one would know her or what had happened to her. Any city where she could get lost would do.

Claiming to be a soldier's widow left alone in the world to raise the young child she carried, she ought to be able to make a decent life for herself and her baby. At least, no one in a strange new place would know that her baby was part Sioux, and her child would be spared the hurtful stigma of being called a half-breed. The baby would probably have light skin and eyes, so it was doubtful that anyone would question her story.

A pang of regret rocked Starr at the thought of denying her child knowledge of his Indian heritage, but she didn't know how else to protect the baby's future. If it was known that her child was a quarter Sioux Indian, that his mother had been married to an Indian, both mother and child would be outcasts. As for herself, it didn't matter, but she couldn't do that to the tiny being growing in her womb. It would be hardship enough for it to grow up without knowing his father.

Once the baby was born she might find a job teaching school. She could even hire an attorney to see about claiming her own inheritance and using those monies that her parents might have left her to open her own school. A small school for refined young ladies would be nice.

Starr pulled her buffalo robe tighter. Was it her imagination or was the weather growing colder? She suddenly realized that the wind had picked up, its biting gusts now coming from the northeast to cut through all the warm clothing she wore and chill her painfully. She buried her nose and chin in her robe and hugged herself in a futile attempt to get warm.

"It's going to snow," Daniel Blue Eagle said, calling her attention to the gray sky. "We'd better make camp."

"Here?" Starr asked, looking around at the flat terrain which could not even boast one tree for shelter.

Daniel Blue Eagle didn't bother to answer her, dismounting instead quickly to construct a small shelter with sticks and hides he'd brought on a spare pony from the village. When the *wickiup* was finished, it was just barely big enough for the two of them, and Starr hesitated before she entered it, not trusting herself to be in such a confined space with Daniel Blue Eagle.

It was then the first snowflakes touched her face, and she reluctantly crawled through the small doorway to escape from the cold.

The temperature inside the hastily built structure was amazingly comfortable. Getting in out of the wind had made an immediate difference. "What about the ponies?" she asked, straining for something to say that would ease the tension between herself and the man who shared the tiny space with her.

"They'll just turn their backs to the wind and wait

271

out the storm," Daniel Blue Eagle said easily, not seeming the least bothered by or concerned about their proximity.

For some reason, that made Starr angrier than ever. If it weren't for his decision to take her to Fort Lincoln, they'd both be back in their own tepee with a fire to keep them warm, instead of here. How could he act as if none of this bothered him? How could he sit there chewing *pemmican* as if he were not freezing to death?

"You better eat," he said, holding *pemmican* out to her.

"I'm not hungry," she lied.

"Suit yourself, but you won't be as cold if you eat."

Begrudgingly taking the food, Starr said, "Thank you."

"You're welcome," he returned, the amused grin on his face belying the fact that his heart was breaking.

"When will we reach Fort Lincoln?"

"Maybe tomorrow afternoon if the snowstorm doesn't last too long."

"I see. Will you go into the fort with me?"

"I don't think so. I'll watch until you're safely inside, and then I must return to my people."

Your people, my people. What happened to our people, Daniel Blue Eagle? What happened to the man who said I was a gift to him from the Great Spirit? The man who told his father I was the very air he breathed? How could you have changed so much? What did I do to make you not want me anymore?

"Are you cold?" Daniel Blue Eagle asked, noticing

272

that Starr's fingers and lips were blue.

"No, I'm fine," she shivered, her body giving lie to her words.

"Come here and we'll keep each other warm," he smiled, opening his buffalo robe so she could come into his arms.

God, how she wanted to fling herself into those arms! How she wanted to be wrapped in their security forever and ever. She wanted to hold on to him and never let go. She wanted to beg him one more time not to send her back, but she didn't. It would be useless. She knew what his answer would be. He wasn't going to change his mind.

"I'm not cold," she said stubbornly, drawing her knees up to her chest and hugging her buffalo robe closer around her.

"But I am, and the best way to keep warm is lying with another human body," he said, edging close to her and pulling her into his robe with him, despite her feeble protests. "Now, isn't that better?"

"I suppose it is," she had to admit, allowing herself the luxury of snuggling her nose into the curve of his neck to smell the intoxicating smell of him one last time.

Chapter Sixteen

"Listen," Daniel Blue Eagle whispered as he cocked his ear.

Starr did her best to hear what he was listening for. "What is it?"

"Horses," he growled, hurriedly crawling out of the *wickiup.* If it hadn't been for the wind, he would have detected the sound of the approaching hoofbeats sooner. As it was, there was not even time to mount up and ride away. He could already see a company of soldiers approaching them.

They were on the reservation, so there shouldn't be anything to fear, but a dark premonition seized Daniel Blue Eagle. "Stay inside and be quiet," he ordered Starr, walking toward the white soldiers who had just arrived at their campsite.

"What are you doing out here by yourself?" a young lieutenant asked him.

"I was waiting for the snow to stop," Daniel Blue Eagle explained truthfully.

"Where is the rest of your tribe?"

"They're east of here. I was on my way to their village when the snowstorm hit."

"There ain't no Injun villages east o' here, Lieutenant!" a gruff master sergeant informed the officer. "Who's in that there *wickiup*? You wasn't ridin' all three o' them ponies by yerself, was ya?"

Daniel Blue Eagle knew he should just give his wife to the soldiers and ride back to his own village. But he didn't trust them. Until he saw with his own eyes that she was safely inside the fort, he couldn't leave her.

"Private Higgins, go see who's in there!" the lieutenant ordered a young man, who responded immediately by hopping off his mount and hurrying toward the little shelter.

"That won't be necessary, Lieutenant," Starr said evenly as she stepped outside.

"I'll be gawdamned!" the master sergeant swore. "He's got him a captive white woman! Take him, men!"

"Wait a minute," Starr protested, moving alongside Daniel Blue Eagle. "This man isn't my captor. He was taking me to Fort Abraham Lincoln."

The lieutenant studied her as he removed a glove and pulled a folded poster out of his coat. He examined the poster and then looked from Starr to Daniel Blue Eagle and back down at the poster again. "Do you deny that you are Starr Winfield who was abducted from a church in Yankton last summer by a band of Sioux renegades?"

"No, I don't deny that. It's just that this man isn't—"

"I beg yer pardon, ma'am," the master sergeant

interrupted, offering her his copy of the same poster for examination. "There's his picture," he said, pointing to a sketch that looked remarkably like Daniel Blue Eagle. "Right there alongside yers."

"I don't understand where you got this picture, but he isn't the Indian who took me! It was—"

"I was the one, Lieutenant," Daniel Blue Eagle confessed, deliberately cutting off Starr's words before she could disclose the name of Gray Wolf.

Starr's head jerked around to protest Daniel Blue Eagle's words, but the look he shot her said that if she revealed the name of his brother he would not rest until he'd had his revenge on her.

"Tie his hands, and let's get him back to the fort. The captain's going to be very pleased," the lieutenant said to his men.

The trip to Fort Abraham Lincoln seemed an eternity to Starr. Not only was she cold, colder than she'd ever been in her whole life, but the chill shaking her body went far beyond cold weather. Seeing Daniel Blue Eagle bound and treated like a criminal was more than she could bear.

Several times she had attempted to drop back and speak to him; but she'd been thwarted every time, either by the armed men riding all around him, or by Lieutenant Hildegard who had kept up a steady conversation of cheerful small talk since they'd first mounted the horses and headed northeast toward the fort.

She wanted to tell Daniel Blue Eagle that once they reached the fort, she would convince the authorities that he was not the guilty party without revealing Gray Wolf's identity. The one thing she couldn't understand was how Daniel Blue Eagle's likeness and description, right down to his blue eyes and name, had gotten on that Wanted poster. Had he been taking part in illegal activities of some sort that she was unaware of? Of course, that was a possibility. He'd often been gone from the village in the months they'd been together. But he had always discussed his activities with her when he had returned. No, she refused to believe he was a criminal. There had to be another answer. If she could just talk to him, make him understand that she would find a way to gain his freedom without implicating Gray Wolf in the process.

"Miss Winfield, did you hear me?" Lieutenant Hildegard laughed politely.

"I'm sorry, Lieutenant. My mind was somewhere else. What is it you were saying?"

"I was saying, I imagine you'll be glad to get out of those animal skins and back into clothing fit for a civilized person."

"Actually, these 'animal skins', as you call them, are quite comfortable," she returned angrily, deciding to put an end to his incessant jabbering. "As a matter of fact, there are many things about the Indian way of life that I prefer to those of the white world. The clothing is just one."

"I see," Lieutenant Hildegard said with an indignant cough.

"I don't think you do, Lieutenant. For one thing, I prefer the Indian custom of keeping silent unless there is something important to say."

"I don't think you're being fair, Miss Winfield," he protested. "I was only trying to make this miserable

277

journey a little more pleasant for you."

"Well, you haven't," she said crossly, her blunt retort bringing a look of surprise to the young officer's handsome features. "And as for being fair, you are the guilty party on that account too. I tried to explain that Daniel Blue Eagle saved me from the renegades and was in the process of taking me back to the fort, yet you persist in tying him up and treating him like a captive. Don't talk to me about fair, sir!"

Lord, that felt good. It may not have changed anything, but it certainly was a relief to say what was on her mind, and it had shut the lieutenant up for a minute.

She glanced back over her shoulder at her husband, who silently rode between two soldiers, his stoic posture and expression giving her no clue to what he was thinking. If only they would untie his hands.

"But the likeness on the poster—"

"Hang the likeness. I'm telling you he's innocent!"

"That's for someone else to decide."

"Who, Lieutenant Hildegard? The Army? The very same men who believe the only good Indian is a dead Indian? The men who've sworn to kill every Indian on the Plains? Please let him go, Lieutenant. If you take him to the fort, he won't stand a chance. As far as they're concerned, he's already guilty because he's an Indian."

"Your loyalty is commendable, Miss Winfield, but I can see we have nothing further to discuss." The lieutenant smiled sympathetically and spurred his horse ahead of Starr's.

She glanced back at Daniel Blue Eagle again, her expression heartbreakingly helpless. He wouldn't even look at her. He hadn't even seemed to notice her looking in his direction.

However, the forlorn look on Starr's face had not escaped the sharp eyes of her husband; and it was all he could do to continue looking straight ahead, keeping his own expression blank. He couldn't let the soldiers know that he cared about the woman they'd 'rescued', since they might decide to use her to get information from him. He'd already seen the way the enlisted men were watching her, and now that the lieutenant seemed to have lost interest, one of the others might use any excuse to take her against her will.

So, the rest of the way to Fort Lincoln, when she thought no one was looking, Starr directed her frightened, imploring looks at Daniel Blue Eagle time and time again. But each time she turned to him, he tightened his fists and clenched his teeth with determination, refusing to acknowledge her need, resisting the temptation to lock his gaze with hers to tell her without words how he felt about her, that he understood her fear was for him and not herself.

When they arrived at the sprawling Army post just below Bismarck on the west bank of the Missouri River, Lieutenant Hildegard took Starr directly to the camp headquarters. Unconcerned with the way the soldiers and scouts who lounged around the huge fort stared at his companion, he left her waiting outside the rough-hewn log building while he went to report to the commanding officer.

Bundled up as she was, no one could know that she was white, and as soon as the lieutenant disappeared through the door she became the brunt of more than

279

a few ribald comments. But the rude words didn't bother her. She didn't hear them, for she was too shaken by being forced to watch Daniel Blue Eagle dragged from his horse and thrown into the stockade by soldiers who kicked and beat him as he was taken away. And then, just as he had been about to be removed from her sight, he finally looked at her for a brief moment, no longer able to hide his feelings.

"Miss Winfield, the captain's ready to see you," Master Sergeant Kirby announced, bringing Starr's attention back to the hefty non-commissioned officer's presence.

"Yes," she said acidly, ignoring his hand and dismounting from her pony without assistance. "I'm ready to see him too. Is he the commanding officer? I don't intend to waste my time with any more junior officers."

"He's the acting commander, Miss Winfield. Colonel George Custer is in Washington, D.C.," the man explained, amazed that a woman who'd been captured and abused by the Indians for the better part of a year could still display such fire and determination.

"Then take me to him, Sergeant. The sooner I speak with him, the sooner this will be straightened out," she said, walking up the porch steps and through the door into the office without waiting for him.

"This way, Miss Winfield," Lieutenant Hildegard said, standing in an open doorway that led into an office off to the side. Behind him, she could see a blue-coated officer with his back to her.

Starr swept proudly past the young lieutenant, carrying herself with unyielding determination.

"Thank you, Lieutenant," she smiled coolly, completely undeterred from her mission by her deer- and buffalo-skin clothing and rawhide moccasins. "Captain, there has been a grave error," she began quickly, compelling the man in the office to turn around and look at her.

"That will be all, Lieutenant," the captain said softly, his voice a gravelly mix of emotion. "Close the door, please."

Not bothering to wait until the lieutenant could no longer hear her, Starr spoke. "Captain, there has been a terrible mistake. You must free—"

"Miss Winfield," the captain said, slowly turning to face her.

Starr stopped speaking in mid-sentence, her mouth hanging open. "William!"

"Welcome back to civilization, Starr."

"Is it really you? I—I thought you were—were dead," she stammered, knowing she should be so happy to find him alive that she would automatically run to him and embrace him. Instead, she stayed rooted to the spot, staring incredulously at the handsome blond officer she had once thought she loved.

"And I you—until recently," William answered stiffly, though the smile on his face seemed natural, exactly as Starr remembered it.

Suddenly, panic rose in Starr's throat. Her first impulse was to turn away and run out of the room. Her husband was alive and she had married another man, if not legally, at least in her heart. She was going to have Daniel Blue Eagle's baby.

Starr was certain she was going to be sick. It was so hot. She was desperate to get out of the stifling, stove-

281

heated room, before she fainted, but she couldn't leave. Her feet wouldn't move. "I must sit down," she apologized, looking around helplessly for a chair.

"I can understand that this takes some getting used to," William said, holding a chair behind the stunned girl, noticing that her breathing was coming faster and faster. "I shouldn't have done it this way. I should have had Lieutenant Hildegard prepare you," he apologized.

William knew he should touch her, embrace her, but somehow he couldn't bring himself to do that—not while she was dressed in those clothes, not when her hair was in braids like an Indian squaw.

"What happened, William?" Starr finally asked. "I saw you shot down along with the others. How did you escape? Is there anyone else? What about my parents? Is either of them alive?" she asked hopefully.

William shook his head sadly, finally gathering the stomach to take her hand in his. He patted the rough skin, trying to ignore the calluses on her once-soft palms and the broken and chipped nails at the ends of her long fingers. "I was the only one. The others perished in the fire."

Starr nodded her head with resignation. For a brief moment she had allowed herself to believe that by some miracle they were all alive, that none of this had happened, that somehow it was part of a bizarre nightmare. "I see."

"But you're not alone, Starr." William said solemnly. "You still have me. I will take care of you, no matter what has happened in the past."

"Oh, my God," Starr groaned, hugging her middle

as she remembered the tiny baby growing in her belly and his father, Daniel Blue Eagle, who at that very moment might by lying unconscious in a cold cell. The realization that legally she was married to one man, yet carried another's child, hit her with the force of a kick in the stomach, and everything before her blurred. The combination of shock and the heat in the small room became too much for Starr, and she pitched forward to the floor, escaping into the blessed oblivion of unconsciousness.

Later, when she awoke, Starr looked around the semi-darkness at her strange surroundings, unable to understand where she was. Not really caring in that moment when she hung suspended between the worlds of sleep and wakefulness, she closed her eyes again and tried to go back to sleep. It was so warm that she reached down to throw off her cover. But instead of the expected buffalo fur robe, her hand come in contact with a smooth muslin sheet.

As though she had been seriously burned, Starr jerked her hand away from the strange-feeling sheet and sat straight up in bed to look around. She was in a room, evidently a bedroom—not a tepee, but a room in a house. She realized she was in the middle of a soft, canopied bed, surrounded by pillows and warm quilts. How had she gotten here? Glancing nervously down at herself, she saw that she was no longer wearing deerskin but was clothed in a long-sleeved, white flannel gown.

"Are you feeling better?" a petite dark-haired woman asked shyly as she rose from her seat in the corner of the room and came toward Starr.

"Who are you? Where am I?"

"I'm Emily Thacker. My husband is a captain with the Seventh Cavalry. You're in Captain Howard's quarters, dear. I understand he's already sent for the chaplain to finish your wedding ceremony," the woman chatted nervously. What did one say to a young woman who'd spent all those months living with the Indians, having who knows what tortures and degradations heaped on her? Who knew how many of the filthy savages had had their way with her, how many diseases she had caught from them? "Just awful, the way the minister was killed before he could pronounce you man and wife!" Emily chattered nervously, shaking her head sympathetically, though she was unable to hide the look of revulsion she felt at being in the same room with the young woman.

"Did you say we're going to finish the wedding ceremony? Does that mean that William and I aren't already married?" Starr asked, not bothering to hide the excitement in her voice.

However, Emily took Starr's elation for agitation and hurried to calm her. "You are so fortunate that after all that has happened, Captain Howard still wants you for his bride. There aren't many men who would take you back."

"Yes, I'm very fortunate," Starr agreed, but for different reasons. She tossed off the covers and threw her feet off the bed to stand on shaky legs. Grabbing the bedpost for support, she said, "Mrs. Thacker, I must see William immediately. Where is he?"

"I'll get him for you," the young woman eagerly offered, thankful for an excuse to get out of the room.

Why Captain Howard still wanted to marry this woman was beyond Emily's understanding. The girl had a strange, wild look in her eyes. Oh, she was attractive, all right, and once her hair was washed, there was no doubt she would be quite lovely, but still—those crazed gray eyes. It was as though she'd crossed over the line between civilized and savage, as if she was now more Indian than white.

In a few minutes, William entered the room to find Starr searching the drawers of the wardrobe for other clothing. "What is it, my dear?" he asked suspiciously.

"Is it true that we aren't married?" she asked over her shoulder before going back to the clothing she recognized as that which she'd sent on ahead before the wedding. "And that you're willing to go through with it after all that has transpired?"

"It's the least I can do, Starr—after all you've suffered," he said nobly, as if expecting her gratitude.

"But I can't let you do that, William."

"What?" The smile on his lips tightened, his expression one of surprise.

"Your career is too important to you. The scandal will be horrendous. It's asking too much to expect you to accept a damaged bride," she insisted. "No, I will go away to spare you the disgrace."

"But I still want to marry you. Hang the disgrace."

"It is truly good and noble of you to say that, so can I be less noble than you? I can't allow you to make such a sacrifice. And while I'm on the subject of nobility and sacrifice, the Indian brave they brought in with me is innocent. He rescued me from the renegades and was bringing me here when we met with the soldiers. You

285

will release him, won't you? I would feel terribly guilty if an innocent man were punished for a kindness to me."

"We'll straighten all that out after our wedding, Starr," William said calmly. "Now, get dressed—I think you'll find everything you need in there," he said indicating the wardrobe. "The chaplain is already waiting in the parlor. Do you want Mrs. Thacker to help you dress?"

"William, didn't you hear what I said? We can't marry now. I'm not the innocent, untouched bride you deserve. I've known another man!" she admitted aloud, thinking to shock him out of his ridiculous obsession with marrying her.

"You will not speak of that again. We will both forget it ever happened. I still want you for my wife."

"William, you can't mean it!" she cried out. "What will people think?"

"What will they think if I turn my back on you, Starr? So, unless you want the Indian's life on your conscience, you will be bathed and dressed in thirty minutes and prepared to say your vows to me."

"You'll release him if I do it?"

"Of course I will, love. If you say he's innocent, then I will believe you," he said agreeably. "Just as soon as we are truly man and wife," he added.

"I'll get dressed, William," Starr conceded. William left the room.

At least Daniel Blue Eagle would be safe, and this way her baby would have a father—if she could convince William that the baby was his and three months early. *It's crazy. He'll never believe it. And if the baby has dark hair, what will I do then*?

"You'll just have to worry about that when the time comes Star Winfield!" *Right now, the only thing that* matters is Daniel Blue Eagle's freedom. Nothing else!

With her thick hair still damp from a vigorous shampooing, Starr stepped into the parlor exactly thirty minutes later. Her appearance matched her mood, a fact that did not go unnoticed by William Howard. Having parted her hair severely in the middle and twisted it into a bun at the nape of her neck, she wore a somber gray wool dress and high-heeled boots—hardly the attire for a happy bride.

Refusing to let her disgrace him even further than she already had by letting everyone in the room know how hesitant she was to marry him, William fixed a smile on his mouth and hurried forward to greet her, placing a kiss on her dry lips. "Here's the lovely woman I am to marry," he said for all to hear, adding for Starr's ears alone, "Smile, Starr, if you want that Indian to be freed."

Starr smiled at William, as if he'd pulled the string controlling the muscles of her face. Of course, that was exactly what had happened. William held the strings, and she had no choice but to act as his puppet, obeying his every command as long as Daniel Blue Eagle was his prisoner. There was nothing she wouldn't do to gain his freedom—even if it meant smiling and playing the part of the happy bride when her heart was breaking.

"Chaplain Conners, allow me to introduce my lovely bride, Miss Starr Winfield, soon to be Mrs. Captain William Howard," William said with a proprietary hold on Starr's shoulders as he turned to face the others. "And of course you've met Mrs. Thacker and Lieutenant Hildegard. This is Captain Thacker, and my aide and his wife, Lieutenant and Mrs. Ross Waters."

William indicated each person in turn, and Starr smiled and dutifully nodded her head at each one. As long as she didn't have to talk to them, she could manage the smiling.

The ceremony was over quickly, and William brought out a bottle of brandy. There was a hurried toast to the bride and groom, and the guests left almost immediately afterwards, finding it admirable—if not downright saintly—that William was so concerned that his beautiful wife who'd gone through such an ordeal might get overly tired and become ill.

Once the last guest had departed, Starr dropped her act of happy bride and turned to William, who was already pouring himself another generous glass of brandy. "What about the Indian, Daniel Blue Eagle?" she said, trying to make her voice casual, but knowing she was failing completely. She shouldn't have appeared so anxious.

"Oh yes, the Indian," William laughed, as though at some cruel joke only he was privy to. "Let's go take care of that little matter right now. Then I will have my darling bride's undivided attention," he suggested, downing his brandy and pouring still another. "Get your cape."

"You don't need me to go, do you?" Starr wanted desperately to see Daniel Blue Eagle one last time, to be certain he was all right if nothing else, but she couldn't bear the thought of the look in his eyes if he saw her with William.

"Of course I need you. After all, you are the one who pleaded his case so eloquently. It is only right that you should be there when I tell him the news."

"I really don't feel well, William. Can't you go alone?"

"Oh, my dear, I didn't realize," he apologized. His voice sounded sincere enough, but something in the way he was watching her sent a shudder of apprehension through Starr. "The Indian can wait until tomorrow," he said, "or whenever you're feeling better."

"I'll get my cape," Starr said with resignation.

"Are you certain you're up to it?" he asked solicitously, the expression in his cold eyes sending another shiver rippling along her spine.

"I'm fine, William. The sooner he's off my conscience, the sooner I will be able to concentrate on my life as the wife of an U.S. Army officer," she promised, offering him a strained smile.

Minutes later, with his new wife on his arm, Captain William Howard entered the stockade area. "I'm here to question the Indian brought in today, Private," he said to the young man on duty, who looked at Starr with a puzzled expression on his face. No one took a lady into this area, and certainly not when a prisoner was being questioned. Sensing the private's confusion, William hurried to explain. "My wife is needed to make a positive identification."

"Yes sir!" The soldier saluted, nervous that the captain had caught him questioning an order. "He's in the first cell on the right," the eager guard told them, taking a ring of keys off a nail by the door and handing them to William. "That one opens the cell doors."

"Thank you, Private Barton," William said, returning the guard's salute and walking toward the door of the cell block.

As soon as he opened the first heavy door, Starr immediately dropped her hand from his arm, but William grabbed it and replaced it in the bend of his elbow, with a satisfied smile of victory on his face. "Come, come, Starr, you wouldn't want me to change my mind about releasing the Indian, would you?"

"No," she admitted, her voice hardly more than a weak whisper.

"I didn't think so," William said, but Starr didn't notice the bitterness in his tone. She was too intent on where they where going. They stopped outside a door of iron bars and looked in.

No matter how she had schooled herself not to react to whatever she might see in the cell, she couldn't have been prepared for the sight before her eyes, and she couldn't suppress the tortured groan that leapt unbidden from her throat.

Daniel Blue Eagle was chained like a wild animal to the stone wall of the cell and appeared to be only half-conscious. At the sound of Starr's groan, he raised his head to look at them with his one good eye. The other was swollen shut, and blood streamed from his nose.

He looked at her for a long moment, studied her hand on William's arm, and then directed his hate-filled gaze directly into her eyes, cutting the remainder of her broken heart to shreds.

Chapter Seventeen

"What have they done to him?" Starr shrieked, rushing forward and pressing her face to the bars of Daniel Blue Eagle's cell. "I told you he wasn't the one who kidnapped me!"

"So you did, my sweet," William answered silkily as he approached her side and slipped a hand around her waist to pull her against him. "But kidnapping is only one of the crimes he's accused of." He spoke as if talking to a child.

"What crimes? He's committed no crimes! I would have known!" She turned to William and beat on his chest. "You said you would release him if I married you!"

William glanced at Daniel Blue Eagle who was watching the drama outside his cell with a puzzled expression distorting his beaten face even more. "Such concern over a savage who means nothing to you, my dear? Or is it that this uneducated heathen is more to you than just the man who supposedly saved you from the renegades?" The smile on his face was cold, challenging, knowing.

Starr's head jerked around to see Daniel Blue Eagle, chained and helpless, and then back at William, smiling and pleased with himself. If she denied she cared for Daniel Blue Eagle, the man she loved would believe her words too, yet if she admitted how important Daniel Blue Eagle was to her, William would never let him free. "What do you mean?"

"No need to be coy, my love," William said, snaking his hand under her cape to squeeze a firm breast, taking obvious pleasure in the wince of jealousy that twisted the savage's face. "This man stole what was rightfully mine, and he will die for it."

Shrinking from the cruel touch on her breast, Starr tried to back away from William, but found her way blocked by his other hand on her shoulders. "I told you he isn't the one who took me from the church," she protested weakly, unable to bear the hurt and rage on Daniel Blue Eagle's battered face.

"I'm not talking about that, Starr," William laughed cruelly as he jerked her cape off her shoulders and stepped behind her to wrap his arms around her and cup both of her breasts painfully in his hands. "I'm referring to these!" He lifted upward on the lush mounds and laughed. "How many times has he touched them, tasted them?" he asked bitterly.

A wild animal growl tore from Daniel Blue Eagle's throat as he strained against the manacles and chains until they cut into his wrists.

"Now we will leave your Indian lover to his own last thoughts while you and I go and consummate our wedding vows." He turned to Daniel Blue Eagle, who continued to struggle, and laughed viciously. "Do you

292

know what *consummate* means, savage? It means I'm going to bed her over and over again. It means I can do whatever I want with her because she is *my* wife!. By tomorrow morning, she will be so sated that you will only be an unpleasant memory to her. Come, my wife," he added, with emphasis on the words, *my wife.*

All the way across the open parade area to William's house, Starr could hear Daniel Blue Eagle's curses and struggles against the chains. Each shout, each rattle, stabbed into her soul, embedding itself permanently in her mind with the memory of that one haunted hate-filled blue eye staring after her as she walked helplessly out of the stockade with William.

William kicked open the door to the house and pushed Starr inside with such force that she tripped and ended up sprawled on the parlor floor in front of him.

"Get up and get out of that ugly dress," he ordered, jerking her to her feet and roughly shoving her toward the bedroom door.

"William, why are you doing this?" Starr sobbed, not only afraid for her own life, but fearing for her unborn baby and its father. If William's rage was not checked, he would kill her and then there would be nothing she could do for Daniel Blue Eagle, the husband of her heart. "You said you love me."

"Love? You?" he growled, pouring himself a glass of brandy and greedily downing it before splashing more into the glass. "A filthy Indian's whore? Who would love *you*?" He downed the second drink and started to pour another, but thought better of it.

Tipping the bottle to his mouth, he guzzled loudly.

"Then why did you marry me? Why didn't you just let me go away so I wouldn't be a disgrace to you? I don't understand!"

"Oh, you don't? Well, let me enlighten you." He took another swig of the brandy, draining the bottle this time, and looked around for more. He found a bottle of bourbon in a cabinet and quickly began to work on it, taking huge swallows between his words. "For your information, your father left you a healthy inheritance. That damned Indian cheated me out of my virginal bride, but he won't cheat me out of the money too. That money is mine. I deserve it.

"But unfortunately, the law disagreed with me on that score, for when I went to claim it as the surviving husband of your father's only heir, I was informed that the wedding was not legal since the ceremony was unfinished. They also pointed out that no one could inherit your money for seven years—or until you could be proven legally dead."

"In that case, let me go. I'll sign it all over to you. You'll be rich and can arrange a quiet divorce so that you can remarry a woman with a less tarnished reputation," Starr suggested eagerly, hurrying toward the writing desk to pick up pen and paper. "I'll go back to the Indians, and you will never have to see me again."

"It's too late for that now, Starr. I didn't think I'd ever want to see you again once Melanie and Dorcas told me you'd lived as that Indian's wife for all those months."

Starr's heart raced. So that was how he'd known. And the wanted poster on Daniel Blue Eagle had probably been drawn using a description given by Melanie and Dorcas. Starr hoped she never saw those two again. She wasn't certain she wouldn't kill them if she did!

William went on after taking a long drag on his bottle. "But I find myself anxious to taste the delights of your body that I waited for so respectfully before our wedding, delights you willingly gave to that savage. He took a step toward her, staggering as he did. "Now, get that old woman's dress off or I'll rip it from you." His words were starting to slur.

If she could delay him a bit longer, perhaps he would pass out. That would at least give her time to think of a plan. "Please, William, don't do this. Don't destroy everything we once felt for each other," she started, speaking slowly as she fumbled with trembling fingers with the top button on her bodice, thinking to use undressing as another delaying tactic.

William watched her hands, four of them it seemed, at her collar. When it filtered through the drunken haze in his mind that she had not proceeded any further than the one button, he crossed to her with two unsteady steps. "Ya need shum help?" he mumbled.

"Yes, please," she lied, thinking that he was so intoxicated that it would take him forever to undo the tiny buttons. "What will become of Daniel Blue Eagle?" she asked, refusing to cringe as William clutched at her bodice with uncoordinated fingers.

"He'll be tried and hung in the morning. But it doesn't matter. It won't be long before all of those filthy Sioux dogs are wiped off the face of the earth."

Something in the way he spoke told Starr that his

words were more than the ramblings of a drunk. Was a large scale attack by the Army actually in the offing, as Daniel Blue Eagle had suspected? "What do you mean?" she asked, making every effort to keep her trembling voice under control.

"Dumb savages meet every summer for a big rally. The stupid animals come from all over for their big celebration. But this year, when they gather at the mouth of the Rosebud, they're not the ones who're gonna be celebratin'. Army's gonna converge on 'em from three different directions an' get rid of 'em all in one grand scale attack. Yep," he said, when the final button was released from the tiny hole in her bodice, "General Gibbon's comin' from Fort Ellis and General Crook's gonna hit 'em from Fort Fetterman, while the 7th will ride out of here with General Custer."

"That's quite a plan," Starr said, forcing a smile. "When is this all to take place?"

"No more talk now. Take off that damned dress."

"But I find it so interesting," she delayed.

"Off," he growled, reaching for the bodice and ripping it from her shoulders.

Realizing she had to give herself to William or he would rape her, Starr made the only decision she could. She couldn't take a chance on hurting her baby by fighting him physically.

"Yes, William," she said obediently, untying her petticoat ties and letting them fall to the floor with her skirt.

"Everything," he hiccuped, taking a drunken step back to take off his own clothing.

"Can we turn the lights down?" she asked timidly,

296

hesitating with her fingers at the strings of her camisole. She hadn't put on a corset when she dressed
because she hadn't wanted to ask anyone's help in
lacing it.

"No," he growled, peeling his shirt from his broad
chest and concentrating on his belt buckle with
clumsy fingers. "I'm gonna see it all," he said, his
words sounding like a terrible threat.

"All right," she whispered, knowing that her skin
was burning brightly with shame as she raised the
camisole over her head.

"Drawers too," he bellowed, reaching for the waist-
band of the flimsy underwear and tugging on it until
the drawstring cut into her skin, finally breaking.

The drawers dropped around her ankles in a limp
pool of white, leaving Starr standing naked before the
drunken man she had once thought to be so perfect.
Her first instinct was to cover herself with her hands,
but somehow she knew that her fear would ignite the
fire burning in William's eyes. If she acted afraid, it
would be worse.

Relax and it might not be so bad, her mother's
consoling words came back to her suddenly, as they
had one time before. Only that time she did fight.
This time she wouldn't. No matter what, she would
not risk her baby's life.

Starr straightened her shoulders and let her hands
hang at her sides, her fingernails digging into her
palms. She took a deep breath and waited, her eyes
refusing to veer from William's drunken face. Funny,
she had thought him the most handsome man she'd
ever seen. Handsome and perfect. Starr laughed silently at the misconceptions of her youth.

297

"Aren't you going to fight and beg?" William asked, dropping his pants around his ankles and stepping out of them, almost falling when he lifted a foot off the floor.

"No, I won't fight you." She refused to show her revulsion. Starr swallowed hard to keep back the bile that rose in her throat.

"Why?"

"You're my legal husband, William. I won't deny you your rights." The words were forced through clenched teeth. There was something warm and wet and sticky in her left palm. She knew it was blood, her injury self-inflicted. She consciously relaxed her fists. If Daniel Blue Eagle could bear the torture of the stockade, she would bear this.

"That's right," he slurred as he walked naked to the almost empty bottle of bourbon and drained it. "I'm your husband, and you're my property, my possession. I have the right to do what I want with you."

"Yes, William," she agreed, hating the tear that trickled over the bottom lid of one eye and made a lonely, forlorn trail down her face.

"Go get in the bed. I'll join you when I find another drink." He ripped open cabinets and drawers all over the room until he found what he was searching for.

A wave of temporary relief washed over Starr with her escape to the bedroom. Standing there before him as though unbothered by her nakedness, and his, had been one of the hardest things she'd ever done.

Quickly crawling into the bed, Starr pulled the covers up to her chin and lay there waiting for the final blow to descend. She wished she'd had some of William's brandy or whisky to dull the ache in her heart, but she had to have all of her wits about her. It wouldn't do for her to be drunk and unable to think.

Once William was through with her and had fallen to sleep, she was going to get dressed and go get Daniel Blue Eagle out of the stockade, even if it meant her own punishment and death for aiding a criminal. Somehow, she had to find a way to free him and give him the information about the summer attack on the Rosebud gathering.

Starr was brought back to the horror she was experiencing by the sound of William bellowing loudly as he ripped the covers from her, leaving her exposed and helpless. "Such modesty, my dear? Were you so modest with your Indian lover?" he asked, not expecting an answer and not getting one.

With no further warning, William fell across her vulnerable nakedness and bit her shoulder until she couldn't help but cry out in pain. He laughed and leaned all his weight on her chest to clumsily lift himself above her. His fingers digging painfully into her breasts, he swung a leg over her to straddle her hips.

It was all too much—the pain, the nausea, the feel of his flesh touching hers, the revolting sight of his drunken face looming over her. Starr finally allowed herself the luxury of closing her eyes so she wouldn't have to see. She bit the inside of her lip to hide the grimace that her face made involuntarily.

But it wasn't necessary to hide her feelings. William was numb to them. He could see only his own drunken rage, his own hatred for the woman beneath him. She was a whore. An Indian's whore. How dare she lie there like some sacrificial virgin awaiting the slaughter?

William ungracefully rolled off Starr's prone body, and her eyes opened in shock. Wasn't he going to—? Had she been granted a reprieve? But in the next second, she knew the answer to her question as William's cruel laugh echoed in her ears. There would be no reprieve.

"Turn over on your belly," he ordered crudely as he grabbed at her and began to turn her.

"What?" Starr gasped.

"On your belly! I don't want to look at your Indian whore's face," he growled, finally succeeding in forcing her to lie face down on the bed. "Besides, isn't that what you're used to? Isn't this the way animals couple?" He lifted her hips upward and thrust a pillow beneath her.

Oh, God, let this be over. Let it be a bad dream, she prayed silently. *Daniel, don't let this happen to me. Please help me.*

Starr lay on her stomach, holding her breath, no longer trying to stop the flow of tears that streamed from her tightly-closed eyes, wetting the sheet beneath her shame-contorted face.

But as she waited for the inevitable attack on her unresisting body, she suddenly became aware of another sound in the room, a sound besides her own pitiful whimpers and rapid breathing.

It was snoring! Someone was snoring right beside her ear. In the very same bed with her!

Starr cautiously opened one eye, then the other. She blinked them several times to be certain she was not imagining things.

William was snoring, his head only inches from her surprised face! Lying sprawled and naked on his back, his lower jaw slack and hanging open, William had passed out!

Snoring! He was sleeping and snoring! Never had Starr heard a more blessed sound. Her prayers had been answered.

Fighting the desire to laugh her relief aloud, Starr tried to raise her head. But strands of her long hair were caught under the dead weight of William's head, immediately reminding her of her precarious position and bringing her back to reality.

She had to get away from him to go help Daniel Blue Eagle, but she must be careful. One false move might awaken William. Then all would be lost.

With calculated slow motions, Starr inched her hand toward her trapped hair. Slowly. Slowly.

Almost there now. Her hand was almost touching her hair. Just one more inch to go.

William snorted and mumbled something incoherent. Starr's heart leapt in her throat. She froze, waiting a full minute before resuming her task.

Barely breathing, her heart thudding so loudly in her ears she was afraid he could hear it, she finally managed to reach her hair and wrap first her thumb, then one finger, then two, three, four fingers around the caught tresses. *Close your hand over the hair, Starr*, she thought.

She waited another minute to be certain William was not aware of what was happening. Gently tugging on her own hair, then waiting, tugging and waiting, tugging and waiting, she was able to free her hair at last.

Then the process began all over again as she carefully scooted herself across the bed and away from William, one laborious, guarded inch at a time.

Somewhere a dog barked, and Starr froze where she was on the edge of the mattress, one arm and one leg already off, the tip of her toes just touching the cold floor. Again she waited.

William's breathing continued to be even, his snores louder and louder. Just as she decided it was safe to continue her escape, William drew a loud breath, sighed and rolled over on his side, smacking his lips loudly as he did. Wait.

Finally, after what seemed like hours but was in fact not more than ten minutes, Starr managed to get out of the bed. Knowing he would awaken for certain if he was cold, she took an extra minute to cover William up and blow out the lamp before she left the room to gather up her clothing and dress in the parlor.

Minutes later, with a bundle of warm clothing, food, first aid supplies, pistols and a bottle of whiskey under her cape, Starr stole across the parade grounds toward the stockade. Approaching from an unguarded side, she left the bundle of clothes and food in the dark corner.

Glad for the moonless night, she made a dash toward the corralled horses, spotting Daniel Blue Eagle's ponies in the midst of the Army horses. Giving a soft whistle that she knew the Indian ponies would respond to, Starr only had to wait a second before the three ponies came to her, waiting patiently for her to fashion a rope halter on each of them and lead them out of the roped-off area.

Looking both ways before stepping away from the corral, Starr couldn't help thinking the Army was awfully confident that the Indians wouldn't attack them. Otherwise, why would they leave so few guards on duty? She hurried the three animals back to the stockade and ground-tied them. Carefully securing the bundle of supplies on one of them, she took one final check of her preparations and made her move.

Stepping out of the shadows, she walked boldly toward the guard who stood leaning against the wall, his rifle cradled in his arms, his head nodding softly.

His head shot up, his rifle in readiness. "Who goes there?"

"It's Mrs. Howard, Private," she said, her voice exceedingly friendly.

"Mrs. Howard, what are you doin' out at night?" He looked from left to right, expecting the Captain to come forward any minute.

"I couldn't sleep, Private," she said, drawing near him and laying her hand on his sleeve, making certain the unspoken suggestion in her eyes and voice was easy to read.

"You shouldn't be here, ma'am."

Standing so close to him, Starr could see beads of sweat pop out on the boy's forehead and upper lip, and she scolded herself silently for feeling guilty about what she was doing.

"You don't have to call me ma'am, Private. I'll bet I'm not much older than you are. Why don't you call me Starr?"

"Ma'am, I mean St—Starr, you ought not to be here," he stammered, looking around nervously.

"I thought you might be cold, so I brought something to warm you up." She rubbed her hand along the young man's peach-fuzz-covered jaw.

"Oh, my god," the guard groaned, certain what she had in mind to warm him up. What he wouldn't give to take her up on her offer. But she was the captain's wife—he'd have to be crazy to do what she was suggesting. He'd be court martialed. Hung!

"We could have a little drink first—just to ward off the chill," she suggested, producing the bottle of whiskey from under her cape and uncorking it without waiting for his answer.

"I s'pose one little drink ain't gonna hurt none."

"Of course it isn't. And it just might help me get to sleep." She lifted the bottle to her lips and pretended to drink. "Now, your turn," she giggled, holding the liquor up to his mouth, forcing him to drink the laudanum-laced whiskey or have it poured down the front of him. "My turn," she laughed sweetly, taking another feigned swallow. "Your turn again."

By the time the gullible private had his fourth 'turn', he had propped his rifle against the stockade wall and was finding himself quite dizzy.

"Are you all right, Private?" Starr asked, the concern in her voice sounding totally sincere.

"Oh, yes, ma'am."

Starr raised her eyebrows and smiled her disappointment.

"I mean Starr," he said, taking the next offered swig.

"Go on, drink all you want," she encouraged. "I know where I can get more." The guard took her advice and quickly drank more of the drugged liquor.

"Why don't we sit down?"

"I b'lieve I will," the boy agreed, stumbling forward to sit with his back to the wall, hardly able to keep his eyes open.

"You stay right there and I'll be right back."

"Where're ya goin', Starr?" he mumbled, not bothering to open his eyes.

"Why, Private, what a question to ask a lady!"

"Sorry."

"I'm going to step inside and take off some of my warm clothes. Maybe you'd like to come with me?"

"Gotta stay out here. On duty. Maybe 'nother time, Starr," he mumbled, toppling over and landing with his face on the cold ground.

So much for demon rum being all bad. That's two times tonight it's saved me, Starr told herself silently as she grabbed the key ring from the nail over the unconscious guard's head and hurried toward the stockade. *Three keys. One for the door, one for the cell, and one for the manacles. Please, let these be the three.*

Trying the first one at the heavy door, she quickly found it didn't fit. Nor did the second one. *Well, it has to be this last one,* she told herself certainly, finding it necessary to hold the key with both hands to steady her trembling fingers enough to insert the metal into the lock.

Click. Unlocked.

I'm here, Daniel. I'm inside. I'm coming, my love.

Shoving on the heavy door, she took a last anxious glance over her shoulder to be certain the guard was still asleep.

So far, so good.

305

Starr hurried to the cell where she knew Daniel Blue Eagle was and quickly found the key to that lock, leaving only one unused key on the ring. *It has to fit the manacles.*

She rushed to the heap in the corner that was Daniel Blue Eagle and struggled to drag his weight to a sitting position, "Daniel Blue Eagle, wake up. We have to hurry. I'm here now. I've come for you. But you have to help me."

After quickly propping the barely conscious man against the wall, Starr hurriedly inserted the key in the manacle on one of his wrists, purposely steeling herself against the wet stickiness on the iron, knowing it was Daniel Blue Eagle's blood where he had cut himself struggling against the terrible shackle.

Certain she had already had more than her share of luck this night, Starr rolled her eyes heavenward and said a hasty prayer, pleading for yet another favor.

She took a deep breath, bit her lower lip and turned the key. Nothing happened. Her luck had run out!

"Oh, God, no!" she gasped, twisting frantically on the key.

"Turn it over," Daniel Blue Eagle mumbled.

"What? she shrieked. "Daniel, I can't open the locks! What are we going to do? How will I get you out of here?"

"Turn the key over," he said again, finding it difficult to talk because his mouth was so dry.

Starr looked down at the key and manacle in her hand and laughed aloud. It was upside down in the lock. She yanked it out of the keyhole and inserted it again, this time easily unlocking the metal bracelet.

"Thank you," she whispered to heaven and hurriedly undid the chains on Daniel Blue Eagle's other wrist, his ankles and his neck.

"We've got to hurry, love. I don't know how long we've got. Can you walk?" She tugged on him, until she could get under his arm. Calling on strength she didn't know she possessed, she finally helped him to stand.

"How'd you get in here?" The expression on his abused face was confused, as if the danger they were in meant nothing to him.

"It doesn't matter now. We'll talk about it when we're away from here. We're still a long way from free, Daniel. We must hurry!"

Wanting to refuse her help but knowing he probably couldn't make it across the cell without her, much less outside, Daniel Blue Eagle leaned heavily on Starr and let her take him out of the stockade.

They moved cautiously past the unconscious guard toward the waiting ponies. "Thank you, Firebird," he coughed, dragging himself up to his pony as he spoke. "You'd better go back to your husband now before he discovers what you've done."

"Go back?!?" she blurted angrily, catching herself in the middle of the first word and lowering her voice to an angry hiss. "Not on your life, mister! There isn't an army big enough to make me go back there. I'm leaving here with you!"

"I can travel faster alone," he said stubbornly, silently cursing the unexpected weaving his body did at that very moment.

"Of course you can! Just look at you. Why, you're using every bit of strength you can muster just to stay

307

on that horse! Just how far do you think you'd get without me?"

"But your *husband*," he protested.

"I only have one husband, Daniel Blue Eagle, and Captain Howard is not that man," she said, mounting her own horse purposefully.

"He said—"

"I don't know why we're having this conversation when the entire United States Army may be down on us any minute," Starr interrupted patiently. "But it was my husband, the one who has a law degree from Harvard, who told me that a marriage is not legally a marriage if it is not consummated. Now can we leave?" She kicked her pony's soft sides and led the spare pony out of the shadows toward the corral area.

"You mean he didn't—" Daniel Blue Eagle caught up to her and rode beside her, hopefully waiting for her answer.

"Yes, I mean he didn't," she smiled, knowing now that Daniel Blue Eagle loved her no matter how many times he tried to deny it. And as long as he loved her, he would never be able to get away from her again.

Chapter Eighteen

Rather than give in to the hammering desire to gallop full speed from the fort, Starr and Daniel Blue Eagle rode slowly across the open space in case there were any witnesses to their escaping. Their eyes and ears alertly tuned to every movement and sound around them, neither of them spoke until they reached the horse corral.

"It might be a good idea to let their horses lose so we can ride part way with the herd to disguise our trail," Daniel Blue Eagle whispered as he leaned down to loosen the rope that enclosed the cavalry mounts. But a sharp jabbing pain in his side caused him to swoon and nearly fall from the saddle. Cursing himself for not having the strength to complete such a simple task on the first try, he clenched his teeth and pulled himself upright in the saddle again, certain the dizziness would go away after he rested a minute. Then he would try again.

Starr couldn't help seeing the wave of agony that passed over Daniel Blue Eagle's face but knew there was no time to stop to check on his injuries. "Here, let me do it," she offered, riding between him and the rope barrier.

She reached out and easily slipped the rope off the post, letting it drop to the ground, thinking the simple action would free the horses immediately. However, she quickly discovered that the entire enclosure didn't fall, only the one section did. So she hurriedly left Daniel Blue Eagle's side to ride silently around the corral, carefully removing the rope from each post that circled the horses.

Daniel Blue Eagle wrapped his arm over his own waist and pressed on his aching ribs as he watched her capable maneuvers with frustration. He felt like a fool because he couldn't help. But he was having so much trouble keeping his balance on the horse that he knew he'd be more good to her if he just concentrated on staying mounted. If he fainted, she would never have the strength to get him back on the pony.

The horses in the pen didn't seem to realize that the ropes were down until Starr whispered loudly enough for Daniel Blue Eagle to hear. "Let's go," she hissed as the last section of the horse corral fell away.

Suddenly aware that the restraints confining them in the small area had been removed, the nervous horses began to snort and neigh; and in their confusion, they crashed into each other in their rush to be free.

Hearing the disruption of the quiet night, sleepy soldiers in various stages of undress poured out of a nearby barracks with rifles in hand. "What the hell's goin' on?" one hollered, frightening the confused horses into making their bolt for freedom.

Pandemonium broke out. As if of one mind, the liberated horses ran away from the shouting soldiers, trapping Daniel Blue Eagle's mount in the midst of them.

In his weakened and groggy state, Daniel Blue Eagle had to use every bit of effort and strength he possessed to stay on his pony by clinging to the animal's neck, knowing for certain he'd be trampled by the others if he went down.

When he finally managed to gain control of his own pony and work his way to the edge of the stampeding herd, he was one or two miles from the compound.

Looking around expectantly, he quickly realized that Starr was not there!

A wave of panic rocked him. He had assumed she was with the herd, and a cold shiver of worry shook his weakened body at the discovery that she was not on any of the horses that now stood scattered over the flat terrain.

Starr had in fact never left the corral. The same rush of horses that had taken a helpless Daniel Blue Eagle out onto the open plain had disabled her in a different way.

Unaccustomed as she was to riding bareback, Starr's perch on the Indian pony was at best tenuous. So when the spooked cavalry horses began to run, it took only the slightest unexpected lurch of her own pony to send her tumbling to the ground.

As the Army's terrified horses, together with her mount and Daniel Blue Eagle, sped away from Fort Abraham Lincoln, Starr lay unconscious in a crumpled heap on the cold hard ground, unaware that only a few yards had kept her from being crushed by the pounding hooves of the entire herd.

Roused slightly by the angry voices that surrounded her, Starr opened her eyes slowly. But seeing the sea of soldiers' faces surrounding her, she knew she had failed and closed them again.

"It's that white captive we brought in today!" a soldier announced as he stepped into the trousers he'd carried from the barracks when he'd run into the open. "She looks diff'rent in them clothes, but I'd reco'nize that face anywhere."

"What the hell's she doin' out here?" a handlebar-mustached sergeant asked, lifting Starr to a sitting position and slapping her cheeks lightly to bring her around.

Starr opened her eyes and stared blankly at the man, aware of the nauseating smell of tobacco and whisky on his warm breath as he leaned close to her face. Her lids fluttered downward again.

She could hear the conversation around her, but none of it seemed important now. There was no reason to open her eyes. She knew what she would see—Daniel Blue Eagle being dragged off to jail again, or worse! She remembered William's promise to hang him in the morning.

All was lost. She had failed to free Daniel Blue Eagle and nothing else mattered if she lost him. She just wanted to sleep. It was the only escape open to her now.

"Ya think she's the one that let them horses go?"

"Naw," one said certainly.

"Then what's she doin' here?"

"Damned if I know, but we better git 'er inside," the sergeant said, easily lifting the lethargic girl in his arms and walking toward the barracks.

Starr was vaguely aware of running footsteps approaching. She peered indifferently through thick fluttering lashes, listening to the men and conversation around her as if she were witnessing it from some far away place.

"That Injun done 'scaped!" a voice shouted excitedly.

Starr grew more alert, though she kept her eyes closed. Was it possible that Daniel Blue Eagle had gotten away after all? Optimisim surged in her heart.

"How the hell'd that happen?"

"He musta got lose an' hit the guard an' taken off. The guard's still out."

"Cap'n's gonna crap!"

"Ya s'pose she was helpin' 'im git away?" one asked, the tone in his voice unbelieving.

"Why would a white woman help a Injun?"

"What I think happened was that Injun was tryin' to steal 'er agin, got caught and had to abandon 'er when we all come out."

"What're ya gonna do with 'er, Sarge?" one excited voice asked.

"I'm gonna take 'er in outta the cold, and then I'll decide what ta do 'bout 'er."

"Ya know who she is, don't ya?"

"Sure. She's the white captive Lieutenant Hildegard brought in today."

"She's the cap'n's wife!"

The man carrying Starr stopped in his tracks. "Naw!"

"They say she was kidnapped by them damned redskins right in the middle o' their weddin'."

"We better take 'er to his house if we know what's good fer us."

"I guess so," the voice Starr had come to recognize

313

as the sergeant's answered, the disappointment evident in his tone.

Whatever he had planned to do with her, Starr found herself tempted to choose that over being taken back to William for punishment. And she knew without a doubt that she would be punished. No matter what the soldiers believed, William would know she was trying to escape and would make her pay.

Minutes later, the small party of men, some dressed only in longjohns and boots, took Starr up the steps of William's house. It was a long time before he came to the door, causing the men to wonder if the Indian had injured the captain while stealing his wife. Just as they were ready to break into the house to check on him, a drunk and groggy William finally opened the door.

"What is it?" he growled, doing his best to look sober, though he couldn't stop weaving from side to side in the doorway.

"Cap'n, sir, that Injun done 'scaped and tried to take yer wife with 'im," the sergeant said, taking care to ignore the fact that his superior officer was exceedingly drunk.

For the first time, William seemed to notice Starr in the sergeant's arms, but he made no move to take her from the man. "Where'd you find her?"

"The Injun scattered our horses, and when we all heard the ruckus, we come runnin' out to see what was goin' on. That's when he had to let 'er go. We figure she fell off the horse he had 'er on!"

"I see. Put my wife on the sofa, Sergeant," William said, pointing to the interior of the house. "Then go

314

and inform Lieutenant Hildegard what has happened before you send men out to round up the horses."

"Yes, sir!" the sergeant said sharply as he crossed over to deposit the captain's wife on the couch. He gave no indication that he thought it was very peculiar that the captain didn't seem more upset about what had happened, or more worried about his wife. "Will that be all, sir?" he added as he left.

William didn't answer, allowing the slamming of the door behind the departing soldier to serve as his only response. "Well, Starr, is what that man said true?" he asked as he crossed the room to stand over Starr, the accusation in his voice deadly. "Did your Indian lover manage to free himself from his chains and come after you? Or was it the other way around?"

Starr kept her eyes closed, thinking that if he thought she was unconscious, he might leave her alone. But of course that was foolish thinking on her part. Being ignored only made William more angry.

"Answer me, slut!" he screamed, gripping her shoulders and jerking her to a sitting position so roughly that her head snapped back and her eyes popped open.

Starr remained silent, staring into his drunken, rage-filled eyes. There was nothing but contempt in her expression.

"Did you release him?" William stormed, his voice high and hysterical.

"You already know the answer to your question, don't you, William?"

Her response made him livid. How could she be so calm about it? How could she stare at him with those big gray eyes as if she pitied him?

"I ought to kill you with my bare hands," he sputtered, wrapping his fingers around Starr's exposed throat and making the pressure of his strong grip known, but not cutting off her oxygen.

"But you won't, will you, William?" she said, carefully keeping her voice cool and taking care that her gaze didn't waver from his, despite the fact that she wasn't the least bit certain he wouldn't kill her right then and there. "I doubt that a husband can inherit his wife's property if he is her murderer," she pointed out sensibly.

"It would almost be worth losing the money to see you dead!" he threatened, pressing his thumbs on her windpipe.

"But not quite," she rasped, managing a knowing smile.

"Not quite," he agreed angrily, releasing his grip on her throat and throwing her back down to the sofa. "But as soon as I get my hands on your father's property and money, I may not be so easy to manipulate."

The threat in his voice was very real, and Starr felt she had tested him to the limit, so she said nothing.

"In the meantime, you won't go out of this house again without my knowledge," he laughed bitterly, dragging her toward the bedroom, where he pulled a rope from a trunk and bound her hands and ankles before throwing her onto the bed and leaving her.

As afraid as she was, as cutting as the ropes were, Starr couldn't help being relieved. William wasn't going to rape her, not now anyway. And Daniel Blue Eagle had escaped. That was all that mattered to her

316

right then. Nothing else. That was all she would think about. He was free!

Starr closed her eyes and tried to sleep. She wouldn't worry about what William would do to her. Nor would she let herself wonder if the fall from the horse had hurt her baby, or think about where Daniel Blue Eagle was right that minute. She would believe they were both all right and that the man she loved was safely on his way back to the People.

If only I'd had time to tell him about the summer attack the Army was planning to make, she worried silently as she finally drifted into a restless sleep, her total exhaustion impossible to deny any longer.

But Starr would not have been able to sleep had she known at that moment Daniel Blue Eagle was anything but safe. For rather than riding to safety as she supposed, he was foolishly making his way back to the fort, barely avoiding detection by the soldiers that now covered the plains in search of their scattered horses.

Afraid that Starr had been thrown and was lying helpless somewhere on the ground, his immediate impulse when he had discovered she was not with her pony had been to turn back and retrace his route from the fort. But to go back the way he had come, without so much as a tree or shrub to hide behind, would have meant certain capture, and would do neither of them any good. There had to be another way to go for her.

Forcing himself to fight the instinctive impulse to ride head-on into the soldiers in his hurry to go back for his wife, Daniel Blue Eagle decided on a more sensible course. Instead, he would travel further away from the fort before turning east toward the river, thinking to make his way back to Fort Abraham Lincoln from the river side.

When Starr awoke in the morning, she was aware of the bright sunlight beaming through the bedroom window onto her bed and warming her to the point of being uncomfortable. Scooting off the bed, she managed to stand up, despite the fact that her hands and ankles were still bound, though not as tightly as she had thought. At least she still had some feeling in her fingers and toes.

Looking around the bedroom inquisitively, she spied the washstand in the corner, and an idea began to form in her mind. The marble-topped chest displayed the expected necessities—a large bowl and pitcher, another smaller pitcher and tumbler for rinsing the mouth, a sponge basin, a bottle of ammonia, and a footbath under the washstand. But none of these things interested Starr. A bath wasn't what attracted her to the well-equipped washstand. What she wanted was probably going to be in the little drawer of the washstand, or in its cabinet.

Starr took an anxious glance at her bedroom door and cocked her head to listen for William moving about in the other room, but she heard nothing. Reasonably certain no one was in the house with her, she hopped across the space between the bed and the washstand, determined to put her plan into action.

Though her hands were tied behind her back, she managed to open the drawer to the chest. In her nervousness, she jerked too hard on the brass handle and pulled the whole drawer out, dumping its contents on the floor at her feet.

"No!" she gasped, hastily examining the spilled items scattered around her. There was a bootblacking kit, shaving soap and brush, a small tin pot for hot shaving water, a package of paper for wiping razors and—

Where were William's razors? He had to have them. Every man had a case of razors, a different one for each day of the week, just like the ones in her father's dressing room. They had to be there somewhere!

There! Under the rocking chair!

Starr dropped to her knees and anxiously moved over to the wooden rocker, stretching her arms as far behind her as she could manage in an effort to reach the razor case. She patted her hands on the floor but couldn't locate the razors.

Sighing in frustration, she turned around to determine the location of the evasive case, then tried again until she finally felt its soft leather and drew it out from under the chair.

With shaking fingers, she hurriedly unsnapped the clasp and gingerly took a razor out, hardly noticing when the sharp blade nicked one of her knuckles. It would be worth a little blood if she could cut her ropes and free herself. If she could escape before William returned, perhaps she could get to Bismarck.

As she sawed away at the rope binding her wrists, periodically slipping and accidentally taking another piece of her skin, she reminded herself of the way the Indian women mourned the loss of loved ones by cutting bits of flesh from their arms and cutting their hair.

In a way, that was what she was doing. Mourning.

She was mourning the fact that she would never see Daniel Blue Eagle again. The fact that her baby would never know its father. If only she could go after him. But she didn't have any idea where to look for him. The tribe would have moved several times before she could get back to the Black Hills—if she could find her way back at all—and he might not even be there.

As the final strand of the rope gave way, Starr shook her hands out of the rope and hurriedly untied her ankles.

She listened again for William. Except for her own rapid breathing, the house was silent.

Realizing she was still alone, she had the optimistic thought that she might escape yet. And that thought gave her the incentive to promise herself that if this attempt failed, she would simply try again until she was successful, or dead. But no matter what the outcome, she vowed she would never give up until she'd left William Howard and Fort Abraham Lincoln behind her.

With determination bordering on panic, Starr washed her cut hands and wrists and wrapped them in bandages before changing into a riding habit and warm cape she found in her wardrobe.

Planning to sneak out the back door of the house and hide somewhere until nightfall, Starr pulled her hood up over her head and hurried to the kitchen.

Spotting a loaf of bread on the counter as she passed through the kitchen triggered an unexpected reaction. Her stomach growled loudly, reminding her that she hadn't eaten since the day before. She hadn't even realized she was hungry. But now there was no doubt, and she hurriedly tore off a chunk of bread and bit ravenously into it while stuffing the rest of the loaf into her pocket.

Deciding she was as ready as she would ever be, Starr crossed to the back door and, taking a deep breath, extended her hand toward the brass knob. But just as her fingers came in contact with the cold metal, she heard bootsteps on the back porch, and her heart leapt in her throat. What if it was William? No, it couldn't be. He would use the front door, wouldn't he?

Starr looked around frantically. She had to hide fast. If he came in and found her untied and dressed for the out-of-doors, he would know what she was doing and would make her next escape attempt even more difficult.

Spying the large pantry, she hurried into it and closed the door behind her, leaving it slightly ajar so she could see what was happening. If William came in, he would probably go to the bedroom immediately to check on her, and she would have only a few moments to scurry out the back door before he discovered her absence. If she was very careful and didn't panic, she could slip out the door the second he was out of sight, and hide herself under the house until it was safe to head for the river and Bismarck.

Starr heard the boots pounding on the back porch again, but no one came inside. What was he doing out there?

Though she was expecting the door to open any second, Starr, scarcely daring to breathe, couldn't refrain from emitting an involuntary gasp when the doorknob actually moved before her eyes.

Balling both fists against her mouth to silence herself, she quailed back against the shelves of the pantry and pressed her arms against her chest, certain it was necessary to muffle the deafening pounding of her heart to keep whoever was coming through the door from hearing it.

Hypnotized by the turning knob, Starr could only wait until the door began to open, first a crack, then an inch, then several inches, then enough for a man to step through.

Suddenly, there was the crash of someone coming through the front door, and the back door slammed shut again. Starr shrank further back into the pantry, huddling helplessly in the darkest corner.

William was in the house now, and she could tell by his cursing that he had already discovered she had freed herself and was no longer where he had left her. She could hear the sounds of wardrobes being pulling open and rooms being searched as his steps drew nearer and nearer the kitchen.

When William's shadow crossed in front of the narrowly open pantry door, Starr thought she had been discovered; but she quickly realized that he went directly to the back door and opened it.

"Has anyone gone out this door?" he roared to someone outside on the porch.

"No sir," a man mumbled. It must be whoever had started to come inside the house. William must have stationed guards at the doors. How would she get out now?

William slammed the door without questioning the guard further and raged back across the room, stopping just short of the pantry.

"Did you think you could make me believe you were gone?" he laughed suddenly, snatching open the door that hid Starr. "Were you going somewhere, my dear?"

Cowering in the corner, Starr felt like a trapped mouse about to be a hungry cat's next meal. The rage in William's eyes was so great she knew there would be no reasoning with him, no manipulating him, no reminding him about her father's money. He was going to kill her. She could see it in his eyes.

Well, if he did, she wasn't going to die cringing in a dark closet. He would have a fight on his hands, she decided as she stood up to face him.

William took a step toward her, and she gripped the shelf behind her for support.

When her hand touched the cold metal of the butcher knife laying on the shelf, her fingers jerked back in surprise. But it was only an instant before she realized what she was touching and her hand wrapped around the handle.

William laughed menacingly and reached out for her.

"One more step, and I'll kill you, William," she warned, the expression on her face now as angry and determined as his as she held the knife in front of her.

"The kitten has claws," he laughed, his voice maliciously amused.

"Get out of my way, William, or I swear I'll use this!" Her voice rose with each word. Her hands began to shake violently.

"Put that thing down," he ordered, taking another step in her direction.

"If you touch me, I'll make so much noise you'll

323

never live down the scandal," Starr shrilled hysterically, waving the knife nervously.

Where nothing else could have penetrated William's rage, the word *scandal* was the magic key. It was bad enough that he was forced to play the part of a forgiving and compassionate husband to get the money of a woman with a tarnished reputation. But if she publicly rejected him and left, it would be too much. It would destroy all of his plans to become a leading politician in the Dakota Territory once he had made a name for himself in the Army. There was nothing that could hold back a rich war hero, not even a wife with a questionable past. But without a great deal of money and with it known that his wife preferred an Indian's bed to his, there would be no hope for his political career.

"All right," William said, smiling patronizingly and holding his hands up in defeat, though the anger in his eyes still burned vividly. "Just come on out of the pantry and we'll talk."

"We have nothing to talk about. I'm leaving you and you're not going to stop me," she said, moving toward him, bravely brandishing the knife in front of her.

Without warning, William's hand shot out and grabbed her wrist, bending and squeezing it. "You're not going anywhere!" he snarled as he exerted even more pressure on the fragile bones of her wrists.

Pain burned its way along Starr's arm, but still she clung to the knife as she kicked out at William's shins and screamed at the top of her lungs. She realized some pleasure in the knowledge that the guard outside would hear her and would know how William

Howard treated his wife.

"Shut up, you damned whore!" he ground through clenched teeth as his strong hand clamped over her mouth, muffling her screams, but not silencing her altogether.

Finally, unable to ignore the pain in her wrist any longer, her fingers opened and the knife fell to the floor, clattering loudly in a cruel reminder that she had failed to escape once more.

With the final bit of defiance she could muster, Starr bit down on the hand that covered her mouth.

William yowled angrily, the expression on his face stunned, and then crazed, telling Starr that he had forgotten all of his reasons for keeping her alive.

Still gripping her wrist with vicious pressure, he drew back his throbbing hand and clenched it in a tight fist, obviously planning to slam it into her face.

Starr squeezed her eyes shut as she awaited the blow that would send her to oblivion. The blow never came.

William made a choking sound and released his hold on her wrists.

Starr's eyes flew open in time to see a blue, uniform-clad forearm wrap around William's neck from behind. He was gasping for air and his eyes were bulging with fear as he struggled against the hold on him, his hands grasping ineffectively at the uniform sleeve.

"That's no way to treat a lady, Captain!" the attacker said, wheeling William around and crashing his own hard fist into the young captain's astonished face.

Chapter Nineteen

"Daniel Blue Eagle!" Starr flew across the space that separated her from the only man she would ever call 'husband'. "Where did you come from? How did you find me? What are you doing in that uniform? Why did you come back?" she babbled as she threw herself into his strong arms and rained joyful kisses over his face. "I didn't think I'd ever see you again!"

"You should've known better, Firebird," he smiled, wincing slightly as she squeezed him to her. "I couldn't leave my wife with that animal," he said, indicating the unconscious man on the floor at their feet.

He had called her his wife!

"Before we left the village, you said we weren't married anymore, yet just now you called me your wife," she said hesitantly, needing to hear Daniel Blue Eagle say it again, needing to believe that he still wanted her, that he hadn't meant the words he had spoken before they left the village.

"I was a fool. You will always be my wife, Firebird," he vowed, the light in his eyes telling her that she would never have to doubt his feelings for her again.

He held her away from him so he could examine her for injuries. To his great relief, her face was marked only by tearstains. "Did he hurt you?"

She shook her head, dismissing his question as unimportant. She was still his wife! Nothing else mattered. Starr raised her hands to caress his face.

Then his eyes lit on her bandaged hands and wrists. "What happened? I'll kill the son of a bitch!" Daniel Blue Eagle cursed, turning to raise his hand and punch William again.

Starr clutched at Daniel Blue Eagle's strong arm. "No, don't, Daniel. He didn't do it. He tied me up so I wouldn't run away again, and I cut myself getting lose. It's nothing serious. Believe me!"

"Are you sure? If I thought he injured you—"

Nodding her head, she smiled her assurance, saying, "Being your wife is all that is important to me now."

Daniel Blue Eagle sighed uncertainly, finally dropping his arm and relaxing his fist as he took one last look at William's unconscious form. "Well," he finally said, "if you don't want to be a widow in the next few minutes, I suggest we leave Fort Abraham Lincoln immediately."

Daniel Blue Eagle's words reminded Starr that they weren't out of danger yet, and she looked around helplessly. "How are we going to get out of here? He has guards on the doors, Daniel!"

The smile that crossed his face was mischievous as he bent to hogtie William securely before gagging him and hurling him into the pantry, a little more roughly than necessary. "Make that guard, not guards."

Suddenly it came to her why the man's voice at the back door had a slightly familiar sound to it. It had been Daniel Blue Eagle.

"You!" she squealed, not knowing if she wanted to laugh or to cry. "It was you at the door when he came home! You actually talked to him! Where's the real soldier?"

"Under the house, sleeping off a nasty bump on the head. I'll tell you all about it later on. Right now, show me where the captain keeps his spare uniforms; and then go tell that guard out front to saddle two horses for us. Tell him your husband's going to take you out for a ride to show you around the fort."

"What are you going to do?"

"I'm going to get promoted from corporal to captain. Then I'm going to take my wife for a ride."

"You'll never pass for William! You're about the same height, but one look at your dark hair and you'll be spotted."

"Do you have a better suggestion?"

"I'll show you where his uniforms are."

"I thought so," he chuckled.

"Daniel?"

"Hmm?" he grunted as he moved the heavy kitchen table in front of the pantry door.

"Will you hold me for just a minute before we go?" Starr's voice was very small and her bottom lip trembled as she gallantly, though not successfully, fought the tears threatening to tumble down her cheeks.

Knowing how frightened she must have been, how

afraid he'd been for her, Daniel Blue Eagle smiled and held out his arms to Starr. Even though there was not a moment to lose, even though their very lives depended on precious seconds, he could not have denied her request.

She ran gratefully to him and melted into the security of his warm embrace, the embrace she had been certain she would never know again. "I was so afraid," she sobbed softly against his shirt front, drawing on his strength as she pressed herself against him.

"I was too, Firebird," he choked, turning her face up to his to kiss her damp eyelids, her nose, her mouth, as if by so doing he could erase all the bad memories of the past twenty-four hours. "But you don't have to be afraid anymore. I'm with you now and I won't let him hurt you again."

Starr placed her hands on Daniel Blue Eagle's face and smiled into his serious eyes; her own filled with joy. "That's not what I was afraid of, Daniel. I was afraid I'd never see you again—never know the feel of your arms around me again, never hear you call me Firebird again. I was afraid I would never have the chance to tell you how much I love you. But I'm not going to wait any longer. I love you, Daniel Blue Eagle. I love you!"

She loved him! How long had he waited to hear her say those words? How long had he wanted to tell her what was in his heart? But why now? The timing was all wrong. Why, when it was too late?

Unable to hold back his feelings any longer, Daniel Blue Eagle hauled Starr to him, holding her head to his chest. "And I love you, my sweet Firebird. God

329

help us both. I love you," he told her, even though he now knew they would never have a future together.

His mouth came down on hers, his tongue probing deeply into the moist warmth to make love to her the only way he could right then. "Now, we'd better go," he rasped with frustration, forcing himself to push her away from him.

It would have made what he had to do so much easier if neither of them had ever said the words. Yet, the words had been spoken and there was no way to take them back now, not that he would have even if he'd been able to. His heart was soaring, despite the fact that he knew her love for him would bring her only sadness.

Minutes later, Daniel Blue Eagle stepped into the parlor, his hair cut short, and wearing William's uniform, which fit him surprisingly well. "How do I look?"

"Very handsome, my love, but nothing like William."

"Give me time!" Daniel Blue Eagle promised, grabbing up the hat and overcoat William had thrown over a chair and putting them on, taking care to turn up the collar of the coat and pull the hat down on his head. "Better?"

"Better," Starr agreed, although the expression on her face told him how worried she was.

"Then let's go," he said, kissing the frown lines on her forehead to ease her apprehension as he pulled her hood up to cover her bright-colored hair.

Daniel Blue Eagle opened the front door for Starr. She took a deep, stabilizing breath and swept out onto the porch, deliberately placing herself directly

330

between her husband and the young guard who was giving the 'captain' his smartest salute.

"I see you've found a horse for me, Private," Starr complimented gaily, directing her most radiant smile in the private's direction.

"Sure thing, ma'am!" the soldier stammered, not even noticing the captain's bored answering salute, which conveniently hid the side of Daniel Blue Eagle's bruised face as he passed closest to the young man. "Just like you asked for."

"Thank you so much. I'm so looking forward to this little outing," she prattled happily, bringing the innocent soldier even further under her spell. "I hope you don't think it's too terrible that I prefer to ride astride rather than use a sidesaddle." At this point, she actually batted her eyelashes at him—a disgusting device she had seen other young women use, and one she had sworn she would never use.

"Oh, no, ma'am. That's jest fine!" the boy blushed.

Standing between the horses with his back to the soldier and Starr, Daniel Blue Eagle cleared his throat pointedly, and she shot the guard a helpless *you-do-understand-why-I-can't-stay-and-visit* look and dashed down the steps to quickly mount her horse with no assistance.

As the two rode away, the young private smiled after them. He'd heard the terrible fight the Howards had had earlier, and came to the conclusion that the row must have been over whether Captain Howard would take Mrs. Howard for a ride or not. It was obvious the captain wasn't too happy about taking his wife on a tour of the fort. But after seeing Mrs.

Howard, it was easy for the soldier to understand the reason the captain had given in. His wife had gotten her way this time she probably always would. Whenever there was any kind of disagreement, the poor captain wouldn't stand a chance in hell.

Starr nervously looked around the lobby of the Merchants Hotel in Bismarck. What was Daniel thinking of, coming to a public place like this? There were people everywhere, steamer crews, prospectors stopping off on their way west, tradesmen, business men, soldiers, and well-dressed women—many of questionable professions. She felt as if everyone in the lobby was staring at her, as if they all had seen her face on that poster and recognized her. Unintentionally, Starr reached up and pulled her hood farther down on her face, focusing her eyes on the tips of her boots peeking out from under the hem of her dress.

The escape from Fort Lincoln had been relatively simple, and Starr had finally begun to relax when Daniel Blue Eagle had informed her they were going to Bismarck instead of directly back to the Black Hills.

When she had protested that Bismarck was only five miles from the fort and that they would be captured again, he had merely said that he had business to attend to and didn't think he would be back this way for some time. What business could he have that was as important as getting away from Fort Lincoln as fast as they could to warn the People about the Army's plans?

"Mr. Edwards!" Starr heard the friendly desk

clerk call out. "Or should I say Captain Edwards? When did you join the Army?"

She looked up in surprise to see her husband shaking hands with a small, baldheaded man, about forty years old, who had rushed forward to greet him.

"Max Beecher, it's good to see you!" Daniel Blue Eagle returned, deliberately ignoring the man's question about the Army. "The last time I saw you, you were thinking about heading west to look for gold."

The man laughed good-naturedly and slapped Daniel Blue Eagle on the back. "Yeah, well, I got ta thinkin' I wanted ta keep what little hair I got left! Decided it looks better on my head than on some redskin's belt!"

Starr, her gray eyes wide with indignation, gasped aloud and took a step forward, ready to give the bigot a piece of her mind. Fortunately, Daniel Blue Eagle placed a restraining hand on her arm and interrupted before she could say anything.

"Max, I would like for you to meet my wife! Max is an old friend, dear," he said, narrowing his blue eyes purposefully, telling her without words that he was counting on her to play her part, just as he was playing his. And playing her part did not allow room for taking exception to statements against the Indians.

"Howja do, Mizz Edwards. I'm real pleased ta meet ya," the little man said, smiling as he took her hand and bowed to kiss it.

"Mr. Beecher," Starr replied coolly, removing her hand from his sweating palm as quickly as she could. She might not be able to tell the man what she thought of him, but she certainly wouldn't spend any

333

more time in his presence than absolutely necessary.

"We'd like a room, Max," Daniel Blue Eagle inserted, drawing the desk clerk's attention away from Starr before he could look too closely at her face.

"Sure thing, Captain Edwards. How long ya gonna be with us?" Max asked, scurrying around behind the registration desk. All business now, he shoved the cumbersome book toward Daniel Blue Eagle.

"Just for the night. We're on our way to Fort Stevenson," Daniel Blue Eagle lied adeptly as he picked up the offered room key from the desk, after signing the register, *Capt. and Mrs. Daniel Edwards.*

Safely in their room a few minutes later, Daniel Blue Eagle hurriedly crossed to the window to look down on the main street of the bawdy town of Bismarck. Saloons and brothels lined the street, and he breathed a sigh of relief when he saw that there weren't more than two or three enlisted men on the streets right then, and no officers. Luck was with him for a little while longer. But he knew he was going to have to handle his business quickly if he wanted to be back in the room before off-duty soldiers from the fort came to town as they did every evening.

"Daniel, are you going to explain this to me? How do you know that desk clerk? What are we doing in Bismarck?" Starr asked as she threw her cape across the bed, the fire in her gray eyes lighting up her entire face.

Daniel Blue Eagle took another quick glance at the street below and then turned back toward his wife. He smiled at the picture she presented, fists on her hips, the strained bodice of her dress rising and

334

falling rapidly. Was it his imagination, or were her breasts fuller than he remembered?

"Well, are you going to answer me? What is going on?"

"I'll explain everything when I return, my love. Right now, I'm going to take care of my business," he said, crossing to the door, seeming not to notice Starr's agitation. "Lock the door behind me, and don't let anyone in but me."

"You're not going to leave me here alone!" she announced angrily as she snatched up her cape and hurried toward him.

"I'm sorry, *Mrs. Edwards*, but with your bright hair and lovely face, you'd call too much attention to us. I'll be less apt to be noticed if I go alone."

She wanted to argue with him, but knew he was right. "How long will you be gone?" she asked.

"Not long at all. And I'll order a bath and hot food brought up just as soon as I get back! All right?" he chuckled, lifting her chin so he could give her a consoling peck on her lips.

"All right," she laughed, "but you'd better hurry or I'm going to come after you! I saw the way those painted women downstairs were giving you the eye!"

"What painted women? The only woman I ever see is you. Other women don't even exist, as far as I'm concerned."

"And it had better stay that way, *Captain Edwards*! Now go on, before I decide to entice you to stay."

"I love you, Firebird," Daniel Blue Eagle mouthed as he tweaked the end of her nose and disappeared through the door.

"And I love you, Daniel Blue Eagle," she whispered, leaning happily on the closed door, refusing to let herself worry that he would not come right back.

"Lock the door," his low voice reminded from the hallway.

His mouth must have been touching the opposite side of the door, at the place she rested her head, and a thrill of anticipation shot through her body. His lips were separated from her ear by only the piece of wood.

Starr wheeled around and saluted the closed door. "Yes, sir!" she answered, slamming home the bolt in the lock.

"Good girl," she heard from the other side of the door, and then he was gone.

Rushing over to the window, Starr pulled back the curtains slightly so she could see where Daniel Blue Eagle was going. It was a while before he stepped out onto the street, and his hat and overcoat hid his face, but she still would have known him anywhere. No other man had his graceful, confident walk.

Watching her husband below, Starr's heart was so full of love that she tapped on the window, thinking to get his attention and wave at him. But he didn't hear her, and Starr didn't try to make him notice her again because his attention was drawn elsewhere and her heart leapt into her throat.

She was sick with disappointment, for her husband was speaking to a statuesque blonde in a red dress who had slinked out of an alleyway and attached herself to Daniel Blue Eagle's arm, obviously glad to see him. Starr's stomach turned over painfully.

No wonder he didn't want me along, was Starr's

336

first thought; and though she knew she would only be hurt if she continued to watch the two in the street as they made their plans, she couldn't move away from the window.

The blonde, about the same age as Starr, maybe even younger, was talking animatedly to Daniel Blue Eagle, who was listening intently to what she had to say.

As the woman gave Daniel Blue Eagle a particularly sultry smile, Starr decided she couldn't bear to watch any more and started to turn away. However, it was just then that she saw her husband's strong hand cover the prostitute's fingers on his sleeve.

"Oh," Starr groaned in disappointment, sickened and hurt by the sight before her eyes, yet unable to tear herself away.

Just when she thought he was going to go with the woman, Starr realized that Daniel Blue Eagle had touched the woman's hand to gently, but firmly, pry it from his arm before stepping aside and walking away from her.

"Oh!" Starr squealed, clapping her hands together gleefully as she thrilled to the sight of the irate woman screaming curses at Daniel Blue Eagle's retreating back until he disappeared into the telegraph office. Once he was out of sight, the prostitute forced another friendly red smile on her face and accosted the next potential customer who had the bad fortune to step off the hotel porch into her path.

Ashamed of herself for spying on Daniel Blue Eagle and for not trusting him, Starr dropped the curtain and walked around the hotel room, finally deciding to lie down and nap until he returned.

When she awoke much later, the room was dim, and panic set in. It was late afternoon! The sun was already beginning to go down. Daniel Blue Eagle had been gone for hours! Maybe he wasn't coming back! Something dreadful must have happened to him or he would have returned by now.

Someone could have recognized him and attacked him! He might be lying in some alley wounded and bleeding, or dead!

"I have to go look for him," she resolved, not stopping to think that she had no idea where to look. She just knew she couldn't stay in the hotel room another minute when her husband, the father of her child, might be lying in some dark alley dying!

Wrapping her cape securely around her shoulders, Starr unbolted the lock and ripped open the door to the room, prepared to tear the entire town of Bismarck apart until she found her husband.

Daniel Blue Eagle was surprised as he wrestled, to no avail, to balance the stack of boxes in his arms as Starr ran headlong into him, sending the packages scattering over the floor. "Hey!" he shouted, "I told you not to open that door until you knew it was me! Where do you think you're going?" he asked, suddenly noticing she was wearing her cape again.

"I was going out to look for you! Where have you been? I've been worried frantic! You told me you'd be right back!"

"I wasn't gone but a couple of hours," he defended, gathering a stack of boxes and shoving them into her hands before bending to pick up the rest.

"What is all this?" she grumbled, tossing the boxes on the bed and turning back to him. She wasn't going

338

to let him off the hook so easily. He had scared her out of her wits and he was going to explain!

"New clothing," he announced, opening a box and taking out a mauve traveling dress and holding it out to her.

"Where did you get all these things? What are they for? How did you pay for them?" Starr's voice sounded slightly hysterical, even to her own ears. What was wrong with her? She'd done nothing but harp at him ever since they'd arrived in Bismarck!

"I wired my grandfather's bank in Yankton, and they wired the bank here and told them to give me whatever I needed."

"Oh."

"What did you think I did? Rob a dress shop?" He was amazed. Most white women would have grabbed at the boxes, never giving a thought to where the money had come from.

"No, I didn't think that. I didn't know what to think. But what are we going to do with all these things? I would have thought denim pants and flannel shirts would be more practical for riding horses back to the village."

"We're not going to be riding horses for the next few days," he started, wishing he didn't have to tell her what his plans were.

"What are you talking about? Aren't you planning to return to your father's village right away to warm them about the soldiers?"

"Yes, I am, but—" A knock on the door mercifully interrupted Daniel Blue Eagle's confession, and he rushed to answer it. "Who is it?" he asked holding a newly purchased pistol toward the door and listening.

"It's Max, Captain. I brung your supper myself."

"Come on in, Max," Daniel Blue Eagle laughed, tossing the pistol in a chair and opening the door.

Max hurried in with a tray laden with fried buffalo steaks, potatoes, hot bread, steaming coffee, and a whole apple pie.

Seeing and smelling the food, Starr's mouth watered as she realized how ravenous she was. Her stomach rumbled loudly, and she responded by hurriedly clearing a small table in the corner for Max to set the tray on. It was all she could do to wait until Daniel Blue Eagle had paid the man and closed the door behind him before she dug into the huge portion of food on her platter. "I'm starving to death," she confided with a full mouth, not even bothering to wait for her husband to join her.

"I see you are," he laughed as he sat on the edge of the bed and tasted the food on his plate. "Should I have ordered more? Or do you think this will be enough?"

Starr laughed self-consciously. "I'm sorry to act like this, but except for a bite of bread earlier today, I haven't eaten since yesterday."

And I'm eating for two, she added silently, wondering when the best time would be to tell Daniel Blue Eagle he was going to be a father. Never good at keeping secrets, she ached to tell him right then; but he had so many things on his mind, she knew it would be unfair to add another worry to the growing list. Once they were back with the Lakota, the time would be better.

Later, when Starr was washing down the last bite of her second piece of apple pie with a swallow of coffee, another knock came at the door. Her nerves strained by the experiences of the past few days, she leaped from her seat with a jerk, spilling coffee down the front of her dress.

"It's just your bath, Firebird," Daniel Blue Eagle whispered, though the smile on his face didn't hide his concern as he crossed the room. "Who is it?" he asked sternly, holding the revolver in readiness as he leaned his ear to the wooden door.

"It's the bath you ordered, Captain," a young girl's voice answered.

Daniel Blue Eagle signaled for Starr to step behind a dressing screen, then opened the door cautiously, taking care to stay out of sight with his gun poised for an attack.

But all of his guarded actions had been unnecessary, for the girl had been who she said she was and the bath was a welcome sight to Starr. Once the girl was gone, taking the dinner tray with her, Starr hurriedly took off her clothing and donned a silk wrapper that she found among Daniel Blue Eagle's packages. "I don't know what good this will do me when we're back with the People," she laughed as she stepped from behind the screen, "but it's very nice."

Daniel Blue Eagle didn't answer, and Starr looked up from tying the sash on the robe to see her husband stretched out on the bed, his head against the headboard. He was fast asleep.

Smiling at how sleep seemed to erase the worry lines from his sensitive face, making him seem younger than his twenty-six years, she blew out all the lamps in the room, save one, and then carefully removed Daniel Blue Eagle's boots before covering him with a blanket she found in a chest of drawers.

After taking a leisurely bath in the hot water that stung the nicks and cuts on her hands, Starr quickly toweled herself off and slipped between the cool sheets. Secure with the sound of her husband's even breathing in her ear, she snuggled next to him and drifted easily to sleep.

Chapter Twenty

A thumping noise, followed by a man's low muttered curse woke Starr suddenly, cruelly drawing her away from a pleasant dream about Daniel Blue Eagle and their baby. Turning over on her side, she plumped her pillow angrily and tried to recapture the beautiful experience her imagination had created for her.

But it was impossible. There that noise was again. Thumping and cursing.

Her eyes opened grudgingly.

It took a moment for her sleep-heavy eyes to adjust to the darkness of the room, and another moment to remember where she was. As she gained her sight and memory she came to the frightening realization that there was a man standing at the foot of her bed. What did he want? Was he there to rob them? To kill them in their sleep? What should she do?

Daniel Blue Eagle, she tried to call out, but when she opened her mouth, nothing came out but a raspy, choking sound. Reaching out to warn her husband that they were in danger, she patted the bed beside her and found herself with nothing but a handful of blanket. She gasped aloud.

Daniel Blue Eagle was not there. He was gone. Had the intruder already killed him?

The thought assaulted Starr's half-asleep brain with the force of a deadly tornado, and she bolted straight up in the bed, not caring about her own safety. "What are you doing in here?" she yelled, groping under Daniel Blue Eagle's pillow for one of his new revolvers.

Bump. Thud. Splash. "What the hell?"

"Who are you? What do you want?" she cried out, aiming the gun toward the shadowy shape that stood between the bed and the window. "Speak up or I'll shoot." She clicked the hammer on the pistol.

"Put that damned gun down, you little fool!" Daniel Blue Eagle ordered, diving to the floor as the moonlight reflected off the barrel of the weapon in Starr's trembling hands.

"Daniel Blue Eagle? Is that you?"

"Who did you think it was?" he asked, raising a bath towel in the air and waving it anxiously as he cringed at the foot of the bed until he was certain Starr wasn't going to shoot him.

"What are you doing down there?" she asked, able to see quite clearly now that the bulky figure of her husband was no longer blocking the window.

"Is it safe to come out?" Daniel Blue Eagle asked warily, giving his 'white flag' a final shake in the air above his head. "Are you still going to shoot me?"

"I thought you were an intruder!" she apologized, returning the revolver to its place under the pillow.

"Why aren't you asleep?"

"I was taking a bath," he explained, standing up cautiously, peering suspiciously at Starr to be certain the gun was no longer in her hand.

"In the dark?"

"I didn't want to light a lamp and wake you. I thought you needed to sleep."

The more accustomed to the darkness she became, the more aware she was of the moonlight on Daniel Blue Eagle's muscled torso, turning his tanned skin the color of antique gold.

"That was very thoughtful of you," she mumbled softly, suddenly growing self-conscious as he turned to the side and the light beaming in from the window reflected off the taut muscles of his buttocks.

The realization that Daniel Blue Eagle was wearing no clothing sent an exciting shiver over her, bringing her entire body to life with unexpected desire, and she bit her lower lip to keep from moaning aloud.

Squirming uncomfortably, Starr flinched involuntarily when the silk robe she wore over her own nakedness slithered seductively, agonizingly over her hardening nipples. Embarrassed by the feelings that shook her at the sight of her husband's broad-shouldered body as he stood watching her from the foot of the bed, Starr had no idea how appealing she was to him.

Her long hair was disheveled and wild, a perfect halo for her face. Her eyes were open wide, the pupils dilated and glistening with what he recognized as desire equal to the need in his own loins.

And the way the robe molded to her curves, falling

345

open almost to her waist. He wanted to rip it from her to see if the twin buds that pushed against the adhering silk were real. He licked his dry lips in anticipation of the taste of those buds so unsuccessfully disguised by the shimmering cloth.

"Is it safe to come back to bed?" he asked, his voice catching in his throat as he watched her moisten her lips as he had moistened his own.

"It's safe," she smiled bashfully, wishing he would hurry back.

The mattress shifted under Daniel Blue Eagle's weight as he knelt on the bed beside her and reached out to brush a wisp of hair off her cheek with the back of his fingers. "I love your hair," he murmured softly, wrapping some curls around each of his fists and using them to draw her to him.

"Then I'm glad I didn't cut it," she whispered, her face only an inch from his.

Daniel Blue Eagle drew back from her, an ache in his eyes. "Why were you going to cut your hair?"

"When I thought I wasn't going to see you again, it was as if you were dead, as if I had died too, Daniel. I wanted to mourn my loss.

"When I was using the razor to cut the ropes William put on my wrists, I welcomed every cut into my flesh, as if the pain would take away the ache in my heart. I thought about cutting my hair, like the Oglala women do when they lose a loved one, but something stopped me. I must've known you would come for me."

Daniel Blue Eagle took her hands and turned them palms up, kissing them in turn before he touched his lips to each of the tiny cuts on her wrists. "I'm sorry,

Firebird," he lamented. "I never should have taken you there."

"There was no way you could have known," she comforted, thrilling to the electricity of his merest touch.

"I want to make love with you, Firebird." Daniel Blue Eagle's voice was husky as he nibbled his way to the sensitive bend at her elbow to run his tongue over the tender creases he found there before continuing his lazy journey up her arm.

"I want to be inside you," he murmured against her skin as he pushed aside the loose sleeve and nipped at her skin with his teeth.

"Oh, I want you there, too," Starr moaned, luxuriating in the feel of his mouth on the flesh of her inner arm. A spiral of fire ignited explosively within her body.

Leaning back on one elbow, Starr cried aloud as she instinctively moved her straining breasts toward Daniel Blue Eagle's mouth, begging him, tempting him to kiss them and end her agony.

Drawing a ragged breath, Daniel Blue Eagle lifted himself over Starr, straddling her thighs and splaying his hands around her ribcage to pull her to a sitting position. With all the urgency he had held in check since he had falsely told her he didn't want her for a wife, his lips came down to devour hers.

His kiss was demanding. It told her he shared her deep need.

Intent on mapping her mouth's hot interior, his kiss became leisurely, as though he wanted to prolong their pleasure. He delved into every sweet crevice, until he grew intoxicated with the delights he discovered in his erotic search.

Continuing his thorough study of her mouth, Daniel Blue Eagle lowered Starr's shoulders onto the bed, releasing her lips from his kiss only so he could sit back and relish the beautiful sight before him.

He gloried in the rapture on her face, and his mouth watered to taste the beaded nipples standing out invitingly against the clinging material of her robe, but he held himself back.

Instead, he fanned his hands over her silk-covered breasts, barely touching them, though they rose up invitingly to meet his palms. He gently teased and caressed her body, leaving her skin burning wherever he touched her, drawing an urgent response from her as she moved under him in a desperate effort to urge her point of need closer to his hands.

When his teasing touch had her moaning, Daniel Blue Eagle slid his hands upward. Lifting and weighing her breasts from the sides, his thumbs feathered back and forth over the pearling peaks as he thrilled to the results of his touch.

Thrusting herself higher and higher against his hands, Starr was unable to bear the absence of his mouth on her any longer.

Watching him through lust-clouded eyes, she reached up and threaded her fingers into Daniel Blue Eagle's dark hair, still damp from his bath, to guide his head down to the shadowy cleavage between her breasts where her kimono gaped open.

He nuzzled the sweet-scented gorge, made even deeper when he circled her breasts from their undersides and lifted them together, squeezing, massaging, sending a quickening response spreading along Starr's veins like a warm rush of fire.

"You taste so good," Daniel Blue Eagle murmured huskily against her flesh as his mouth scorched its way along the opening of the robe.

Sitting back on his calves, Daniel Blue Eagle locked his gaze to Starr's, holding her his captive with glistening eyes that seemed more black than blue in the moonlit shadows.

His weight pressed her bottom down into the sheets, causing her to lift her hips upward to meet him. Her hands rested on his thighs, nails digging urgently into his hard, muscled flesh.

No longer able to deny himself the pleasure of seeing her beauty unveiled, Daniel Blue Eagle untied the sash at Starr's waist with slow, measured actions. As though uncovering a long-desired and valuable treasure, he ran his hands up the center of her body to gingerly smooth the silk away from her skin, exposing her lush breasts to his hungry vision at last. He could not stop the gasp of pleasure that escaped.

The robe fell away to reveal her dusky-tipped breasts to his spellbound gaze.

Starr cried her delight as he dipped his head and hungrily drew a rosy peak into his mouth to tug and caress it with his lips and tongue while his hands molded and kneaded both breasts.

Continuing to caress her fullness, now wet and glistening from his kiss, Daniel Blue Eagle blazed a trail of liquid fire to her other nipple. He eagerly drew that neglected tip deep into the moist warmth of his mouth to fully love and adore the stiff peak.

Starr arched her body upward, unable to keep from moving in animal anticipation. She was on fire. Heat

349

radiated from her breasts to her whole body. She didn't remember her breasts ever being so sensitive before.

She moved her hands up and down Daniel Blue Eagle's sweat-slicked back as she lifted her head upward to kiss and bite at his shoulder.

Rolling off her, Daniel Blue Eagle lay on his stomach at a right angle to Starr's squirming body, continuing his mouth's assault on her gently rounded belly. He dipped his tongue deep into her navel as his fingers slid over the downy fur that guarded the soft, slippery pleats of her womanhood.

"Oh, Daniel," Starr whimpered, unable to stop herself from shuddering as he brought her passion to exploding fulfillment. "So good, so good," she mumbled, impatiently bending her upper body toward Daniel Blue Eagle and reaching out for him, needing to bring him closer to her, to be one with him.

Her lips grazed his narrow waist and her hands pushed urgently on his hip to roll him to his side so that she could caress his strength, now hard and erect, its smooth skin stretched tight.

Tentatively at first, then with determination born of an overwhelming urgency to touch and possess all of the man she loved, Starr trapped his shaft between her warm palms and made love to him with her hands. Her touch sent bursts of fire raging uncontrolled through Daniel Blue Eagle's powerful body, rendering him weak and helpless.

Glorying in the loving caresses, he flopped over on his back, carrying Starr to a kneeling position over him. Again her own quivering need ascended to volcanic proportions with the feel of his warm breath on her moist curls. The need for him was so great it actually hurt. Her adoring kiss descended to his pronounced desire as he drew her to him to lave her to another glorious completion.

Afraid he wouldn't be able to control his desire if she continued her worshipful attention much longer, Daniel Blue Eagle turned Starr to her back with one agile motion and entered her body with a sure thrust, magnificently filling her emptiness.

"I love you, Daniel," she cried out as she raised up to hold him even further within her warmth.

Deeper, faster, he buried himself within the sweet haven of her body.

They moved as one force, with one need, climbing to the glorious zenith that could be reached only when their bodies were united, only when they were one.

"I love you, my wife," Daniel Blue Eagle breathed heavily into her ear as he collapsed on her.

"And I love you, my husband, with all my heart, my soul. You're my life," she vowed, choking back the tears of joy that suddenly rose in her throat.

"Are you crying?" he asked, confused. He rose up on his elbows to look anxiously into watery gray eyes.

"Yes, and I don't even know why," she blubbered helplessly. "It's never been this perfect, and I'm just so happy," she giggled tearfully, hugging Daniel Blue Eagle to her.

"That's no reason to cry, is it?"

"No," she agreed readily, but that did nothing to turn off the tears. In fact, they came harder. "No reason at all. But I thought I'd never know the feel of your arms around me again," she sobbed, realizing she was being foolish, but unable to stop crying now that she'd started. "I thought all I had left of you was our ba—"

Starr clamped her mouth shut on the rest of her word, and her eyes rounded nervously. She couldn't tell Daniel Blue Eagle about their baby yet. He had so much on his mind. She wouldn't add to his worries.

"What did you say?" he demanded, incredulous. "What was the only thing you had left of me?" he asked suspiciously.

Fear rippled through Starr, and she could feel his body withdrawing from its warm nest inside her, leaving her feeling empty and afraid. "M—m—memories. All I would have left were memories," she improvised, withering pitifully under his scorching gaze.

Now it all made sense to him. Her unexplainable tears, her insecurity, her increased appetite, her irritability, her enlarged breasts, her sweetly rounded belly. Why had he been so slow to realize? Why hadn't he known?

She's going to have a baby! My baby! The blow hit him with gale force. *Not now. Not when I have to send her away*, he cried silently. *Not when I may not live to see it!*

"How long have you known?" he asked, rolling over onto his back to stare with unseeing eyes at the cracked ceiling.

Starr knew there was no point in lying to him. "I've suspected for a while, but I wasn't certain until just before you returned from the Comanche village." She studied the ceiling too, hurt and disillusioned.

352

She had known he would be surprised, had expected him to be worried. But it had never occurred to her that her husband, the man she loved with all her heart, wouldn't be happy. But he wasn't the least bit happy. Not only was he unhappy, he was downright angry that she was pregnant.

"Why didn't you tell me?"

To Starr, the question sounded more like an accusation, as if she'd hidden something from him for her own selfish purposes.

Now she was angry!

"Why didn't I tell you?!?" she shrieked. Clutching the robe around her, she sat up in the bed to glower at the man who had taken her heart and torn it to shreds with his reaction to the fact that she carried his baby nestled in her womb.

"What do you think I was trying to do the day you waltzed in and told me you didn't want me for a wife anymore?"

"You could have said something on the way to the fort."

"And have you throw it up to me that you didn't want me *or* my baby? Believe me, if I'd known how you would hate the idea of me having your child, I would never have told you."

"Is that what you think this is about? You think that I hate the idea of you having my baby?"

"Well, don't you?"

"No, I love the idea of my child growing, safe and warm, inside you," he said earnestly, extending a tentative hand to her belly to cup his palm over the soft roundness there.

How could she stay angry with him when he talked

353

like that? "Then why are you so mad at me?" she wept, no longer able to control the tears that flooded down her cheeks.

"I'm not angry with you, Firebird. Never with you." His voice was resigned and tortured.

"Then what? Is it because I didn't tell you sooner? I didn't want you to worry about me when you have so many other things on your mind. I wanted to tell you, but I thought it would be better if I waited until we got back to the village."

"But that's the problem, love. I can't take you back to the village."

"Why not? Where are we going?"

"Not we, Firebird. You. You're going back to Yankton, and I'm going back to the Oglala. This may be the last time we're together."

"You can't mean it!" she inhaled frantically. "You can't send me away!"

"If William told you the truth and the soldiers come to attack our summer conference, there is a very good chance that many Indians will be killed. I will probably be one of them," he said gently, as if talking to a child, unable to hide the truth from her any longer. He couldn't let her go on hoping. "Though I've done everything I can to stop a war, if it comes, I can't turn my back on the People when it does."

"Then I'll go with you. Don't leave me. Do you want your baby to have the kind of childhood you had? Of two worlds and belonging in neither?"

He smiled at her reasoning, but it was something he'd already thought of before he'd made all of his arrangements. "You'll go to my grandfather's house as the widow of Captain Daniel Edwards. I've con-

354

tacted my lawyers and left everything to you."

"I can't go to Yankton. People will know about the marriage to William, about the Indians taking me." Couldn't he see how ridiculous his whole plan was?

"I found your marriage certificate in William's desk when we were at the fort and have taken the steps to annul that marriage by filing the proper papers. As far as the law is concerned, you aren't married to him. He won't be able to bother you. And as far as the other goes, you can say Captain Daniel Edwards saved you from the renegades and that you married him."

"But there are people who know the truth."

"Your word against theirs."

"Daniel, this is crazy. You're not going to die. Take me with you! Please," she begged, throwing herself over his chest and wrapping her arm tightly around his waist. "I don't want to live without you."

He gripped her arms and lifted her over him, shaking her angrily. "Don't ever say that again! You have to live. I'm counting on you to tell our child how much his father loved him, how much I wanted to be there to see him grow up, how many wonderful things I wanted to share with him, how much I hated leaving him a legacy of war.

"Firebird, you must live to tell him the truth about the Lakota, to make him see that the only way the People can exist is to be one with the whites. You must see that he never forgets what strong people he is descended from. Give him pride in both his white and his Indian heritage. Don't let him be ashamed of his Lakota blood. Do you understand me?" he asked roughly, not bothering to hide the tears glistening in his blue eyes. "Promise me, Firebird."

"We'll teach our baby those things together, Daniel," she insisted, her statement a plea.

"It's too late, Firebird."

Starr stared forlornly around the interior of the rail car. Daniel Blue Eagle had thought of everything—a private sleeping compartment, luggage with new clothing in it, the annulment, a place to go, what to tell people, money to live on—everything she could want. Yet, she would have given all of it up gladly to be able to go back to the Oglala village with him. Why couldn't he understand?

Tears streamed down her cheeks as she leaned her forehead against the glass window for a last longing look at Daniel Blue Eagle, who stood outside the rail car amid buggies, wagons, horses, late-boarding passengers, and people seeing the train off.

Tall and handsome in a Stetson hat, a black sack coat that strained over his broad shoulders, and tight-fitting nankeen trousers that molded to his muscular legs and were tucked into tall leather boots, the miserable expression on Daniel Blue Eagle's face mirrored the desolation on Starr's.

"Please," she mouthed, placing the flat of her small hands pitifully against the car window. Where the heel and ball of her palms and the tips of her fingers pressed desperately against the glass, the flesh flattened out and turned a deathly white.

Death! That's what Daniel Blue Eagle was suffering by sending her away. His death and hers. The thought of never seeing her again was unbearable and tore at him with vengeance.

As if needing a final reminder that his wife was alive, and that he was doing the right thing by sending her to his grandfather's house, Daniel Blue Eagle stepped close to the rail car and pressed his hands against hers, imagining he would be able to feel her warmth through the glass. But the pane was cold—cold and dead like his heart.

With the see-through barrier between them, they stayed like that for long moments, hands pressed together.

"All aboard," a man's voice sang out at the same time a puff of steam curled around Daniel Blue Eagle, forcing him to step back. When the haze cleared, he looked to the window for one last, torturous time. But she was gone, as if she had evaporated with the white cloud that had obliterated her features a moment before.

Knowing it was best that she had been strong, Daniel Blue Eagle stood watching the darkened window, hating himself for wanting just one last glimpse of her, but wanting it just the same.

The conductor leaned out the side of a car and signaled the engineer ahead, but still Daniel Blue Eagle watched the empty window.

Amid the noisy hiss of steam and the piercing scream of the whistle, the wheels screeched in place for the briefest instant before the train jerked forward.

"No!" Daniel Blue Eagle bellowed, leaping into action to jump onto the slow moving train as the end of a car rolled by.

"Daniel!" Starr cried as the train moved past the place where she stood with her luggage on the platform, seeing her husband as he disappeared into the car. She gathered her skirts in her hands and ran screaming after the train that was gaining speed. But it was no use. She couldn't catch it.

The train pulled out of the station, leaving Starr standing alone in its wake.

"Looks like we had the same idea," Daniel Blue Eagle said from the opposite side of the tracks, looking sheepish and relieved.

"Just don't say anything, Daniel," Starr cautioned evenly, her hands knotting into fists at her side. "I'm not going to run away and hide in Yankton. I'm going back to the Lakota where I belong, and if you won't take me, I'll go alone. But I am going," she shuddered, all her heartache and frustration roiling to the surface.

"All right, Firebird," Daniel Blue Eagle said softly, holding tight rein on every muscle in his body to keep from leaping over the tracks and taking her into his arms.

"You can't stop me from going," she continued before the meaning of his words penetrated.

What had he said? Had he said *all right*? Was that a smile she saw on his face? It was. It was a smile.

Her gray eyes clouded with confusion, then glossed with emotion.

He wanted her. Daniel Blue Eagle wasn't going to send her away!

Taking the tracks that separated them in two long strides, Daniel Blue Eagle stood before Starr, looking down at her with love shining from his sparkling blue eyes. "You never did know what was good for you, did you?"

"Oh, I don't know about that," Starr answered tremulously, feeling like laughing and crying. "I think I've got a pretty good idea about what's good for me, not to mention what's good for you, Mr. Daniel Blue Eagle Edwards!"

Chapter Twenty-one

"Crazy Horse's scouts have spotted us," Daniel Blue Eagle informed Starr through clenched teeth. "We should have company before too long."

Frightened for the first time since they'd left Bismarck by riverboat two weeks before, Starr's head automatically jerked around to see what he meant. "Where?"

"Don't make any sudden moves," Daniel Blue Eagle ordered harshly, though he didn't look at her. "Keep your eyes straight ahead and smile when you talk. It'll be all right if you don't panic."

"Where are they? What do they want?" Starr choked, doing her best to follow her husband's directions and act as though nothing was wrong.

"They just want to watch us right now. They haven't decided if we're friendly or not."

"Can't you give them some signal, so they know you're Oglala, too?"

"When they get a little closer," he whispered.

Her eyes shifted nervously from side to side, Starr

moved her mare closer to Daniel Blue Eagle's mount and asked, "What if they shoot us before you can identify yourself?"

"I don't think they will, not when there are so many of them and only two of us. They'll want to know what we're doing here, especially when one of us is a white woman." His smile was mischievous, teasing, deliberately disguising his own concern. Unfortunately, he wasn't nearly as certain as he sounded that Crazy Horse's renegade warriors wouldn't attack first and ask questions later; and he mentally upbraided himself again for not having the strength to leave his wife behind.

Starr didn't say anything else, nor did she return her husband's smile. Instead she made a herculean effort to think of things other than the possibility that at any minute arrows might whiz out of the brush and kill them both as they traveled south along the Powder River in the Montana Territory.

Though the long hours spent on horseback during the past week as they moved up the Yellowstone River, and now the Powder, had been exhausting, the trip the week before up the Missouri River on the sternwheeler, *Western Queen*, had been wonderful. She would think about that, not her aching back, her sore bottom, or her fear.

Starr recalled how, not wanting to take any more chance of being recognized than absolutely necessary, she and Daniel Blue Eagle had spent most of the week on the steamer inside their cabin, talking and making love.

It had been a wonderful, idyllic time which had allowed them to escape temporarily from their problems, as well as bringing them closer together than ever before. During the long, sweet hours on the riverboat, they had shared thoughts, fears, and dreams neither of them had ever spoken of to another soul. They had talked, laughed, and cried.

And they had made love, spending long hours leisurely investigating and loving each other.

He had marveled at the changes her pregnancy had already made in her figure and anxiously anticipated the future alterations his baby growing inside her would bring to her slim body. Showering kisses over her expanding belly, he had assured her that he would love her when she was 'fat and ugly'—*her* words, not his—dispelling any doubts she might have had about how much he wanted their baby and her.

She, in turn, had kissed every scar on his body and made him tell her where, when and how each and every one of them had come to mar his smooth skin.

One particular scar gave Starr more insight into Daniel Blue Eagle than any other. It was the tiny, almost invisible line just under the ridge of his strong chin. Not heroically earned in battle or some Indian test of courage, he had attained that injury when he was six years old and had challenged Gray Wolf to a foot race.

"I was certain I would win and was showing off," he laughed, remembering the race from twenty years before with bittersweet thoughts. "I turned around and ran backwards for a few steps, teasing and goading him unmercifully."

"You ought to be ashamed."

"I am, now. But when a boy is six years old and the oldest child, there's a certain amount of picking on his younger brother he feels it's his right and his duty to carry out. Anyway, in the next minute, I got my reward and a lesson that has lasted my whole life."

"What happened?"

"Gray Wolf was so mad, he was almost crying. He leaped forward with a burst of speed that brought him alongside me, and he passed me before I knew what was happening. I turned around and ran like hell but I couldn't catch him."

"Did Gray Wolf win?" Starr asked, feeling the younger brother's frustration as if it were her own.

"Just wait a minute," he shushed her. Building the suspense, he finally went on. "We were almost to the finish line and I was still a step behind Gray Wolf. I kept thinking about how my friends would laugh if my little brother beat me in a foot race. I couldn't stand the thought. Winning was all that mattered. I threw my body forward, parallel to the ground, and flew over the finish line to win the race by one very bloody chin."

"Poor little chin," Starr murmured, tickling her tongue along the tiny raised scar. "But it did serve you right."

"Actually, that little accident taught me a lesson I could never have learned in books. I not only learned that winning isn't all it's cracked up to be and often can be downright painful, but it showed me that if the strong push the weak too far, the weak will fight back, and they just might win, or at least do a lot of damage trying."

Starr knew he was relating the race from long ago to the boiling conflict between the plains Indians and the whites. It was the foot race all over again. The

363

strong would be the inevitable winners, but in the end, both sides would be the losers. And a man whose heart pumped both white and Indian blood would feel the losses doubly, as would his wife.

"What about this one?" Starr asked, deliberately indicating a more recent scar on the inside of a corded forearm. "What lesson did you learn from this experience?" she asked about the white line that was identical to the one on her own arm.

"I learned a man with a redheaded wife has more trouble than he can handle and that he hasn't got a chance in hell of winning," Daniel Blue Eagle growled with pretended anger. The light in his sapphire eyes told her that his black mood had been successfully banished, for the moment anyway.

He shifted his weight to his side and arranged Starr comfortably against his muscular length. "I learned that women with red hair are stubborn, contrary, and impossible."

"Just how many redheads have you known, Mr. Edwards?" Starr asked indignantly, rising up on one elbow to glare into his mischievous eyes.

"You're more worried about how I came by my information than the actual information," he laughed.

"We've already established that *I'm* stubborn, contrary, and impossible. What I want to know is how many other redheads you've studied to make the statement that we're all like that!"

"Hmm, let me see," Daniel Blue Eagle said thoughtfully, rolling to his back again and holding up one hand. He made the motions of counting redheads on his fingers. When he held up his other hand and began on it, Starr sat up in a huff and grabbed his wrists and held them down.

"How many?" she asked again, holding his arms over his head as she straddled his middle.

"I was counting," he defended, enjoying the view of her full, ripe breasts swaying above his face, and the feel of her long hair draping over his skin in a sensual caress. "You interrupted me, so I'm not really sure, but if I made a wild guess, I'd say about—mmm—"

"How many?" she ground out through clenched teeth, looking as threatening as she could manage.

"One."

"Are you certain?" she asked, arching a fine eyebrow with feigned suspicion. "Because if I thought you were lying to me, I'd strangle you right here," she said, dragging her long hair back and forth over his exposed neck and upper chest. "With my stubborn, contrary, impossible red hair!"

"I'd die a happy man."

"Would you, Daniel? Would you die a happy man if you died this very minute?" Her gray eyes were now serious.

"Very happy. The Lakotas have a saying, Firebird. We say, *Hoka hey*. It means 'It's a good day to die.' That is how I feel with you."

"I'm happy too, Daniel. I love you so much," she whispered, bringing her mouth down to cover his in a kiss that ended further conversation. . . .

A low, eerie bird call brought Starr's attention back to the present with a jolt, and she looked questioningly at Daniel Blue Eagle.

He cupped his hands over his mouth again and

365

repeated the call a second time.

After a moment, his call received an answer, to which he responded with another, slightly different, sound. "Now they know we know their signals. Let's hope they have the good sense to come a little closer before they start firing on us."

"I thought you said they wouldn't shoot us."

"Well, if they come close enough to recognize me, they won't. But in these clothes, I'm not so sure," he admitted apologetically.

Starr's heart began to hammer its staccato rhythm with a vengeance. She looked around frantically, imagining Crazy Horse's braves hiding in every wild plum bush, behind every cottonwood tree growing along the Powder River. "Daniel Blue Eagle, why didn't you tell me?"

"I didn't want you to worry."

Before she could respond, an arrow suddenly streaked across the trail, embedding itself in the ground in front of the two riders.

Starr's heart catapulted to her throat, miraculously plugging the scream that started there.

The first arrow was followed by a second, then a third, all three landing within inches of each other.

Daniel Blue Eagle and Starr reined in their horses, and he held up a hand in a sign of peace. "It is Daniel Blue Eagle, son of the Oglala chief, Man of the People," he called out in the Lakota language. "We've come to see Crazy Horse."

"Why do you wear the clothing of the *wasicun*, Daniel Blue Eagle?" a brave asked as he walked into the path, stopping beside the three arrows. The lithe and sinewy warrior was not particularly tall, but spoke with a quiet dignity and confidence that immediately told Starr she was seeing the famous Oglala war chief, Crazy Horse, in person. A young man to be a chief, he appeared to be about thirty-five years old and was very handsome in a melancholy way. Starr could see now why many people thought Crazy Horse was a white captive who had been raised by the Sioux. His skin was as light as Daniel Blue Eagle's.

"The soldiers took my wife, and I had to wear this clothing to travel in their midst, Crazy Horse," Daniel Blue Eagle responded as he dismounted. He indicated Starr with his hand and introduced her. "This is my wife, Firebird."

"Your *winyan* is white," Crazy Horse said bluntly, his black eyes roving over Starr's gray-wool-clad figure, his detached gaze lingering on the wisps of red-gold hair that had worked their way out from under the hood of her cape.

"You, my friend, above all others, should know that one must be judged by what is in his heart, not by the color of his skin. My woman's heart is Oglala, as though she were born among the People," Daniel Blue Eagle said, looking straight into Crazy Horse's eyes and smiling sincerely.

"Is this true?" Crazy Horse asked Starr directly. His black eyes bored through her, as if he could see into her soul to verify or refute Daniel Blue Eagle's words.

"*Ohan*, my husband's friend. In my heart, I am Oglala," she answered respectfully, taking care to keep her eyes downcast, rather than meeting the hard gaze. She was glad that so far she'd been able to follow the conversation between Daniel Blue Eagle and Crazy Horse.

"She speaks our language," Crazy Horse said to Daniel Blue Eagle, the tone in his voice a mixture of surprise and delight.

"She is a good Oglala *winyan*," Daniel Blue Eagle told the other man in an offhand manner, lassoing his desire to smile his pride in his wife. He could tell she'd made an impression on Crazy Horse.

The suspicious chief's face broke into a hearty laugh, and he raised a hand in the air. The clearing was immediately filled with mounted braves who, just as Starr had feared, had evidently been hiding in the cottonwood trees and thick brush of wild plum bushes until it was determined that Daniel Blue Eagle could still be trusted.

"You will spend the night in my camp, and tomorrow I will have some of our braves escort you to your father's village in the valley of the Mizpah," Crazy Horse said as he mounted the pinto one of his men had brought out to him.

"We appreciate your kindness, Crazy Horse," Daniel Blue Eagle returned, remounting his own horse and following the young chief, who was known to the whites as the greatest Indian tactician of battle strategy ever to live.

Daniel Blue Eagle gave Starr, who was still holding her breath, an encouraging wink and smile to tell she had done well and how proud of her he was.

Placing Starr and her mount between himself and Crazy Horse, Daniel Blue Eagle spoke again, his tone very serious. "While she was held captive by the whites, my wife obtained some information that could prove very important to the Lakota people."

"What information is that?" Crazy Horse said, speaking directly to Daniel Blue Eagle's wife.

Starr looked hesitantly at Daniel Blue Eagle, her face paling with panic. She hadn't planned on being the one to relay the important facts to Crazy Horse. Her understanding of the Lakota language was reasonably good, but speaking it aloud was another thing altogether. What if she said something wrong and the chief misunderstood?

Daniel Blue Eagle read her concern on her face and patted her hand in an open show of affection. "My wife is unsure of herself when it comes to using a newly-learned language to convey such serious knowledge, so I hope you will understand if she speaks slowly and allows me to assist her."

Crazy Horse nodded and Starr began, choosing her words slowly and carefully, looking often to Daniel Blue Eagle for encouragement and for the confirmation of a word.

"The soldiers plan to converge on the Lakotas from three different directions and destroy them all. There is a Colonel Gibbon who is supposedly bringing men from Fort Ellis in the west. I was told General Crook is coming from Fort Fetterman in the south and that General Terry is supposed to march from the East with Lieutenant Colonel Custer's Seventh Cavalry."

"When?" Crazy Horse asked.

"Probably next month, during the Moon of Making Fat, when we are all gathered for our annual meeting," Daniel Blue Eagle interjected, relieving Starr from the strain of having to answer questions. His expression told her she had done well, but that she could now relax and just listen. "They know that for as long as anyone can remember, all the Teton Lakota have come together once a year for this great meeting. It would be a perfect time for them to attack."

"The one your wife refers to as Gibbon is already here. He is camped at the mouth of the Rosebud with about five hundred men. He has sent out scouting parties but doesn't seem to be preparing to attack, as if he was waiting for something. Now we know what it was. He was waiting for those famous Indian killers, Custer and Crook, to join him." Crazy Horse's lip curled when he said the hated names.

All the Sioux and Cheyenne had good reason to hate the very sound of the names Custer and Crook above all others of the despoilers of the Indian lands. Known to the Indians as "Three Stars," General Crook was responsible for the attack on the peaceful, sleeping Cheyenne camp two months before. That attack and burning of the village had left hundreds of Cheyenne homeless and without food, many of them dying from exposure as they had made their way through the snow to Crazy Horse's camp for aid. He still ached with the memory of the beaten, half-frozen people when they had come into his village three days after they had lost everything.

Then there was Lieutenant Colonel George Armstrong Custer, known as "Long Hair" to the Lakota. He was even more hated than General Crook. It had been Custer who had broadcast the news of gold in the Black Hills, bringing the prospectors onto the Indians' lands, and it had been Custer who eight years before had led his Seventh Cavalry into Black Kettle's sleeping camp on the Washita River, killing and scalping the long-suffering peacemaking chief and over a hundred others, most of them women and children. "Long Hair" had been commended for that "victory," Crazy Horse remembered, choking down the bitter bile that rose in his throat at the thought of the glory-seeking officer.

"If they attack, we will be ready for them this time," Crazy Horse said aloud, though the words were uttered as if he were speaking to himself.

During the rest of their visit with Crazy Horse and his wife, Black Shawl, Starr didn't hear Daniel Blue Eagle and the war chief discuss the Lakota's problems with the whites again. So by the time she and Daniel Blue Eagle rode into Man of the People's camp two days later, she could almost forget that the United States Army might descend on them at any moment. She was too happy to be home, too anxious to see Prairie Moon and tell her about the baby.

The same evening Starr and Daniel Blue Eagle rode into Man of the People's camp on the bank of the Mizpah, Captain William Howard made the first entry into the journal he planned to keep to detail the Seventh Cavalry's campaign against the Sioux.

17 May 1876
Dakota Territory, west of Fort Abraham Lincoln
   The Seventh Cavalry of the United States Army left Fort Abraham Lincoln this morning, marching smartly to the sounds of the military band playing, 'The Girl I Left Behind.' As we passed by the Indian quarters, the old men,

squaws, and children moaned their farewell, and the 40 Indian scouts going with us, mostly Arickaras under Bobtailed Bull, beat on their drums in answer to the gloomy chant.

In front of Laundress Row, the little children formed their own troops and mimicked the soldiers by marching alongside us. The women cried and waved and held their babies in the air for a last look as the 7th Cavalry moved out of sight. It must have been an impressive sight to watch 1,200 brave men, three Gatling guns, a herd of cattle, and 150 wagons carrying over 250 tons of supplies disappear into the early morning mist.

Colonel Custer almost didn't get to take part in this campaign because of political differences with President Grant. But General Terry, who was given the command when Custer was removed by the president, is inexperienced in fighting Indians, so he arranged for Custer to go as second in command. The Colonel confided in me that he plans to cut loose from Terry during the campaign. He says once we get there we won't be slowed down by some over-cautious general.

I personally think he wants the publicity and glory all for himself. He has even brought along a newspaper reporter from the Herald. There are many who suspect he plans to use this campaign to make his name even more popular so that he can run for president.

Well, Custer isn't the only one who plans to make a name for himself during the next few

*weeks. I too expect to eliminate my share of
thieving Sioux and claim a little bit of fame for
myself. If I have to "cut loose" from the others
to do it, I will.*

"It's so good to be back among the People, isn't
it?" Starr commented with a weary sigh as she rolled
out their buffalo robes.

"Very good," Daniel Blue Eagle agreed, smiling at
the way his wife still turned her back away from him
when she removed her clothing, as though he hadn't
seen and touched and loved every satiny inch of her a
hundred times.

"Are you going to come to bed soon?" she asked,
reaching for the red silk kimono she had taken to
sleeping in. No matter how much she felt like one of
the Oglalas, she had never gotten used to sleeping in
her clothes or in the nude. She slipped her arms into
the sleeves and reached down to tie the sash.

"Allow me," Daniel Blue Eagle offered, sliding his
arms around her from behind. But instead of tying
the belt, he opened the robe to look down the length
of her pregnant body. "Our baby is growing," he
whispered as he smoothed his open hands lovingly
over her round belly, his tongue moving lazily along
the outer rim of her ear as he spoke.

"Allow you to what?" she murmured, leaning her
head back against his shoulder to fully savor the
luxury of his embrace.

"To do this," he breathed, his tongue spiraling
along the sensitive tissue of her ear. "And this," he
whispered against her neck, dragging his tongue

373

along the pale flesh at the bend of her shoulder. Chills rippled along her skin.

His warm hands circled over her stomach. "And this," he teased, trailing a finger along the rim of her navel before dipping it inside the tiny hollow.

His hands encircled her ribcage and whispered up her body to cup and weigh her breasts, already growing heavy in preparation for the baby that would nurse from them in the fall. He covered her breasts, rubbing the centers of his palms over her tender nipples until they were hot and hard, pressing achingly against his hands.

Keeping one hand busy massaging her breasts, Daniel Blue Eagle slid his other hand downward to explore and tease the delicate flesh between her thighs.

"Does your back still hurt?" he asked, lifting her thick hair and kissing the sweet hollow at her nape.

"It'll be all right," she sighed, trying to turn in his arms but he held her in place, deliberately pulling her back against his hard length.

"Lie down on your stomach and I'll massage it for you," he ordered, slipping the robe from her shoulders and giving her a little prod toward the buffalo robe.

Starr followed his directions and lay down, her arms under her head. Her back really did ache, and a massage sounded awfully good.

Something cold touched her skin in the small of her back and she jumped involuntarily. "What are you doing?"

"It's just a little of that oil I bought in Bismarck," he explained, quickly spreading the liquid over her back in a bone-melting massage. "I'll warm it the next time in my hands," he promised as his nimble fingers squeezed and kneaded the tight muscles of her shoulders and back.

Gripping her at the waist, he circled his thumbs along the vertebrae, giving each hard nub special attention. "Thank you," she finally said, certain that if he kept up the delightful ministrations much longer, she would go mad with frustration. "Why don't I do you now? You rode just as far as I did."

"I'm not through," Daniel Blue Eagle said, pouring more lotion in his hand and allowing it to warm for a second before he spread it over her bottom and the backs of her thighs. Before he would be through he would smooth the sweet-smelling oil over the soles of her feet, between her toes, along her calves, taking time out to kiss the backs of her knees.

"Your skin is so soft," he whispered, ducking his head to kiss the back of a well-shaped thigh and run his tongue along the half-moon crease that divided her leg from her buttocks. "Are your legs sore from riding so long?"

"Not anymore."

He gripped the tops of her thighs and ran his thumbs down between them, pressing upward. He was pleased to find her warm and moist with desire. "How about there?" He slid his fingers into the honeyed cave that was moving rhythmically under his hand. "Are you sore here?"

"I'm not certain 'sore' is the word I would use," she groaned, rolling her hips from side to side and up and down on his probing fingers.

"What is the word?" He withdrew his hand.

"Empty," she admitted, rolling over on her back

375

and holding her arms up to her husband, who knelt beside her. "Come fill me, my husband. Fill me with your strength, your gentleness, your love. Make me feel complete."

Tearing off his own clothing, Daniel Blue Eagle placed himself between her open thighs. Supporting his torso on his forearms so he wouldn't put too much weight on her, he kissed her mouth sweetly and tenderly.

The tip of his tongue moistened itself at her lips as the tip of his manhood bathed itself in the sweet lotion of her body, but he went no further. He moved his shaft along the length of her, from the crest of her desire to the beckoning grotto at the entrance to her body, and his tongue explored her lips until she thought she would scream with need.

She opened her mouth and sucked at his tongue as below she seemed to open and suck at his manhood. Her legs wrapped frantically around his hard thighs and she raised her hips upward, begging him to enter her and end her agony.

"I can't bear to wait any more, Daniel. Please don't torture me any longer," she whimpered breathlessly, her whole body alive with desire.

"I love you, Firebird," he groaned urgently, finally plunging his power into her. Her tunnel of love surrounded him, drawing him deeper into the glorious heat, moving and contracting against him.

Starr's hands roved over the sweaty sinew of his shoulders, back, and arms. She clutched hungrily at him, lifting her head upward to lick and kiss and taste the salty moisture from his skin.

Their united tempo increased to the speed of a

shooting star, their glorious, fiery ride on that heavenly body finally hurling them violently into another sphere to explode into a million tiny lights.

"Does your back still hurt?" Daniel Blue Eagle panted as together they tumbled back to earth.

"Not that I would admit," she answered, her words coming in breathy staccatos. "I don't think I have the energy to have another 'massage' tonight," she laughed, biting at his neck playfully.

"Well, you just let me know when you're ready. I'll be glad to oblige."

"Oh, I will. Have no worry about that."

Chapter Twenty-two

7 June 1876 Montana Territory—South bank of the Yellowstone at the Powder

Rendezvoused with the sternwheeler, Far West, today after three weeks moving across the flat, treeless grasslands of the western Dakota Territory. It is good to see trees again.

The Far West is piloted by the famous riverboat captain, Grant Marsh, and will serve as our supply boat, hospital, and mobile command post. It will ferry Gibbon's troops to this side of the Yellowstone when the time to attack comes. Presently, Gibbon is camped at old Fort Pease at the mouth of the Bighorn.

Messengers brought word that General Crook crossed the Platt on 29 May and that he is on his way from Fort Fetterman with 1,500 men, 103 six-mule supply wagons, and a pack train of 1,000 mules. No other word has been received from him, but General Terry calculates that he

should be somewhere in the vicinity of the head-
waters of the Tongue, about 150 miles away.

Looks like it's all going to happen soon. The
word is that the Sioux are holed up in the
Rosebud Valley. Colonel Custer is so anxious to
get going that he can't hold still. I think he's
afraid someone else is going to kill all the Indi-
ans before he gets there. But General Terry
thinks the Sioux will try to scatter when we go
after them. So to make sure none of the red
bastards get away, he will wait until all the
troops are in position to surround them before
attacking.

I'm just counting the hours until I can kill my
first one. I would give my commission and ten
years of my life to be the one to slaughter that
filthy buck, Daniel Blue Eagle, and his whore,
Starr Winfield. But the most I can probably
hope for is that those two devils are in the thick
of things when we charge and that they are both
punished for what they have put me through.
With each savage I kill, I will imagine those two
dying and roasting in hell.

I'm going to see every last one of those Sioux
vermin exterminated from the West. When this
is all over, it won't only be Custer's name that
people will remember. I plan to see to it that the
name William Howard earns its share of fame
when we destroy the Indians and make this land
safe for its rightful owners—the whites.

The Sioux had always gathered near Bear Butte in

the sacred Black Hills for their great summer assembly; but since their traditional meeting place on the reservation was so close to the roaring gold camp at Deadwood Gulch, they had been forced to move the conference two hundred miles west of the Black Hills.

Possibly the largest gathering of Indians ever to assemble in one place, with ten thousand people, including women and children, the vast Indian camp stretched for three miles along Rosebud Creek in an isolated valley in eastern Montana. Laid out in six tribal circles, the Hunkpapas were at the upstream end of the Lakota camp, followed by the Sans Arc, Miniconjou, Oglala and Brule circles below, with the Cheyenne occupying the northernmost position downstream.

Throughout the huge settlement, men, women and children danced, sang, raced, wrestled, and visited with old friends, while the chiefs from all the bands of every clan met to discuss and settle problems in an eighteen-foot-high tent that stood at the center of the camp.

While Daniel Blue Eagle was meeting with the chiefs, Starr and Prairie Moon watched with interest as specially selected braves and women trimmed away the branches as high as the fork of a felled cottonwood. The tree was being readied to serve as the *Enemy* in the sun dance the Hunkpapa medicine man, Sitting Bull, had promised to dance.

The only son of the Hunkpapa warrior and mystic, Returns-Again, Sitting Bull had become the recognized leader of all the Teton Sioux, in a time when all the chiefs were supposedly equal and tribes rarely extended their loyalty beyond their own clan. He was known for his courage, determination, and distrust of the whites. Aware that a final showdown with the Army was near and that the whites were planning to crush the Sioux once and for all, he was preparing to appeal to the Great Spirit for divine guidance and aid in battle.

"What will happen next?" Starr asked the older woman in the Lakota language.

Prairie Moon answered in English, which brought a smile of pride to Starr's face. "Women paint the *Enemy* red on west side, green on east, blue on north, and yellow on south. Stand in big hole. At top, tie red robe, cherrywood sticks, tobacco offerings and two pieces of dried buffalo hide shaped like man and like buffalo. Sitting Bull will offer up scarlet blanket to *Wakan Tanka* tomorrow."

"Scarlet blanket?"

"He will offer up his own blood. He will give fifty pieces of flesh from each of his arms. Then he will dance and pray, staring at the sun. He will take no food, no water, until he experiences the passing death. When Sitting Bull lives again, he will tell us *Wakan Tanka*'s message for us."

"Ohhh," Starr groaned, rubbing her open hand over her stomach.

"What is it, Firebird?" Prairie Moon asked, wrapping one arm around Starr's waist and placing her other hand on Starr's abdomen. With great concern evident on her wrinkled face, Prairie Moon scolded herself for talking about scarlet blankets and pieces of flesh in front of the pregnant young woman. What if she had said something to make the girl sick? "Are you in pain?"

"No, it doesn't hurt," Starr laughed, feeling foolish now that the fluttering sensation in her belly had stopped. "I just had the oddest feeling. For the briefest instant, it felt like—like—like bird's wings flapping at the wall of my stomach."

"Bird's wings?" Prairie Moon repeated, her worried black eyes shifting from side to side as she tried to translate Starr's words into her own language. "Ah," she hooted suddenly, her face lighting with revelation. "Bird's wings! *Ohan.* Bird's wings!" The older woman continued to laugh and nod her head up and down happily. "Bird's wings."

Certain Prairie Moon thought she was crazy, the look on Starr's face grew flustered. "Well, not exactly like bird's wings, but—Oh! There it is again! I felt it against my hand! Did you feel it?" she shrieked excitedly.

"*Ohan*, like bird's wings. Your *hoksi cala* be much strong already."

"My baby? Is that my baby moving inside me?" she asked the older woman, who continued to nod her head energetically.

Starr's expression became reverent as her heart flooded with recognition of the sweet life that was blossoming inside her. She pressed her palm against her swollen body and waited for the baby to move again. But the tiny being's debut performance had obviously ended.

"I must go and find Daniel Blue Eagle and tell him. He'll be so excited," Starr bubbled enthusiastically as she took off toward the great chiefs' tepee to wait for Daniel Blue Eagle. All thoughts of sun dances, scarlet blankets, soldiers coming, and danger were gone from her mind.

14 June 1876 Montana Territory—Rosebud Creek

I got myself assigned to Major Marcus A. Reno's scouting party, hoping to finally kill some Indians. Though we are under orders not to attack, but to report back to General Terry with what we find, I would like the chance to kill at least one or two redskins before the others get here.

We left the rest of the 7th on the afternoon of the 10th, taking with us six troops, one Gatling gun and crew, about 70 pack mules, and the half-breed scout, Mitch Bouyer, on loan from Colonel Gibbon.

We had orders to go up to the second fork in the Powder, then cross over to the Mizpah and follow it and the Tongue back down to the Yellowstone to rejoin the column. However, the word was that the Indians are all on the Rosebud, so when we crossed to the Tongue, Mitch Bouyer just kept on going until he brought us to the Rosebud.

We immediately located a wide Indian trail going up the Rosebud and followed it. It is obvious a very large tribe passed this way recently. I'm certain this is the main camp we are looking for. The grass all around has been cropped to the roots by ponies, and there are many places where the ground is cut to powder six inches deep from lodge poles being dragged over it. The dust burns our throats and eyes, and the damned buffalo gnats and deerflies torture us and our horses, but if we could be the ones to locate that village, I would not complain one bit.

But we have followed the trail since yesterday morning and have not seen one filthy Indian. They are so close we can smell them, and even feel them watching us, but Major Reno has decided we aren't going to go any further up the Rosebud. He says we will rest here this afternoon and then start back downstream this evening when it is cooler. Some of us argued with him that we should go on, but he is determined to head for the Yellowstone so he can report back to General Terry. I think he is afraid.

Since we are allowed to spend this leisure time as we see fit, I have half a mind to take off on my own scouting expedition while the rest of the troops are lazing away this afternoon. I have the feeling that the village we're looking for is just over the next hill, around the next bend. And if I were to be the one to locate the Sioux and get a count of their tepees, I could make a real impression on General Terry. He would probably give me my own command, maybe even this one when he learns that Reno was too cowardly to take the initiative and follow through on the lead we have.

"The whites will not attack us. We are too many," one chief said bombastically, looking to his nodding friends for support of his theory. "They only attack small defenseless villages, never anything as large as this united camp."

"We appreciate your views, Broken Nose," Crazy Horse said to the older chief whose face left no room for doubt as to where he had gotten his name. "And I hope you are right, but I have reason to think that you are wrong."

"Just yesterday, we spotted a scouting expedition coming up the Rosebud from the north," Gray Wolf, who had been put in charge of the guard that constantly circled the perimeter of the large Indian village, pointed out.

"And I myself saw the large column camped to the south at the fork of Goose Creek and the Tongue," Crazy Horse reminded the others patiently. "They are coming, and we would be fools not to be prepared for them."

"But surely they know how strong we are," Broken Nose tried one more time.

"That doesn't make any difference to the whites, my friend. They think they are invincible," Gray Wolf laughed, his comment drawing many grunts and nods of heads.

"Man of the People has convinced me that it would be wise to give the *wasicun* a last chance to leave our lands once and for all. So I've asked Daniel Blue Eagle to go to Washington, D.C. and explain our position to their president," Crazy Horse told the others. "I don't think we will be able to avoid the battle that seems destined to take place while we're all here, but if there is a chance Daniel Blue Eagle can convince President Grant to withdraw his troops permanently, we need to try."

"In the meantime, what will happen?" one chief

asked.

"I think we should kill the scouting party to the north and attack the troops at Goose Creek," another voiced his opinion.

"We have women and children to think of. We can't leave them unprotected," another argued.

"We will move our camp across the Wolf Mountains to the Greasy Grass River after the great Sitting Bull completes his dance. The soldiers will expect us to still be here. We'll watch for them and attack first if they do come," Crazy Horse promised. "The guard around our village will be doubled and will watch day and night."

The chiefs, old and young, grunted and nodded their heads in agreement.

"If they come, they will come as conquerors and to kill us. We must be smarter than they are if the People are to be the victors."

During the heat of the afternoon, when many were resting and visiting, it had become a regular event for Starr to read to some of the young children in the tribe from the book of *Grimms' Fairy Tales* that Daniel Blue Eagle had purchased before leaving Bismarck. It had been a whim, but he had wanted to buy something for their baby, and since owning a book was a sign of intelligence, he had bought one for their unborn child.

The first time Starr had sat in front of her tepee leafing through the pages, two curious little girls had come over to see what she was doing. That day, she had read to them from the book, in English, immediately translating the story into the Lakota language; and the girls had delighted in the tale of princesses and kings and monsters. And Starr had delighted in their delight.

The following day, Starr had looked up from the beadwork in her lap to find six pairs of large black eyes focused on her, waiting solemnly for her to bring out the *book*. She did, and the process of the day before was repeated—reading in English, translating into Lakota. Day after day they came to hear Firebird's wonderful stories, until this day there were at least fifteen eager, black-haired children gathered around her.

As she read to the children, a sudden feeling of uneasiness ghosted over her. Someone was watching her. Someone besides the children. She stopped reading, oblivious to the groans of the children who waited anxiously for her to continue, the puzzled expressions on their small faces serious.

Her head snapped up and around as her anxious gaze shifted away from the book in her lap.

There, just a few feet away from Starr's tepee, stood Gentle Fawn. She was motionless except for her black eyes which moved rapidly from Starr's face to the children, and back to Starr again. What was she doing here? What did she want? What mischief had she come to do now?

It was the first time Starr had seen Gentle Fawn since she and Daniel Blue Eagle had returned from Bismarck, and she couldn't help but notice there was something different about her. Was it just the becoming rosiness in her healthy young cheeks that made her seem changed? Or was it something else? Was it

Starr's imagination, or was there an attractive new maturity on the lovely eighteen-year-old's face that had not been there before? Could that possibly be a beseeching plea for forgiveness that she saw shining in Gentle Fawn's black eyes?

Starr studied Gentle Fawn for a long time, trying to determine what had brought the young woman to this spot, trying to figure out what she wanted.

Then, as if jarred by an electrifying flash of lightning, Starr's qualms were all expunged. Her own life was so complete, brimming with such unqualified joy, that there was no longer any room in her heart for distrust or anger. Of Gentle Fawn or anyone else. There was only room for love and understanding.

Gray eyes met and held black eyes, and Starr's mouth curved upward in a gentle, sincere smile. "Hello, Gentle Fawn."

"Hello, Firebird," Gentle Fawn returned uneasily.

"How have you been?" Starr asked, not certain what it was the younger girl wanted, but willing to give her a chance.

"I have been fine. And you?" Gentle Fawn stayed where she was, her hands nervously fidgeting with the fringe on the sleeve of her dress.

"Why don't you come sit with me while I finish the children's story? Then you and I can visit."

Gentle Fawn nodded her agreement silently, but made no move to sit down with Starr and the children.

When Starr had finished the fairy tale and sent the children back to their own tepees in spite of predictable whines and pleas for "just one more," she turned back to Gentle Fawn, the smile on her face very happy. "I think I enjoy the stories as much as they do," she admitted. "I actually look forward to this time each day."

"The stories are very beautiful," Gentle Fawn said, taking a few hesitant steps toward Starr, and then stopping.

Had Gentle Fawn been listening to Starr's stories on other days? She curiously studied the girl who stood with her head bowed, her huge black eyes welling with tears. *She looks so miserable.* "Please sit with me," Starr encouraged with a welcoming pat on the ground beside her.

"Why would you want me to sit with you? Don't you hate me?"

One piteous tear trickled down a smooth tan cheek, and Starr's heart went out to Gentle Fawn. "No, I don't hate you. As a matter of fact, I've missed your friendship."

"But I was no friend to you. I tried to hurt you so that I could have your husband. I don't deserve your friendship."

"Why don't we put that behind us and start all over?" Starr wondered why she felt so much older than the other girl.

Gentle Fawn's almond-shaped eyes rounded with surprise, and hope illuminated her face. "Do you think that is possible?"

"I think anything we want is possible. Would you like to be friends?"

"Oh, yes, Firebird, I would like that very much!" Gentle Fawn cried, dropping to her knees beside Starr. She hesitated only a moment and then threw her arms around the red-headed young woman, who

389

returned her embrace warmly. "Please forgive me."

"You're forgiven," Starr chuckled with a maternal pat on Gentle Fawn's arm. "But only if you tell me if what I've been hearing about you is true or not."

"What have you heard?"

"Prairie Moon says that the braves line up outside your tepee every night for a turn to stand under the blanket with you," Starr said lightly, watching Gentle Fawn's face break into a broad grin. "She says sometimes there are eight or nine in the line at a time. Is that true?"

Gentle Fawn laughed aloud. "I think Prairie Moon exaggerates. There have never been more than three or four at one time."

"Three or four!" Starr coughed, able to imagine the handsome young braves waiting impatiently outside Gentle Fawn's parents' tepee for a chance to spend a few minutes wrapped in a big blanket with the pretty girl.

"But from now on there will only be one," Gentle Fawn said mischievously, anxious to tell Starr her news.

"Who?" Starr urged with excitement. "When did you decide? Is he anyone I know?"

"I don't think so. He is from the Cheyenne camp."

"And?" Starr prodded anxiously. "Come on. Don't leave me in suspense. Are you going to marry him?"

"His name is Tall Feathers. He is eighteen summers old and already as tall as Daniel Blue Eagle. He's very handsome, and when he and his friends came to our first social, I asked him to dance with me. Then he came to visit my tepee the next evening, and we stood under the blanket and talked. He is very popular with the other girls, but when they asked him to dance at the social that night, he told them he would dance only with me."

"Has he asked you to marry him?" Starr asked, feeling a tiny bit of guilt that part of her own excitement might be caused by the relief she would feel when Gentle Fawn posed no further threat to her own marriage.

"He talked to my father last night," Gentle Fawn admitted, the pleasure on her face telling Starr that she had been foolish to think that Gentle Fawn still had any feelings for Daniel Blue Eagle.

"Well?"

"My father gave us permission to be married when the tribes assemble on the Greasy Grass River tomorrow."

"Tomorrow!" Starr shrieked with astonishment. "You must have a million things to do!"

"I do, but I could not do anything until I had begged for your forgiveness. Now that you have given it to me, I will go into my marriage with a light and happy heart." Gentle Fawn looked up at the sun and, noticing the time, jumped up to leave. "I promised my mother that I would go to the hills and dig for prairie turnips, so I'd better be on my way if I don't want her to beat me like a little child on the day before I become a married woman!"

"No, we wouldn't want that to happen," Starr agreed.

"Would you like to come with me, Firebird?" Gentle Fawn asked, suddenly uneasy again.

Starr thought for a minute about all she needed to

do and decided that it could all wait until later on. "I'd like that very much, Gentle Fawn."

14 June 1876 Montana Territory—Rosebud Creek. (About five miles south of the spot where Major Marcus Reno decided to turn our scouting party around.)

Using a pair of binoculars, I am looking down on the largest Indian village that any white man has probably ever seen. The west bank of the Rosebud is crowded with hundreds of tepees for as far as the eye can see, even with the glasses. I have tried to count the number, but gave up after five hundred when I realized I wasn't even halfway down the line.

I wouldn't be surprised to find out that every single Sioux bastard in the world is down there right now, including Daniel Blue Eagle and his whore. What a great opportunity it will be for us if we can manage to get our troops into position around them and attack before they have a chance to scatter. It will be the greatest battle ever to take place on this continent. It will be known as the day the Sioux Nation was wiped off the face of the earth! The day Captain William Howard made a name for himself and was promoted to Major, or even Colonel.

It's obvious they don't realize that soldiers are in the area. What would they do if they knew they were all going to be dead before much longer? They'd be running in every direction trying to escape. It would look like a disturbed ant hill down there.

But they aren't running. In fact, it looks like they are celebrating. It looks like they are having a huge party. Everywhere there are people visiting from tepee to tepee. I can see groups of children playing games in the open, and braves are racing their ponies down long stretches of land as if they haven't got a care in the world. And the women are idly combing the hills searching for something, onions or turnips I suppose, as if they're on a Sunday picnic.

At the center of the camp, there is a giant circular arbor covered with pine boughs, and there seems to be some sort of big spectacle going on there. I can't see what it is because the crowd of singing, drum-beating, chanting Indians surrounding it is blocking my view. But it must be something important to draw such a crowd. I can see that at the center there is a painted pole with what looks like a buffalo skull and some other things tied to it.

My curiosity has gotten the better of me. I think I will go a little closer just to see if I can determine what it is that has all those savages so damned fascinated. I've still got plenty of time before I need to leave. Major Reno won't be pulling out before dusk.

Daniel Blue Eagle stood beside his father and brother at the inner edge of the great circle formed by hundreds of weaving and chanting Lakota and Cheyenne braves. Moved by Sitting Bull's demonstration of courage and greatness, they were waiting for the words of prediction that would come when the great medicine man finally ended his sun dance by collapsing.

Now in its final moments, Sitting Bull's immolation had begun the day before with the priests painting his hands and feet red and his shoulders blue. Sitting and leaning against the specially prepared *Enemy* tree, his legs outstretched, he had chanted his wailing, singsong prayer as his adopted brother, Jumping Bull, had used a needle-pointed awl in one hand and a sharp knife in the other to slice fifty pieces of skin from each of Sitting Bull's arms. All through the scarlet blanket sacrifice, the expression on Sitting Bull's face had not changed, and there was never the slightest alteration in the tuneless prayer he wailed for all to hear as his arms were cut from wrist to shoulder.

Dripping blood from his motionless fingers, Sitting Bull had risen from his place against the sacred tree and faced the sun. He began to bob up and down, praying as he danced, looking directly at the sun. He had danced all that day and through the night with no food or water, deliberately driving himself to a state of complete exhaustion.

Daniel Blue Eagle noticed a change in the rhythmic dance that had lasted for eighteen hours. Sitting Bull's step slowed to an occasional stomp of a foot or jerk of an arm, and his chant had become a senseless mumble. His eyes were glazed and watering from so many hours of looking at the sun, but still he danced.

Then suddenly it was over. Sitting Bull stood motionless for a long moment, and then staggered a few steps, falling over into a dead faint, *the passing death*.

The vigilant witnesses to what was happening waited anxiously, silently. They knew that the first words out of Sitting Bull's mouth when he regained consciousness would tell them what they wanted to know. Were the soldiers coming? Who would be victorious?

No one touched the exhausted man on the ground, and as he slowly opened his eyes, their look was dazed, sad, and concerned. The witnesses leaned forward, straining to hear the message sent by *Wakan Tanka* through the fearless leader.

"Out of the mists that surrounded me as I reentered this life, I saw human forms taking shape. They were soldiers and they were entering the Lakota camp," Sitting Bull rasped weakly, his glazed eyes still watching his vision.

The men who could hear him gasped aloud. Was he saying that the soldiers were coming and that they would defeat the People?

"But the soldiers are not the victors," Sitting Bull went on more strongly. "The soldiers I saw were falling into our camp like grasshoppers from the sky. Their heads were bent in defeat."

Shrill yells of triumph rose from the crowd. The People were going to be the victors. That was what Sitting Bull's vision had told them! They were going to defeat the soldiers when they came. The Indian whoops rose in ear-shattering joy.

But Sitting Bull wasn't through, although only those closet to him heard his next words. "The soldiers will be gifts to the People from *Wakan Tanka*. We can kill them, but we must not take their guns or horses or belongings. If we do, it will prove a curse to the Lakota People that will never be rescinded."

The look on the medicine man's countenance was sad, for he knew the braves would never be able to resist taking the soldiers' belongings when the time came. And if they took them, the victory would be the beginning of the end for the Lakota people.

Chapter Twenty-three

Using a tool made from a buffalo's shoulder-blade, Starr hoed at a telltale clump of blue flowers that divulged the hiding place of the prairie turnips she and Gentle Fawn were seeking. During the past hour, they had each almost filled a basket with the tasty roots as they slowly worked their way farther and farther up the gray hill and away from the village.

Exhausted, Starr tossed her latest find into her basket and straightened her back, gripping her waist and rotating her shoulders and neck wearily. "That's all for me," she sighed, feeling guilty that she tired so easily since she had become pregnant. But she just had to stop. "My back is beginning to ache from bending over so long," she explained apologetically as she walked past a patch of green-and-white-petaled Spanish dagger plants to sit under a tree.

"I'll dig just a bit longer," Gentle Fawn called over her shoulder as her search for the blue flowers carried her off to the left. "Then we'll go back."

"I'm in no hurry," Starr returned, lazily leaning

back against the cottonwood and closing her eyes. "I'll just sit here and rest in the shade."

"All right," Gentle Fawn acknowledged, her voice sounding far away as Starr dozed off.

Minutes later, Starr awoke with a jerk, her gray eyes popping open with alarm.

With mysterious, choking tentacles of dread, spiraling through her she sat up straight and looked around anxiously.

Gentle Fawn was nowhere in sight.

A chill of apprehension scuttled over Starr's flesh. *She's just on the other side of those trees*, she assured herself, listening carefully for sounds of Gentle Fawn's hoe as it hacked at the ground to upturn the hidden prairie turnips. She heard nothing. Even the birds were silent.

Starr opened her mouth to call out to the other girl, but her cry was interrupted before she could give it voice.

A twig broke directly behind her, the loud cracking noise sounding almost like gunfire in her ears.

Her heart leaped into her throat.

Starr's head flew around, but nothing was there. No one. She was completely alone.

Just a rabbit or something, she decided, desperately fighting the inner voice that told her the twig had been broken by something much larger than a rabbit. She drew herself up to her feet and took a shaky step away from the tree.

"Ge—Ge—Gentle Fawn?" she squeaked out uncertainly, but she received no comforting answer from the Indian girl. "Are you about through?" she asked as loudly as the constricting lump in her throat would allow.

"Don't make another sound or it will be your last," a deep voice ordered from behind her.

Starr recognized the sound of a revolver hammer being cocked. She whirled around.

His dark uniform blending into the obscure shadows, making him nearly invisible from where she stood in the light, the appearance of a man in the dense brush accosted her unguarded senses cruelly. She staggered back a step. Her gray eyes showed horror and disbelief. "William," she gasped.

"Yes, William," he agreed, showing even white teeth bared in a diabolical grin as he motioned with his revolver for her to come to him.

Starr's feet remained rooted to the ground, where she stood on shaking legs. "How did you find me?"

"Let's go," he growled, ignoring her quavering question.

Starr looked over her shoulder in the direction she had last seen Gentle Fawn, afraid for the girl as well as for herself.

"You'll have the whole Sioux Nation down on you in a matter of minutes if you fire that gun." Starr knew her stalling words were a bluff. If anyone did hear the shot, there was so much noise and activity in the giant camp below that they would just think it was another celebrating brave letting off some steam.

"That may be, but you and your little friend won't be around to see it happen," he laughed, obviously not very worried.

As Starr stood staring woodenly at the barrel of William's gun, Gentle Fawn hurried back to the place where she had left Daniel Blue Eagle's wife resting.

She had gone further than she had intended and felt guilty for being away so long; but she had spotted a particularly thick patch of the little blue flowers in the distance and hadn't been able to resist them. Telling herself that Firebird would understand, she called out, "Firebird, are you ready to go back to the camp?"

William pointed his gun in the direction of Gentle Fawn's voice. "If you don't want that little piece of Indian baggage to get a bullet in her head when she gets here, you'd better move fast," he sneered, the threat in his tone very real.

Starr could easily see that as soon as Gentle Fawn came over the rise, William would have a clear shot at her. She wouldn't have a chance.

Gentle Fawn would be dead in seconds if Starr didn't do something immediately.

"Gentle Fawn! Run!" Starr shouted, throwing herself across the space that separated her from William, deliberately hitting his arm with the full force of her body. His aim diverted, the bullet he fired was sent harmlessly into the trees overhead.

"You damned little fool," William cursed viciously, jerking Starr to her feet by her hair as he struggled to retain his own footing. "You're going to pay for that," he ground out, heaving her over his strong shoulder and pushing his way farther up the hill to where his horse was tethered in a dark clump of cottonwoods.

The baby! She had to protect the baby!

"William, please," Starr begged, very aware of the hard shoulder pressing painfully into her belly. "Put me down. I'll go with you. I won't give you any more trouble. Just put me down."

Apparently, her fears that the pressure could injure her baby were not unfounded, because the tiny human being chose that moment to make his displeasure known by kicking out against the squeezing discomfort.

She tried again. "William, I'm pregnant. You're hurting my baby. Please put me down!"

William stopped for a moment in his tracks. The revulsion he felt at hearing her words distorted his face. It was bad enough to think of the woman he had considered so good and pure lying willingly under a grunting Indian.

But a baby! God! It made him want to vomit.

The seed of a Sioux dog is growing inside her body, and she wants to protect the little bastard. I ought to kill her right here and now. I'm not sure all the money in the world is worth the disgrace of having people see her and know she's carrying a savage brat in her belly.

It would have been so much easier if that Bismarck lawyer hadn't come to the fort with those papers not long after Starr had left. How the hell had she gotten that annulment? The lawyer had said some Yankton lawyer named Edwards had filed for her.

If it weren't for that damned annulment, I'd kill her and her half-breed bastard right now. I'd say the Indians did it and would play the part of the bereaved widower while I collected her inheritance. But now if I want the money, I'm going to have to marry the cheating, whoring bitch all over again.

If the money were the only factor, it might have been worth the loss to see Starr dead. His hate and abhorrence were that great.

401

But could he turn his back on the money and the hero's recognition he was sure to gain for "saving" his wife from the Sioux village? Americans loved stories of romance and valor, and any man who was brave enough to single-handedly face thousands of wild Indians for his woman would immediately become a national hero. Could he pass up that chance at immortality?

When news of what I've done gets out, they'll write books about me. Compose songs about me. My name will be in all the newspapers. Little children will want to be just like me. Buffalo Bill Cody, Kit Carson, Wild Bill Hickok and me, Fearless Bill Howard!

"Please let me walk," Starr implored, bringing William's attention back to the present.

"All right, but I'm warning you. One more dumb move and you and that half-breed bitch bastard in your belly can kiss this world goodbye."

"Yes, William," Starr responded dutifully. "I won't do anything else to upset you. I'll be good. I promise."

A smile of satisfaction crossed William's face as he lifted Starr onto his horse, then quickly mounted behind her, in his thoughts already basking in the glory that would soon be his.

Instinctively reacting, Gentle Fawn dropped to the ground at the sound of a gun being fired in the area where she had left her friend. She inched her way under a bush and waited, listening intently. But Firebird didn't call out again. Gentle Fawn heard what she thought was a man's voice. But it was muffled and far enough away that she couldn't be sure.

What should she do? Should she go and find out what had happened? Or should she run back to the camp for help? If she went toward the spot the gunfire had come from, someone might be waiting to shoot her too. Then she would be no help to Firebird. On the other hand, if Firebird had been injured, she could be seriously bleeding and might die before Gentle Fawn was able to run all the way to the camp and come back with help.

The Indian girl's face hardened with resolve. She had no choice.

Pulling herself forward with her elbows, Gentle Fawn slithered silently through the brush on her belly just the way her brothers had taught her when they were all too young to understand that a girl could never become a warrior, no matter how good she was at a man's skills.

She lizarded along the ground with surprising speed, spying the tree where she had left the other girl dozing. But though the grass where Starr had been sitting was still pressed flat and her basket of prairie turnips waited undisturbed for its owner to return, Firebird was gone.

Gentle Fawn cocked her head and listened. She heard someone running. Heavy, noisy steps. No moccasion made that much sound. It was white man's boots!

Quickly dragging herself away from the concealing cover of the brush, Gentle Fawn crouched low and followed the rustling, crunching sound.

The footsteps stopped. Gentle Fawn froze in her

tracks. Hunkering down, she squinted her eyes and listened intently. She heard the hushed sounds of a man and woman speaking. The man was angry, the woman afraid, pleading. They were so close she could almost make out what they were saying.

A horse whinnied just ahead. Her heart lurched into her throat, spurring an immediate dive into a nearby bush, where she waited anxiously, oblivious to the scratches on her arms and face.

Stealthily moving aside the thick cover of leaves and branches of the concealing shrub, Gentle Fawn peeked out in time to see a horse and two riders exit from a thick grove of trees right in front of her. They were so near she could see the terror on Firebird's face and the malice on the soldier's. She could see the way Firebird kept glancing down at the gun the soldier had against her belly.

Gentle Fawn fought the immediate inclination to leap out and attack the passing soldier. Perhaps she could catch him by surprise. But she didn't dare try.

Knowing that if she made the slightest sound Firebird could be killed, Gentle Fawn held her breath as the two passed so close she could have reached out and touched the man's boot.

The instant the horse and riders were out of sight, Gentle Fawn bounded from her hiding place and hiked her dress up. Frantically bolting into a dead run, her speed increased as she raced down the hill for the camp.

She ignored the agony gripping her side, the crushing ache in her lungs and the stinging perspiration pouring into her eyes.

She had to get help. Nothing else mattered. She

had to save Firebird.

Run—run—run—run—run—, she chanted to herself, forcing her mind to numb itself to the messages of pain her body was sending to her brain.

Blind with determination, Gentle Fawn was so intent on her mission that she didn't notice the lone brave riding up the hill toward her until he leaped from his horse and grabbed her, his hands parenthesizing her shoulders cruelly.

"What is it, Gentle Fawn?" Daniel Blue Eagle shouted to the distraught young woman, his fingers digging hard into her upper arms. He shook the panting girl so hard that her head snapped back and forth. "Where is Firebird? What have you done to her?"

"So—so—soldier," she gasped, "t—took her!" Her chest heaving rapidly, Gentle Fawn pointed up the hill to the place where she had last seen Daniel Blue Eagle's wife.

Daniel Blue Eagle's face contorted viciously. If he had had the time, he would have killed the deceitful girl right then. "I'll take care of you later," he vowed, hurling Gentle Fawn away from him and making an agile leap to his pony. "If anything has happened to my wife, I swear you'll pay for it," he threatened angrily as he rode with breakneck speed toward the spot the Indian girl had indicated.

Gentle Fawn stared after the departing rider, stunned. He was blaming her for his wife's disappearance!

It was easy for Daniel Blue Eagle to pick up the soldier's trail. A broken twig here, a turned blade of grass there, the telltale impression of a horseshoe in a soft patch of earth, tiny betraying plants that had been crushed, and even fresh horse droppings strung along the ground, indicating a ridden horse rather than one able to stop at will.

Because the soldier had left such an obvious trail, Daniel Blue Eagle was able to move quickly. But the fear that he wouldn't arrive in time tore at his gut. When he thought of how easily he could have stayed with the other braves as they celebrated Sitting Bull's revelation, a chill swept over his strong body, leaving him weak with anguish. Only by chance had he decided to go to his tepee and check on his wife to be certain she was feeling well enough to make the move to the Greasy Grass River that afternoon.

Remembering the panic he had felt the instant he had discovered that Starr wasn't at the tepee, Daniel Blue Eagle shook his head, forcing himself to concentrate on the trail he was following. It wouldn't do any good to keep thinking about it. He had to count himself fortunate that he *had* gone back and that Prairie Moon knew where Starr had gone.

He would never forget the sinking feeling of anxiety that had seized him when his aunt had revealed that Starr was out of the village hunting prairie turnips and who she was with. How could she have been so foolish to trust Gentle Fawn? After all the girl had done to her!

He didn't know how Gentle Fawn had managed it, but he had no doubt that she had betrayed Starr again. And he swore it would be the last time she would have the chance to betray anyone!

The trail Daniel Blue Eagle was following crossed a narrow creek but didn't come out on the other side.

Evidently the soldier had realized that someone was following him and had decided to walk in the water to conceal his trail. If the man traveled upstream he would be going back the way he had just come, but if he went downstream he would meet the Rosebud about four miles below the Sioux camp. No doubt that was the direction he was headed.

Daniel Blue Eagle guided his pony into the stream and started north, keeping his eyes alerted to signs of the soldier's horse leaving the water.

Suddenly, without warning, a shot rang out, grazing Daniel Blue Eagle's temple. A woman screamed.

Before he could react to the bright red streaming down his cheek and over his jaw, or to the woman's scream, a second, truer bullet whizzed through the air to embed itself in his flesh. The woman screamed again.

The impact of the cartridge propelled Daniel Blue Eagle backwards and off the startled pony, to land face down in the icy mountain stream. The water churned around him, instantly turning murky and red with his blood.

"If you scream again, I'm going to forget my decision to keep you and that damn half-breed in your belly alive," William snarled, jerking Starr out of the concealing brush and toward the stream where Daniel Blue Eagle lay motionless.

"You monster," she shrieked, trying to pull loose from the constricting grip William had on her upper arm. "You've killed him!"

He chuckled at Starr's useless efforts to gain her release. "So it would seem, but let's just make sure." William raised his gun again, aiming for Daniel Blue

Eagle's head.

"No!" Starr screamed, wrenching herself free with a strength born of desperation. She jerked upward with her interlocked fists. Using her clenched hands as a club, she swung her arms around to knock the revolver from William's hand and hit him in the side of the head.

"You damned whore!" William spat out, raising his own fist to hit her. But the blow was never carried out.

Instead, wet hands grabbed at William's ankles and yanked his feet from under him, dragging the surprised soldier into the stream.

Bleeding and weak from his injuries, Daniel Blue Eagle fought like a madman, directing blow after blow to William's middle and face, and it was all the man could do to defend himself.

However, Daniel Blue Eagle's sudden extraordinary strength lasted only through a few well-aimed blows before it began to fail him. Each of his punches carried less and less clout as the loss of blood from his head and shoulder wounds took its toll on him.

The flesh around one blue eye began to swell on William's angry face, and blood flowed freely from his nose and the corner of his mouth. But the injuries to his face were only superficial. The damage to his ego was much greater—so great that killing the Indian who had ruined things for him was all that mattered now. Not the fame. Not the money. Only revenge.

The toe of a heavy black boot came out of the water, clipping Daniel Blue Eagle's chin. The weakened man staggered backwards drunkenly, his head reeling. Using every fragment of effort to focus on his blue-coated opponent, by some miracle, he managed to retain his own footing in the rushing mountain stream. But it wasn't enough. He was too weak. His blood loss too great.

Still he fought.

The look on his bleeding face crazed, Daniel Blue Eagle stumbled forward, his fists jabbing at William but missing him with every punch. Blinded with blood and sweat and anger, he didn't see William's boot when it rose up out of the water again, this time to sink its ferocious weight deep in Daniel Blue Eagle's groin.

Grunting his astonishment with the forced expelling of the oxygen in his lungs, Daniel Blue Eagle gripped his mid-section and doubled in half.

Senseless with pain, he didn't even feel William's final blow, the rock-hard fist that slammed into his jaw to send him down into the water. Nor did he know when William leaped on top of him, straddling his middle.

The shock of the icy water covering his face roused him slightly. Coughing and sputtering frantically, Daniel Blue Eagle tried to raise his head out of the water to get his breath.

William buried his fingers in the thick hair at Daniel Blue Eagle's temples; and using his vicious grip on the hair, he forced his victim's face under the water again. This time there would be no doubt about the Indian's death!

The last thing Daniel Blue Eagle saw was the leering grin of triumph on William Howard's face. He didn't see Starr standing on the bank with William's revolver in her trembling hands. Neither did William.

"Let him up, William," Starr ordered, her voice high and strained. She had watched the entire fight with the gun in her grip, but had not dared to shoot it. She had never fired a gun and wasn't sure she could hit a stationary target, much less a moving one. Besides, even if she could hit what she was aiming for, the chance was too great that Daniel Blue Eagle would move between her and William and catch the bullet. "Get up, William." The tremble in her voice matched that in her hands.

Turning around to see Starr pointing his own weapon at him, William dropped his hold on Daniel Blue Eagle and raised his hands in surrender. The smile on his face was menacing, frightening.

He stood up and took a step toward the bank.

"Stay where you are," Starr spat out, the revolver now shaking violently in her hands.

"You're not going to shoot me, Starr, and you know it. So give me the gun and we'll forget this happened." He walked toward her, his hand outstretched.

"I will, William. I'll shoot you if you come any closer."

William could see the fear in her gray eyes, and he was certain she would not be able to pull the trigger. "No you won't."

"I will!" Starr repeated, squeezing the trigger as a warning. The shot didn't come anywhere near William, but it was close enough to tell him she would try again. He shrugged his shoulders in defeat. "All right. What do you want me to do?"

His agreeable change of mood took Starr off guard,

and her resolve faltered. What did she want him to do? She wanted him out of her life forever. That's what she wanted. But could she pull the trigger that would end another human life? No matter what he had done to her, could she kill a person she had once thought she loved? For that matter, could she kill anyone?

A movement behind William suddenly diverted her attention.

The instant he saw her concentration move away from him, William lunged across the space that separated him from the armed girl. He knocked her to the ground, easily twisting the gun from her grip as he did.

"Now, what do you want me to do?" he laughed at the stark terror on her face as he raised the revolver to her head. "Do you want to come back with me and be a good little wife, or do you want me to kill you now and leave you with your lover for the buzzards?"

Kill me now, Starr's mind cried out. *I don't want to live without Daniel Blue Eagle. He's my life*, she wanted to scream.

But did she have the right to deny life to Daniel's baby? If she died, the baby would die. If she lived, a part of Daniel Blue Eagle would still live. What choice did she have?

"I don't want to die, William," she whispered. "I'll go with you." The resignation in her voice told him that she wouldn't fight him again.

"I always knew you were a smart girl," William laughed, standing up and offering a hand down to Starr, who lay on her back staring at him with unseeing gray eyes.

She was beaten. Money and fame would be his at last. Nothing would stop him now!

An eerie swishing sound the barest instant before it sliced into his chest was the only warning William had of the arrow streaking silently through the air toward him. As if they had a life of their own, his hands grasped at the arrow protruding from the spot over his heart. His face grimaced into a ghoulish grin of surprise as the fact of his own death registered in his confused brain. He toppled over backwards, landing on his back, half in the stream, half out.

It took a moment for Starr to comprehend what had happened, but when she did, she leapt to her feet. She didn't question where her reprieve had come from. She just knew it had come. She prayed that Daniel Blue Eagle was still alive.

She ran heedlessly into the stream, oblivious to William's lifeless body that bobbed up and down in the water as it stared up at the sky. Tramping anxiously through the knee-deep water, she cried, "Daniel Blue Eagle, you'd better not be dead. I'll never forgive you if you die!"

When she reached the spot where Daniel Blue Eagle had fallen down for the last time, she circled in confusion. He was gone. His dead body had obviously washed downstream toward the Rosebud. She would never see him again.

Starr didn't notice when Gray Wolf and Gentle Fawn stepped up to the bank, obviously relieved to find her alive, and then panicked when they realized Daniel Blue Eagle was nowhere to be seen.

Dropping to her knees in the water, Starr sobbed her anguish. "How could you leave me, Daniel?

Why?" she moaned, sitting down in the water and hugging herself.

She rocked back and forth, wailing her sorrow as she watched the fast current swirl downstream. The water had stolen her love, her life.

She wished for a knife so she could cut her hair and slash her forehead and legs as all Lakota wives did when they mourned their husband's death. If she spilled her blood and cut her hair here in the stream where Daniel Blue Eagle had died, part of her could follow him to the afterlife. Part of her would be with him forever.

Determined to find something sharp enough to help her make her mourning sacrifice, Starr searched the rocky stream bottom for a sharp stone.

She didn't see Gray Wolf and Gentle Fawn as they came toward her in the water.

But she did hear her name being called. "Firebird," the breeze seemed to whisper. "Don't cry, Firebird. I love you," the breathy voice rasped. "Help me, Firebird."

Starr stood up and cried out to the wind voice, "Daniel, don't leave me. Wait for me. I'm coming," she wept, taking several faltering steps downstream.

"Firebird, come with me," Gentle Fawn said, blocking Starr's stumbling progress. "Everything's all right now."

Starr stared at the concerned Indian girl for a long time, as if she were searching her memory for a name and face that were no longer familiar.

"It's Gentle Fawn, Firebird. I'm here to take care of you." She took the shivering girl into her embrace.

"Daniel Blue Eagle needs me, but I can't find

413

him, Gentle Fawn," Starr said forlornly, looking north toward the Rosebud. "Will you help me find my husband? I want to go with him, but I don't know how to find him. Will you help me?"

"I'll help you," Gentle Fawn promised, gently turning Starr around to see Gray Wolf stepping out from behind a large boulder on the opposite bank of the stream. He was half-carrying, half-dragging another man.

Chapter Twenty-four

Disoriented and confused, Starr directed her bewildered gaze toward the two men who approached her in the water. She recognized that Gray Wolf was the strong Indian who supported the weaker brave. But who was the second man?

His clothing was soaked and he had obviously been injured. His head was bent, as if it required more strength than he could muster to hold it up, and his arm was draped listlessly over Gray Wolf's shoulder. In fact, the only thing keeping the man's legs from collapsing beneath him was Gray Wolf's strong arm wrapped around his chest.

Unaware of the surprised looks exchanged by Gray Wolf and Gentle Fawn, Starr continued to study the poor, wretched man her brother-in-law brought toward her.

"Firebird," the man moaned forlornly, his head hanging down. "Firebird, I need you."

Starr's mouth dropped open, and she gasped for life-renewing air. With her vision blurred by tears, her eyes widened with shock.

Recognition assaulted her. It sounded in her head

with the force of exploding cannonfire, repeated in her heart with the speed of a Gatling gun.

Was it possible? Could Daniel Blue Eagle be alive?

"No," she insisted, squeezing her eyes shut and shaking her head from side to side. She refused to believe the trick her mind was playing on her.

It couldn't be Daniel Blue Eagle leaning on Gray Wolf. Her husband was dead. She saw William shoot him twice and then beat him to unconsciousness. She had seen William hold his face under the water to drown him. To let herself hope for even an instant that he was still alive, that he hadn't been killed and washed downstream, was a cruel joke.

The man raised his head weakly and looked directly into Starr's glazed eyes, his own blue eyes filled with pain and confusion. "Firebird," he gasped as his head dropped back on his chest.

Starr looked helplessly at Gentle Fawn, then to Gray Wolf for confirmation, the expression on her face unbelieving.

They both smiled and nodded their encouragement.

"Daniel?" she ventured uncertainly, peering suspiciously at the wounded man.

The man was aroused slightly by her voice, but he couldn't keep his head up and let it fall again.

"Oh, my God, Daniel! It is you!" she cried, leaping forward and embracing him. She put her hands on either side of his face and lifted his head to kiss his eyes, his nose, his chin, his forehead, his mouth. "I thought William killed you, Daniel. I was certain you were dead and that I would never see you again," she wept. "I looked for you but you were gone. I was sure you'd been washed downstream. I knew I had lost you. I was so afraid."

"Come, Firebird," Gentle Fawn said softly. "We need to get you both back to the village."

"He must have regained consciousness enough to drag himself to the edge of the stream," Gray Wolf explained to the two women, knowing Daniel Blue Eagle's wife still hadn't grasped what had happened. "I found him behind that boulder, with only his head and one arm out of the water. He was clinging to a tree root that protruded from the bank. That's the only thing that kept your fears from being true." Gray Wolf's voice cracked with emotion. "We could have lost him for good."

"Oh, my sweet, sweet love," Starr breathed compassionately, slipping her arm around her husband's waist to support his other arm.

Gentle Fawn worried that Daniel Blue Eagle's weight on the pregnant woman's shoulders would be too great, but she knew that it would take an act of *Wakan Tanka* to stop Firebird from assisting her husband. Wisely, Gentle Fawn didn't suggest it. Instead, she slid her own arm around Starr's waist and let the other woman lean on her, thereby taking some of the burden of her friend.

The three carried Daniel Blue Eagle to the bank and laid him down. "His head is bleeding again," Starr stated matter-of-factly, the concern in her eyes rational again, rather than hysterical. She was in her natural element now, nursing and caring for her husband, the man she loved above all else.

Everything would be all right. It had to be!

Starr stood up and unabashedly removed the

drawers she preferred to wear under her deerskin dress.

"Don't look so surprised," she laughed at the stunned expressions on Gray Wolf's and Gentle Fawn's faces when they saw the strange white undergarment appear from beneath Firebird's clothing.

"All the *wasicun*'s customs aren't so terrible. There might even be some you would like, Gray Wolf," she teased the avid hater of the whites, seeing in his eyes for the first time how much he truly cared for his older brother. "Besides, they're perfect to keep on hand for emergencies, aren't they, Daniel?" she added, speaking naturally to the semi-conscious man as she ripped the muslin into strips.

"Are we tearing up your drawers again, my love?" Daniel Blue Eagle mumbled, making a weak attempt at a smile, though his eyes remained closed. "I'll buy you more. A dozen next time."

"Maybe a gross would be more like it!" she laughed with relief as she efficiently wound an improvised bandage around Daniel Blue Eagle's head. She looked up at Gray Wolf as she finished. "One bullet just grazed his head, but the other may have to be removed."

They both looked at the significant tear in Daniel Blue Eagle's shirtfront and then back at each other. Without further hesitation, Starr ripped away the buckskin shirt to expose a gaping bullet hole in Daniel Blue Eagle's shoulder.

"The cold water must've stopped the bleeding," Gray Wolf suggested, looking uncertainly at the wound in Daniel Blue Eagle's flesh. He'd seen dozens of injuries much worse—larger, bloodier, more seri-

418

ous—but seeing his brother so weak had a devastating effect on him. He had wasted years hating him, being jealous of him, resenting him, and today he had almost lost him. Lost him without telling him that he didn't hate him, that he in fact loved him, admired him for standing by what he believed.

"There's no exit wound," Starr worried, lifting Daniel Blue Eagle's shoulder gently off the ground to check. "It's still in there."

"We need to get him back to the village," Gray Wolf suggested nervously, glancing around for Gentle Fawn and the four horses she was gathering up. He knew what his brother's wife was going to say before she said it, and he dreaded hearing the words.

"I'd better take it out now. The longer we wait, the more the wound will close around it, and the harder the bullet will be to remove. Besides, he won't feel the pain as much while he's half-conscious."

"That's easy for you to say," Daniel Blue Eagle grumbled.

"What do you want me to do?" Gray Wolf asked, knowing Starr was right and resigning himself to helping.

"Tear off a piece of his shirt and put it between his teeth for him to bite down on. Then hold his hands and keep him still."

Gray Wolf hesitated a moment, hating his sudden weakness where his brother was concerned, but unable to move.

Starr smiled, understanding exactly what her brother-in-law was feeling. It had been a shock to the warrior to realize how much he cared for his brother, and then to almost lose him.

419

"Hold his hands, Gray Wolf," she repeated gently, taking Gray Wolf's hands in her own and wrapping them around Daniel Blue Eagle's limp fingers. "He needs you now. Let him draw on your strength."

Gray Wolf nodded his head and did as Starr told him, his uneasiness abating only slightly.

Carefully placing the index and middle finger of each hand on either side of the bullet hole in Daniel Blue Eagle's shoulder, Starr separated the torn, red flesh gently. "I don't think it's very deep," she muttered, speaking more to herself than to Gray Wolf. "We're fortunate the water kept the skin soft and pliable. It hasn't started to swell and close up yet. I may be able to reach in there and retrieve it."

Starr ran the back of her arm over her sweating forehead to push stray wisps of hair off her face. "Daniel, bite down. I'm going in for it. Hold on to Gray Wolf, love," she encouraged, biting her lower lip.

Taking a deep breath, she inserted her finger up to the first knuckle into the open wound, bringing on a fresh flow of blood. "I don't feel it," she reported, using her arm to wipe at the perspiration on her forehead again.

She buried her finger deeper in the wound, finally touching what she thought was the bullet—or a bone.

"I think I've found it," she announced breathlessly, hunching up her shoulders one at a time to wipe her face again.

Steeling herself against the grimace of pain on her husband's ashen face, she circled her finger in the wound to ream out the narrow tunnel the bullet had made in the muscle. "Are you all right, Daniel?" she asked.

His lips were colorless, the muscles in his jaw clenched tightly. "Mmh," he responded, his knuckles turning white where he clung bravely to his brother's hands.

"Well, hold on just a bit longer." She withdrew her finger and then reinserted two, stretching and separating the wound as she slowly worked her way back to the bullet. She had to be careful that she didn't push it deeper.

When she touched it again, she wiggled her two fingers back and forth to widen the area around the bullet so that she could pinch it between her fingers and draw it out.

It was slippery with blood, but finally she managed to get a tenuous grasp on the metal in Daniel Blue Eagle's shoulder.

"Got it," she breathed.

Holding her breath, she began the torturously slow withdrawal of her two fingers gripping the elusive bullet. A fraction of an inch at a time, she drew it toward the opening.

Just when she had it almost to the point where she could use her other hand to grab it, the fingers she was using as forceps slipped, and the bullet slid back up the bloody canal. "Damn," she hissed, starting over again.

This time it was easier, and it was only a few minutes until she had the bullet out. There was a collective sigh as Starr sat back and held up the bullet.

"Will you wash these bandages, Gentle Fawn?" she asked the girl who had finally located Daniel

Blue Eagle's pony and brought it back. "I'm proud of you, Daniel," she beamed happily, even though she knew he was far from being out of danger. "Thank you for your help, Gray Wolf," she smiled. "We couldn't have done it without you."

"Thank *you*, Firebird," Gray Wolf returned. "*I* certainly couldn't have done it without you!"

"You might've surprised yourself." She accepted the wet rags from Gentle Fawn with a smile and pressed one onto the bullet hole. Leaving the wet compresses in place, she tore the remainder of Daniel Blue Eagle's shirt and wrapped the wound tightly. "We need to get him back to the village so Prairie Moon can do a little bit of her *washtay pejuta* on him."

"Seems to me like you just did a bit of good medicine yourself," Daniel Blue Eagle praised weakly, the color beginning to return to his face.

"Well, don't tell Prairie Moon! She'll think I'm trying to replace her!"

"It'll be our secret," he promised, managing a wink in her direction.

"How are we going to get back with him? He might fall off his pony if he tries to ride," Starr worried.

"He'll ride on my horse with me," Gray Wolf said, in control of his thinking and emotions once more. "With me holding him, he won't fall."

"Then let's go," Starr demanded. "I want to put this place as far behind me as I can." A shudder rippled through her body.

By the time the weary foursome arrived back at the gigantic village on the Rosebud, the tepees were all down and had been loaded onto packsaddles and moved across the Wolf Mountains toward the Greasy Grass River, called the Little Bighorn by the whites.

As they rode through the deserted camp, they repeatedly saw the signs of Sitting Bull's prediction on painted rocks, in drawings and other symbolic displays. More than once they saw pictures drawn in the sand of falling soldiers losing their hats.

They saw two buffalo skulls—one a bull, one a cow—facing each other with a pile of stones between them. Beside the bull's skull, there was a stick pointing toward the cow. Gray Wolf explained that it meant that when the soldiers came the Lakota would fight like a bull, and the *wasicun* would run like a frightened cow.

The attack that for so long had seemed like something that would never really happen, suddenly became very real to Starr. "They're coming soon, aren't they?" she said to Gray Wolf and Daniel Blue Eagle.

Both brothers nodded sadly.

"Is that why the camp was moved this afternoon? Is this why they didn't wait until tomorrow morning to leave?" She made a pointed sweep of her hand to encompass several descriptive sand drawings.

Gray Wolf answered, "The soldiers know we've been camped here, so this is where they will come. Our main objective is to get the women and children to safety. Then Crazy Horse will lead our warriors back to fight if necessary."

"The soldiers are all here now, Firebird," Daniel Blue Eagle said softly, his eyes reflecting the hopelessness in hers, "just as you warned Crazy Horse. Crook and Terry, together with Gibbons and Custer. They could come any day now. Maybe even tomorrow. They will be expecting to attack an unsuspecting village full of women and children. But this time, their heartless method of murder won't work. The women and children will be gone, and armed braves will be prepared to strike back."

How it hurt him to see the shock on his wife's beautiful face! Why had he brought her back? What had he been thinking of to let her convince him to bring her with him? How could he have been so weak where she was concerned? Why hadn't he been firm and left her behind? Now it might be too late. Too late for any more talks with the government. Too late to get her to safety. Too late for anything but fighting.

While Daniel Blue Eagle was worrying about his wife's safety, she was thinking only of his. A wave of relief flooded through her with the realization that her husband would be too weak to go into battle with the other men.

Then a rush of guilt consumed her. She was thinking only of herself. What about the other braves who would fight in the coming battle? What about the wives and mothers who would wait anxiously for their men to return? How many of those men would die? How many women and children would be left to mourn them? Would Gray Wolf live or die? What about Man of the People? Even Gentle Fawn's betrothed, Tall Feathers, might not live to see another winter. The shattering thoughts shook Starr to her very core. The people she knew and cared about could all be killed!

"Is there nothing we can do to stop this madness?" Her tone was desperate as she searched her husband's face for the answer she knew would not be there.

"I was supposed to go to Washington to speak to the government for the People, but now I don't know if I will go or not." His answer sounded so final and so devoid of hope.

"What will you do?" Starr's voice was rife with dread. She knew what Daniel Blue Eagle was planning. She wanted to scream out her protest, but she couldn't. She could not disgrace him with her own lack of courage. "What, Daniel?"

Daniel Blue Eagle sought understanding in his wife's expression. But how could he expect her to understand when he himself didn't? He had been so certain he could find a way for the People to live in peace with the whites. But he had failed her, failed himself, and failed the People.

He sucked in a slow agonizing breath, holding it for a long time, finally releasing it in a sorrowful, defeated moan. "I have no choice, Firebird. When the time comes, I will strip for battle and put on the war paint."

There! He had said it. He had uttered the dreaded words aloud. Fighting the tears that sprang to her eyes, Starr looked helplessly at Gentle Fawn and Gray Wolf. Neither of them spoke, both embarrassed that they were hearing a conversation that should have been private, between husband and wife.

Starr glanced thoughtfully at her own hands gripping her pony's reins so tightly her knuckles turned white. Consciously, she relaxed her hold on the rawhide strips. "But your injuries," she protested weakly, her voice a tortured whisper.

Daniel Blue Eagle put his hand to his injured

425

shoulder and smiled. "Healing already," he returned. "Thanks to your fast thinking and *washtay pejuta!* In fact, since we're going to be riding on to the Greasy Grass River, I'll ride my own pony the rest of the way." He said the last to Gray Wolf.

Damn my washtay pejuta! Why didn't I make him ride back to the camp with that bullet in him? He'd be in such pain right now he certainly wouldn't be talking about putting on warpaint and going into battle!

Was this where it was all to end? Was this what the last ten months of her life had been leading up to? Had she really been so foolish as to believe that loving each other and being together would be enough to ensure a happy future? Had she actually fought to stay with the man she loved just to watch him ride off and die in a war that could not be won?

It would have been better if she had never loved him, or conceived his child, she thought bitterly. But no sooner had the thought entered her mind than she discarded it. Nothing could have been better than to have loved and been loved by Daniel Blue Eagle.

The rest of the way to the Greasy Grass River, the travelers were somber and quiet, each lost in his or her own thoughts.

Finally, Daniel Blue Eagle spoke. "I owe you an apology, Gentle Fawn."

The others looked at him questioningly.

"I thought you had something to do with Firebird's disappearance. I'm sorry I blamed you unjustly."

"You owe me no apology, Daniel Blue Eagle."

"But I do. That and a lot more. I owe you my life. If you hadn't brought Gray Wolf when you did, I might not have made it, and Firebird would have still been a prisoner."

Gentle Fawn smiled and blushed at the praise.

"And while I'm on the subject . . ." He looked at his younger brother, the smile on his face full of love and respect. "Thank you, Gray Wolf. Thank you for being there when my wife and I needed you."

"Yes, thank you, Gray Wolf," Starr added sincerely, her eyes telling the brave that her heart no longer held any malice toward him.

"Do not speak of it. It does not mean I have changed my feelings about our differences," he blustered uncomfortably, suddenly afraid someone would see how he felt.

Daniel Blue Eagle smiled knowingly. He understood Gray Wolf's feelings. They were the same as his. "But the blood that binds us is stronger than any differences that separate us, isn't it, my brother?"

"It is stronger," Gray Wolf agreed grudgingly, feeling good about his relationship with his brother for the first time he could remember.

When they arrived in the Oglala tribal circle on the Greasy Grass River, Starr realized that Daniel Blue Eagle's shoulder was bothering him, despite his repeated denials. She wanted to get him bedded down as soon as possible. However, it was too late to erect her own tepee, the one that Prairie Moon and some of the other women had kindly taken down and packed when the village left the Rosebud so suddenly.

Even though Daniel Blue Eagle's aunt was now married to Running Fox and no longer living alone, she had plenty of room and would be glad to have them. So they spent the night in Prairie Moon's

427

tepee.

Long after her husband fell asleep, Starr lay awake worrying about the future. Finally her exhaustion won out over her fears, and she slept.

When the first gray light of dawn seeped into the lodge through the smoke flaps, Starr rolled over and snuggled closer to her sleeping husband. Suddenly, memories of the day before came crashing into her half-awake mind, jarring her to full awareness.

Starr regretted the need to leave the security of the buffalo robe cocoon made warm and cozy by their combined body heat. But she had work to do. Glancing sleepily around the shadowy interior of the tepee, she eased herself away from Daniel Blue Eagle and sat up, careful not to disturb him.

On the opposite side of the tepee, Running Fox and Prairie Moon were wrapped in their own buffalo robe, contentedly snoring in unison as they lay in each other's arms. Starr smiled at the older couple. Then worry marred her features. What would become of Prairie Moon and Running Fox when the soldiers came?

Starr shook her head sternly, reminding herself that she had vowed to think only about things that required her immediate attention. She had decided to live and enjoy one day at a time and had promised herself that she would not allow her fears about the future to ruin the present. As long as the soldiers hadn't come, she could still hope.

Starr turned back to Daniel Blue Eagle and placed her hand on his forehead. No fever. That was a good sign. His breathing was easy, not labored. Evidently, he was not in pain. She gently drew back the cover and looked at his bandages. Dry. No fresh bleeding. Her husband was going to recover.

Starr said a silent prayer of thanks, gathered all her nerve and leapt to her feet, facing the chilly morning air with determination.

By the time Prairie Moon awoke, Starr had breakfast started and had tied her own lodge poles in place beside Prairie Moon's tepee. Since they considered themselves one family unit, despite the fact that they had two lodges, they always took their meals together and erected their tepees next to one another. And when Daniel Blue Eagle stumbled out of Prairie Moon's tepee around noon, Starr had finished putting up her tepee and unpacking their belongings.

Approaching her at the cookfire, he threaded his fingers through his sleep-rumpled hair that was still too short to braid. "Why'd you let me sleep so late?" he grumbled irritably.

"Good morning," she smiled happily, refusing to waste even one of the few precious moments they might have left by getting angry with him for the tone of his voice.

In the morning light, she could see that his chin was swollen and bruised, and noticed that he walked stiffly. Her first inclination was to rush to check his wounds, every cut, every bruise. But she was determined not to hover over him the way her nurturing instincts called out to her to do.

"How are you feeling? How's the shoulder?" she asked casually.

"Fine," he growled. "Prairie Moon changed the bandage and said I'm already on the mend."

"Does it hurt?"

429

"No, it doesn't hurt!"

"How about your head wound?"

"My head doesn't hurt either," he returned angrily.

"Then, would you mind telling me just what *is* wrong with you?" Her patience was growing short. She'd done nothing to deserve this kind of treatment and had no intention of putting up with it, precious few moments or not!

"Nothing's wrong," he yelled cantankerously, stomping stiff-leggedly away from her and into the tepee Starr had just raised.

Standing with her hands on her hips, exasperated and confused, Starr watched Daniel Blue Eagle disappear through the doorway.

What had she done? Starr searched her mind for a clue to his strange behavior. Nothing! She had done nothing that could have made him angry.

Had she said something to upset him? No!

Who does he think he is talking to me like that? I have a right to be concerned about his wounds. I'm his wife!

Then without warning, as though it were taking place in a theatrical production, a scene from the day before replayed in her mind.

Starr knew what Daniel Blue Eagle's problem was.

"Poor thing," she sympathized. *To take a kick like that and then ride a horse all afternoon!* She fought the giggle that threatened to escape through her tightly-clamped lips. But it was no use. The laugh sounded deep in her throat in spite of her efforts. *I ought to be ashamed*, she chastised herself sternly, frowning to force a more serious demeanor. "No wonder he's in such a bad mood," she snickered aloud, the stoppered laughter impossible to dam a moment longer. "Ta—lk about injur—ed pr—ide!" she told herself between hiccupping, snorting, hooting fits of laughter.

"I'm glad you find it so amusing," Daniel Blue Eagle said as he stepped back into the open, his voice indignant.

"I'm so sorry, my love. I didn't mean to laugh. I don't really think it's funny," she insisted, shaking her head from side to side, her choking words of denial doing nothing to thwart her uncontrolled hilarity. "Honestly, I don't. It's just that—just that—" She stopped talking to wipe the tears from her eyes. "It's just that I can't help thinking how glad I am that you got shot in the shoulder and kicked—you know." She raised her eyebrows suggestively and indicated his tender groin with her hand. "You've got to admit it would've been a lot worse if you were kicked in the shoulder and sho—ot in the—" She doubled over with new peals of laughter, unable to finish her sentence.

"You're going to pay for laughing at my pain," Daniel Blue Eagle threatened sternly, striding stiffly toward Starr with a mischievous sparkle in his eyes. "I'm going to have to punish you for your inexcusable behavior."

He caught his wife up against his hard chest and hugged her, not caring who was watching. Public display of affection was one of those *wasicun* customs that he thought the Lakota might do well do adopt. Another one was kissing.

With that his mouth closed over Starr's, muffling her giggles in a searing, branding kiss. Raising his lips from hers, Daniel Blue Eagle laughed at the stunned expression on his wife's face. "Do you want to step into our lodge for the rest of your punishment, or do you want it right here?"

Starr looked from left to right, very aware of the people at the other lodges who were pretending not to notice what was happening, the way people have to do when they live close together. "Daniel, people are watching us!" she protested, pushing her hands against his bare chest, careful not to hurt his shoulder.

"Out here? Or in there?" he asked, squeezing her closer against him and kissing her nose.

"But we can't—I—I mean, a—aren't you—won't it hu—?" she stuttered.

"Come inside, and we'll find out if you've got any of your *washtay pejuta* left for my 'injured pride'!"

"My father thinks I should leave for Washington as soon as possible," Daniel Blue Eagle told Starr the next day.

"But your injuries aren't healed," she protested. Here it was only the second day after he had been shot, and he was talking about taking a long trip to Washington to see the President of the United States. She was fully aware that his recovery had been quite remarkable, but his body simply needed more time to mend.

"But there is no more time," he said, seeming to read her thoughts. "The soldiers are all around us. Someone has to make the whites understand the crime they are committing against the People by

432

sending the soldiers to steal our lands and slaughter our women and children."

Starr studied the set expression on her husband's serious face. She knew it was useless to argue with him. When it came to doing what he thought was best for the People, there was no changing his mind. Besides, if he were gone when the soldiers came, he wouldn't be able to go into battle. That was some consolation. Even if they were parted, at least she would know he was alive.

"How long will you be gone? Will you be back by the time the baby comes?" The thought of not having Daniel Blue Eagle with her when their child was born sent a wave of loneliness through her, and she scolded herself for her weakness. Oglala women had babies all the time without their husbands there. Starr straightened her shoulders. *If they can do it, so can I.*

"We'll try to be back by then," he promised.

"We? Is your father going too?"

A secret smile flashed across Daniel Blue Eagle's face. "No."

"Then who? Surely not Gray Wolf. Somehow I can't see your brother as a diplomat. I should think he would already be stripped and painted for battle."

"Not Gray Wolf."

"Will you stop looking at me with that silly smirk on your face and tell me who's going with you?"

Daniel Blue Eagle continued to 'smirk', the light in his blue eyes impish and exasperating.

"Then don't tell me," she huffed, turning her back to him and crossing her arms over her chest. "I don't really ca—Is it Sitting Bull?!?" she shrieked, wheeling around to face him again. "That's it, isn't it?

Sitting Bull is the one going to Washington with you!''

"You," he divulged at last, enjoying the play of emotions that crossed her face: uncertainty, disbelief, shock, joy. "You're the *who* I'm taking with me."

"Me?"

"Man of the People feels that an intelligent white woman who has lived among the Lakota may be even more effective than an educated 'Indian'."

Starr threw her arms around her husband's neck and hugged him exuberantly as she planted appreciative kisses over his smiling face.

"Well, what do you think?" Daniel Blue Eagle asked, holding her at arm's length. "Do you want to go or not?"

"Do I want to go?" she squealed. "When do we leave?"

"Tonight," he announced.

"We can't go tonight! I promised Gentle Fawn we'd be at her wedding ceremony!"

"We'll go afterwards. If we travel at night and rest during the day, we should be able to get to Cheyenne without being spotted by the soldiers. From there, we'll travel by train."

"Daniel, will we be able to get to Washington in time to do anything to help the People?" Starr asked, suddenly serious.

"I don't know, Firebird. I just don't know." Daniel Blue Eagle took his wife in his arms and held her close to him, the expression on his face pensive.

434

Chapter Twenty-five

Gentle Fawn's wedding that evening was similar to Starr's marriage ceremony, except there were even more people at this one. Not only Oglalas from Man of the People's band were present, but also the Cheyenne from Tall Feather's tribe, as well as anyone else who happened to wander by and realize there was a celebration going on.

Under normal circumstances, it was the custom for the groom to build a shelter away from the camp where he could take his bride for a honeymoon, a week spent all alone when they would give all their attention to each other and think of nothing else.

However, with the soldiers all around the area, it had been decided that Tall Feathers and Gentle Fawn would stay in the camp for the honeymoon.

As their wedding gift to the young newlyweds, Starr and Daniel Blue Eagle had offered the use of their own tepee for the week, planning to take up temporary residence themselves with Prairie Moon and Running Fox. However, since they were leaving that night, it had been decided that Gentle Fawn and Tall Feathers would continue to care for and use Starr's tepee until Gentle Fawn could sew her own.

Shortly after the happy wedding couple had been escorted to their flower-decorated tepee with great celebration and teasing from family and friends, Starr and Daniel Blue Eagle retired to Prairie Moon's tepee to finish their own preparations for leaving the village shortly after dark.

"I think Gentle Fawn will be happy, don't you?" Starr said to her husband as she packed the last of their *wasicun* clothing in carpetbags brought from Bismarck. "They seem very much in love."

Daniel Blue Eagle didn't answer. Instead, he stood up straight and held his finger to his lips, cocking his head to listen. Starr grew silent and listened too. The thunder of horse's hooves and the sounds of shouting people filled the air.

Curious about the commotion, Daniel Blue Eagle hurried outside the tepee, with Starr following close behind.

The cause of the disturbance was immediately apparent. Cheyenne scouts had stirred up a billowing cloud of brown dust as they heedlessly rode their lathered horses through the Oglala camp. Before the lodge of Crazy Horse, the agitated braves dismounted at a run and entered unannounced, oblivious to the dust and squealing people scattered in their wake.

"What is it?" Starr asked, a feeling of apprehension enveloping her like the dust curling at her feet.

"I don't know," Daniel Blue Eagle returned, worried. "Go back into Prairie Moon's tepee and wait for me. I'll see what I can find out."

Panic rose in Starr's throat. "Don't go, Daniel!" she begged, grabbing his arm and trying to stop him. "We have to finish packing for our trip! We have to leave soon!"

"I won't be long, Firebird," he promised, tearing himself away and leaving her standing in front the tepee, a feeling of dread choking her.

She watched until her husband disappeared into Crazy Horse's lodge, and then turned to reenter Prairie Moon's tepee, her posture one of defeat. Already she could hear the criers spreading the word for all the chiefs to meet with Crazy Horse immediately.

Absently studying the carpetbags that sat in the middle of the tepee, packed and ready to go, she was unaware of the tears that trickled down her cheeks.

It's the soldiers, she thought dejectedly, dropping to her knees beside her packed bags and laying her cheek against the rough carpeting material. *I knew it was too good to be true. Now we'll never know if we could have done anything to stop the war.* Starr buried her face in her hands and cried. Cried for the People, cried for Daniel Blue Eagle, for herself, for their baby.

Then, with the courage and determination all good Oglala wives had to possess in order to survive, she rummaged among the packs they'd planned to leave with Prairie Moon for safekeeping. When she found it, she clutched Daniel Blue Eagle's war bundle to her heart for a long moment before placing it carefully in the middle of a buffalo robe in readiness for her husband. Next she hurried to where Daniel Blue Eagle kept his ponies and selected his two best

437

mounts, one to be ridden, the other to act as a spare.

By the time Daniel Blue Eagle rushed into the tepee a few minutes later, Starr had saddled one of the ponies and was spooning pieces of boiled meat from the cooking pot into a wooden bowl.

Seeing the preparations his wife had made, Daniel Blue Eagle knew that Starr had correctly interpreted the meaning of the Cheyenne scouts' ride into the camp, and his heart broke anew. How could he bear to hurt and disappoint her again? She had never really asked anything of him. All she had wanted was his love and to be allowed to stay with him. Now he had to leave her again, maybe for the last time, maybe forever. "I'm sorry, Firebird," he sighed. "I have no choice."

"I know that, Daniel Blue Eagle," she said woodenly, vowing she wouldn't be cowardly and cry. But she knew she couldn't look at him if she wanted to remain true to that promise. "You will need to eat to keep up your strength," she changed the subject, holding the bowl of meat out to her side, taking care not to look around.

"The Cheyenne scouts spotted 'Three Stars' and his troops at the headwaters of the Rosebud, not more than forty miles from here." Though she had asked for no explanation, he felt compelled to give it to her.

"I suspected something like that."

"Crazy Horse has argued for an immediate attack on them before they can locate this village and try to destroy it. He's hoping that if we ride all night we will be able to surprise them in the valley of the Rosebud."

"I see."

"Firebird, look at me," he pleaded, taking the offered bowl of food and placing it down before turning her to face him. "I have to go, Firebird. Can you see that?"

"I see that, Daniel Blue Eagle."

"Then tell me you understand," he begged, his intense eyes boring into hers.

"You are a man of peace, Daniel, not a warrior, so don't ask me to understand why you must go to war. Ask me to accept, and I will. I do! I accept that I may never see you again. I accept that our child may grow up without a father. But don't ask me to understand it! Not any of it! Don't ask me to understand why men must kill each other. Don't expect me to understand why Gentle Fawn may lose her husband on the day of her wedding. And don't ask me to understand why I may be forced to spend the rest of my life without you. Don't ask that of me, Daniel," she whispered, her voice small as the tears she had promised not to shed spilled over the rims of her frightened eyes.

Daniel Blue Eagle drew her to him, placing her damp cheek against his hard chest. Resting his chin on the top of her head, he smoothed his hands over her silky red-gold hair, marveling at how good she always smelled, how perfectly the curves of her body fit the contours of his.

"I won't ask it, love. I won't ask you to understand. Just know that I will do my best to come back to you and to our child. But if I can't, I know that you will raise him or her to be strong, giving, a lover of all mankind. Perhaps our child will grow to be the person who finally achieves what I've tried to do and

439

failed."

Starr watched as Daniel Blue Eagle stripped off his buckskin shirt and leggings. Wearing only his breech-cloth, he knelt on the buffalo robe and untied his war bundle. He took out his paints and studied them for a long time. Though they had been a gift from his father years before, he had never found the need to use them until now. With sad resolution, he picked up the first color.

Using Starr's mirror, he drew a black line down the center of his face, painting the right side white and the left side red. He then outlined three teardrop shapes in black on his left cheek, filling them with blue, yellow and white. His hair was too short to braid, so he simply tried a rawhide thong around his forehead, securing a blue eagle feather and a red cardinal feather in its knot.

Standing up, he placed a knife in the sheath at his waist and slipped a buckskin quiver and bowcase over his shoulder. Picking up a late-model repeating rifle and a cartridge belt in one hand and a decorated rawhide shield in the other, he looked at Starr one last time. He took a step toward her, then shook his head and stopped. "I have loved you with all my heart, Firebird."

"And I have loved you, Daniel Blue Eagle," she choked in answer, fighting the urge to throw herself at the painted warrior and beg him not to leave her. Her weakness would change nothing. He would still go, remembering only her lack of courage.

Determined to imprint everything about this last moment on her memory, Starr studied her husband from head to foot. The symbolic feathers in his hair, the sad determination on his painted face, his bandaged shoulder that he still favored, his muscular arms and broad chest, his long legs and moccasined feet—She had made and beaded those mocassins herself!

This moment might be all that she had left of him. *No, that's not true. I have his baby and memories enough to last my whole life through. As long as he lives in my heart, he can never die!*

"I will always love you, Daniel Blue Eagle. No matter what happens, I will never regret one moment of our love. Even if I never see you again, I will consider myself fortunate because I have known your love."

"My sweet, sweet Firebird," he groaned, crossing to her in one easy stride and crushing her against the hard wall of his chest. "I don't know what I did to deserve your love, but I know that I am a better man because you have loved me. *Hoka, hey,*" he said, his voice breaking. At last he turned to go, leaving Starr standing alone in the tepee, the tears silently trailing down her face.

Finally gathering the courage to step outside the tepee, Starr met Gentle Fawn. At the sight of the bride's tormented face, her heart constricted painfully in her chest. *She didn't have even this one night. The memories she has are so meager compared to mine. I have Daniel's baby. What does she have?*

Feeling guilty that she had only been thinking of her own loss, Starr opened her arms. The frightened girl ran into her embrace. "They'll be back before we know it, Gentle Fawn," Starr soothed, holding the girl tight against her and letting her cry. "Then you

441

and your husband will have all the time in the world to love each other and make many healthy babies."

"What if he doesn't come back, Firebird? What if he is killed?" Gentle Fawn sobbed helplessly.

"Then he will die knowing he was loved by a beautiful girl he adored, and he will say, 'It was a good day to die.'"

"There was so little time, Firebird. I won't be able to bear it if he does not come back," Gentle Fawn choked tearfully. "I will die too."

"No, you won't die. A part of you may want to, but you know that isn't what Tall Feathers would want. He would want you to go on living. At first you will live for him, so that he won't have died in vain. Then little by little, you will learn to live for yourself again." Starr wasn't certain if she was talking to Gentle Fawn or to herself, but they both drew strength from her words.

Turning arm in arm, Starr and Gentle Fawn sadly watched the procession of braves as they streamed out of the village, their war bonnets trailing impressively down their backs, their rifles held high like banners. The warriors passed through the village of frightened women and excited children, quickly disappearing over the hills and heading toward the Rosebud Valley, their yells and high yips and howls audible long after the last rider had disappeared from view.

"What do we do now, Firebird?" Gentle Fawn asked, mistaking Starr's calm exterior for inner peace and wishing she could be more like the white woman.

"We wait, Gentle Fawn. We wait and pray."

Considered the Army's top Indian-fighter, General

George Crook was certain the Sioux were camped in one giant village on the Rosebud to the north of where the creek bent toward the Yellowstone. Having spent the night before at the headwaters of the Rosebud, his troops had resumed their march before dawn on the seventeenth, planning to push on for a surprise attack on the unsuspecting village.

About eight o'clock that morning, an overly confident General Crook was convinced the Sioux had no idea he was in the area and called for a rest stop in a flat open area west of the great bend of the Rosebud. Ignoring the advice of the Shoshoni chief, Washakie, and the Crow scouts who pointed out that the surrounding hills could serve as perfect vantage points for the enemy, he had his men unsaddle their horses and let them graze.

Certain the Sioux were nearby, the Indian scouts were very nervous and incredulous that the general and his men were casually resting in such a vulnerable spot. Some actually played cards! To ease their own fears and guard against a surprise attack, the Indians stationed warriors on the northern ridges surrounding the valley while they sent others out to look for the Sioux.

In the meantime, while most of Crazy Horse's warriors rested after the hard night ride from the village on the Greasy Grass River, Sioux scouts were sent up the largest hill north of the bend in the Rosebud to see if they could locate the soldiers.

As the Lakota scouts neared the top of the hill, they suddenly heard horses coming up the other side. Dropping from their ponies to crouching positions, the scouts listened, their ears and eyes straining as they waited.

The instant the Crow scouts crested the hill, the Lakotas fired on them, and the Crows returned their gunfire, both groups suffering injuries and wheeling to race back to their commands with their warnings.

With both the Indians and the soldiers deprived of the advantage of a surprise attack, the Sioux rode up the hill shouting their war cries, finally swooping down on Crook's column nine miles away.

In one of the few battles between Indians and soldiers where the two were of equal strength, the fight went on all day. Choking in dust and gunsmoke, men and horses died, finally leaving thirteen Lakota braves and twenty-eight soldiers dead on a field that had earlier been rich and fragrant with wild roses, but was now defiled by blood and the stench of death.

Both leaders claiming victory, General Crook turned back to his headquarters on Goose Creek for additional supplies and ammunition, not daring to venture out again for a month and a half, while Crazy Horse led his warriors back to the Lakota village on the Greasy Grass River, ready to fight another day.

Together with Prairie Moon and Running Fox, Starr and Gentle Fawn waited as the whooping, celebrating warriors rode through the large camp, peeling off a few at a time when they neared their own tepees. Both young women grew more and more anxious as hundreds of braves paraded down the human corridor created by the women, children and old men of the camp, and still there was no sign of Daniel Blue Eagle or Tall Feathers.

444

"They've been killed. I know they have," Gentle Fawn worried over and over again, looking to Starr and Prairie Moon for reassurance.

"I will not believe that Daniel Blue Eagle is dead," Starr threw back sharply, her nerves taut from the strain of waiting and being strong.

Knowing she would explode if she stood still another minute, she stepped away from the crowd to work her way down the line of braves. Her eyes burning from the dust stirred up by the hooves of the tired horses, she doggedly searched the jubilant faces of the returning warriors.

He was there somewhere. She just knew it.

All around her, husbands were openly embracing their wives and children were jumping up and down with pride in their fathers and older brothers, some laughing gleefully as they were tugged onto ponies' backs to ride through the cheering crowd with the warriors.

"Where are you going?" Gentle Fawn cried out, running to catch up with Starr.

"I'm going to look for my husband," Starr shouted with determination above the noise, refusing to look back at the girl in case Daniel Blue Eagle, or someone she could ask about him, should pass by. "I'll find him if I have to walk all the way back to the battlefield." *And he won't be dead*, she added silently. *I won't let him be!*

Examining the faces of every returning warrior, the two young women anxiously made their way to the Hunkpapa tribal circle at the southern end of the village, a mile and a half from the Oglala camp.

Most of the warriors had passed by; and the

welcoming crowds had thinned out. Only a few people remained, people like Starr and Gentle Fawn, who had yet to find their loved ones. Reaching the farthest edge of the camp, Starr gazed numbly at the few stragglers who still rode out of the hills into the camp, bringing with them the wounded and dead.

Starr waited anxiously until the last riders entered the village, her chest rising and falling painfully as she realized that Daniel Blue Eagle wasn't among them. Her fists clenched tightly, she looked down at her mocassins, trying with all her will to remember the things she had told Gentle Fawn about living on if her husband didn't return from the battle. But she couldn't remember one word.

As though able to sense her doubt, share her sorrow, her unborn baby pounded a reminder of its existence on the walls of her womb, bringing an unbidden smile to her sad face. "Yes, my sweet love, I know I have a reason to live," she whispered, rubbing the flat of her hand over the spot where a tiny foot kicked at her belly.

Starr turned to the other girl who continued to watch the hills, the look in her black eyes desolate. "We may as well go back, Gentle Fawn," she said softly, putting an arm around the girl's drooping shoulders.

Gentle Fawn lifted a hand and pointed toward the hills, making a feeble attempt to speak.

Starr's head swiveled around so she could see what the Indian girl was pointing to, and her own mouth dropped open.

Coming over the top of a hill was a pony that looked like Daniel Blue Eagle's. It was riderless and pulling a travois, but the closer it drew, the more certain she was that she recognized the paint and the brave who limped alongside it.

Starr broke into a run, with Gentle Fawn close on her heels. "Daniel Blue Eagle! Where have you been?" she cried, the tears of joy blurring her vision, but not stopping her from throwing herself against her husband. "I had given up!" she confessed.

Daniel Blue Eagle caught his wife in his arms and kissed her mouth hard, not certain if the salty tears he tasted were hers or his own. "I told you I'd be back."

"What took so long? The others have been back forever."

"My other pony was killed and I had to walk," he admitted sheepishly.

"The travois," she began, finally able to tear her gaze away from the beloved face she had been afraid she would never see again, "who—" she started, but it wasn't necessary to finish asking her question.

The brave on the travois was sitting up and embracing Gentle Fawn, the grin on his handsome face belying the pain in his leg and chest where he'd been injured.

"Tall Feathers," Starr uttered happily, wrapping her arm around her husband's waist and helping him lead the weary pony the rest of the way to the Oglala camp.

Despite the 'victory' on the Rosebud, a peace council had decided that if anyone were going to speak to President Grant for the People, it had better be soon. So in spite their hesitation to leave Man of the People and the others behind, Daniel Blue Eagle and Starr had been persuaded to depart for Washington. Following a tearful goodbye with their loved ones, they had left the valley of the Greasy Grass River the day after the warriors returned from the Rosebud.

Riding only at night and sleeping during the day, the trip from the Indian village to Cheyenne was more difficult than Starr had expected. By the time they rode into Cheyenne two weeks later, they were both exhausted.

Sprawled over the high prairie east of the Laramie Mountains, Cheyenne was a chief outfitting point for gold prospectors heading northeast to the Black Hills. It was where they would be able to board an eastbound Union Pacific train.

Dressed once more in their *wasicun* clothing, Mr. and Mrs. Daniel Edwards checked into Kelly House on O'Neil Street for a much-needed bath and rest while they waited for the arrival of the train in two days.

"You go first," Daniel Blue Eagle said, glad they had seen the poster advertising the Kelly house and its Bathtub In Every Room. "I'll watch," he added with a mischievous twinkle in his blue eyes as he tested the water the landlady's daughters had brought to fill the tub.

Starr didn't need to be told twice. Completely unconcerned with modesty, she quickly peeled off her clothing and stepped into the warm water, sighing contentedly as she lay back in the short tub.

Watching the water splash her silky skin, Daniel

Blue Eagle groaned aloud. Without hesitation, he stripped off his own shirt and trousers and knelt beside the tub. "Need some help?" he asked, snatching up a floating sponge and lathering it with soap.

"My back could stand a little scrubbing," she sighed, holding her hair up and leaning forward to give him access.

Daniel Blue Eagle massaged her skin with the sponge, finally tossing it aside and using his hand to scoop the warm water up over her back.

"That feels so good," Starr moaned, rotating her neck lazily.

Suddenly Daniel Blue Eagle stood up and placed a long foot beside one of Starr's thighs in the tub. "What are you doing?" she shrieked with a giggle as his second foot landed in the water next to her other thigh.

"I want to take my bath while the water's still hot," he explained, bending to lift her out of the water to a standing position. "We'll take our baths together."

"There's not enough room in here for both of us, Daniel," Starr protested as he slid down into the water, his legs now between her feet, his knees bending to fit all of him into the short tub.

"Let's find out," Daniel Blue Eagle smiled, his blue eyes smoky and passionate as he offered his hands up to her.

"It won't work," Starr laughed, shaking her head doubtfully as she allowed herself to be drawn down to a kneeling position straddling her husband at the bend of his lap. "Daniel!" she squealed, her gray eyes opening wide with surprise when she encountered his erect manhood against the soft flesh of her stomach.

"It's been two weeks, Firebird," he explained, encircling her waist with his hands and lifting her upward to impale her on the hot spear of his masculinity.

"Yes, it has," she moaned with delight, wiggling her bottom from side to side to settle herself more fully around his strength. She tangled her fingers into his thick black hair and pushed her body against his, tickling her jutting, passion-tightened nipples back and forth over the hard flesh of his chest, deliberately tantalizing him.

"Mmm," he grunted, moving subtly under her in response to the gentle milking motions her twitching sex worked on his virile length. "You'd better stop that or we'll never finish our bath," he threatened, obviously enjoying her actions, but picking up the sponge and soap anyway.

He glided the slippery sponge under her chin from ear to ear, back and forth over her upper chest, lathering under and along her graceful arms, round and round each rosy-tipped breast, leaving both of the heavy globes crested with soap bubbles. Next, he concentrated his attention on her very pregnant belly that rounded against his own flat stomach, finishing the sensuous bath by slipping his soapy hands between their bodies to gently massage the petals of her femininity that held him snugly within her body.

The urgency of her movements on him, around him, and against his hand increased as she washed his strong neck, muscular arms, the ladder of ribs above his lean waistline, and the deep navel at the center of his belly. She bent to kiss the soap bubbles

450

from his flat brown nipples, lingering to work the tiny nubs to hard points of desire with her tongue.

Unable to endure the teasing lovemaking any longer, Starr moved her mouth over Daniel Blue Eagle's broad chest. She covered his firm corded flesh with her kisses as her hands continued to worry his nipples and her hips rotated over him, the muscles of her desire tightening and relaxing around his shaft. Oblivious to the sound of the water sloshing gently around their bodies, she began to rise and fall on him, each lunge more intense and more demanding.

She looked deep into his passion-drugged blue eyes and saw her love mirrored there in the picture of a woman crazed with desire. A soft growl escaped her lips.

Her hands traveled eagerly over his flesh as her tongue darted in and out of her mouth over his face, tickling his nose, the corners of his mouth, delving deep into his ears in rhythm to her slow seductive movements on his manhood. Feverishly, her tongue sought his mouth, sinking hungrily into it as she ground eagerly against him, her body pleading with him to end her agony.

"I can't wait," Daniel Blue Eagle suddenly gasped, gripping his hands around her ribs and hurrying her movements to match his own frantic rising and falling, carrying them both to a crashing, convulsive climax. "Now!" he shouted, his voice rough with his passion.

"I love you, Daniel," Starr cried out as she felt herself catapulted over the edge of ecstasy, groaning helplessly as she collapsed against his heaving, water-slicked chest.

She wrapped her arms tight around his waist and squeezed with all her might. "What a bath!" she laughed tearfully.

"Beats that little tub of yours in our lodge, doesn't it?"

Minutes later when they had lovingly rinsed and dried their bodies, Daniel lifted Starr in his arms. "You're heavier than I remembered," he grunted, pretending to stagger with the strain of her added pounds as he carried her to the large four-poster bed and stretched her out on the chintz counterpane.

"You promised you would still love me when I was fat and ugly," she reminded him, pouting prettily.

"Love you, yes!" he returned. "But lugging you around is another thing altogether!" he said, with a kiss on her cheek as he lowered himself to the bed beside her.

"Oooh," she jumped, touching her stomach. "Your child has decided it's time for somersaults."

Daniel rolled over to lay his cheek against Starr's naked stomach and listened intently. "He's talking to me, Firebird."

"In Morse code?" Starr joked as the baby thumped out its message, making funny little lumps pop out and disappear on her pale flesh, as it often did when she lay on her back.

"Go ahead and laugh if you want, but I tell you, this baby is speaking to me," he said, rubbing his open hands over the smooth expanse of her stomach, which seemed to have doubled in size during the past two weeks.

"What is our little one telling you, *Ate*?"

"He's telling me he's growing so fast that his

'lodge' is becoming crowded. He says he doesn't want to wait three more months to meet his parents. He is telling me that he's the child of the future, a child of white and Indian blood who will be the one to teach mankind to live in peace with people of all colors."

"What if 'he' is telling you that *he* isn't a *he* at all, but a *she*, Daniel?" Starr asked seriously, looking worried as she gazed down at her husband's dark head pressed against her belly. She ran her fingers through his hair. "What if 'he' is asking, 'Will you still love me, *Ate*, if I am not a *hoksila* but a *wicinca*?'"

Daniel Blue Eagle raised his head and looked into his wife's teary gray eyes, berating himself for being so thoughtless. Then he looked back at her belly and spoke directly to the baby within. "Yes, my *hoksi cala* I will love you if you are a *wicinca*. How could I not worship any child that is part of your beautiful *ina*—a baby that is part of me, created by my love for your *ina*?" He then planted a moist, noisy kiss on the spot where the latest kick had distorted the shape of Starr's stomach. The kiss quickly turned to playful nibbles that worked their way over her flesh to her breasts.

Suddenly, Daniel Blue Eagle raised up with an idea. "Do you suppose that wild Indian in your stomach would behave if you sat up?"

"Well, our little wild Indian doesn't like for me to lie on my back. That's for certain," she giggled, pulling herself to a sitting position and throwing her feet over the edge of the bed. They both watched her stomach for a minute. There were two determined thumps on the supple skin of her belly, then all was quiet.

"That's more like it, little one," Daniel Blue Eagle whispered, kneeling on the floor between Starr's knees and gathering her to him so he could kiss her stomach again.

He ran his tongue over her plump belly, worshipping her body, her pregnancy, their love. "I love you, Firebird," he murmured against her taut flesh as he rose up to include her ripe, full breasts in his sensuous foraging. He opened his lips and eagerly clamped onto one extended bud, greedily sucking it into his mouth to nurse at her, while his hands wrapped around that breast and squeezed it in a kneading, milking action.

Starr groaned and clutched his dark head to her breast, unable to stop the gentle movements of her groin against his chest. "That feels so good," she whimpered, throwing her head back and pushing her chest harder against his mouth.

"This is where our baby will get his nourishment," Daniel Blue Eagle said, rolling her nipple with his tongue. "I'll be jealous every time our baby nurses here," he admitted, opening his mouth wide to suck hard at her breast, as though he could taste the delicious mother's milk already.

"You don't have to be jealous, sweet husband. I will always have enough love and time for you," she whispered, moving her body so that he would know how desperately her other breast needed his attention.

Daniel Blue Eagle fully loved and worshipped both her breasts and then rose up to kiss her mouth as his hands moved around to cup her round bottom and scoot her closer to the edge of the bed. Kneeling between her thighs, he crushed his torso to hers from breast to groin as he sank his tongue deep into her mouth. She could feel the imprint of his masculinity pressing against her belly, and she leaned into it, rocking from side to side against his hardness.

"Not yet," he whispered, burning a trail of hot kisses over her neck and shoulders. She felt as though boiling lava was flowing over her skin as his tongue scorched its way along her tingling flesh to the red-gold delta of fur that hid his goal from his greedy eyes.

"Oooh," she jerked as the hot tip of his tongue tentatively darted out of his mouth to tease the sensitive point of her desire. Chills tore through her body, causing her to clutch at his shoulders and dig her fingers into the rippling sinew as she pulled herself closer.

"Want me to stop?" he asked.

"Noooo," she admitted throatily, her head reeling deliriously with the effects of his loving. "Oh, God, Daniel!" she cried out, tangling her fingers into his hair as she was carried to heaven to soar with the eagles. His name became a song on her lips as she repeated it over and over again, mumbling words of love as he coaxed her to a point of exploding release.

Reaching for him, Starr tried to lie back and take her husband with her, but he shook his head and stood up. "I don't want to wake our little one," he laughed, pointing to her still tummy. "Come over here," he said, taking her hands and bidding her to follow him to a chair in the corner.

Daniel Blue Eagle sat down and drew Starr onto his lap and hardness, insinuating his hand between her legs to touch and caress her femininity as he moved within her, slowly and gently.

When the peak came this time, it was for both of them and was as sweet and lasting as their love for each other, bringing tears to both their eyes. "I love you, Firebird. I will always love you. I want only to make you happy," he told her emotionally.

"Don't you know by now that all it takes to make me happy is to be with you?" she smiled, kissing his forehead and eyes. "You and our baby are all I want, Daniel Blue Eagle!"

"Would you like to have our wedding repeated by a minister?" Daniel Blue Eagle said suddenly.

"What brought that on?"

"I thought you might feel that we weren't really married."

Starr kissed her husband's worried brow and hugged him to her. "I couldn't feel any more married to you than I already do, Daniel Blue Eagle, but I would marry you again, every day of my life if I could, just to show you how much I love you."

"In the white world, our marriage is not considered legal," he went on. "Our baby will be considered a bastard by some."

Starr didn't say anything. She hadn't thought of that before. As far as she was concerned, she was married. It had never occurred to her that anyone would doubt the legality of their marriage.

"I think we should marry again, Firebird. Not only do I want you to marry me willingly this time, but I want to ensure that you and our children can always hold up your heads in the white world."

"Whether we remarry or not, Daniel, our children

and I will hold our heads high in the white and Indian world, because we will know that we are loved by a man who represents the best of both those worlds."

"Don't you want to marry me?"

"Of course I do. I love you. I just want you to know that a piece of paper isn't important to me. I want only you—legal or otherwise!"

"We'll get married today, and then we'll board a train tomorrow and go to Washington. With you by my side, I should be able to straighten out the government's thinking in no time at all!"

"Well, you'll always have me on your side, Daniel Blue Eagle, until death do us part!"

"Until death do us part," Daniel repeated reverently, bringing his mouth down on Starr's to seal their vows to each other.

Epilogue

Washington, D.C.—August, 1881

"Mr. Edwards! Mr. Edwards!" an eager young newspaperman called out to Daniel Blue Eagle as he stepped off the wheezing, steam-spitting train. "Did the fact that you're half Sioux have anything to do with the reason the territorial governor has appointed you the Special Supervisor of Indian Affairs for the Dakota Territory?"

"Why are you in Washington, Mr. Edwards?" another shouted. "Does it have anything to do with Sitting Bull turning himself in?"

Daniel held up his hands to quiet the overzealous reporters, but questions continued to be hurled at him. All he could do was smile and wait patiently for the noise to die down.

"Are the Sioux going on the warpath again?"

"Did you know Crazy Horse personally?"

Realizing he was not important enough news to warrant being greeted by the more seasoned reporters, the tall man in the white shirt and black business suit didn't mind. In fact, he was glad. He enjoyed the youthful exuberance of the zealous reporters, most of whom were too young to remember Daniel Blue Eagle Edwards' visit to Washington following the Battle of the Little Bighorn in 1876, the year no one had wanted to hear what he had to say, the year no one could be convinced of the truth about Custer's attack on the Lakota camp on the Greasy Grass River.

A part of his heart continued to ache, after all these years, when he remembered the pain and frustration he had experienced the day he had read the newspaper account of the battle.

It had been July 3, and he and Starr had been ready to board the train in Cheyenne when a newsboy had run through the station hollering, "Extra! Extra! General Custer's regiment massacred by the Sioux! Extra! Extra!"

"Give me a paper, boy!" Daniel Blue Eagle had ordered, his voice strained. Tossing a coin to the boy, he had snatched up the paper, devouring the words on the front page with a frantic look.

Her eyes wide with shock and worry, Starr clung weakly to her husband's shaking arm as she too read the biased accounting of the Battle of the Little Bighorn. "Daniel, look!" she choked, pointing with a trembling finger to the paragraph that told of General Terry's troops finding ten 'squaws' dead in a ravine. "What if Prairie Moon is one of those women? What are we going to do?"

"I don't know, Firebird," Daniel Blue Eagle had said, dropping the hand holding the newspaper to his side.

"This paper says the Indians obviously scattered.

Where would Man of the People take his band? We must go back and help."

"I want to go to them, Firebird. Every bit of my heart is crying out to return to my father's band, now, today! I'm not sure I can bear not knowing if they are alive or dead." Daniel Blue Eagle bent his head and spread his hand over his forehead, circling his thumb and forefinger over his eyebrows. "But I'm not certain I can indulge myself and return. Now the People will need a spokesman more than ever. Who else is there to stand up and tell the whites the truth about this 'massacre'?"

"Only you, Daniel," Starr whispered with resignation. "You are the one Man of the People wanted to speak for him. We must go on to Washington and try to make the government understand what happened."

So, with hearts filled with grief and doubt about whether they were doing the right thing, Starr and Daniel Blue Eagle had gone to the East Coast. They had talked to government officials, newspapers, political clubs, humanitarian groups, even to an aide close to President Grant. But their pleas for understanding had fallen on deaf ears, and they had finally given up and gone back to Yankton in time for the birth of their first child.

Not long after their return to the Dakota Territory, they happily located Man of the People and his band living on the reservation once more, as were most of the Lakota. By the end of the following year, even Crazy Horse had brought his people in. Only Sitting Bull had stayed out. Now, after five years, the last of the renegades had come in, too. The Sioux War was officially ended at last.

During that same five years, the tide had changed ever so slightly. More and more humanitarian organizations had taken an interest in the plight of the Indian and wanted to hear what Daniel Blue Eagle had to say. Slowly he had become a renowned Yankton attorney who was asked to speak for the People all over the country, finally leading to his appointment by the territorial governor to the newly-created position of Special Supervisor of Indian Affairs for the Dakota Territory.

"Ate, Ate!" a five-year-old boy who was an exact miniature of the tall man on the platform, blue eyes and jet black hair included, squealed impatiently from his position at the top of the rail car steps. "Can we get off now?"

There was a hush over the crowd of reporters as a beautiful woman stepped up behind the little boy and shushed him gently. Dressed in a beaded dress that was an unusual mix of Indian and white styles, the woman's red-gold hair was duplicated in the hair of the three-year-old girl at her side, and in that of the eight-month-old baby in her arms.

The reporters couldn't miss the warm look of love that passed over Daniel Blue Eagle's face with the appearance of his wife and children in the doorway, and they smiled too.

"Gentlemen," he said, holding up his hand and finally managing to raise his voice over the noise of the train station and the clamoring reporters.

"If you'll ask your questions one at a time, I'll be glad to answer them," he laughed. "But I hope you will permit me to introduce my family first."

He turned back to the train car and swung the

giggling five-year-old to the platform beside him. "This is my son, Danny, and this beautiful little thing is my daughter, Felicity," he chuckled proudly, setting the little girl down beside her brother.

Felicity immediately hid behind her father, clinging to his leg as she peeked out at the crowd of laughing reporters.

Next, Daniel Blue Eagle took the baby from his mother's arms. "This big boy is Davey," he went on, completely unembarrassed by the fact that the baby immediately latched onto his father's nose with a chubby little fist. Last, he offered his hand up to Starr, who took it and descended the steps with the grace of a queen. "And this, gentlemen, is my wife, Firebird," he said, the love shining brightly in his eyes.

The reporters were immediately smitten with the handsome family before them, and a strange, warm silence enveloped the entire crowd. Only the coldest heart could not be affected by the love that radiated from the Edwards family.

Riding away from the train station later when they had finally escaped from the friendly reporters, Starr leaned against her husband's shoulder and sighed happily. "This time they will listen, won't they, Daniel? This time they want to hear what we tell them. Maybe finally the people of the United States will learn to love each other and live together as one people."

"Like we have?" Daniel Blue Eagle laughed, pulling Starr into his arms and kissing her mouth firmly.

"Daniel!" Starr squealed, pushing on his chest to move back from him. "People can see us! What will they think?''

"They'll think we're practicing what we preach— love the Indians!''

"Well, if it will help our cause, I'm all for it!'' she laughed and threw her arms around her husband's neck. "I love you, Mr. Indian.''

"And I love you, my sweet wife. With all my heart. I always will.''

"Always is a long, long time, Daniel Blue Eagle.''

"Not long enough, Firebird.''

"Not nearly long enough,'' Starr agreed softly. Hugging her husband and her children closer to her, she smiled contentedly, knowing without a doubt that if this was not her happily ever after, it was certainly close enough!

Author's Note

Research shows that Wild Bill Hickok and Calamity Jane didn't actually ride into Deadwood until April, 1876, but in that this is a fictional work, I have taken liberties with the dates, having them arrive seven months earlier. This way they can be there when Starr is—I couldn't let her get all the way to Deadwood and not meet such famous people. And although Deadwood was in existence in the fall of 1875, it didn't really become crowded until the spring of 1876, reaching a population of 25,000 that summer, so I've taken a poetic license with this date also. Since there were 800 to 1000 prospectors in the hills then, I let myself imagine that they were all concentrated in and around Deadwood.